THE RULE OF WAR

THE RULE OF WAR

Aoife Feeney

SOMERVILLE PRESS

Somerville Press,
Dromore, Bantry,
Co. Cork, Ireland

First published in 2011 by Somerville Press Ltd

Designed by Jane Stark
Typeset in Adobe Garamond
seamistgraphics@gmail.com

'Storms are promised . . .' by Dermot Healy
reprinted on pages 146 and 147
by kind permission of the author and the Gallery Press
Loughcrew, Oldcastle, County Meath, Ireland
from *A Fool's Errand* (2010).

ISBN: 978 0 9562231 4 2

Printed and bound in Spain
by GraphyCems, Villa Tuerta, Navarra

For John

CHAPTER 1

William and Rosanne Roycroft first saw the Ranelagh house on an autumn day in 2006. Its delicate redbrick was hidden by a virulent covering of Russian vine, paint peeled from rotting window frames, and the garden was a mess of discarded furniture, nettles and briars. They stood at the gate, stared at the dismal edifice, and hoped against hope that this might be the bargain they could afford.

The estate agent turned the key and pushed the front door, but it didn't budge. He pushed again, to no avail.

'Put your shoulder to it,' the estate agent muttered to himself. 'Come on now. One, two, three.' And then the door opened and bits of ancient plaster fell down from the lintel. There was dust everywhere – falling from the ceiling, rising from the floor – as the couple moved into the hall.

The estate agent remained at the front door and was surprised to see Rosanne dash past him back into the front garden. She shook her head, and shouted something that was muffled by her heavy scarf. She bent over, flung away the scarf, tore off her coat, her fingers felt her ears, ran through her hair. She shook her head again and again.

William was standing in the hall, staring at the yellowing walls, the stained radiators. The long search must continue, he decided; this house, along with so many others, was not for them. Then the estate agent nudged him and pointed towards Rosanne, who was still jumping and gesticulating in the front garden.

William rushed back down the hall towards his wife, tripped on a loose floorboard, and tumbled forward, landing on his hands and knees among a thousand escaping earwigs. 'I'm fine,' he exclaimed. 'It's nothing,' though when he pulled up his trouser leg, his shin showed a long and bloody gash.

The estate agent rooted in his briefcase, and held out a bottle of disinfectant. 'I always carry it with me,' he said.

'There's a spider in my hair,' Rosanne shouted as she ran back into the hall. 'I felt it moving.' She shook her head violently in the estate agent's face.

The estate agent recoiled. It was not part of his job to examine a client's scalp. He did not, however, relish the idea of a row, so he parted a few strands of her hair, removed a woodlouse, and pronounced the all clear. Only then did Rosanne search her bag for a handkerchief to staunch the flow of William's blood.

'Well that's another one off the list,' William said, as Rosanne pulled up his bloody sock to keep the handkerchief in place.

The bottle of disinfectant in her hand, Rosanne marched down the hall and trampled determinedly on all the living creatures she could find, finishing off the job by pouring disinfectant over their corpses, then handing the empty bottle to the estate agent. She looked at William and sighed. Another failure. The estate agent shrugged.

One last look at the decaying floorboards, one last look up the dismal stairway, and with the last rays of evening sun, the high round-headed window on the landing flung itself into Rosanne's gaze. The return had not been built out – how could she not have noticed? She touched the banisters, shabby with some of the uprights missing, but they would be beautiful when restored. She looked through the living room doors, and a Victorian marble fireplace came into view. A few careful paces and there was an amazing ceiling above her with intricate stucco cornices. In terrible condition, but nevertheless....

William and Rosanne crept upstairs. Rosanne's eyes kept returning to the landing window: vivid red and blue panes lit up in her imagination. That window, with its subtle geometry of curves and rectangles, which had somehow remained in place through years of neglect, was the deciding factor for her. Those panes of glass, filthy and barely translucent, would one day again disperse variegated morning light on stairs and ceilings. Rosanne had looked at so many houses, there had been so many disappointments, and she decided then and there that this *had* to be the one.

'Two storeys over basement,' she whispered as they left the house. 'Victorian. End-of-terrace. Nine excellent rooms.'

Although the house was practically derelict, it was selling for a great deal of money. A gift from William's parents formed a substantial deposit, and while Rosanne could find no common ground with those two elderly people, she kissed and hugged them. 'Thank you,' she said, and meant it.

The work of transformation got under way.

'Our new home,' they murmured to one another when they visited with their two baby girls, the tinier held close to Rosanne's breast in a baby pouch, the older wrapped up warm in a comfortable pushchair. They stood around and watched in the cold months after Christmas.

Then March arrived and Rosanne had had enough of the long wait. They camped in the upstairs bedrooms, cooked on a two-ring stove, stored milk and yogurts in a tiny fridge, while wholesale destruction and rebuilding continued below.

In the kitchen, beauty board worktops were replaced by stainless steel; an Aga stood in calm authority where the ugly gas cooker had been; an island unit was positioned to accommodate a sink, dishwasher, recycling unit; a fridge for wine was put in. Paint was stripped off period fireplaces, ceiling cornices were remoulded, walnut floors and underfloor heating installed.

By the time May came, their budget was gone and William cancelled the order for hand-made wooden sash windows. They would have to make do with factory look-alikes, he said with a crestfallen air.

'No, William,' Rosanne wailed. 'The rest of the house is so lovely. Could we increase the mortgage?' she asked on a sudden impulse. William shook his head, and when Rosanne looked again at the figures, she had to agree that they had reached their borrowing limit.

Rosanne had endured cheap aluminium windows during her childhood. She could not bear it. She *would* not bear it. Without telling William, and scarcely telling herself what she was doing she drove very early one June morning to Kilkenny, and from there to Bennettsbridge. Before 10 o'clock she rang at the bell of the crumbling Georgian house, pushed at the unlatched front door, walked through the draughty hall, then entered the kitchen, wondering where her in-laws could be.

Which of them should she ask? She stood in the kitchen and put that question to herself for the first time. Of course her father-in-law would be at work in Kilkenny, so the only person to talk to was William's mother. Rosanne shuddered. She pressed her lips together, regretting the necessity that had forced this mission upon her. She would have to go through with it, she realised; she would have to steel herself. The alarm on her mobile phone went off, and the screen told her that she had a meeting with the Arts Council in four hours time.

'Sugar!' she whispered to herself. She was pressing for an increased bursary as well as substantial financial backing for her next book, and this would be the meeting to clinch it. 'Damn.'

It was a big, high-ceilinged, old-fashioned kitchen. A tap dripped into the square enamel sink, where a food-encrusted casserole dish had been placed. Unwashed crockery was piled high on the draining board. The remains of breakfast, which looked as if it had been shared by a large number of people, was still on the table. The walls needed painting, some of the cupboard doors hung loose on their hinges, piles of newspapers and magazines were stacked on the tiles.

Rosanne wondered had it been wise to drive down? Am I going to ask this person to lend me money, and then rush away to my meeting? she thought. Am I really? All the old irritations surged back into her mind.

She began to clear the table, opened the dishwasher and discovered that it was full of unwashed dishes, found dishwasher tablets and set it to work. There were voices coming from other rooms, and from time to time people carrying books and stacks of chairs walked through the courtyard behind the kitchen.

She asked if anyone had seen Mrs Roycroft, but the people she questioned stared at her in an odd way. Some made incomprehensible gestures, and Rosanne began to wonder if her father-in-law was running a psychiatric clinic from his home.

Her mother-in-law, clad in a worn grey overcoat, at last shuffled into the kitchen, dragging alongside her two shopping bags filled to overflowing with loaves of bread.

'Thank goodness you've come, Mother Roycroft,' Rosanne said. 'With all the armies of people, the to-ing and fro-ing, it looks as though you're running a clinic or a soup kitchen.'

'For the conference, dear.' Mrs Roycroft said, as she returned her daughter-in-law's embrace. 'I've to take the butter out of the fridge, boil up the eggs, cut ham and tomatoes, wash the lettuce.'

'What conference?' Rosanne said. 'Is Daddy Roycroft running a conference? Does William know?'

Mrs Roycroft sliced bread, set eggs to boil, all the time talking about genetic disorders and their causes.

'But Mother Roycroft, you're retired now,' Rosanne said. 'You don't have to worry about that stuff any more. And Daddy Roycroft should be retired too. It's too much for him at his age.'

'The funding's been cut back,' her mother-in-law replied, and her sentences began to wander among missing chromosomes, abnormal eggs.

'Mother Roycroft, dear,' Rosanne interrupted softly, 'we have to ask you a big favour.' She licked her lips. 'We're going to have to borrow a little more money from you. William was too embarrassed to ask. After all, you've already been so generous.' Rosanne held the tips of her fingers against the sticky edge of the table, then hurriedly withdrew them. 'Leaking windows, the girls' bedrooms, coughs and colds,' she managed to say.

Mrs Roycroft, after casting a sharp glance at her daughter-in-law, rambled on, slicing tomatoes, buttering bread. A pile of sandwiches was growing on the kitchen table as words and phrases – *aneuploidy, Turner mosaicism, karyotypes, monsomy*, an indecipherable stream of consciousness so far as Rosanne was concerned – spilled for no apparent reason from her mother-in-law's mouth.

Rosanne felt something horrible whirring in her head. She should have guessed that this trip would be a disaster. She would be late for her meeting with the Arts Council, and the journey would all have been for nothing.

'But, Mother Roycroft, we're family,' she shouted over the droning old woman's voice. 'Surely that counts for something! I can't live with those windows. I'll die.'

William's parents eventually sent the extra money, and today in 2011, five years, almost to the day, after the crazy meeting in the old couple's kitchen, the Ranelagh house looks out on the world through wooden sash windows made to the highest specification. The casual viewer gazes appreciatively at flower-boxes on windowsills, curved garden paths, leafy bowers, a tiny rockery.

The house is set on a solid middle-class road that meets and complements others of its kind. There are strong, wide footpaths, trees, shrubs and railings, mile after mile of settled redbrick. And just across the road from the new house, at the epicentre of this inner suburb, is a charming park where the children can be brought to play. Little gems of flowerbeds, grassy stretches, a duckpond, a tiny waterfall, tall deciduous trees. It is a place where weddings are photographed every day of the week among the flowers, where each night foxes range among the trees, and in the dark recesses of certain bushes soft anal corrugations are explored.

Rosanne is relieved that her children are girls, although she would not say this to anyone, not even to William. Boys ruin gardens. It has happened with her friends. Grass destroyed by soccer on the lawn, plants broken in two by a miskick of the ball. William has suggested having another child. She feels he hankers for a boy, although he does not say this. Rosanne has no intention of having other offspring. There is the environment to consider. Disposable nappies fouling up the ecosystem, among all the other wastes produced by a new being. There is the cost of bringing up a new child in a country whose economy seems to have collapsed, although for William and Rosanne that has not yet become a personal worry. None of their friends have more than two children. Most find one quite sufficient. It is a question of responsibility, Rosanne maintains.

Their paternal grandparents' home remains a mystery for Rosanne's daughters, Maeve and Deirdre. They have little idea of Bennettsbridge, its broad river, rambling gardens. Occasional short visits have taken place, but Rosanne considers it a dangerous environment for her daughters. The girls are too young, she tells the old couple, the distance from Dublin too great, and their weekends are taken up with tennis, swimming, ballet, horse-riding, violin lessons.

The girls do occasionally – when no alternative babysitter can be found – spend nights with Rosanne's parents in the outer Dublin suburbs, in a semi-detached 1950s' Kimmage bungalow. The children dread these nights. The bungalow is cold and dark, their grandparents watch them with suspicious eyes and feed them thin tasteless soup which has been simmering on the gas cooker over several days. An equally tasteless rice pudding follows. The grandparents spend many hours, or so it seems to the girls, kneeling at prayers. William shudders when Maeve and Deirdre talk of his parents-in-laws' unhappy way of life, then explains carefully the cultural forces that combined to produce the narrow fearful outlook of their world.

'How lucky you are that it's only for a night or two.' Red blotches appear on Rosanne's face and down her neck as she listens to her daughters' complaints. 'I grew up there. Think what that was like.'

Then the day comes when the girls – aged six and a half, and eight – pat the tops of their heads, and say, 'they poured water on us'. Rosanne's breathing almost stops. 'They said lots more prayers,' Maeve adds, and William rushes for the phone.

They could not have done it, Rosanne tells herself. How dare they? She looks at her children again, still unable to contemplate the horror that has been done to them, then turns away and staggers, hands over her ears, to her study.

Outside the door the children look at one another. They had not expected this dramatic response to their revelations. The water had not hurt them, but now they fear that there may be horrible repercussions. And they also recall that their grandparents had made them promise not to tell. They tiptoe around the house, careful not to disturb their mother, fearful of what will happen next.

In the study Rosanne paces, her heart palpitates. How dare her parents interfere with her life? How dare they baptise her children? How dare they try to force their miserable dark and prejudiced world into her enlightened one? She makes a final firm resolution that her children will never again spend a night with her parents.

Now comes the struggle to regain her equilibrium. She sits at her desk, one hand on her throbbing heart, the other tracing with loving fingers the illustration on the cover of her most recently published poetry book. She must regain her courage, turn away from the entrapment of that dark corner of her life.

Slowly, breath by breath, her chest frees itself. One by one she calls to mind all the assurances that tell her that she has escaped the closed world of her youth, where she and her four siblings bowed their heads to the nightly rosary.

'My poetry,' she whispers, touching one by one the titles of poems as they appear on the contents page. She moves on to whisper her husband's name, then slowly and deliberately intones the names of her closest friends – the talented men and women whom now she calls her real family.

'William,' she says, and glances towards the bookcase where first editions of his four historical monographs stand side by side. 'Risteard O'Toole.' She hesitates. Poor Risteard; in any other country he would be a crowned laureate. In Ireland he must make do with being named a *Saoi*. 'Tina Foley.' Her nose quivers a little. Tina is a great painter – strange landscapes, bare arid places. 'Wendy Boothe,' she murmurs, 'journalist'. 'Blaise Boothe – film-maker', 'Derek Garvin – novelist, essayist, art historian.' Rosanne's heart lifts as she whispers Derek's name; he is her special confidante. 'Finn Daly,' she says, and then tries out the name again. 'Finn Daly – novelist.' Perhaps he is too beautiful, too unstable for inclusion in the group. 'But time will tell,' she says. 'Time will tell.'

Rosanne's hands caress her pale oak desk. After some minutes of meditation her heart stops thumping. Slowly she recites her mantra. She breathes carefully, regularly. Over and over she repeats the incantation, searching out that plane of detachment where she may hover, and contemplate the world from which she has escaped as if it were elsewhere, far away, a distant planet.

CHAPTER 2

'It's us,' Miriam Daly says as she comes out of the cinema on a September night. 'It's our story.'

Finn grunts. 'We'll walk home,' he says. 'It'll save the bus fare.'

'I love going to the cinema,' she says. 'Sitting in there with you in the dark, all cosy and warm.' She squeezes his arm.

Werburgh Street. Steaming bags of chips, tender succulent fish. 'The cod melts,' Miriam says. 'It melts in your mouth.' And they walk up past Iveagh Buildings, relishing the quick bite and swallow, the sting of vinegar that stays on their lips. Etched in the redbrick of the flats is the date they were built for the city's poor by a benevolent employer – 1905.

'A hundred and six years old,' Finn says. 'They built them well. I like looking at old buildings, knowing they've served generations.' He drops his empty chip bag on the ground, and Miriam quickly picks it up and pushes it into an overflowing bin.

'You were mysterious to me,' she says. 'Everything before you was quiet and ordinary. You were like a hurricane that blew into my life. An outlaw from a foreign world.'

'Not foreign. Germany's not exactly foreign.'

'But you were different from all the others. They were easy to understand. I could read their faces, and know exactly what they wanted. With you, it was something else. You were just this beautiful mystery. The first time I saw you, I wanted to have sex with you. I never wanted that with anyone else.'

'Ten years in Leipzig. Jesus! My bloody parents. A provincial dump. And then my fucking mother goes and dies. Jesus!'

'We're both orphans,' she says.

'If I hadn't made my father send me back to Ireland, I'd never have met you. That frightens me. It needed that coincidence for me to find you.'

'It was fate. We were meant for each other. *Bonnie and Clyde.* Me lying on the bed, bored to insanity. I look out the window just for something to do. And there you are with a golden halo. How lucky was that?'

'I've seen it before.'

'But it's not the same on television. You have to see it in the cinema to get the feel of it. *Hey, boy, what you doin' with my Mama's car?*'

'I never stole your mother's car. I should have.'

'You stole me. And we took a few things with us.' She offers him her bag of chips. 'Finish them,' she says. 'I've had enough.' And she counts on her fingers the items they have taken. 'CD player, coffee-maker, those nice plates they never used, sheets, two duvets, the fish knives, reading lights…. Oh and that fantastic tablecloth.'

'They didn't need them. We liberated them. We gave those things a better life. Your parents had too much stuff.'

'Not any more,' she says, and they walk in silence for a while, thinking of the apartment in Alicante to which Miriam's parents have retired. Miriam and Finn have not been out to visit. They cannot afford the airfare, and Miriam's parents no longer have surplus money to pay for their tickets.

'We'll have to take Jeremy out there sometime,' Miriam says. 'It might be fun.'

'Not a hope in hell,' Finn says. 'We can barely hang on as it is. Up to our necks. That bloody house! If they hadn't paid a deposit, we'd be better off. Maybe we should just bail out – cut our losses.'

'Lovie, they thought they were doing us a good turn,' Miriam says quickly. 'It's not so bad. I mean we've both got jobs. We're lucky.'

'I can't stick mine much longer. They hate me in there. Fucking teaching. Jesus.'

They walk along Kevin Street, cross the intersection at Wexford Street. Miriam looks up at the Cuffe Street flats – a series of dark balconies where lines of washing flap dismally against bicycles and surplus furniture.

'I never told you this,' she says, 'but one day when I was pregnant I was sitting in Stephen's Green. One of those delicious hot summer days – it was my lunch break, and I was sitting there and it was gorgeous. And a mother comes along pushing a buggy with a baby in it. She was from those flats.' Miriam gestures towards the high balconies. 'I know because I followed them afterwards. There was a little boy walking beside her, and he wanted to paddle in the fountain. A nice little boy – he didn't whinge or anything. So eventually she said he could. She was strict; she warned him there'd be trouble if his shoes and socks got wet. You could tell she didn't have much money. And she walked off with the buggy, and the little boy put his shoes and socks on the edge of the pool and tested the water with his toes. He was only about four or five; I was surprised she'd left him. Then he was paddling around, holding up the ends of his shorts, happy. And I was happy watching him, thinking about our baby, wondering would it be a boy. And the sun was lovely, and the trees and flowers – it was perfect.

'But just a few minutes later some girls came along with a toddler, about one and a half, like Jeremy is now. Tottering along, the toddler saw the shoes, and before anyone could stop him, he threw them into the pond. All the happiness disintegrated. The little boy started to cry in this terrible desolate way. He took his soaking shoes and socks and ran after his mother. And I followed because I wanted to say to the mother that it wasn't her son's fault. But she was gone, and he ran across the road still crying. Then he got to the flats, and I lost my nerve because by then I was angry with the mother for leaving him to cross a dangerous road by himself. I was afraid I'd shout at her for not staying to look after him. Every time I pass here, I think about it. I suppose it haunts me.'

'Why didn't you tell me? I'm here for you to tell me these things.' And he kisses the top of her head. 'It was alright. You sent good vibes to that little kid. I bet he's thriving now.'

She smiles up at him. 'You know what I was thinking? If The Female State took me on full-time, maybe you could give up teaching. If you could just get something…. It wouldn't have to be much. You know that grant they give writers? I was working out the figures, and I think it would be alright.'

'If you're talking about Aosdána, Miriam, you can forget it.' He is flexing his fingers. She hears his knuckles crack and she flinches. 'I know what the Aosdána people of the world are like.' His voice has gone heavy like gravel and she holds her jacket tight against her body to deflect his words. 'It's a self-electing corrupt organisation. It claims that it supports artistic talent, but in reality it destroys it. Remember: I lived in East Germany. I was only a kid when the Wall came down, but they couldn't stop talking about what it was like before. I know about what happened in their bloody Writers' Association.'

'But East Germany was a Communist state, a dictatorship. Ireland and East Germany have nothing in common, Finn.'

'Yes they do!' he shouts.

'Careful,' Miriam says. She holds her husband's arm as a tram making a mooing noise passes along Harcourt Street.

'Yes they do,' he says more quietly. 'Bloody Anna Seghers was an excellent writer until she got mixed up with them. After that she wrote shit. And she stayed president of the Writers' Association for twenty-six years. How evil is that for a start? In all that time she never challenged the regime, never defended a fellow writer. You've got Wolf Biermann, who was a good Communist, who criticised the regime the way you'd criticise someone you love. They took his nationality away, threw him out of the country. Anna Seghers said nothing. Just stood by, let it happen. It's hard to believe, but before she joined that bloody Writers' Association she was a good person.'

'Then what about applying for an Arts Council grant?'

'Arts Council. Call that a fucking Arts Council! I wouldn't touch those greedy, exploitative bastards. Venal cunts who squeeze blood out of the artists they're supposed to protect. They know all the tricks. And the ones they let into their rotten cosy Aosdána club feel so damned privileged, they won't utter a squeak. For Christ's sake, Miriam, why should the State pay you for writing? Why would they pay you for writing unless they want to control you?'

'Finn, I don't think this argument is making sense. It'd be just to tide us over. Aosdána would give you space. You'd have enough money so you wouldn't have to teach.'

'Look, Miriam, if the State wants to encourage writing or art or whatever, what should it do? I'll tell you. It should subsidise small publishing houses, proper art galleries, different music sites. So that people have outlets for their work. It shouldn't pay them to do that work.

You don't pay plumbers a special wage, do you, if their work isn't bringing in enough? And they're a lot more damn useful than most writers. Plumbers create beauty. A lot more beauty than bloody writers. Copper pipes laid out in burnished symmetry.'

'But how does someone like you manage, if they want to write but can't afford to give up their job?'

'You close your eyes and jump. It's the only way to do it.'

'We wouldn't be able to pay the mortgage.'

'That fucking house! It's a millstone.'

'If we didn't have Jeremy, I'd say fine, give it up,' she says. 'But we need it for him. We'd still have to rent somewhere with two bedrooms. And we'd get a terrible price, so we'd have to go on paying back the mortgage. In the end, we'd be worse off.'

'We could just walk away,' he says. 'Dump the keys in the bank's letterbox. Fuck negative equity.'

They reach Leeson Street Bridge. The lights are red. They step into the roadway, Miriam stumbles to her knees. 'Ouch,' she says. 'I slipped.'

'Come on,' Finn calls from the opposite footpath. 'It's dangerous. The cars won't see you.'

'I'm fine,' Miriam says as she gets up.

An Aston Martin, travelling fast, takes the turn from Leeson Street into Mespil Road. It is an illegal turn, and Miriam does not see the car coming, until Finn screams and the car's horn sounds.

Then the Aston Martin is gone and Miriam is lying on the roadway and Finn is running towards her, strange howls coming from his mouth, and he is gathering her up into his arms. A knot of people begins to form on the footpath.

Miriam looks up into her husband's face. 'What a fright,' she says. She smiles at him. 'Some benevolent god intervened just there.'

'Jesus,' he says, 'what would I ever do if I lost you?'

2014

CHAPTER 3

It is September once more. A cold early morning wind whines around the dirty façades of Heuston Station, jostling sweet papers and cans, rolling and rustling them across the greasy tarmac.

Derek Garvin holds his cigarette between two yellowing fingers. He is shaking a little at the shock of cold dank air blown from the Liffey as he watches Wendy Boothe and Tina Foley drag themselves from the taxi, scramble for their handbags and shoulder bags, stumble into a slow, awkward run towards the train.

When they're in their seats Wendy opens her laptop, while Tina's mournful gaze moves from her reflection in the train window to her image in the tiny mirror of her powder compact. 'You dragged me out before I'd even woken up,' she says to Derek.

'I needed you. If I had to bring Philip, I think I'd go mad.' Derek's hand goes to smooth his puckered forehead, rests there a moment. 'It's all very well for you heteros. You bring home a lover, your parents see romance and moonlit dinners. With us, all they see is spunk and arses. This sickness stuff, they'd probably wear masks. I tell them Philip's busy. Pass the water, Tina, pass it.'

'Your mother? Is she the one with the big hair?' She pulls off a boot, then a sock and flexes her toes against the table's edge.

He grabs the bottle of water, gulps it down. 'You met her at your last opening. Paintings of derelict sites – all the shades from vomit yellow to brown. I hope she won't remember. You were as pissed as a newt and very insulting. Luckily, these days she's grateful for anything in skirts.'

'I never could see what grabbed you about Philip.' Tina opens the other boot. 'Was it just the money?' She picks a piece of fluff from between her toes. 'I love fluff,' she says. 'Comes from nowhere to find a home between my toes.' She sniffs her fingers, recoils. 'Jesus!'

Derek watches her spit into the palm of one hand, stir it with an index finger, gaze into the greeny white-flecked globules.

'They're saying there's a new strain of HIV that passes in spit,' Tina says dreamily. 'Think of all the dickheads I'd be able to infect with this little gob.' She spits again, rubs the saliva into the toe of her boot. 'So is he going to die? Leaving everything to you?'

'You know that's rubbish.' Derek's eyes fix themselves on the toe of Tina's boot, shiny with spit. 'Philip isn't going to die. He's got some sort of recurring flu, that's all. And you can go back on the next train.'

He thinks of the nervous twitch that has recently developed in Philip's right eye. Perhaps it's part of the illness? How did he come to get it? When Derek asks himself this question, he forgets to breathe and his chest overfills with air.

Urban sprawl recedes. The train moves through pastureland, Charolais cattle, tall elegant horses, carefully maintained wooden fencing. Then, after an hour, Tullamore in a heavy grey dawn. A wreckage-strewn halting site beside the tracks. Pools of water, mud, no solid ground. Pieces of clothing cling to a hedge. A child stands facing the tracks, her back to the sewage works. Dirty face, wild tangled dark hair. Derek's flesh contracts as he surveys the scene. His eyes, for an instant, catch those of the child. 'We're all going down there,' he whispers; 'we're falling apart.'

He looks away, watches Wendy tapping at her laptop. Pale blonde hair, slim fingers tucking it behind delicate ears, the glitter of earrings against the creamy skin of her neck. Wendy can work anywhere, he thinks. And then she looks up, rubs the back of her neck, gazes out of the train window at the grey sky.

'I'm cursed,' he tells her. 'Cursed with being on the margins.' Numb with depression, he watches Wendy stretch her long body.

And then she's trying to comfort him, telling him he needs a massage, that she's found a great person. Gay, she's shouting it loud and clear, he thinks. His jittery yellowed fingers dance on the formica.

'People recognise you,' she says then. 'They respect your work.'

'That's stupid.' The way she wants to round off things, to make things good, is beginning to irritate him. 'My publisher's un-contactable. I've sent him the new novel – no word and every time I phone, he's in another bloody meeting.'

She tells him about some festival, until she sees his scowl and quickly adds, 'But I know you hate them.' Carelessly running a finger across the edges of her mouth. 'I should have brought lip cream.' She talks as if he had no feelings. 'Have a look at the paper.' She pushes *The Irish Times* across the tabletop towards him. But all he sees is the photograph and its caption – central Warsaw, men and women crowded together, their mouths open in a common scream of rage, the Virgin Mary's statue held high.

'They're savages over there,' he says, shoving away the newspaper.

'If you think your life's fucked,' Tina says, tapping a number into her mobile phone, 'what about mine? Finn Daly's not taking my calls. Screwed him a couple of times, and it's like goodbye. That's the trouble with men. The good ones run.' She lights up a cigarette. 'Next time you're reading with him, Derek, you can bring me along.'

'There won't be another reading, and for Christ's sake put out that cigarette. It's illegal.' Finn Daly, he thinks. A lethal beauty. Drinks, but that adds to it. Golden skin under stubble, crazed eyes. Exudes an indefinable lustre. Charisma. The fair hair carelessly falling across his forehead, harassing his audience, yet they ache for more. Stand cheering at the end. Then comes Derek's surrealist prose. A dumb silence. His fists clench at the memory.

What, he wonders, is the point? No one has ever appreciated what he has given them. The distant, delicate touch. Falling apart, Derek thinks, the three of us. All falling apart. Even Wendy, tapping there at her keyboard. Books, books, books, Derek thinks dejectedly: they give you nothing. He gets up, and walks off down the carriage. And as he walks, all the words in the world batter his head, surging and colliding with the rhythm of the train.

'Coffee and biscuits,' he says, sharing them across the table. Wendy holds the paper cup, her little finger crooked against it. Tina takes hers in both hands, stares into it. She sips, makes a face. 'Tastes like shit.'

Wipes her mouth with the back of her hand.

They sit in silence. He finds himself examining Tina's strained face, the lines around her mouth as she lights her third cigarette. He remembers how she used to be lovely. Soft, curling, black hair, huge russet eyes, warm skin. The hair is a harsh black now, the skin faded to a greasy white.

'Falling apart,' Derek whispers to the train's rhythm.

CHAPTER 4

'You might have tried a bit harder to get here in time for the Mass.'

Derek's sister hands him a gin and tonic. He takes a gulp. 'Poor Uncle John,' he says. 'I always liked him.'

'Look at the way you're dressed,' she tells him. 'You could have shaved.'

'I'm sorry he died.' He touches her arm to try to appease her, takes another gulp. 'Really, Alice, there was nothing to be done. The train was late.'

'The train's always late.' She shrugs off his fingers. 'I warned you. I told you! You should have come last night. After all, it isn't as if you had a job to go to.'

He is looking at the ground, not knowing what to say, when their mother comes from the other side of the room to stand between her children. 'Don't be cross, Alice,' she says. 'We're delighted that Derek could come. And I especially asked him to bring his friends.'

Derek kisses his mother's wrinkled cheek in gratitude, touches the soft skin furrows of her face with the tips of his fingers. She moves away slightly so that his nicotine-stained fingers fall to her shoulder, where they rest awhile.

He looks around the room, searching for something to admire. There is Belleek pottery on the mantelpiece, framed watercolours on one wall – his mother is a member of the Irish Watercolour Society – a large embroidered cloth on another. 'It's lovely, Mum. Did you get it on your African trip?'

'I think it was very inconsiderate.' Alice's irritated voice erupts over his mother's reply. 'Clumping in at the end of the Mass. And that person….' She gestures sideways at Tina, who is sprawled on the sofa, a large brandy on the carpet beside her. 'Does she not know how to dress for a funeral?'

'She's an artist, Alice,' his mother explains. 'They can't help wearing peculiar clothes.'

'The other one doesn't look too bad, I suppose, though I don't see what you had to bring them for. Everyone turned around to stare at them. You should know the way people talk.'

Derek watches as Mrs Garvin becomes that steely thing he was so desperate to escape from.

'Alice, dear,' she says, 'that's exactly why it's important for Derek to bring along his friends. We all know the way people talk and we don't want to give them more to talk about than absolutely necessary, do we?' She smiles tightly at her daughter.

'All very well for those who don't have to live here,' Alice says, and flounces away.

Galway city is as Derek remembers it: the same stinking canals, offal and plastic bags floating among surface bubbles. The same toytown façades of city centre apartments, even dirtier now and more decrepit. Beer cans, Buckfast bottles, a drowned cat, trapped in the sluice gates at Nun's Island. Market Street, the boys' primary school, five of Derek's worst years spent in those miserable classrooms, bullied and taunted, until he learnt to bully and taunt better than anyone.

As he walks in the funeral cortège, it is as if time thrusts him backwards, and the same two hundred drenched children still play in that concrete yard. That same lone teacher huddled against the wall. Abbeygate Street, Mary Street, the dark unwelcoming cafés. The delivery vans idling at the roadside, exhaust fumes tainting the sodden air. Eyre Square's heaving, dripping shoppers. Anoraked, shapeless creatures, heads bent against the wind, shuffling as they always had, across the city's innumerable roundabouts. On the city's outer perimeter, nameless housing estates cover every hillside, every field, their grey walls lit only by the purple lichens which bloom on damp plaster.

'Your parents have a gorgeous house,' Wendy tells him as they sit into the evening train. 'Late Georgian, isn't it? I didn't think Galway had a Georgian period.'

For Derek, the sense of relief at having escaped from home is immediate and almost overpowering. He feels light-headed. A sensation of joy courses through him as he folds his coat and places his bag on the overhead rack.

'Blaise and I used to come down here when we were engaged.' Wendy rubs her wedding finger, looks down wistfully at the small stone in her engagement ring. 'We were poor back then. Poor but happy. I love Galway. It's bright and vivid and friendly. You can go into a pub and talk to anyone.'

'So what about that festival then?' Derek asks her. 'I feel better now that I've got away. The sense of dread all the way down in the train. And now it's gone, so you can tell me.'

'It's still under wraps, though the Roycrofts will be big in it. They'll have been let into the secret. You should talk to Rosanne.'

'If I talk to Rosanne, she'll try to manage me. I'll be frogmarched into the festival whether I like it or not.'

Now Tina is slapping the formica table, chuckling. 'A pale blue g-string,' she's saying. 'I forgot to tell you. Orange bush and a pale blue g-string. The bush peeking out all over the place. One of those nights we were shit-faced down in The Swamp and the two of us had to piss in the same pot.'

'Rosanne's never drunk', Derek says. Still, when he thinks of her in a g-string, he has to smile. Rosanne, so upright and respectable, pulling down the g-string, sitting with her large pink bottom on the black marble toilet.

And Tina's laughing back at him. 'There's another side to Rosanne, you know,' she's saying. 'She's not all suck Risteard O'Toole's dick. Anyway, she did the oddest thing after she'd wee'd. A funny little handshake with the lady attendant in the john. She thought I was still wiping my ass. But I was looking. I thought, secret society, what the fuck. You know her poetry's got all that esoteric shit in it. And then I thought, no, the woman in the toilet is probably her mother, and Rosanne's slipping her a tenner, so she doesn't give her away.'

'Her mother can't work in a nightclub,' Wendy says. 'They don't take old women, even in the john. Anyway, the nightclub women are all Eastern European. I did a piece on them for one of the red tops.'

'Well, this one was ancient and ugly, and for me she was Rosanne's mother.'

And now Wendy's going on about Rosanne's poetry, and Derek begins to feel sick again: that nervous sickness he feels when someone else's work is praised.

'I can't read it in the Irish,' Wendy is saying, 'but in translation it's fantastic. Really fine. I think she'll overtake Risteard.'

Derek floats his mind to a new clean space; no point in getting annoyed, he decides. He rubs the window with the flat of his hand, peers out at gloomy low-lying fields. 'Goodbye, Galway,' he says. Little flashes of joy keep dancing around him. Hard to understand it. Perhaps he should come to Galway more often just to experience those feelings of relief and pleasure when he leaves.

'I'm thirty-five,' Wendy says. 'I want a baby and Blaise doesn't. So what am I to do?'

Tina's squinting into her little mirror, rubbing pink blusher on her cheeks. 'What d'you want a baby for?' she's asking, but Wendy doesn't answer, just looks at her laptop as if she might cry.

'The other thing is....' and Wendy is still looking sad as she switches on her screen, 'Blaise told me to tell you, Tina, that he wants the flat back. He's planning to sell the building. I'm sorry, but he's got a buyer.'

Derek winces. Blaise doesn't care who hates him. That's the weird part of it. Out of the corner of his eye he sees Wendy look anxiously into Tina's face, then lower her gaze to the screen. 'I thought I should warn you,' she says. 'That way, you can look around.'

And now Tina is staring wide-eyed at Wendy. Her powder compact and lipstick drop from her grip onto the table. Her brain must be churning, Derek thinks. All that brandy at the wake.

'It's *my* flat,' she says. 'I put a hundred thousand into it. And I'm paying off the rest. I've been giving you paintings, haven't I?'

'Blaise says he … doesn't want any more paintings,' Wendy says, not looking up. 'He's gone off landscapes. And the flat's in his name. So….'

'But you know I did that because I couldn't raise all the money. And Blaise said it made sense for him because he could put it in as a loss-maker and save on tax.'

'But now it makes sense for him to sell. He's trying to float a new production and he needs cash. He says he'll give you back your capital.'

'Bastard.' Tina's mouth clamps shut; she folds her arms and looks into her reflection in the darkening windows of the train.

'So what about that festival?' Derek tries again. 'Come on, Wendy, tell me now.'

'They're saying that we have to rise above all the economic disasters; we've got to stop being depressed about ourselves. That this will be a way of giving us back pride. Pride in being Irish, so they want it to be massive. They're calling it Summer Twenty-Sixteen. Ireland as cultural dynamo for the world. That's what they told Blaise, though he says it's trying to promote a sort of ultra-nationalism, a regeneration of the Irish nation. Looking back to the European Dark Ages – with the idea that we Irish provided the single light in the world – our magnificent monasteries, Annaghdown, Kilmacduagh, Glendalough. Ireland's huge influence in Europe, Book of Kells, Book of Durrow, John Scotus Eriugena. St Brendan sailing to America.'

'So they think the crackheads and illegals will play along?' Tina rolls her eyes, traces a fingernail across her throat. '*Proud to be Irish*, they'll shout, as they smash the next little old lady on the head. Anyhow, what the fuck are they calling it Summer Twenty-Sixteen for? What's that about?'

'You know perfectly well,' Derek tells her. 'It's recalling our dead heroes, the nation's martyrs. Our very own tiny revolution. Remember Padraic Pearse? James Connolly? The 1916 Proclamation?'

Tina examines the red chipped varnish on her fingernails. 'You heard what else they're planning? We're all going to be fingerprinted. How does that fit with our stupid revolution?'

'Not fingerprinted,' Wendy says. 'They're taking our biometric data. A single hair and we'll be on their radar for ever. It's happening across Europe. They're cloaking it in virtue – telling us they're mapping disease tendencies in different populations, so that the correct medical response can be ready and waiting. Imagine a European DNA bank – how corrupt would that be? Though after the looting here, people want someone to be strung up.'

'Blah, blah, blah,' Tina says. 'You said you were going to read the bloody article, Wendy. So do.'

Derek sits watching Wendy read aloud from her screen. Her fingers from time to time run lightly across her mouth, push a trailing curl of hair back behind her ear.

Wife of Finn Daly, he hears, *fledgling poet; she might have stepped from a mediaeval painting. Soft, deep, dark eyes, clear pale skin, tumbling dark hair…. A slim volume of Miriam Daly's poems is to be published this spring by Sparrow.*

Sparrow is Derek's publishing house. He had set it up as a trailblazer – poetry as a subversive art form, which would needle and undermine existing power structures while demonstrating Derek's contempt for established poetry imprints. But the poems have never risen to their task, and every title causes Derek to lose money. Sparrow is a stone around his neck. Sometimes the sales go as low as fifty copies, and he can be certain that those buyers are all related to the author.

Three months ago, when Philip had his first attack of fever, Derek decided that his publishing venture was over. And that very evening Miriam had phoned him. He hardly knew her then, but something made him say, 'Okay, send me the poems.' Miriam will, he resolves, definitely be his last published author.

As he sits at the train window, he imagines Miriam sitting opposite him. He is savouring her skin, her deep blue eyes. She is leaning forward, towards him, her soft lips slightly open. Miriam is whispering to him and he is leaning closer and closer to catch her words.

Derek's best friends have always been women. Tina and Wendy, Rosanne Roycroft. Now Miriam. Whenever he looks at Miriam, whenever his eyes search her face, the sense of shock at her beauty confuses him; his sentences peter out into stammered words.

It's hard to explain but the instant I met Finn, it was like I'd always known him. It was just so powerful…. A feeling so powerful it was an earthquake, like just absolutely shaking all your molecules around and rearranging them…. Way beyond mere sexual attraction. He told me that if we didn't marry, he wouldn't see me again because he couldn't bear to see me and not be married to me.

Derek lets Wendy's words wash over him in a haze. He knows that they are ridiculous, and that Miriam could never have said these things. Veronese's *Venus*, he thinks. The horse, Mars, and the cherubs. It's the figure of Mars that makes the painting great. Derek as swarthy Mars. He could grow a beard.

Poems finely honed and haunting. Derek grits his teeth as Wendy quotes his own words. *They house vagrant voices. Deceivers, savants, uncertain fugitives….*

He tries to dream away Wendy's voice. Aristophanes, he thinks, the Androgynes, their state of eternal bliss. Then punished by the gods, split in two, into man and woman. And ever since we search through the world for our beloved other half. Since first meeting Miriam, Derek has had the peculiar sensation that he has come home, that he has at last found the creature who is his other half.

… not as fallow as a woman married to a businessman. My consciousness challenged, stimulated….

'For Christ's sake, Wendy,' he finds himself bursting out. 'Miriam couldn't have said that rubbish. She doesn't even talk like that.'

And Wendy is looking up at him defensively, for once not trying to placate him. 'Listen,' she says, 'I don't have time to do interviews. I talked to her over the phone and then I lost my notes.'

'You don't have to make her sound like such an imbecile. Why would I publish her if she's that stupid?'

Wendy shrugs. '*The Irish Times* wants her to be wholesome and dedicated, but also looking out to the wider world, and that's what I tried to do. Anyway it's only dressing for the photo.'

'I always thought your job was sick,' Tina's saying. Derek watches Tina put on lipstick, deep red, pouting at herself in the train window.

'I love her,' he tells them then.

'And if she wasn't beautiful?' Tina has that sneering smile on her red lips.

'I love her,' he says again.

'I can't see it being a long *amour*. She'll irritate the fuck out of you. *The soft blancmange of her mind* – I remember you saying that.'

'I didn't know her so well then,' he says.

'She fancies you because you're this gay sophisticate, so she thinks you'll never try to get into her knickers.'

Derek grimaces as the laptop closes.

'I liked her,' Wendy says. 'She's different from us.'

'Why do we have to keep on about Miriam?' Tina says. 'I just want to screw her fucking husband again.'

CHAPTER 5

Saturday morning, Dunnes, Rathmines Road. Miriam Daly holds a wire supermarket basket, feels in her pocket with her other hand. The mask is there. Finn would be furious if he caught her wearing it, but when she sees everyone else with one on, it's hard not to follow. Quickly she puts on the mask, adjusts it over nose and mouth. She picks up her basket again, moves through the throng of shoppers with a sleepwalking sense of unreality. Her skin is numb. Jeremy had woken three times in the night. A recurrent nightmare: cloaked figures, a tiger with open claws. Each time she and Finn got out of their warm bed, quietened the little boy, slid him back under his duvet. Shivering, they returned to bed, but had only just warmed up and were sinking into sleep when the screams started once more.

Like an automaton she gathers tins of beans, spaghetti hoops, frozen pizzas, dilutable orange juice. A bottle of Pays d'Oc for herself and Finn. Sausages, sliced pan. She queues at the meat counter for a kilo of minced lamb. Her eyes take in the cracked and blackened ceiling, the broken light fittings. The back of her hand unconsciously presses her forehead; presses away the tiny worry lines. These days shopping takes such a long time. And with so many wearing masks, she has the sensation that each human person is becoming anonymous. She looks at the throngs of people pushing shopping trolleys this way and that. The mask presses into her nose, and she hates the feel of it.

A lingering flu epidemic across Ireland. Some say it's from Eastern Europe, a mutation of the flu that killed Ukrainians in 2006. Others say it's a type of malaria, or a new strain of HIV. Miriam knows these rumours are probably nonsense, but in crowded supermarkets she feels afraid.

Newspapers have regaled their readers with stories of people collapsing in the streets, people falling down dead in their homes.

At last the shopping is over, and Miriam carries the heavy bags into the chemist's to buy a small treat of bath salts and hair conditioner. Then she is standing waiting for the 18 bus. She takes off her mask, and it is as if she has taken off a layer of skin. Her pores are open and the air is chilly as it rushes against her face. When she gets home, she will have a long bath to help revive herself. She will wash her hair, shave her legs, do her nails while Finn takes Jeremy to the park.

After thirty minutes she gives up waiting for the bus, and prepares to walk home through Ranelagh to Donnybrook. At the top of Appian Way she stops to rest, clenches and unclenches her fists to restore circulation, examines the deep red marks on her palms. She sets off again and on Morehampton Road catches a 46A. All the seats are taken. Standing in the bus, she piles her bags around her and reattaches her mask. Finn would be angry, but she cannot help that.

'Malaria passed through spit?' Finn's lip curls in contempt. 'We all know it's a load of bollocks. Media-induced panic. It suits them to keep the population in a state of terror. Like that, we're more malleable.'

Miriam blinks several times to dislodge Finn's angry face from her mind. But when she opens her eyes and grabs at a shopping bag which is threatening to fall over and disgorge its contents on to the bus's floor, his face is still there, angrier than ever. He is shaking a newspaper at her.

'Bloody profile,' he is saying; 'that rubbish about molecules, did you say that?' His fist clenches around the pages so that her image crumples.

Miriam had not mentioned molecules in the interview, but as she tries to rebalance the two shopping bags against her legs, and at the same time hold on to the overhead bar, she accepts that the words Wendy wrote in the article are essentially true. Even though the way she put it was corny, her words express exactly what Miriam feels about Finn. She had said it to her friend Yvonne, but Yvonne could not seem to understand that Finn's physical beauty might continue to do that to another person.

'The first time you met him, maybe,' Yvonne said. 'But you've been married for six years. Get a grip.'

The bus does not stop at Donnybrook church, although Miriam presses the button repeatedly, and she has to walk back along the Stillorgan Road. At the newsagent's stall outside Donnybrook Church a tabloid photograph catches her eye. A crowd of young people carrying buckets, mops and bottles of detergent. She reads the caption: *Belgrade's Red Light Clean-up.* She frowns. Is that good or bad? she wonders. She crosses the road, walks up along the Dodder to the down-at-heel housing estate she calls home, and at last is opening her front gate. And there is Finn at the door. Despite her exhaustion and the weight of the bags, she feels that same joy and bewilderment as at the first glimpse of his beauty. It always happens.

'I've got to feel free,' Finn had shouted on a still summer night.

Miriam looked up from her knitting. 'I've dropped a stitch,' she said.

'That's exactly what I mean. Here I am, driven by demons, going out of my mind, and all you can do is blather on about knitting.'

'It's just that I was in another world. It always happens when I knit.' She rolled the knitting into a ball and put it to one side. 'And, lovie, you *are* free.'

'You're an albatross hanging around my neck.'

'Albatross. How could I be an albatross?'

'Open marriage,' he shouted then. 'We're supposed to have an open marriage! If you're not availing of it, what use is it? It puts that Catholic guilt thing on me.'

Miriam looked anxiously at him, her finger to her lips. 'You'll waken Jeremy,' she whispered. 'Okay, I'll try.' And in the discussion that followed, she had promised to carry a condom to every party she went to, and to try to find someone to use it with.

Later that night, once Jeremy had been coaxed back to sleep, carefully placed in their big bed, Miriam inserted her diaphragm, shuddering at the feel of cold sloppy jelly, and sat in the wicker chair in the bathroom waiting for Finn. Thinking about everything.

Then Finn came into the bathroom, and Miriam forgot that he had called her an albatross. He kissed the mole on her thigh, and the tiny one under her arm, and she pressed her body to his. But just as her orgasm was beginning and she was gasping and loving him, her head thrown back, the door handle started to rattle.

'Daddy, Mummy, let me in! I've got to go wee.'

'Go in the basin in our room, Jeremy,' Finn called. 'Mummy and I are busy.'

But the little boy beat at the door. His cry grew to a scream. And Miriam, her clitoris still aching and convulsing, had to detach herself from Finn, pull on a dressing-gown and open the door to her four-year-old son. Finn had not yet ejaculated. He stayed in the bathroom, pretending to read the *Socialist Review*, but by the time Miriam returned – it had taken her a full half-hour to coax Jeremy back to sleep – he was too cross to continue.

'Open marriage,' Miriam said to herself with a little sob, as she rinsed her diaphragm in warm soapy water.

October leaves scud along wide footpaths. Blasts of icy wind. Miriam is hurrying through the dark autumn evening. At the Roycroft's garden gate she takes off her sensible shoes, replaces them with high-heels, removes her ugly coat, stuffs everything into her shoulder bag, and rings the doorbell.

Rosanne opens the door and stands there immobile for a moment, examining her guest. Her large freckled face recoils from Miriam's cold cheek. 'Where's Finn?'

'Babysitter problems.' Miriam smiles apologetically, but Rosanne, with a click of her tongue, has already turned away. Her streaked ginger hair lies dull and flat against the back of her head. 'I've to finish the pavlova,' she calls over her shoulder, and disappears in the direction of the kitchen.

Miriam stands at the edge of Rosanne's yoga group, taking in the room's deep blue walls, painted cornices, sandalwood cabinet. Paintings hang everywhere – Camille Souter, Phelim Egan, Gwen O'Dowd, Basil Blackshaw. And others, lots of others.

When the babysitter phoned to say she couldn't make it, they had tossed a coin. Finn cheered when he lost. 'One of us has to go to their fucking party,' he said. 'Anyway, the Roycrofts make me sick. They can go screw themselves.' And he had pushed her out the door. 'Go on,' he said. 'Jeremy's upstairs. Get going before he realises.'

Miriam sometimes dreams of a gentle little daughter who would curl up on her lap, kiss her softly. But they cannot have another child. Not in their tiny house, which gobbles every penny that comes in. Two small bedrooms, a leaking flat-roofed extension – bathroom above, minuscule kitchen below. Apart from some chairs and a low table, removed surreptitiously from Miriam's parents' house, they had found everything in skips, or had bought them in the Make Poverty History shop. Miriam has painted these items, stitched cushion covers for the sofa, hung the walls with prints, placed a flotilla of tiny ornaments on shelves and windowsill. Every afternoon, when Jeremy returns from school, his games destroy the fragile beauty of Miriam's composition. Each evening when he has gone to bed, she lovingly reconstructs it.

The problem, Miriam reflects, as she stands in limbo with Rosanne's yoga group, is that she cannot coldly have sex with someone without having feelings for them. The idea is repugnant. There have been people she liked at recent parties, but something or other – they were married (which Finn does not consider a barrier), or had bad breath when Miriam got close, or were too eager – something has always put her off.

Miriam tried to explain Finn's idea of freedom to Yvonne, walking behind her as Yvonne carried a basket of washing to the clothesline in her small back garden. Yvonne turned to stare at her.

'Open marriage?' she said. 'The guy's a scumbag. He makes you work all the hours, and then he screws around. You should leave him *now*. Once they start going on about open marriage, you can tell they've been fucking everything that moves for years. Anyhow, he's a fool. You're much better-looking than him.'

'People have to be free,' Miriam said. 'I'd hate Finn to feel trapped.'

'So if he'd suggested this open marriage thing from the beginning, you'd have still married him?'

'Back then I wouldn't have understood. I'm more mature now. I understand that things change, that you can't stay the same.'

'Leave him,' Yvonne said again. She began to hang out the clothes – tiny dungarees, a little girl's dress. 'What's sauce for the gander…,' she said eventually. 'You can screw anyone you like. And how will Finn feel about that?'

'He's completely open. I'm the one who's not so keen. Other men's bodies don't really appeal to me.' Miriam did not say that Finn handed her a condom each evening as she left the house. That, she knew, would be too much for Yvonne.

Miriam takes a step back from the yoga group, and slides away.

'Miriam Daly?' A man with pimpled cheeks and pointy features is greeting her as if he knows her.

'Hello,' Miriam says. She cannot think where she might have met him.

'You know the way Tintoretto's *Annunciation* is almost brutal in its forcefulness,' the man says and Miriam sees that his receding mousey hair is tied back in a stringy ponytail. 'The angel crashing through the wall, followed by a battering ram of cherubs. The world we glimpse behind him, an apocalyptic wreck, dark with chaos.'

'Oh yes,' Miriam says. If Finn could listen to this, she thinks, he'd understand why I don't want to have sex with people. She looks around to see if she can slide back to Rosanne's yoga group. But the man grips her arm. Miriam looks at him, startled. There is an expression of contempt on his face, and she wonders if she might, by some inadvertent facial movement, have betrayed her thoughts.

'Careful,' she says. 'You'll spill my wine.'

'You're a pathetic little fuck.' Thin venomous words penetrate her head. His hand squeezes her arm, shakes it, wine threatens to spill over her dress. And now she sees that his eyes are crazed, red-ringed.

'Stop it,' Miriam says. The man grabs a clump of her hair, pulls her face up against his. Over his shoulder she can see that people are taking notice. 'Let go,' she whispers. She can feel the wine slopping around her glass, but she cannot look down to see where it is spilling. He is forcing her to stare into his eyes; his hand is entwined in her hair.

'You're the little fuck,' he says, 'who sees yourself as Botticelli's Virgin, demure and helpless. The golden scum of semen pouring in a fine stream over your beautiful ghastly head.'

More people turn to look as his voice rises. Miriam glimpses William Roycroft among them. Surely William will come to help me, she thinks; surely someone will hear what the man is saying, though maybe they'll imagine that this is an embrace. She tries not to see the cratered facial skin, narrow dark nostrils, sparse hair follicles, but his face is so close she has no choice.

'Let go of me,' she says. 'Let go or I'll scream.'

'A golden shower of piss flowing over your breasts and cunt.'

She squirms away. He yanks her back. She tries to breathe steadily. It's a hallucination, she decides. This doesn't happen at parties. I'll shake my head and it'll go away. But when she tries to shake her head, his fingers tear at her skull. His voice grows and amplifies until it seems to occupy the whole room. Why, she asks herself, does someone not intervene?

'We are the golden shower.' A roar from his mouth, rancid breath scorching her face. 'We had an idea once that we, the cultured ones, were the scourge of the state, of big business and consumerism. Now we know we've always been their anointed handmaidens. We were the golden shower, and it is spent. All we have ever done, all we can do now, all we could ever do, is screw each other, and screw everyone else.' He stares into Miriam's face, recoils from her. Her hair, her arm, her wine glass are suddenly free.

'How dare you come on to me like that,' he says. 'Are you drunk?' And she sees that her wine has spilt down the front of his trousers. 'Nymphomaniac,' he mutters, and the guests standing nearby look at Miriam strangely. There is no sign of William, and Miriam stares in confusion at the parquet flooring. Wine-stained patches are damp on her black dress. No one speaks to her. No one defends her.

A touch on her shoulder.

'William,' she says, and the word comes out as a sob. She staggers, almost falling into his embrace in her relief.

William is several inches shorter than Miriam, a round bald patch on the top of his head, clumps of fuzzy black hair sprouting from each side. A cosy tub of a man. Miriam leans against his plumpness, gratitude flowing through her warm body into his.

'Blaise Boothe,' he says, stretching out one hand to the man who assaulted her, 'good to see you. Writer? Critic? Film director? Which hat are you wearing tonight?'

Miriam blinks in surprise. William is speaking as if he had noticed nothing. As if the crotch of Blaise Boothe's fawn trousers is not stained with red wine. As if Miriam's hair is not tossed and tangled. Others have turned away to separate conversations and Miriam, as she tries to regain her equilibrium, wishes that she could go home right now.

'Blaise is Wendy's other half.' William says. 'And speaking of Wendy, she did a good job, Miriam. Splendid profile, really strong. You've read it, Blaise?' His arm caresses Miriam's shoulder and guides her across the room to safety. 'I need a little help with the *vinaigrette*,' he whispers.

Miriam touches the red pressure marks on her arm. 'What's wrong with that person?' she asks, but William does not respond to her question. As if that madman's attack on Miriam had been nothing. Though perhaps her voice is inaudible, coming out of her mouth like a thin wisp of smoke. Then she's glancing back at Blaise Boothe's pock-marked cheeks. Is he really Wendy's husband? she wonders. Can he really have said all the appalling things I thought I heard?

'I think I should go home,' she says to William, and she walks into the hall. But the hall is full of people, and Miriam hesitates. She will have to make her way past them, pick up her bag, which is by now buried under a mountain of coats.

'You've to send me your poems.' William's voice comes to her through a confused mist. 'I've heard they're quite something.'

Miriam shakes her head. 'I can't stay.'

Then, with a trembling sense of relief, she sees Derek Garvin, moody and decadent, disentangling himself at the front door from Rosanne's welcoming embrace. Miriam wants to cry out and run to him, hold him tight. 'Derek', she whispers, and the misery lifts from her shoulders. 'Derek.' She will tell him everything, and he will make all these crazy happenings go away, so that the world will once more become comprehensible and secure.

Miriam and Derek's first encounter happened in the foyer of the National Gallery into which Miriam had retreated to escape a rainstorm. The big doors closed behind her and she bent forward, shaking out her wet hair. Somehow she had tripped over a foot, which turned out to be Derek's foot, and grabbed on to his jacket to prevent herself from falling.

'I'm so sorry.' Miriam looked at the forehead scrunched into disapproving convolutions, the umbrella tapping the tiles in irritation. But Derek had smiled then, and she had smiled back, and they had started to talk. As they talked, they climbed the stairs from the Millennium Wing, wandered the old section of the gallery, stopping from time to time to discuss a painting – Titian's *Ecce Homo*, Nolde's *Two Women in a Garden*, Heimbach's *Evening Meal* – but mostly they just talked, and eventually emerged through the main door. Under the shelter of Derek's capacious umbrella, they crossed the road, and wandered through the leafy rain-sodden spaces of Merrion Square.

During that first meeting they had discussed all the issues in the world, as it seemed to Miriam, and by the end of their conversation she felt she had known Derek for ever. Dark good looks, dark eyes, a laugh that rang out. When Miriam told him about the condom which she was supposed to bring everywhere with her, and which never got used, he had laughed and laughed.

'I'm gay,' he said, and Miriam had laughed too.

During the succeeding weeks Derek had several times brought Miriam to eat in the Winding Stair restaurant on the Quays. There one evening, after swapping forkfuls of duck and monkfish, he told her that his partner, Philip, had some mysterious illness, terrible fevers that came and went. Nobody knew what it was. Bruises on his legs. Kaposi's sarcoma, they thought at first. Except it wasn't that. The tests were all negative. Derek's mouth had closed in a thin anguished line. He grasped her hands across the table.

'I'm okay, Miriam,' he whispered. 'There's nothing wrong with me. But I feel as if I'm going insane. I look at people wearing those stupid masks and I want to vomit. Because that makes them think they're protected, and the real stuff happens only in Africa, or bloody Russia or somewhere. And when some poor bastard like Philip gets sick, there's nothing for him. Just drugs and more drugs. And everyone treating him as if he's a leper. It's the spirit of the age, Miriam. Individualist, fragmented. No one cares, no one steps outside themselves.' And he squeezed Miriam's hands tightly. 'We're going to fight that fragmented spirit, Miriam. We'll make it our mission. You and I together.'

'The *vinaigrette*,' William whispers. He is leading her back along the hall, down a small flight of stairs to the kitchen. Miriam stares around the enormous room. It is strange to have come from the buzz of conversation so close at hand into this pure silence: terracotta tiles, a long oval pale ash table, pristine worktops, a deep blue Aga, and miles of floor space.

'What a great kitchen,' she says and William holds her hand lightly in his.

'Olive oil,' she says. 'Extra Virgin, that would be best.' She tries gently to disengage her hand. It is not a successful attempt. William's other arm stretches around her body and clutches her to him. His lips press her chin, then her lips; his tongue attempts to enter her mouth.

'Please, William.' She slithers from his grasp. 'Salad dressing. What about the salad dressing?'

William stands staring at her helplessly. 'You're looking so lovely,' he says at last. 'And you handled Blaise marvellously, poor fellow. You didn't bat an eyelid. With those disasters he's had, it's all been too much. And then you leaned against me, and your courage touched me…. I knew something wonderful had to happen.' He runs two plump hands through the curly edges of his hair.

Miriam represses a shudder. There is a wet look in William's eyes which makes her feel sick. She walks to the draining board. 'Garlic crusher?' she asks. 'Peppercorns?' She looks out at the coloured lights, the beautiful fairy-like garden, feels her breath coming in little jumps.

'Don't be cross, Miriam. Rosanne and I – we want to help the two of you, we really do. We know what a struggle it is when you're just starting out.'

William stands beside Miriam, holding out the garlic crusher and olive oil. She feels his hot breath on her shoulder.

'We've a new literary magazine on the go,' William is whispering against her bare shoulder. 'It'll define once and for all where Irish intellectual life is at. It'll be Finn's thing. We want him on the editorial board. All the most important names gathered together. Risteard O'Toole's also. We'll publish your best poems.'

'Lemon?' Miriam says. 'I'll need some lemon. And honey?' But William's fingers, seemingly of their own volition, move once more towards her breast.

'William!' She twists her head this way and that, trying to avoid his mouth. In the midst of this embrace, the kitchen door opens and Rosanne's red, flustered face stares in at them.

'Rosanne....' Miriam says helplessly.

After a second's indecision, William releases Miriam and rushes across the room to take his wife's outstretched hands in his. 'It was Aosdána, Rosanne. You did ask me to break the news to Miriam. I couldn't do it in public.'

'You're supposed to be welcoming guests.'

Miriam winces at the way Rosanne spits the words, at the bulky body made ugly in its anger, the orange hair gone damp.

William walks backwards as he leaves the kitchen, and Miriam quickly follows him.

'You mean Finn didn't get Aosdána?' she says to him, and a new weight of depression begins to settle on her. Finn will be glad – that's the worst of it, she realises. Her body is trembling. She notices that beads of sweat have appeared on William's forehead.

'Talk to my parents.' He wipes his forehead with a large handkerchief, turns away from her. 'You'll find them in the living room. They're lonely.'

Miriam walks slowly up the stairs. She tries to calm her breathing. How will she rescue the situation with Rosanne? How will she and Finn manage? The mortgage, she thinks, three months behind, and she had been counting on Aosdána.

In the living room she slides unhappily past the knots of people drinking, talking, laughing. I should go home, she thinks, but if I get home too early, Finn will be angry. And there is Derek across the crowded room lounging against the patio doors. He is looking out for her, catches her eye. A red neckerchief is tied carelessly at his throat.

'Derek,' she calls. But the patio door opens from the outside. Rosanne briefly appears, and draws Derek with her into the October night. Miriam sighs, and turns to find William's parents. At least they're old, she thinks; they won't try to assault me or say terrible things.

Risteard O'Toole is standing by the window, in deep conversation with Tina Foley. Risteard's brocade waistcoat, the rose in his lapel. She looks a moment at the thick greying hair, the strong profile. Finn is too harsh, she thinks. Risteard's poetry is pure genius, so it doesn't matter how he dresses.

She finds William's parents side by side on a sofa, and smiles at the elderly couple. They look vaguely at her, and Miriam dredges her mind to discover some common ground.

'I know your two granddaughters,' she says. 'My son Jeremy has just begun at the same school. Junior infants. He's not five yet.' She smiles again. Perhaps he's too young, Miriam thinks now. Maybe that's why he's so cranky all the time.

'We came to see the children,' Mrs Roycroft says softly. 'We came to see our granddaughters, but they're not here.' They sit looking sadly into the crowd, and Miriam glances uneasily from one wrinkled face to the other.

'It's a nice school, isn't it?' Miriam says.

Mrs Roycroft shakes her head, speaks so quietly that Miriam is unable to make out what she is saying. And Miriam is immediately assailed by her own doubts. Something about the school that she cannot articulate, and to which Finn is oblivious.

'What did you say?' she says. But then the moment is over, because someone is touching Miriam's arm. She turns to see Tina Foley's ring-bedecked fingers beckoning her.

'Come and meet Risteard,' Tina says. 'Come and talk to our great poet.'

CHAPTER 6

A child's bedroom on a November morning. Pastel shades on walls, a white coverlet on the bed, floorboards polished to a restrained shine. Plenty of space for the Victorian wardrobe, the desk, the comfortable armchair in which to curl up with a good book. Excellent floor space for the thousand-piece jigsaw of Louis le Brocquy's *Family*, recently begun.

Maeve Roycroft looks out briefly on the winter garden, where feathery Mimosa leaves touch the bare pale bark of the silver birch. Then she draws her initials in red poster paint on the lower part of the sash window. She dips her brush in water, sprinkles a few drops of the pinkish fluid on the windowsill, chooses green to make an outline around the letters. The paint runs down the glass. 'Oops.' Maeve quickly halts the escaped greeny-red paint with a rub of her pyjama sleeve. 'Too watery.'

With her finger, she applies undiluted green in widening spirals to the window. She cleans the residue from her hand onto her pyjama trousers, then applies the red paint in the same way until the lower section of the window is covered in an interlacing pattern.

'Hmm,' she says, sitting back to survey her work.

'Maeve?' The door opens slowly.

'Go away,' she says. 'I'm busy.'

'Oh, Maeve, what are you doing?' Her sister trails into the room, carrying a small stuffed dog. 'You'll get in trouble.'

'Why do you have to nose in on everything? I'm painting the Book of Kells if you must know.'

'On the window?'

'I looked "illuminated" up in the dictionary. It means lit up. That's why it has to be on the window. You're such a baby.' Maeve presses her palm to the window to check if the paint is dry, rubs her hands again on her pyjamas. 'I was dreaming about this,' she says. 'I'm going to put yellow in all the spaces that are left.'

'But we're not allowed have paints in the bedroom.'

'I know. I sneaked them home from school. Think of Muinteoir Róisín's face when she sees they're gone.'

'Mummy'll be cross.'

'Mummy bummy.' Maeve looks at her sister. The two girls giggle.

'Anyway we can wash it off,' Maeve says. She gets out the yellow paint and begins to apply it. 'Hmm, maybe I'll mix the yellow and red and make some orange. I've got clean pyjamas under the bed. I'll put them on when I'm finished.'

Downstairs, William and Rosanne Roycroft sit at their pale ash table, frowning over *The Irish Times* and *The Guardian*. Coffee is brewing on the Aga, croissants warm in the oven. Large, ginger-haired Rosanne grinds her teeth and reads the words *entrepreneurship, statecraft, unabashed materialism* for the tenth time on this particular morning.

'The croissants, William,' she says and watches irritably as he stumbles towards the oven. Outside, the crumpled leaves are scuffling on the patio, begging to be swept up. The sound reminds Rosanne that she has earmarked this morning for tidying the garden.

Today, however, she knows that she is helpless. What have I done? she asks herself, rubbing a finger across the bridge of her nose. But why shouldn't I? she answers, staring at the bald red centre of William's head, at the cleft of his fat buttocks where the trousers have slipped down as he bends to the oven.

Why shouldn't I? she says again and for a moment Finn Daly's body tingles against her fingertips. She looks down in confusion at her hands. It should have been nothing: two adults spending a few nights together during a conference in Belfast.

Finn had been too drunk to climb the stairs, and Rosanne had helped him, led him step by step, brought him to her room, laid him on the bed, then opened his trousers and struggled to take them off. Eventually they were both undressed enough to have sex, and even though Finn lapsed from time to time into unconsciousness, the outcome was a moderately successful intercourse.

The following night Rosanne tried again. William was at a conference in Lausanne and the children were staying with friends, so it seemed a pity to waste the opportunity. This time, however, Finn pushed her away, mumbled something incoherent and staggered from the room. Rosanne's face reddens at the memory.

As she chews her croissant, Rosanne thinks bitterly of Derek Garvin. Why did he run to that fool Miriam Daly, instead of to Rosanne, his closest friend? Why did he have to choose such a stupid name for his group?

'We're calling it Sócúl,' Derek said, and Rosanne had laughed her contempt.

'So cool,' she jeered.

'It means "comfort." What's wrong with that? We're comforting sick people; people who've been insulted, humiliated. We want to help give them back their dignity.'

'The ones with that crazy disease that you say isn't AIDS?' she asked sourly.

Derek turned away without answering and Rosanne knew she had gone too far. She put her hand on his knee. 'Sorry, Derek. Of course I'll join your group.'

Sounds of laughter from upstairs, and William, glancing at Rosanne's frown, goes to quell the noise. In the quiet of the kitchen the telephone rings and Rosanne, staring at the ash table, dreams that it might be Finn. Telling her he loves her. Promising to take her away to the earth's ends. She feels a new burst of rage towards William. In fifteen years of marriage he has taught her nothing.

'Hello,' she says, breathlessly, huskily.

It is Finn! And Rosanne smiles inside herself. 'Could we meet for coffee?'

'I've nothing to say to you,' Finn answers. 'Where's William?'

Rosanne goes to call her husband. She will deal with the two girls, whose screams and laughter, now that they have William as an audience, have reached a crescendo.

Rosanne believes that when reason fails, a light slap on the legs can sometimes be a positive element in the parent-child relationship. But when she sees the state of Maeve's hands and face, she is so taken aback that a slap lands on the side of Maeve's head, followed by another and another, so that Maeve falls over screaming on the landing.

'Rosie,' William shouts. He is running down the stairs from the study. 'Rosie,' he pants. 'I had to cut Finn off. What's going on?' He looks at his wife, then at his elder daughter, who is crawling away from her mother across the landing floor. 'You've got it all wrong. We were having a game. Don't tell me you hit her?' He stands in front of his wife, his face pleading.

Rosanne pushes past her husband, rushes down the stairs, grabs the car keys from the hall table.

'Please, Rosanne, please.' William chases her down the front steps, pulls open the Volvo's passenger door. His plump panting face leans into the car. 'What about the children's riding lesson, their violin? How will I manage?'

Rosanne presses her foot down hard on the accelerator. William is thrown aside. His forehead scrapes against the car door, blood drips from a gashed hand. The open car door bounces against the gatepost and snaps shut. Rosanne drives on.

William phones Derek and Philip, and a little after midday they are speeding towards the riding stables in Kilpedder. Derek lounges on the slender back seat, an arm around each of the girls. The soft top is down and the pink-cheeked children, wrapped in warm jackets, scarves and hats, give joyful little shrieks as new bursts of wind threaten to blow them away.

From the front seat, William, hand carefully bandaged, woollen hat pulled down over bruised forehead and ears, glances back at a laughing Derek and reflects, not for the first time, what a deprivation it must be to have no children. He crouches down in his seat against November winds, chats with Philip about the ingenious design of the car's dashboard and wonders about the mysterious illness that has afflicted him. Philip's smooth handsome face lights in a half-smile, his manicured hands rest carelessly on the steering wheel, a carefully constructed air of old wealth about him. Philip seems perfectly well, William decides. Probably the tales that Derek recounted to Rosanne were exaggerated.

Philip is the third son of a Catholic smallholder from Kiltimagh in County Mayo. At the age of twenty he left Ireland. It has taken all these years, he tells his close friends, to rid his nostrils of the stench of silage. The lights of London in the nineties sparkled for Philip. Then one fateful July, on holidays in Sitges, he had met Derek Garvin and fallen in love.

Philip and Derek tried to live in London, but Derek, the writer, had pined for Dublin, the city where he knew everyone worth knowing. A large Victorian house on Leeson Park now serves as both home and workplace. Philip, an independent actuary, makes serious money.

Maeve and Deirdre, deposited at the riding school for their two hour ride-out, climb onto small, fat ponies. The three men drive past the Sugarloaf mountain, marvelling at the deep reds and golds of the bracken. They stop at Hunter's Hotel, tucked away below the main road in a deciduous glade.

'Rosie'll be upset she didn't come.' Derek strides into the old-world hotel bar with its smouldering turf fires and chintz-covered armchairs. He breathes deep satisfied breaths as he ponders russet leaves and sweet turf smoke.

'Loo?' William asks the barmaid, then moves quickly through the hotel lobby. Standing at the urinal, fly open, he phones Rosanne.

'We'll be home before five,' he tells her voicemail. 'Maeve and Deirdre are fine. And, darling, I love you.'

A few dribbles of urine have stained his trousers. He sighs, and dabs at them with a piece of toilet paper, then returns slowly to the lounge, worrying about the door of the Volvo. He had found several paint marks on the gatepost. Will Rosanne blame him? When she sees his cuts and bruises, she will surely soften.

Standing in her study in front of the oak desk and chair, surrounded by her books, Rosanne listens to William's message, and is aware that life is, after all, good. She should be happy. She is on the edge of real fame. Plans for the festival, Summer Twenty-Sixteen, have begun to take shape and Rosanne has been placed centre stage. Her poetry, the committee tell her, will be translated into many different languages. She will be asked to travel throughout Asia as a cultural ambassador. A television profile of her life and work has been suggested.

Rosanne gives a small sob, then finds herself sitting at her desk, her arms embracing piles of books while she weeps. A vision in the midst of her tears, Finn Daly appears. Her hands reach out towards him, but even as she feels the stretch of her arms in the void, the horrible fear comes to her. 'He's sleeping with Tina Foley,' she wails. 'Of course he is.'

Tina had stood in the Roycofts' sitting-room, flicking ash from her cigarette. 'Gorgeous party,' she had drawled when Rosanne thrust an ashtray at her and directed her to the patio. But she hadn't gone outside. Rosanne is certain of that. It makes Rosanne sick to think they had ever bought one of Tina's paintings.

In her angry flight from William, Rosanne drove the Volvo aimlessly through the city, then found herself parked outside her childhood home on Kimmage Road – a mean little house, as she saw it, with three cramped bedrooms, ugly furniture, plastic roses.

Standing in the linoed kitchen, already regretting that she had come, she listened wearily to the familiar complaints.

'We don't go out any more,' her mother said.

'You do, Mummy,' Rosanne answered as she always did. 'Daddy drives you to Mass every day. That's going out.'

'All our shopping delivered. The supermarket's a battlefield.'

'They bring it in and put it away for you. You don't have to carry heavy bags. It's a great service.'

'They stare at me and I don't know what they're thinking, Rosanne. I weed the flowerbeds. Hordes of them outside the garden wall. They speak languages God never invented.'

'It's the language school up at the crossroads, Mummy. It's been there since I was at university. You know that. They're just students going to a language school.'

'The Irish State wasn't made for foreigners.' She walked out of the room, slamming the door.

'I'm writing a letter to the newspapers,' her father said.

'I wouldn't bother, Daddy. They won't print it.'

'It's about the attacks on the Christian Brothers for their treatment of children in the industrial schools and orphanages.'

'It's old news, Daddy. Nobody cares any more. Too much else has happened.'

'*The Irish State was poor.*' He held the page up to the light, put on his spectacles. '*It could not afford to undertake on its own the education, the rescue from moral decrepitude, of all its children. So to whom could it turn in its hour of need? It turned to its great ally, the Catholic Church.*'

Rosanne sat on a kitchen chair. Her eyes listlessly examined the laminated tabletop, still in place since her childhood, the circular green fruit-bowl in its centre, which had never contained any fruit.

'*The Catholic Church undertook the task of educating the children, of running the nation's hospitals, of developing the moral conscience of the people of Ireland. A great purifying reformist drive.*'

'You're talking about how the Church developed the consciences of bankers and property developers?' Rosanne said. 'Really?'

'That greedy scum arrived after we turned our backs on Christ's teaching.'

Rosanne had to bite her lip to prevent herself from contradicting him.

'*The church plucked children from corrupt and perverse home lives, housed and educated them in institutions where these same children could learn a trade and become useful members of society.*'

Rosanne looked up. Her father was glaring at her as if she were the enemy. Contradict me if you dare, his look said. She shrugged and lowered her eyes. Stared at the empty fruit bowl.

'*And did the Church get proper recognition for this extraordinary endeavour? Its work in the schools, in the hospitals, in the re-education of delinquent teenagers. Did it get thanks for rescuing children from the scourge of alcoholic and debauched parents?*'

Rosanne sighed. She bent forward and rested her forehead against the cool of the tabletop.

'*It did not.*' His fist banged onto the table beside her head.

'I don't have much time,' Rosanne said then, and slid from the kitchen chair. 'I have to say goodbye to Mummy.'

Rosanne's mother was lying on a black leatherette settee in the dark front room. 'I wasn't asleep,' she responded testily when Rosanne asked could she turn on the light, then stood up and thrust a skein of wool at her daughter. Rosanne stretched out her arms, held the wool taut between them.

'I've been thinking about that husband of yours.' Mrs Flynn began the task of winding the wool into a ball.

'Please, Mummy. Please leave it alone for today. I'm tired.'

But Rosanne's mother would not leave it alone. 'Your father's upset too.'

William, despite his professional fame, has become for Rosanne's mother a deep disappointment. He laughs at her statues and holy pictures, refuses any religious education for her granddaughters. Maeve is already ten, she reminds Rosanne, and has still not received her First Holy Communion.

'It's not as if he was brought up a pagan. There's not that excuse for him,' Rosanne's mother said, as her arthritic fingers painstakingly wound the string of wool into a tight ball. She no longer uses William's name. 'And he won't baptise his own children. I couldn't leave it another day, Rosanne. I had to do my Christian duty.'

'Let it go, Mummy,' Rosanne said. She is worn out with the issue of that home baptism; worn out with trying, and failing, to convince her parents that they had done wrong. At least they can't force communion on the children, she had thought then.

Sitting inert at her desk, Rosanne cannot remember why she had chosen to interrupt the platitudes of normal conversation with her mother. She decides that she doesn't care. Mothers and daughters are supposed to talk about real things.

'Mummy,' she had blurted out, 'I've been wanting to ask you: did you ever sleep with anyone besides Daddy?'

Her mother's mouth dropped open.

'You must have sometimes been attracted by other men,' Rosanne continued encouragingly, 'like at parties, say, or if Daddy was away?'

'Dirty, dirty,' her mother shouted. 'That man is poisoning your thoughts.'

'This has nothing to do with William. He knows nothing about it. It's me. I ... I think I may have fallen in love.'

CHAPTER 7

'Matthew's nose escapes; put your hand over it quickly, or you may find it in the tree. The tree of idleness. Sincerity is all very well. But not every act of sincerity is correct. If Kevin is sincere, he will call Granny a wrinkled peapod.' Paul Ryan sings a song. He is driving his children to school on a wet December morning.

'What's a peapod, Dad?' Kevin puts his hand up to touch his nose.

'I know a man whose nose escaped. He didn't think it was funny. He was bending down to sniff a flower, and whoops a dog, who thought he saw a butterfly, opened his jaws and snap, snap.'

'That couldn't happen, Dad.' Kevin's hand is still raised to protect his nose. 'A dog wouldn't do that.'

'Give it up, Dad.' Matthew pushes at the back of his father's neck to shut him up. 'Will you bring us to see Santa on Saturday?'

'But the nose was too clever. It jumped out of the dog's mouth into a pond and swam and swam until it found a water lily to use as a boat. It was a happy nose. And Santa invites you and your nose to visit him on Saturday.'

They arrive at the school gate. Paul Ryan opens the car door, gets out onto puddled tarmac.

'Stop singing, Dad.' Matthew pulls up the hood of his anorak, hunches his shoulders against rain-filled air. 'Our friends will hear you.'

'But what about the poor man who lost his nose?' Paul Ryan sings more softly as he takes their schoolbags from the boot. 'Now that's another story. A story for tomorrow. Goodbye,' he sings, plays his air guitar with a final spectacular flourish. And the two boys run in at the school gate. They wave.

He touches the steering wheel, adjusts the air guitar's tuning pegs until he likes the sound. 'How does a nose get so huge?' he sings, and he looks in the rear-view mirror at two-year-old Ben, who is clutching a teddy and reading his favourite book. 'Do you like my song about a nose?' his father asks him. 'A nose who rides a horse and startles hunters?' And Ben nods and continues to turn the pages of his book. 'They set the hounds on it,' his father sings, 'and the nose fights them into smithereens. Then it finds a wall and draws the story of its escapades. Graffiti they call it and they send the nose to prison.'

Roundwood for petrol. Boxes of tiles on the bathroom floor. Abstract thinking about tiles. He would never have made an architect, he muses, yet it comes to his wife, Claire as second nature. She can, in her head, correctly place all those tiles. No mistakes.

'Tyranny is a habit,' he sings. 'It is able to and finally does develop into a disease. What can prisoners do but repeat themselves? Those thousands of days that lie ahead are all the same. Tell the same lie over and over, and the orchestra will play you out. Rage, tenderness, pain, cruelty, and eventually resignation. Man can get used to anything. In every creature a spark of God.'

Kilmacanogue. The salesman offers waterproof adhesive, waterproof grout, and a brightly coloured tiling kit.

The tiling kit sits on the seat beside him. 'Cute, oh so cute,' he sings. 'And how is Ben's nose? Has it run away?' He sees in the rear-view mirror Ben's hand rise to his nose, then return to the pages of the book.

Stillorgan, Kilmacud Road. He lifts Ben from the car, with nappy changes, teddy and extra books.

'Granny,' Ben says, 'I'm going to do a picture for you.'

A quick kiss for his mother, a kiss to Ben, the door closes, and Paul Ryan is back in the car, rejoining the lines of traffic. He has one hand on the steering wheel. The car inches forward, the other hand scrabbles among the odd pieces of equipment, searching for an instruction leaflet.

Maybe he and Claire will start on Friday night after the kids have gone to bed. Claire can be the commander. Two big yellow sponges. He'll do what he's told.

'A nose knows no straight lines. No know nose,' he sings. 'Straight lines, spirit level.' He looks at Claire's diagram. 'Bizarre gaps and blackouts when I work alone. I need Claire.' The car behind him is honking. The traffic has moved without him realising. He presses the accelerator but the lights have turned red. 'Red red red,' he sings, 'why is her face red in my rear-view mirror?'

The list of items. Kneepads, a bag of little plastic crosses. Tile spacers. 'At the television station,' he sings, 'they want me to implicate myself. "Whose side do you take?" they ask. "What do you mean?" I answer, "do you ask it of a wounded eagle?"'

His free hand runs along the trowel's flat metal surfaces, castellated indentations along two of its edges. Blue handle. 'There is a flat space where my nose once was,' he sings. 'I will not scream out against the perpetrators, who hide behind half-truths.'

His phone rings. He pulls up on the path after the traffic lights on Orwell Road and listens. 'I was just having nightmares about that sort of thing.' he says. 'Not a chance. Rosanne Roycroft's a predator. I'm not going in there, I'd be devoured. Anyway, I don't do culture stuff any more.'

Rathgar village. Another traffic jam. Ranelagh might have been quicker. His foot on the brake. 'Time is a roof,' he sings. 'A roof that oppresses us and hides the sky.' And he sits looking at the shop-fronts, puts his hand down to search for the pencil. The carpet on the passenger side is soaking. 'Memories are a house,' he sings. A plastic bag is needed under the soggy carpet. A smell of damp. The car is rusting from the bottom up. 'It's a human being who lives here and walks down the street.'

He thinks of the phone call, the prima donnas of the Irish culture scene, turmoil and rage over nothing at all. His friends across Europe – the new regimes. Attacks on ethnic minorities, on opposition leaders, on journalists. His friends want to get people out; they think of Ireland. And they imagine that he can help them, that he still has clout. 'What a fool I am,' he sings, 'what a fool.'

The traffic is scarcely moving. He smells his musty fingers, reaches down again, feels for the pencil. His heel touches something. He picks up the narrow red cylinder. 'What did I buy you for?' he sings. 'A Christian cannot be the pitying one because he is the one to be pitied.'

A thump against his front bumper, the sudden flash of a child's light hair. A scream comes floating up through damp air. People are stopping on the footpath, staring with shocked faces. On both sides of the road people are moving towards him. Paul Ryan's mind teems, his breath comes in short rushes. He gets out of the car, kneels in the wet road beside the child. A boy in school trousers, anorak, with closed eyes. Skinny, about eight. His son Matthew's age.

Suddenly a single whoop of a siren and the ambulance stops in the middle of the road between two lines of traffic.

'We were just around the corner,' they say, and they lift out a stretcher, place it beside the child on the roadway.

'What happened?' Paul Ryan asks. The child, the roadway, the people standing around appear to him in a haze. 'What happened?' He had been negligent, searching the car's floor for that little red pencil.

An older boy is calling from the opposite path. 'That's my brother.' And miraculously the child sits up, wipes the back of his hand across his eyes. The two ambulance men go to lift him. 'I'm alright,' he says. 'I'm better now.'

'I'll get my mother,' the older boy says.

Paul Ryan feels himself wakening from a nightmare. I'll never allow myself to do that again, he tells himself, never. A woman running around the corner of the street, wiping her hands on her apron. She takes it off and the apron blows into a sail over the top of her head as she runs.

'It's our final call,' one of the ambulance men says. 'We're going back to Emergency, so he may as well be checked out.'

'It wasn't the man's fault,' someone says to the woman. 'The child ran in front of the car. Lucky it was going so slow.'

'You shouldn't let a child of that age cross the road by himself,' someone else says. The mother shakes her head in confusion, and climbs into the ambulance, strokes the child, who is sitting up and crying.

'I didn't get my sweets,' the child says and turns his face away from his mother.

'He's not allowed to cross the road,' she says, and she looks as desolate as the child, rubs the back of her hand against her forehead. She holds out open hands to Paul Ryan as if she is trying to convince him that she is not an irresponsible mother. The ambulance doors close and the scene disappears from a Rathgar street.

Paul Ryan returns to his car. For minutes he sits there, inert. 'Why am I not driving this car?' he sings faintly. His hands tremble.

CHAPTER 8

On a December day Derek feels the city's dreariness, the void around his heart, the lurching queasiness of his stomach, the throbbing hangover beating against his temples. He throws his half-smoked cigarette from the car window, sucks deeply on a blast of cold wet air, then lights another, drops the empty packet on the floor.

Miriam is clutching the steering wheel, peering out through slanting rain, as the one remaining wiper moves sluggishly across the windscreen.

Derek takes a long drag, then another, grinds the cigarette out on the car's carpet. 'It's all very well us breaking our backs getting people things.' He is staring at himself now in the car mirror. He does not like what he sees: a yellow pallor around his eyes, glistening beads of sweat on his forehead. 'Bríd's just selling them on. We might as well stay at home.' The effort of speaking increases the pain in his head. He opens his seatbelt, fumbles through several pockets before he drags out another crushed cigarette packet.

He sees through half-closed eyes Miriam's fingers holding the steering wheel, her anxious glance at his open seatbelt.

They had stood in Bríd's kitchen beside the brightly lit Christmas tree. Derek watched Miriam steeling herself to drink the tea, to eat the slice of barmbrack which Bríd had buttered. He saw her slip the brack into her pocket while Bríd was searching the fridge for fresh milk.

'You heard Bríd say that Terry was on to her.' Derek moves irritably in his seat. 'That can only mean she's selling the stuff. She's drugged out of her brains. Didn't you notice?'

Miriam shakes her head.

'Anyway, I saw you put the brack in your pocket. That was pretty damn rude, wasn't it?'

Miriam flushes. 'I'm sorry, Derek.'

'The consultant said there was no risk. Can't you accept it when he spells it out? I suppose you'll be wanting to wear your bloody mask next?'

'That would hurt Bríd's feelings,' Miriam says. 'Doctors do sometimes make mistakes, you see. And I was thinking standing there in the kitchen: what would Jeremy do if I got sick? You know with Mummy and Daddy living abroad. I mean there's no one else.'

'Who were you with in the Clarence the other night?' The throbbing in Derek's head is becoming an angry pulse of resentment. She had been sitting there, her mouth open in laughter. He had seen her touch her hair with that delicate movement of fingers that he loves. Her beautiful fragile face looking into the eyes of a balding middle-aged man. As Derek contemplated the scene, a rush of jealous rage had overcome him.

'Derek, I never saw you there. It was Peter Brindley. He's a little bit strange – he calls himself Byron. He's rich. He wants Finn to teach him to become a writer.'

Derek feels her hand reach across to touch his. He looks for a moment at the long slim fingers, rubs his thumb across her warm flesh. I'll forgive her, he thinks. I'll love her always.

'Do put on your seat-belt, there's a pet,' she says, and ruins it all.

Bríd had shuffled ahead of them into the kitchen, short skirt, thin bruised legs. Derek and Miriam averted their eyes.

'I never saw those bruises before,' Derek whispered. And then he noticed that his hands were shaking, so that the cot he was carrying knocked against the banisters. 'Sorry,' he said.

'In the Clarence, for Christ's sake.' Derek shakes his head in a vain attempt to clear his irritation. 'I was there with the consultant,' he continues with an effort; 'we were talking about the guy who was brought in last week. Pneumonia.' Derek's eyes close. He leans back against the worn headrest, sees once more the high cheekbones, dark eyes, hears a light tenor voice.

'Called Carthage O'Shea,' he says. 'Does that strike you as marvellous, Miriam? I'm a novelist and I couldn't have come up with a name like that. Doesn't have any visitors, and that's where we come in. He's reading *Anna Karenina.*'

When Derek entered the ward, he thought he heard the young man singing. The Count's serenade, Derek thought, from Rossini. Sung lightly, tremulously, and then the young man coughed and Derek wondered had he really heard singing? Perhaps the sound had come from inside his own head. That aria, sung long ago in a Galway public toilet. That slim gracious boy.

'With a name like Carthage, there has to be something,' he murmurs. 'A Phoenician past. I dreamt last night that I was lying beside him, touching Moloch's temple, Tanit's crescent moon. Drenched in his sweat, licking the sacred droplets from his shoulders.'

'Derek, don't talk like that,' Miriam says. 'It gives me a creepy feeling.'

'I saw him there, Carthage O'Shea, lying under a white sheet, in the hospital all alone. They told me he doesn't speak to anyone. The man has young children. And then he smiled at me and I wanted ... I wanted to do everything for him. I think he'd like you.' His hand reaches out to Miriam's.

'I'm sorry, Derek,' She holds his hand tenderly a moment, then signals left to turn in at the hospital entrance. 'The Female State – I'm working tomorrow. And I've to work at the weekend. Otherwise, I wouldn't be able to do the visits with you.'

'Shit.'

'I have to do it. You see, we can't pay the mortgage. Things are terrible at the moment.'

'Listen,' he says quickly as Miriam pulls up in front of the hospital, 'I'm going to give everyone a Christmas party. They told me Carthage should be out of hospital next week. We'll get him to come with his kids. Bríd and her kids. The others too. I thought we'd have it in Rosanne's house.'

CHAPTER 9

Miriam sits alone in the car in the hospital car park. She feels unaccountably tired. Derek has worn her out. Some days he's lovely, she reminds herself, some days he's lovely.

He has been asking to have sex with her. 'Just a little,' he says. 'Just for fun. To try it out. For a gay person, it's important to know.'

At first Miriam thought he was joking and laughed at the idea. But that had hurt his feelings; he accused her of not taking him seriously and she felt ashamed. Still she could not bring herself to take off her clothes, stand naked in his bedroom or bathroom (because Derek sometimes does suggest his bathroom). It is just not the way in which she has imagined their relationship. And there is the whole problem of Philip's strange illness. Derek says that it's not contagious, but how can anyone tell?

One of the days when she called to collect Derek, he had grabbed her arm, whispered that Philip was out. But although Derek had worn a condom, and Miriam had tried hard, she had been unable to relax.

'It's okay,' he said at the end. 'It's okay. We'll try again soon.'

The glass of the windscreen is misted up. Miriam looks for a cloth. There is none. She searches for a tissue in her bag, rubs at the misted glass. The rain-swept car park reappears, rows and rows of cars, the grey hospital buildings like collapsed aircraft hangars in the distance. She touches her hair, holds the strands between finger and thumb.

A lone figure in the distance moving between rows of cars. She checks her mobile phone, nervous that she might have missed Derek's text. Nothing. Anyway, she reasons, Derek would never walk out in the rain. He would text her again if she failed to pick up his first message. The figure is nearer now, running through the wet car park, and Miriam thinks of the homeless people who sleep in car parks, and sometimes die when drivers back over them. But not today, she tells herself. It's too wet.

She rubs the windscreen with her sleeve. Her breathing is getting faster. A figure running towards her, and she is in a car park with hundreds of cars, in a city where crime is rocketing. A tremor of fear passes through her. She presses the automatic locking button, remembers that it no longer works, reaches across to lock the door manually. But the lock will not go down, and the passenger door is opening, even though Miriam struggles to hold it closed.

'Hello,' Paul Ryan says as he sits into the passenger seat, putting a wet battered briefcase on the floor beside him.

Miriam stares at the dripping hair and beard, the sallow handsome face. 'You're soaking,' she eventually manages, 'and I don't have a towel.'

He sits there panting. 'Saw you passing the door of the hospital.' Shakes his head so that tiny droplets of water spray across Miriam's face.

'What are you doing here?'

He gestures towards the distant hospital buildings. One hand is pressed against his chest and Miriam hears a high wheezy sound come from somewhere inside him. She is about to ask if he is ill, but then his review of Finn's novel surges up in her mind. *This man has crawled far up his own anus*, he had written, *in search of what?*

Her lips tighten. 'You're soaking the seat,' she says. 'And it's not even my car.'

Paul Ryan does not respond and they sit together in silence. Miriam stares straight ahead of her. She would like to turn on the radio, but the car radio is broken.

'A doomed battleship in a sea of corruption,' he says at last.

Miriam fiddles with her hands. 'Please go away,' she says. 'I don't think it's right to get into another person's car without being asked.' He is shivering, still dripping. Why did you run through the rain to find me, she wants to ask. She used to like him, but now, since that review, she feels only anger.

A tiny singing wheeze, and she turns away again, touches a hand to her hair in her anxiety. 'Please don't do this,' she says. 'Please go away.'

'That profile of you in the *Times* was ridiculous.' The wheeze in his voice.

She stares at him. How incredibly rude he is. His fingers tapping the dashboard under Miriam's nose. She turns her head away from the bitten stubs of nails.

'You shouldn't have written that review of Finn's book,' she says. 'It wasn't fair.'

'It was fair. Finn lives in a bubble. He's self-obsessed; his writing's autistic. He deserves everything he gets. But he's not in the same league as the lot you're hanging around with now. They're real monsters.' He presses a hand to his chest and Miriam hears again that whining sickly sound, like a straining car engine. 'I'm telling you, Miriam – Risteard O'Toole, the Roycrofts, Derek Garvin, Tina Foley, Blaise Boothe. Monsters all of them, jockeying for position while everything around them collapses. Ireland, Europe – we're at the centre of a terrible crisis. Day by day things are happening that need to be stopped.'

Miriam turns to him, her hands on the plastic of the steering wheel. 'That's why we're trying to help. That's why I'm here.'

'Think of what poverty and hopelessness do to you,' he continues as if she had not spoken. 'I tell you, Miriam, the racist stuff is only beginning. We should all be crying out. If we wait till it gets out of control, we'll be helpless. But your lot, your friends, are so blinded by their ghastly ambitions that they can see nothing.'

'How can you be so arrogant,' she says. 'How can you believe that you're better than everyone else? Why would we be here at this hospital if we're monsters? If Derek is blind, why did he set up Sócúl? It's an organisation that helps people who are outcasts.'

A memory comes to her. Paul Ryan had been humiliated. He'd resigned from his job in Brussels. Poor Paul, Miriam thinks, despite herself. And now he's down at heel, trying to hang on to his dignity. Attacking everyone else so that they won't notice the frayed cuffs of his jacket.

Ryan is gnawing at a fingernail, asking her about The Female State, and Miriam is making a pattern on the car's side window with her index finger. He starts to talk about a suicide attempt. As if she didn't know, she thinks bitterly, and all her pity for him evaporates. A woman whom Miriam had been trying to counsel. Ryan spoke to the woman's sister, and the sister had blamed Miriam.

'I'm doing an investigative piece,' he says lazily, 'so tell me your side of the story.'

Miriam sits looking straight ahead into the damp misted windscreen. 'We had a misunderstanding,' she says, and her fingers move to touch and twist strands of hair, knowing that there is a reason after all for Ryan to have pursued her. A mean cruel reason, nothing to do with a memory of past warmth.

'She thought I was offering her friendship,' she struggles to explain. 'Sometimes I'm not good at keeping the boundaries distinct.'

2015

CHAPTER 10

The new year is bitterly cold. So cold that a thick layer of ice forms on the canals. Wrapped up warmly in heavy jackets and scarves, people of all ages glide along the frozen water, down under the bridges to the wide expanse of Grand Canal Dock. Audiences form to applaud these skaters. At night music is played, and couples dance on the ice.

Moran's food emporium. Miriam smiles at the security man, presents her bag, passes her Loyalty Card through the identity check, lifts her face to the camera, and then is walking through wide aisles, clear warm air, welcoming the fact that in this supermarket no one wears a face mask. A jar of *confit de canard* is the first item to be carefully placed in her trolley, then an organic chicken from the meat section, followed by salmon pâté and quails' eggs from the delicatessen.

Fresh pasta. Miriam examines all the possibilities, finally settles on little semi-circular pockets stuffed with wild mushroom, pumpkin and sage. *Agnolotti* she reads on the card. Nice, she thinks. Next it's organic vegetables, and Miriam decides that today she will take home baby carrots, spinach, and Spanish tomatoes.

She arranges for the delivery, finds a table in the café, takes off her coat and scarf, orders fresh orange juice and a salad sandwich. And thinks how much she enjoys this clear cold weather and the new arrangement with Peter Brindley.

Finn meets Peter once a week to suggest how a chapter might be restructured, a group of sentences condensed. He tries to correct Peter's grammatical errors, and not to lose his temper. Finn spends his newfound wealth on presents for the redhead. '*Ô toison moutannant jusque sur l'encolure!'* he murmurs. *'ô boucles! ô parfum chargé de nonchaloir!'* The redhead is his current lover. She likes alcohol and cocaine.

Miriam spends her share of the money on new clothes for Jeremy, outings to the children's theatre, a good haircut. Food shopping has become a real pleasure for her. On each new expedition she finds some item of food they have not yet tried.

'Smart move,' Yvonne said. 'How much is he giving?' She had whistled between her teeth when Miriam told her the amount. 'Get him to sign a contract. Then he won't be able to winkle out of it. You know the knack Finn has for getting up people's noses.'

'That's the problem,' Miriam agreed. 'Peter Brindley wanted to put it all in writing. That way he'd be able to use it against tax. But Finn won't sign. He can't bear being tied down.'

'How's lover boy?' Yvonne asked then, and Miriam explained that things were not progressing all that well.

'You see, I'm too nervous. My vagina tightens up and then Derek thinks I'm rejecting him.'

Today Miriam will have to be back at work before two, and sit in The Female State through the whole long afternoon listening to unhappy people who ask her advice about interrupting their pregnancies. She will try to be kind, but not too kind. Lonely desperate people sometimes imagine that Miriam can intervene to save them from the choices they alone need to make.

She looks at her watch – another half-hour before her lunch break ends. She orders coffee, a tiny *tarte aux pommes*, and savours nibble by nibble the delicate taste of baked apple.

The moment comes for Miriam to catch the tram back to work. She fastens her coat, wraps her scarf around her neck and walks out into Ranelagh's cold air, then staggers back against the shop door as a heavy body thuds against her. 'Excuse me,' Miriam says.

Rosanne Roycroft stands in front of her, staring as if at a stranger. The streaked orange hair has been pulled back severely from her face. Miriam tries to look away, to pretend that she had not recognised her, but Rosanne grips her arm and does not let go.

'I suppose you'd better meet my parents-in-law,' she says. '*En route* to the train station. What they are doing here I do not know. A magical place in Bennettsbridge, and yet they insist on doing in their lungs with Dublin exhaust fumes. I'm up to my eyes....'

Miriam's arm is being held and Rosanne's parents-in-law are being thrust up against her. She has no choice but to be polite.

'Hello,' she says.

'Now, are you coming in or not?' Rosanne says. They shake their heads.

'They tried to insist,' Rosanne is telling her, 'that I'd shop in one of those teeming cattle runs, but I wasn't having any of it. I'm not spending an hour in a mask, queuing. Besides mingling with all that unsavoury flesh. Look after them, will you?'

'I've to go back to work,' Miriam says, but already Rosanne has disappeared inside the shop, and William's parents are standing beside Miriam on a freezing street.

'We met at William and Rosanne's party some months ago,' she says. 'I was talking to you about the children's school.'

The old couple's faces are red and cold. Dr Roycroft presses a handkerchief to his mouth. He seems to be trying to stifle a cough.

'The school where your grandchildren go,' Miriam adds. And now Dr Roycroft is coughing and his wife is looking anxiously at him. 'And we were talking to Risteard O'Toole. But I think you had to leave then.' She scarcely knows what she is saying, it is so cold, and something has to be said to fill up the space.

Dr Roycroft coughs into the silence. Miriam stands shivering, wondering what she will say next. 'Could we go in?' she says. 'It's lovely and warm inside.'

The old lady's thin strands of frizzy grey hair shake against a crumpled yellow scarf. 'Risteard O'Toole,' she is saying in her quiet voice, 'is not an admirable human being.' And then her voice goes on and on, talking about human rights and migrant people, a racist amendment to the constitution. Without warning, she calls out loudly, '*Ten years ago it was the entitlement and birthright of every person born on the island of Ireland, which includes its islands and seas, to be part of the Irish nation.*'

Miriam looks at Mrs Roycroft shouting on the footpath, and wonders if she has dementia, then at Dr Roycroft's red crinkled face. He, however, appears not to be discomfited, even to be nodding in agreement.

Suddenly Rosanne is back, and one large freckled hand is clamping down on her mother-in-law's shoulder. 'Mother Roycroft's sounding off. I could hear you through the plate glass window. The security men thought there'd been an incident. Tell me, Mother Roycroft, if it's so unpleasant in Ireland, why do immigrants want to stay here?'

In front of Miriam's bewildered gaze, Rosanne and her parents-in-law begin a heated argument about Daonnacht, the new political party, Rosanne defending it, her parents-in-law attacking it vehemently.

'Licensed xenophobia,' Dr Roycroft exclaims.

'Goodbye,' Miriam says, but Rosanne's hand grabs her wrist. 'I still have to find tofu,' she says. 'I'm making miso soup and sukiyaki. A Japanese evening.'

'Intimidation,' Mrs Roycroft says. 'Extortion. Picking off their enemies on the pretence of serving the community.'

'Daonnacht is a party that sees the whole picture.' Rosanne replies frostily. 'It's the Irish for "humanity", for God's sake. You want to blame it for trying to protect us from chaos? From hoodlums, vandals, drug-dealers? I know that chaos. I visit the Devanney family.' Her mouth twists into a bitter grimace.

When Rosanne volunteered to become a member of Sócúl, she had hoped that its whimsical title might have reflected the quality of those to be succoured, and that she would be ministering to a cultured gay couple, fond of an occasional fish pie or Italian bread. She planned to reorganise their drugs regimes, initiate them into aromatherapy, ci-gong, deep tissue massage. Perhaps cure them completely.

Instead, she has been landed with the Devanney family, and as Rosanne shouted into Miriam's voicemail on the day after the Sócúl Christmas party, Derek has given her degenerates. 'Who could pity them?' she roared. And Miriam winced as she listened.

Miriam can see many reasons to pity the Devanneys. From the photographs on the mantelpiece – men in charcoal-grey suits, women at ease in flowery gardens, holding slim glasses of what she can only imagine must be champagne – she has surmised that this is a family which has come down in the world. Two of their sons have crippling illnesses, with symptoms similar to Philip's. One of them is presently in Castlerea prison. The other, blinded by a brain tumour, sits helplessly in a dumb stupor.

'*Focaccia*,' Rosanne shouted into the phone. '*Orecchiette*.' She had invited them to her house, offered them wine and wonderful Italian dishes. And what had the Devanneys done? Thrown the whole lot in the loo, then layered wads of loo paper on top. Rosanne had to put her hand into the ghastly mush in an attempt to unblock the toilet.

'A family of blacks, or Chinese refugees, would have been better,' she yelled. 'They might at least have been intelligent.'

Miriam did not return Rosanne's phone call. 'Keep away from that appalling woman,' Yvonne said, and Miriam took her advice. Yet here she is stuck in this ridiculous charade on a freezing street, with two mad old people and Rosanne dragging her by the arm.

'What's the good of coming to Dublin if we can't see the children?'

Miriam jumps at Dr Roycroft's sudden inapposite intervention. She stares at him, his purpling nose, his veined and rutted cheeks becoming beefier and more florid as his anger grows.

'Nothing justifies your keeping them away from us,' he shouts. 'We might as well have stayed in Kilkenny. And what are we doing outside this wretched supermarket? We came to Dublin to see the children.' He looks up and down the street, his hands rise in a gesture of supplication. Help me, he seems to be saying. There are tears in his pale eyes.

Some passersby pause expectantly. Miriam looks at the ground. She can scarcely breathe from embarrassment.

'You're getting in people's way, Daddy Roycroft.' Rosanne pushes her father-in-law to the edge of the footpath. 'As well as ruining a perfectly nice shopping expedition.'

'Shouldn't they get in out of the cold, Rosanne?' Miriam says, but Rosanne ignores her, fixes Dr Roycroft with a frigid stare.

'As you know perfectly well, the girls were away with friends this weekend.' People stand listening as Rosanne speaks. They stamp their feet against the cold. Rosanne ignores them, squeezes Miriam's arm, winks apologetically.

'Of course if Daddy and Mother Roycroft would be sensible and come inside with me, they could sit down and have a nice cup of coffee, and all this unpleasantness could be avoided.'

'Loyalty Cards,' Mrs Roycroft says wearily, gesturing at the shop's Edwardian-style door, 'to keep people out. It's a form of apartheid. We couldn't go into that shop.'

'Have it your own way,' Rosanne snaps. 'I've an interview lined up at three,' she tells Miriam. 'Have to get this pair to the railway station first. The English *Indo* wants to interrogate me on what's energising today's Irish culture. I'm putting Joyce into the mix. Poor Jimmy Joyce – he's been almost forgotten lately. So we're rushing in to rescue him. I'm taking the "Wandering Rocks" chapter in *Ulysses*, showing how it registers psychic dislocation under colonial modernity. Daonnacht, here I go. Got to find that tofu first though.'

'Goodbye,' Miriam says again, but Rosanne leans towards her and whispers hoarsely, 'Just one more minute.'

'It made me feel bad,' Miriam says to Yvonne that same evening. 'Standing outside in the cold with two old people. They wouldn't go into Moran's on principle. And up to that, I was loving the feeling of being able to shop there. Not having to worry about money any more.'

'Look, this Peter Brindley fellow gave you the Loyalty Card. He invited you to shop in Moran's.' Yvonne switches on the kettle. *'For persons of good character and their guests* – that always tickles me.' She looks down to where

her own Loyalty Card lies on the counter. 'When my family comes up
from Sligo, it's nice to be able to bring them to a top-class supermarket that
isn't too expensive. What's wrong with that?' Yvonne pours hot water into
the teapot and swirls it around. 'I mean you know what shopping is like
these days. And this one supermarket says, "We welcome you if you have
our Loyalty Card." No queues, great service.'

'But the Roycrofts' point was that everyone is supposed to be equal.
Moran's do a background check. They don't have to give reasons.'

Yvonne stirs sugar into her tea, dips a homemade biscuit into the milky
liquid. 'Listen, it's happened forever in shops. What do you think the
security man is on the door for? Moran's have just taken it a step further.
They've a right to keep out people who can't afford to shop there.'

'And then the Roycrofts talked about the quotas in schools, and
apartments that won't let immigrants rent them,' Miriam says. 'Some
places even specify *No Muslims*. It all sounds so horrible.'

'Those Roycroft people sound like cranks to me. Every school has a
quota. You should know that.'

'They said that we're so confused by the country's continual economic
crises, we've no time to think about the dreadful things that are growing
little by little all around us. That we accept things that we would never
have accepted five years ago; that we wouldn't have accepted last year.'

'Even if you don't agree with the principle of the thing,' Yvonne pours
Miriam a second cup of tea, 'it's a fact on the ground. Why be a total
masochist?'

CHAPTER 11

Tina stares at a space just a little way in front of her where the hot air from the heater mixes briefly with the dust from her studio's crumbling plaster before being sucked up into the February cold. Occasionally she turns her head to look from one canvas to another. She does not feel anything. A girl, really only a kid, has stolen Finn from her.

They had been drinking in Grogan's, standing at the bar talking about seventeenth-century Dutch interiors, the way the light played on a face or a table from a window or more faintly from an open door. The shine on a scissors or bucket. The light moving to the gold edging of a jacket.

'I'm thinking of doing interiors,' she said.

Then Finn saw the girl sitting with other young people. Slim, pale skin, a long curling mass of bright red hair.

Tina mixes paints, sets up the ladder and starts to climb. Halfway up, she hesitates. Maybe she'll ruin it working in this mood. She's already behind schedule, only two canvases finished. Landscapes, she thinks, fucking landscapes. Burnt ochre, pthalo blue – she mixes with a palette knife, her hand scoops up the blended paint and she reaches towards the huge canvas to smear it into place. The palette sits atop the stepladder; she mixes lamp black, cadmium yellow. Another scoop of the hand. She leans into the canvas, smears, raises her eyes, smears again in the area above her head. Pure colour. Its particles combine and aggregate, a chemical reaction which forces deep green from black. Pthalo blue turns a harsh brown. Tina, standing on the ladder in her overalls, leaning into her painting with great smudges of colour, struggles to calm her rage.

Wendy in Tina's studio sipped mint tea. She had brought a bag of muffins with her and a teabag, rinsed the mug Tina offered her with boiling water, then added more, dropped in the teabag, and stirred. Pale blonde hair curved inwards to the nape of her neck, the cut of the scarlet coat accentuated her long, slim figure. She sat on a pile of Tina's coats.

'I'm doing a drugs book,' Wendy explained. 'The underbelly of the city. Case studies, like the boy I bring to the methadone clinic, talking endlessly about his constipation as if it's a person. His shit is like hard muscle. He can't get it out. And all the time in the car, when I'm driving him, his body's straining. I'll interlace the book's narrative with a historical context of drug-taking. Coleridge addicted to opium, Aldous Huxley taking mescaline....'

'So Coleridge wrote "Kubla Khan" because he couldn't shit? And this constipated kid's a creative genius?' Tina sat morosely stirring her coffee, looking into its swirling surface. She became aware of a dull ache behind one of her ribs. Could it be her heart? How does a heart attack begin? she asked herself.

'Blaise wants me to go to California with him,' Wendy said. 'So we can spend time together without all the pressures we have here. I've told them at work that I have to go. They're giving me leave of absence.'

Tina stared at Wendy's throat as it swallowed little fragments of her muffin, at her napkin as it dabbed a crimson, anxious mouth. There was something bad coming. She knew it.

'We'll be gone for a month. Blaise has to sort out some film treatments and a couple of contracts. And I'm going to take the material for my drugs book with me; work on it over there. I've miles of interviews.'

'For Christ's sake,' Tina growled, 'you're full of crap.' She stood up, buttoned her jacket, banged the studio door as she left. The ache in her chest had intensified – a cramp, she decided – and she hunched over as she walked down Blessington Street.

But Wendy ran after her. 'You forgot to lock your studio,' she shouted, grabbing Tina's arm. Tina shrugged her hand away and walked on, but Wendy followed her, and everything became clear.

'You have to let Blaise sell the building,' Wendy whispered urgently. 'The other tenants have all left, so if you'll only co-operate, he'll be able to sell with vacant possession. It'll make a huge difference in the price. He's promised to find you somewhere else. Somewhere nice. Please, Tina. For my sake?'

CHAPTER 12

A March morning arrives – wet and stormy. In the dark bedroom the alarm clock's shrill tones drag Finn from sleep. He groans, rubs his sleeve across stubbled face and gropes his way to the light switch. His toe jabs the base of the dressing-table. Pain shoots up his leg, his body becomes fully conscious, and he feels the room's intense cold.

He shivers and yawns all at the same time, then glares at the calendar on the wall. It comes to him with a feeling of glorious relief that today it is Miriam's turn to bring Jeremy to school. He crawls back into bed, snuggles the duvet's warmth all around him. 'Miriam,' he whispers, rocking her in the bed, 'wake up.' He grasps her shoulder, squeezes it, rocks her again. 'Miriam, get up. You've to bring Jeremy to school.'

Miriam turns in the bed, dark hair tumbling over the pillow. Her eyes open a fraction. 'Finn, I'm feeling really sick. I vomited during the night.'

He tries to hang on to the duvet but she is pulling it away from him. His body, in its covering of thermal underwear, is thrust once more into the cold bedroom.

'It's my period too and I feel awful.'

'So why did you stay out so bloody late? Aren't you working today?'

Miriam raises herself unsteadily on one elbow and Finn can see that her face is very pale. There are stains on her nightshirt, and traces of vomit enmeshed in strands of her hair.

'Please, Finn, I don't have to be in till this afternoon. Maybe I'll have to ring in sick. Could you get me a pad?'

'Bloody hell, where are they?'

'They're in the wardrobe,' she says weakly, and now he finds himself searching the bottom of the wardrobe through tangled piles of Miriam's underwear, until he finally pulls out a packet of sanitary towels and throws it across the room to his wife.

'Thanks.' Her voice is still groggy.

Finn puts Miriam's used pad in the bin. He plugs in the electric heater, resigns himself to the tedious business of getting Jeremy to school.

'Tired. Not getting up,' Jeremy mumbles when his father gives him a morning kiss. Finn pulls off the child's pyjamas, throws them on the bedroom floor, forces a T-shirt over the little boy's head. Follows it with a sweater, pulls underpants up over his bottom, dungarees to cover the underpants and clips them at the shoulders. 'Go and do a wee, Jeremy' he says. He is about to descend the stairs when he hears Miriam's voice calling to him through the wall.

'Finn, I feel so sick. Could you bring me up a cup of tea?'

'What d'you think I am?' he shouts, and he hears in his voice his mother's nagging wail, the voice that had plagued his childhood.

There is a package on the hall floor. Who could have dropped it in? Finn wonders as he holds it in his hand and stands over the cooker, stirring the porridge oats. 'Miserable bastard,' he grunts, kicking the base of the gas cooker as he stirs. Every fibre of his body revolts against this entrapment in a sad kitchen. He tears open the package – it's a book from Rosanne – and he wants to fling it as far away from him as he can. But as he stands waiting for the porridge to simmer, he finds himself opening the book. And then he is sitting at the table poring over it, and the porridge is boiling. He is so engrossed in the book that he forgets he has a child waiting for breakfast, and the porridge burns. If the poems are this good in translation, he thinks, what would they be like in the original? 'I have to learn Irish,' he mutters, and then he smells the burning porridge, and jumps up and scrapes it into the sink. 'Shit,' he says, 'bloody Miriam,' and he searches the cupboard for a clean saucepan, pours in oatflakes, adds milk. She's sick, for Christ's sake, he tells himself then. You saw her face, the vomit in her hair. He brings the porridge to the boil again, stirs, looks around for the child. 'Ready in a second,' he says. 'Find your shoes now, there's a good fellow.'

Jeremy glances a moment at his father, then climbs up on a chair and begins to beat the table with a spoon.

'Okay, Jeremy, enough noise. Okay, cool it. It's just coming. And a little honey on top, the way you like it.'

Jeremy eats while Finn switches on the kettle, and searches the fridge for something for the school lunch. 'Why does Miriam buy this rubbish?' he grumbles. 'We were better off before.' Then he's plucking pieces of smoked salmon from their packet, cutting a thick slice of *saucisson*. He spreads goose terrine on thin oatmeal biscuits. A few mini Roquefort crêpes, everything tumbles into Jeremy's lunchbox.

Finn makes the tea, runs upstairs with it. A growl comes from somewhere deep inside him. 'Where are his shoes?'

Miriam sits up shakily.

'His shoes for Christ's sake?'

'Look under the stairs, or they could be in the hall.'

Finn runs back downstairs. 'We have to go now, Jeremy. You'll be late.' He grabs the shoes from the hall cupboard, a pair of socks from the clotheshorse, forces them onto the child's feet as he sits at the table.

'Not finished. I want toast,' Jeremy says.

'Up and out. Quick, quick, quick.' Finn grabs his son with one hand, the school bag and anorak with the other and dashes out of the house. He hopes they may pick up a lift on the way.

Forty-five minutes later Finn returns home. He runs up the stairs two at a time, bursts panting into the bedroom. 'Miriam, had you forgotten that they're interviewing me today? They texted. They'll be here in an hour.'

'It's on the calendar, Finn. I'm trying to get myself ready. But I feel horrible.'

Finn stares at his wife, who is sitting naked on the bed, razor and soap in hand, a bowl of water beside her.

'What are you doing?' Finn looks helplessly at the long bare legs, stretched out towards him, the white towel under her, the red stain of menstrual blood. Shaving her legs, he thinks. What's wrong with her? 'We have to get the house cleaned up.' The words come out as a lamentation. 'They're bringing a photographer.' He kicks at the dirty vests and underpants strewn about on the floor.

Miriam looks up at him, holding the razor delicately between thumb and forefinger. 'I was so sick, I didn't realise I'd got vomit in my hair and down my nightshirt. I had to wash, and then I thought I'd faint when I was in the shower. Anyhow, let's not worry about the bedroom. They won't come up here.'

She goes back to her task, and he stands looking at one pale pink nipple just visible through strands of dark hair, slim hands holding the razor. 'What are you shaving your bloody crotch for?' he says roughly. 'They're not going to photograph it.'

'I don't know, Finn. Just being sick and all. It's horrible sleeping with vomit all over you. I feel I have to cleanse every bit of me.' She runs the fingers of her left hand down her calves to check that they are smooth to the touch. 'I did my legs,' she says. 'Though I don't know if I'll be able to get up…. Maybe you should do the interview in town.'

'But they're coming to the house! That's the point. It's an at-home thing.' He stamps on Miriam's discarded clothes. You stupid woman, he wants to scream: this is my career, my life. 'We can't let them up here,' he tries to keep his voice steady, 'if the place is a tip. And would you for God's sake stop bleeding on that towel. It'll go through onto the sheet.'

Her pale face looks into his. 'The pad was irritating my skin, so I had to take it off. She points to the floor and Finn makes out the red pad half-hidden by one of Jeremy's sweaters. He kicks it under the bed.

'Could you find me the Tampax?' she asks. 'I'm too shaky.' And again Finn is searching through the bottom of the wardrobe.

'I can't find them,' he says. 'I've got to get ready.' He stands up and pulls at the hangers. 'Grey cords with the blue shirt?' He pulls out a pair of trousers, holds them up. 'Shit, they've got a stain.' He throws them on the floor, pulls out another pair while Miriam uses the edge of the towel to pat her pubic area dry.

'I met Blaise Boothe in Derek's,' she says. 'Maybe the Tampax are in the bathroom. I might have left them there. He came over to me and I didn't want to talk to him. He said he was sorry for being so horrible at the Roycroft's party. Anyway, he loved your book.'

That ugly little faggot, Finn thinks, and stands transfixed, watching his wife rub moisturising cream into her pubic area, the stain on the towel still spreading. 'It'll go through onto the sheet,' he says again, runs to the bathroom, pulls two Tampax out of the packet, back to the bedroom, throws them on the bed.

Then he's clearing the floor, pushing everything into the bottom of the wardrobe. Miriam is pressing the Tampax up between her open legs, and he wants to scream at her to get out of the bed, to help him set the place up so that it will look convincing as a writer's haven.

The pile in the wardrobe is too high. It is top heavy, toppling towards him. He shoves the doors against it but cannot prevent an avalanche. Shoes, trousers and Miriam's underwear pour out onto the floor.

'I'll help,' she says. 'Let me do that.' She gets off the bed, and begins carefully folding trousers and sweaters. 'I'll do a wash later when I feel a bit better. But lovie, don't worry. They won't come up to the bedroom.'

'Don't bother folding them,' Finn says.

'*Principia Ethica*,' she says, and now she's lining up pairs of shoes under the bed. 'It's the book Blaise recommended. He says I'll find it on Amazon. You see, it seems I changed his life. After his outburst at the Roycrofts' party, he was so horrified at himself that he went on retreat to the monks at Glenstal. They were reading *Principia Ethica* by some philosopher called Moore. I wrote it down. And now Blaise follows Moore's ethical principles, and he thinks I should too. He was saying that he used to try to *do good* the way I do, and that's what caused his breakdown, so he's learning instead to *be good*.' She's putting on her dressing-gown now. 'Could you get me the dirty-clothes bag?'

'It's burst,' he calls from the bathroom.

'Okay,' she says. 'I'll put them in a pillowcase. Blaise and I are friends now. We shook hands. He told me I should take up painting again.' She is straightening the covers on the bed, and the bedroom is beginning to look like a bedroom should. Finn clamps his mouth shut. Let her talk, he tells himself; let her talk. She'll run out of steam; just let her yap.

Open marriage. It's the only phrase Finn can use, but he hates it. As if he and Miriam were two empty-headed bourgeois fools. He loves her completely, but if she were his only sexual partner, he'd go insane. Monogamy, for Finn, is disgusting. As if your body could ever belong to another person. Bodies are free. The redhead moves unbidden through his mind. His bowels tighten.

Miriam sits on the tidied bed, holds out long slim fingers. 'Blaise says I'm wasting my talents. And you know it's strange – when I looked at him last night, I didn't find him ugly any more.'

He wills her mouth to close, the soft sounds emanating from it to cease – to give his head a clear space, to construct himself in time for the interview.

'He said that beauty carries its own responsibilities. And because I'm beautiful, it's my ethical duty to guard my looks, to enhance them for myself, for my friends; not to fret them away over miserable women who are getting abortions. And The Female State is a wretched place to work. Everyone's unhappy. Blaise told me that I should definitely give it up. If doing good entails an existence cut off from pleasure and beauty, he says that it must be unethical.'

'For Christ's sake,' Finn shouts, 'that's the most self-serving load of bollocks I ever heard. You know why you work. We need the fucking money, that's why. Dump Sócúl. It doesn't pay. What use is charity? Its only function is to make the giver feel good about himself.'

'Now that we've got Peter Brindley … I told Blaise about him and he says now's the right time. I've got to make a jump, he says, or else I'll find myself getting older and sadder and less beautiful by the minute.'

'I told you not to gossip about Brindley,' Finn says ferociously. 'I told you to keep your mouth shut. I don't want these bastards saying I'm a kept man.'

'Blaise won't say anything. He promised me. He thinks you should have got Aosdána. He said it's only fair that some good Samaritan helps us out. And he said you've got to let Peter pay to fix the central heating if Peter wants to do it. And he does. How can we have an aesthetic life if we're frozen all the time? Oh God, my stomach.' She falls back against the pillow, her hands massaging her slim curves. 'Cramps,' she moans.

'Listen, Miriam.' Finn senses a rising wave of incomprehension between himself and his wife. He can feel his hands rise up involuntarily to clutch the sides of his head. 'First of all, Blaise Boothe's a little shit. He wouldn't know an ethic if it gouged out his eyes. And you can't give up the job. We're not depending solely on Brindley to keep us afloat. We'd be insane to do that.'

'But Finn,' she's whimpering now and he wants to hit her, 'I hate the job. There's all these strange people who've started to hang around outside. They sidle up to me and whisper horrible things like *Baby killer*. Then I come home and it's freezing because you won't get the boiler mended. The only good thing this whole winter has been Peter Brindley. And now you won't let him help us properly. I'm sick, Finn. It's probably because the house is always so cold, and there's that damp smell in the bathroom. Even my legs feel strange. Can't you see how pale I am?' She lies back against the pillow, pulls up the duvet, her hands lying helplessly on its blue and white striped cover.

'Jesus, Miriam, I've to light the fire, for Christ's sake. And clean the living room. Aren't you going to help?'

Her voice comes back to him weak and pathetic. 'Peter's work,' he hears. 'Those chapters he gave you on Friday? I told him you'd have them ready this evening. I can't get up, Finn. I just can't.'

'For Christ's sake, I can't read Brindley's shit every day of the week! It's fucking up my writing. He's calling himself Byron all the time now. I can't stick it.' With his clean clothes over his arm, Finn rushes from the room.

Downstairs he switches on lights and looks at the toy-strewn living room, the disfiguring stain on the sofa where Jeremy had spilt his dinner, the piles of dirty clothes on the kitchen floor. He had meant to tidy the place the night before.

He shoves the clothes into the washing machine, and puts Jeremy's breakfast dishes in the sink. He changes the tablecloth on the living room table, throws a rug over the sofa, piles the toys into a corner. He places his ancient Remington typewriter centre stage, a sheaf of paper alongside. He selects several works – Wittgenstein's *Philosophical Investigations*, Schopenhauer's *The World as Will and Idea*, Nietzsche's *Ecce Homo*, Dante's *Inferno*, Joyce's *Ulysses* – and places them in careful disarray on the table.

Somehow, in the movement of books, of typewriter, of shadow and light, the redhead's face seems to shimmer on the tablecloth's surface. Finn smashes his hand downwards on it. How dare the redhead's brother phone up Miriam? How did he get her number?

He cleans out the fireplace, and lights it anew. He plumps up cushions, places them carefully on the sofa, then stands back to survey the effect.

Finn decides to remove *Ulysses* from the table. It could look as if he were trying to draw comparisons. He replaces it with Zola's *Thérèse*

Raquin. On the other hand, he thinks, the fool they send out will probably never have heard of Zola.

Miriam had stared into the phone in confusion. 'How did you get my number?' she whispered. Finn grabbed the phone but the redhead's brother had already hung up.

'Will we always be close, Finn?' she had asked him then. 'This open marriage thing? Might it drive us apart?'

That's the worst of it, he thinks now, to know everything that goes on in Miriam's head, to look at her and know everything. He loves her, no question about that. But even as he recognises that love, the redhead's almond skin invades his head, her low moan is sucked into his mouth like words from a cloud, fragrant translucent skin at her temples, delicate blue veins.

He looks around. They'll be here any second. A shower? No. A quick wash will have to do. He runs up to the bathroom, splashes water on his face, rubs under his arms with a sponge, dries himself and puts on clean clothes. He looks for his razor, then realises that Miriam has it. The blade will be destroyed. He has warned her often enough, but it doesn't stop her.

He remembers the blank page in the typewriter. He goes down to sit in front of it. He rubs his chin and realises that the thick layer of stubble will not photograph well. He will look gaunt and dreary. Back up the stairs two at a time. Without looking at her, he grabs the razor. Listen, you bitch, he wants to say, don't take my fucking razor again.

As Finn shaves, he curses all women. He places small pieces of toilet paper on each separate cut. Downstairs again. And this time as he types, words flow onto the page.

Why the redhead? Why the redhead? Because the winds blow in the trees. Her hair, the red willow bark, her skin, white leaves trembling. I am obsessed. I am obsessed....

Finn hears the doorbell. His typing is a mess of trees and redheads – a whole forest of them on the page. He pulls the paper out of the typewriter and slowly tears it into tiny pieces. The doorbell sounds once more.

'Alright, alright, I'm coming,' he shouts, but catches a glimpse of himself in the hall mirror as he passes. Pieces of toilet paper are still stuck to his face. 'Oh God,' he says, removing them one by one, 'this is going to be a bad day.'

CHAPTER 13

When Finn opens the door, Paul Ryan is standing on the front step, a child in his arms.

'This wasn't my idea.' Ryan smiles apologetically. 'They know I mind my kid in the mornings.'

Finn looks at him, uncomprehending. For a moment he is too shocked to speak. Words eventually stutter from his mouth. 'What are you doing here?' He starts to push the door shut. 'I told them you weren't acceptable to me.'

Ryan wedges his foot in the door. 'I don't want to be here either. Come on, Daly; I'm not going to mess you over. Things aren't going well at the moment. If I don't do this one, I'm out.'

'Do I give a shit? They told me they wouldn't send you. They *promised.*'

Paul Ryan pushes his way through the hall-door, past Finn and into the living room. The child's arms cling tight around his neck, its face buried in his shoulder. 'That's the way things are in the media,' Ryan says. 'You can't trust anyone.' He sits down heavily on the sofa.

'I'm not giving you a fucking interview.' Finn folds his arms against his chest, stares at Paul Ryan. He knows that he should not have relaxed his grip on the front door. Things will go badly, he is sure of it.

'The photographer'll be along in about an hour,' Ryan says, as if Finn had not spoken. 'I'll be out of here. I don't particularly want it to be known that I've brought the kid. Doesn't go down…. New editor hates my guts.'

He begins to unwind a long grey scarf from around his neck, while phrases from his review of Finn's book run through Finn's head. *Self-obsessed – autistic – unconvincing – incomprehensible.*

'You're to get out of here,' Finn says. 'I won't speak to you,' and he holds the sitting-room door open. But Ryan doesn't move. Instead, he looks down at his child and he begins to sing. 'The street is empty,' he sings. 'And shields of light are breaking apart before the rout and the siege.'

Finn stands uneasily holding the door while Paul Ryan unzips his son's anorak, puts him sitting in a corner of the sofa. 'Here, everyone wants us to leave, but we will not leave,' Ryan sings. He opens his briefcase and Finn stares helplessly at him. 'We've got your drawing book here, Ben. And my notebook and pen. And your crayons.'

'I'll call the police,' Finn says, running his fingers through his hair.

'Good job you're a hardy little fellow,' Ryan sings and Finn begins to discern a melody. 'You don't mind that it's cold in here. Because you're used to it. Strange birds seeking refuge. Among them quails and songbirds with colourful wings, and also birds of prey. In our house we don't turn on the central heating. Our friends use wood and turf. You can't afford to heat your house if you drive your car. No crèche either. Granny helps out, but she's sick today.'

Ryan holds his open notebook on his knee. 'Ben likes me to sing,' he says. 'Now, let's start. Background? Motivation? Plans for the future? I've been given the parameters … so it'll be pretty standard. A colour piece, that's all.' He takes a large greyish handkerchief out of his pocket and blows his nose loudly. 'I've had this cold for weeks. Okay, okay. Your parents? General background?'

Finn is so taken aback by the sight and sound of a large man singing to his child about birds and life's problems that he finds himself hunched over the table, talking about growing up in an anonymous apartment in the suburbs of a German industrial city. No fun, no laughter, never a visiting relation or friend. Dreary, distant parents. Never allowed a pet. His ready belief, being an only child, that this was how all children lived. His doomed attempts to change that life, to introduce noise, laughter, conversation. 'The best day of my life was the day my mother died. It meant change, escape from the tedium. I was able to make my father send me back to Ireland.' His voice trails away, and he sits holding his head in his hands. He had not meant to speak.

Ryan sits in front of Finn, chewing the end of his pen. He does not record Finn's words, and waits through several minutes of silence. Then he begins to sing again, and this time to Finn.

'Now I'll tell you what we'll do,' he sings and Finn thinks he can make out some vague resemblance to a tune from a Gilbert and Sullivan operetta which reverts after a few bars to plain chant. 'I'll begin with the décor "tumbling kaleidoscope of colour, touches of emerald and lapis lazuli, walls a gallimaufry" the readers like the odd word they may not understand, makes them feel highbrow. A gallimaufry of pictures and books.' He looks around the room for inspiration. 'Here a carved elm statue,' he chants, 'there a stained-glass panel, what's it of?' He squints at it. 'Let's say reminiscent of Harry Clarke? Where were we? Okay, a bit of excess. Scatters a mosaic of jewelled light across the stairwell framed by bookshelves as thin as saplings. A bit of poetic licence? Miriam will like that.' He scribbles in his notebook. 'And that painting, huge abstract oil painting – it will bring the excitement of Chicago into the living room. Transatlantic pleasures. And then we get your desk, how you love to write to the patter of little feet, to be in the centre of the household.' He stops singing, gestures towards the typewriter.

'That's what the table set-up is supposed to symbolise, isn't it?' he says. 'You really use that thing?'

Finn walks over to the typewriter and touches its keys. 'The intimacy of the typewriter is what I like. My mistakes, all here in front of me. I write everything down in a copybook. Then I type.'

Paul Ryan follows Finn to the table, looks briefly through the pile of books lying there. Finn shrugs. 'My reference library.'

'Poetry?' Paul Ryan sings. 'You've chosen poetry?'

Finn looks up with a start. He sees that Ryan is flicking through Rosanne Roycroft's poetry book.

'She's good,' Ryan sings. 'Even better in Irish.'

'I burnt the porridge this morning,' Finn admits, 'I got so engrossed in it.'

'I thought there was a bit of a smell.' Ryan sniffs the air and returns to sit beside his child. 'Rosanne can sing. She can write, but she's such a damn bully.... She remains like a wall on our chests, in our throats, like a piece of glass, like a cactus thorn, and in our eyes a storm of fire.'

Finn hunches his shoulders and drags his fingers through his hair until it stands on end. 'In my family the different generations hated each other,' he says. 'My father ran away from home, never spoke to Grandfather again. My dad and I haven't spoken in years. I won't ever let it be like that between me and Jeremy.'

'At dusk a sensation of darkness and gloom floods the chest,' Paul Ryan sings. 'Amassing like silt, closing in like a wall.'

'That's what it felt like.' Finn is standing, making grasping gestures with his hands, opening them and closing them as if trying to catch some attribute or idea of himself. 'I was trapped. Walled in by the past. I didn't have the energy to imagine a future. Germany had stifled me. And even when I got to Ireland, I could hardly breathe. It was only when I found Miriam that I started to live. It's Miriam who gives me courage, happiness.'

'Lovers of hunting,' Paul Ryan sings, 'don't aim your rifles at my happiness, which isn't worth the price of a bullet. What seems to you so nimble and fine, like a fawn and flees every which way like a partridge, isn't happiness. Trust me: my happiness bears no relation to happiness.'

The words that Paul Ryan sings beat against Finn's consciousness. There is something in his head that has to be clarified. 'I've broken the mould.' His hands move to grasp each other, his knuckles crack. 'My grandfather,' he says. 'My father hated him, so I felt that my grandfather and I must have some connection. I wanted to find out everything about him.' Words pour from him in a confused rush – his aunt, his grandfather's diaries, the copybooks that he has found stored away in a small whitewashed cottage in Cavan.

Ryan sits back, gnawing a thumbnail. The child sits beside him carefully colouring. 'Good picture, Ben,' he sings. 'Do a nice sky.'

'Listen to me, Ryan,' Finn hisses. 'It's always been a dream of perfection. Always. And that's where it is. That's why I'm going there every week; I want to piece it together. When I see the world through my aunt's eyes, the story's totally different. Think of it, Ryan: a little whitewashed cottage, a tiny farm. And it's me. I'm part of that. But it's not simple. You can't patronise it. It's immensely complex and real.'

'The crayons go back in the box,' Paul Ryan sings. 'Time to go, Ben. Out of here before the photographer arrives.'

'It was all there in my first novel.' Finn is unable to stop himself explaining. 'That's why I keep trying and trying again. That's why I'll beg or steal to get the work done. Nobody understood that. Nobody understood why. Not even me. *The political unconscious.* That's what Jameson called it.'

Paul Ryan stands up, puts the child's crayons and colouring book carefully into his briefcase. 'It has taken me a long time,' he sings 'to understand that water is the finest drink and bread the most delicious food, and that art is worthless unless it plants a measure of splendour in people's hearts.'

'That's exactly what I'm writing.' Finn's two hands clutch at his head again. He cannot stop a groan escaping from his mouth. 'That's what I've always been writing. Ireland, comfortable and smug, believed itself invincible, believed that it would never be touched by the rot in Europe. Ireland, riddled with greed and corruption.' He sits down and rocks himself on his chair. 'It begins with a mental picture. It's a dream and it eats at me; it gives me no peace. The picture of an abandoned child in torn muddy trousers. She's looking from the outside in through her bedroom window, and she sees her own dead body lying on the floor.'

'Remember the photographer's coming,' Ryan says.

Ryan's little son smiles at Finn. Finn smiles back, watches Ryan carry the child to a battered blue Nissan. He runs upstairs, wets a facecloth in the bathroom sink. Miriam is lying prone on the bed, clutching her dressing gown to her chest. 'It was Paul Ryan, wasn't it?' she says.

'Take it easy.' He presses the wet facecloth to her forehead. 'The photographer'll be here any minute. D'you want to be in the picture?'

'He shouldn't have brought his child here,' she whispers. Her voice trails off into a muttering blur. He stands looking down at her, hears little bleats of words.

'Jeremy's hair,' she says.

'What are you saying, Miriam? Jeremy's at school for Christ's sake.'

'Maybe it has head-lice,' she says. 'Did it touch Jeremy's toys?'

'Miriam, the kid never budged.'

And now he watches as she forces herself from the bed, sits at her dressing table. Her pallor accentuates the contours of her face, the flawless skin. 'What will I wear?' she asks him.

'I should hate Ryan,' Finn says, 'but today he was crazy. He kept singing mad stuff when he could have been asking me questions. And now … I don't hate him. I sort of admire what he does. Ethnic groupings, linguistic interaction, cultural elites. Pierre Bourdieu territory. The European Commission had him working on all the big cross-cultural events. And then he resigned because Irish Immigration strip-searched a Muslim philosopher whom he'd invited to a seminar in Dublin. I suppose he thought his resignation would galvanise people, but it didn't. It changed nothing. In the piece that I read about him, he said you have to follow your principles even if it does no one any good.'

Miriam is still sitting at the dressing-table, looking at herself in the mirror. Finn sits on the bed watching her. He feels his body relax now that the difficult task of being interviewed is over. 'You're beautiful,' he says. 'Even when you're sick, you're beautiful.'

Her mouth softens. The stress lines leave her forehead. 'I'm sorry for being mean about Ryan's child,' she says.

CHAPTER 14

The canals thaw. Spring's buds are everywhere. The freezing mists that oppressed the city throughout the long winter have vanished. A light breeze wafts in from the sea. People are decked out in stylish spring clothes. Everyone is taking long weekend walks – on Sandymount strand, the hill of Howth, Bull Island, the Three Rock Mountain. Miriam takes her courage in both hands and gives in her notice to The Female State. She has not yet told Finn, and when she mentioned her decision to Yvonne, her friend looked at her doubtfully.

'Don't do it,' she said. 'It's dangerous to leave yourself without options.'

But Miriam dreads going to work. And now that she has taken the decision to quit, it is as if a great weight has been lifted from her shoulders.

Peter Brindley is an eager, generous admirer. In addition to paying Finn, he has recently transferred a sizeable sum to Miriam's bank account. He describes it as a nest-egg, tells her to buy new clothes and make-up, fashionable shoes. So far Miriam has not used Peter's money for luxuries like these, but now he has suggested a complete makeover of their little house, and Miriam is tempted to accept.

'No point in doing it piecemeal,' Peter says. 'I know Finn's a bit funny about getting work done, so, if you like, we'll get the ball rolling when he's at his writers' thing in Stuttgart. Give him a surprise.'

Even Jeremy seems to have become a sunnier person. When Miriam collects him from school, they stroll home chatting together. Some days they go to the park and play ball, or chase each other among the bushes. On the way home, Jeremy scarcely ever has a tantrum outside a sweet shop, or whines to be carried.

Miriam is asleep. Her phone rings, and she thinks she is dreaming. 'Hello,' she says. 'Hello.' And then she is awake and Peter Brindley is shouting that Finn has stolen his Harley Davidson. His voice is screaming and cracking with rage. Sitting lopsidedly in the bed, the bedclothes bunched around her, Miriam rubs desperately at her forehead. It's a nightmare, she thinks. I'll wake up soon.

'Calm,' she tells herself, 'calm.' But even as she whispers the words, she knows that the redheaded lover has made Finn crazy. Slim and tall and terrifyingly unhappy, she was standing at the corner of the road as Miriam and Jeremy returned from the shops.

The redhead had walked behind them. 'Just a little part of your life?' she kept saying. 'Just a little part of your life?' Like a famine victim begging for crumbs. Then stood weeping on the path outside their house, her hands grasping and squeezing each other. Her head was bowed, so that Miriam could see only the veil of red hair, hear the thickness in her voice.

'Please stop.' Miriam turned from her front door, whispered urgently. 'Remember there's a child here.'

'She's crying, Mummy.' Jeremy had gazed up under the shielding hair. 'Her eyes are all red.'

'This isn't my doing,' Miriam tried to explain. 'I haven't wanted to hurt you.'

But the girl blindly reached out to stroke Jeremy's head, saying again, 'Just a little part of your life?'

Jeremy ducked and dodged. He hated when people messed with his blond hair. 'Tell her to leave me alone, Mummy.' He had kicked out at the teenager, leaving a mark on one pale, unstockinged leg. The girl flung herself down on her stomach in the tiny front garden as if mortally wounded by what was after all only a touch from a little child.

'But the grass is soaking wet,' Miriam said. 'Please don't. You'll ruin your clothes.'

Afterwards, Miriam brought her inside. She had not known what else to do.

It had not helped. When Finn came upon the redhead sipping coffee in their little kitchen, he had turned on his heel and rushed out of the house, the girl running desperately after him, grasping at his sleeve.

Pearse Street garda station. Finn glares out at Miriam from a dark, rancid-smelling cell. 'We're implicated,' he hisses. 'Don't forget that. It's us who accept his money. We make him respectable. Help him launder his dirty past. And that shit he calls writing. He can fuck off. You tell him from me.'

'Finn,' she says, 'don't do anything rash. Please don't.'

'A young girl on the pillion.' The desk sergeant's nasal whisper drills relentlessly into Miriam's brain. 'Should have been at home in bed, not courting death with that madman.'

Miriam looks at herself in the bathroom mirror, her eyes ringed with shadows, strange sunken eyes. And then blusher, foundation, eye make-up – a painstaking reconstruction of beauty that tears cannot be allowed to ruin. 'Peter's Harley Davidson is wrecked,' she repeats dully to herself. 'Finn has destroyed everything.'

Sitting in her dressing gown in the little wicker chair, Miriam grieves for herself. Sparrow will not be publishing her poems.

'Philip's pulled the plug,' Derek told her last week. 'He's not investing any more money. Says it's a waste.' He shrugged. 'You'll have to find a new home for your poems.'

'But don't you care?' Miriam looked at him in bewilderment. Only the previous day they had discussed typefaces, cover illustrations. She could not believe that it could all end so casually.

'For heaven's sake, Miriam, of course I care. There's just nothing to be done. When Philip gets like that, there's no moving him.'

'See, it's what I told you,' Yvonne said. 'Once they have sex with you, they don't respect you any more. They don't feel they have to put out for you. Little bastard. You're not still doing his dirty work in Sócúl I hope?'

But Miriam explained that Sócúl was organising a big fundraiser and she couldn't pull out now. It would look mean; as if she was taking revenge on Derek. And, after all, it wasn't Derek's fault that Philip had withdrawn his money. When people aren't well, they behave in strange ways.

'You should get back to painting,' Yvonne said then. 'I never understood why you stopped.' She folded the shirt she had ironed and added it to the pile.

'No studio,' Miriam had said. 'And the house is too small. The smell of turps and linseed. Doing it at home is impossible.' She did not explain to Yvonne that Finn hates her paintings. He calls them insipid and sentimental.

Sex with Derek had been very inadequate. Miriam recognises this. He was determined that penetration should occur, so they had used baby oil as a lubricant. Coitus had involved two or three thrusts, and Miriam had felt nothing, apart from the sensation of the condom scraping her vulva.

'That was lovely, Derek,' she whispered afterwards, and snuggled up to him in his big bed. He was lying on his back, his arm covering his eyes. His face was getting thin, she decided, rising on one elbow to gaze at him. He was looking worn out. And then she sank back on the pillow, all the doubts in the world assailing her. Can a condom really protect you? she asked herself as she lay beside him. There was already the feeling of a strange irritation in her vagina. Perhaps it was the type of condom Derek had used. Imagine if she died … and everyone said it was her own fault.

Carthage O'Shea, in his wretchedness, is back in hospital once more. And Derek's passion for him continues to blaze unabated. 'We're two displaced Galway men,' he tells Miriam. 'Adrift in an alien world, we yearn for a country to which we can never return.'

But when Derek sits beside him in the hospital, Carthage turns his face to the wall. Miriam sometimes glimpses his dark eyes, sunken cheeks, teeth gritted in revulsion.

Occasionally Derek manages to surprise Carthage having a smoke on the balcony, emaciated chest heaving into coughing fits as he clutches the railings to keep his balance. Then Derek tries conversation, charming anecdotes, lights up beside him to keep him company. When Carthage returns to his bed, he finds money under the pillow, new books on the bedside locker, cigarettes hidden in the folds of his underwear. He flings these inducements on to the floor, refuses to respond when the ward sister demands that he keep his personal possessions to himself.

The bus travels slowly, halting at every stop – Nassau Street, Mount Street, Northumberland Road, Ballsbridge, Merrion Church. At Rock Road the grey sea broods on Miriam's left, beyond a mess of weeds and rushes, laughably signposted as a bird sanctuary. What self-respecting bird would nest in that scummy undergrowth? she wonders.

CHAPTER 15

Booterstown. The granite gateposts. Dejectedly, Miriam greets the security guards, who raise their hands in response. She stands at the open hall-door, her lip trembling, trying not to recoil while Peter rubs his red-veined cheeks and flattened nose against her hair.

'Dear girl,' he whispers, 'you should have taken a taxi.' He leads her into the panelled sitting-room. A wood fire is burning in the grate.

'Dear girl,' he says again and looks with his bloodshot eyes into her dark, unhappy gaze. 'It's going to be alright.' He takes her jacket. 'He had no permission to take the Harley, but we'll work something out.'

Miriam is shivering, moving from foot to foot on the parquet flooring. 'You see I thought…,' she is saying, 'oh, I don't know what I thought, but because we were meeting today I asked Derek Garvin to come to lunch. It's the Sócúl thing. His fundraising. And then I tried to cancel it, but after all the calls I'd made, I'd no credit left.' She is looking at the ground, her hands clutching each other.

'What time?'

She notes with a little shudder how his voice has hardened once more. 'Half-one,' she mutters. She doesn't want to admit even to herself that Derek's anger is the only thing she fears. Now she is fiddling with the catch of her handbag, now touching her damp hair.

'Okay.' Peter glances at his watch. 'I've an appointment later on, but half-one's okay. It gives us a couple of hours – just you and me.'

And before Miriam understands quite what is happening, she is sitting on the couch, holding the glass of Courvoisier which he offers her.

'One, two, three and down the hatch.' He swallows his brandy in one gulp. Miriam does likewise, grimacing at the fiery taste. She feels the pleasure of the couch's softness, the fire's warmth, the relief that Peter is being kind to her. He pours a second glass, reaches out to touch the folds of her skirt.

'You're so lovely,' he tells her.

Miriam sips her second brandy, closes her eyes. Peter's voice seems to come from very far away. She hears a phone ringing.

'Miracle.' Peter is standing over her. 'Finn's out. I told them not to push it, and they've released him.' He thrusts a bundle of photographs into her hand. 'One of my French houses is empty at the moment. Pézenas.'

Miriam mechanically moves the photos from one hand to another, her mind carefully forming the words: Finn is free. Thank God, she thinks, thank God, and she feels light, like air. Peter's words are strings floating in the air.

'I'm sorry, Peter.' She presses her temples, tries to focus her eyes. 'Could you tell me again?'

'A house I own in the south of France.' She winces at the irritation in his voice. 'Look at the photos. That's what they're there for.'

Once more she moves the photos from one hand to the other, but this time she tries to look at them. Grey walls, vines, pale blue sky. She cannot understand what she is expected to see.

'Why don't you have a go at renovating the interior? I'd give you a budget. Finn can write. Nothing there to distract him; everything to help him concentrate. It has a swimming pool. Stay as long as you like. And while you're there, we'll do up your Dublin place.'

The south of France. What an idea! A smile begins at the corners of Miriam's mouth, hesitates, then stops as Peter's heavy body looms closer.

'But your memoir? How will Finn keep up? I mean he's only looked at the first two chapters,' Miriam whispers feverishly as Peter's fingers begin opening the many buttons of her short, black cardigan.

'Email, pet – it's easy. And I'll come over. I'll want to see you often.' Peter plucks a large white towel from behind the sofa. He lays it carefully on the hearthrug, then, kneeling in front of Miriam, pulls her to her feet, opens the full red skirt and eases it gently down over her hips.

'Finn owes us this,' he tells her, as she stands in front of him in bra and panties. Then he is running his fingers down her back, feeling her buttocks, opening the catch of her bra, and Miriam is gritting her teeth. Perhaps she could plead a period, but he would be unlikely to believe her, and she knows that for some men it's more pleasurable during menstruation. It's necessary, she tells herself. I have to do it.

She stands inert as Peter pulls her knickers down to her ankles. Then lies down on the soft, white towel at his direction. She watches him remove his clothes, notes the expensive underwear, the white, plump, rather hairless body, the greying matter around his pubic area. She closes her eyes when Peter lies down beside her. It would be better not to see what is about to happen.

An hour and many orgasms later, Miriam stands panting and dripping with sweat in the centre of the room.

'No more,' she pleads as Peter directs her again to lean over the back of an armchair while he parts her legs.

'You have the longest tongue I've ever known,' she tells him before her thoughts dissolve once more. 'You're also the best fucker.' She continues to shriek the word 'fucker', her clitoris now irritated to such a pitch of sensation, she feels it may well explode.

As the excitement subsides, she feels Peter's hand leading her again to the soft white towel on the hearth rug. She looks down with affection at the little vibrator lying innocently on the carpet.

'It'll help you to get going,' Peter had explained as he gently inserted it into her vagina. What a revelation it had been. Now, as she lies once more on the towel, Miriam believes that she has never experienced such sensations before. Not with Finn, and she laughs aloud as she thinks of the ridiculous sexual farce she has endured with Derek.

Peter is on top of her, entering with his penis for the first time. Miriam is writhing, dancing on her back, calling out. They are wrestling with each other, fighting, shouting, laughing when Miriam notices that the door is ajar and a white face is looking in at them. Miriam knows in this glimpse that it is Bronwyn, Peter's girlfriend, but she is too busy with the sex to care, taken over by it, aware only of an added glow from the notion of a spectator. Perhaps this is where Peter's girlfriend gets her kicks, she tells herself as she takes control. Swinging Peter over on to his back, she sits astride him and luxuriates in the thrust of his strong, thick penis. She allows her eyes to rest on the lines and sharp angles of Bronwyn's face, smiling as she feels the beginnings of another orgasm. Peter is beginning to ejaculate and, as they both shudder and gasp, Miriam is aware of the door softly closing.

Peter gathers up their clothes and brings Miriam, wrapped in the towel, up to his room. He helps her into the sunken jacuzzi, then sits in the tub beside her, a hand resting familiarly on her thigh while the water gushes around them. 'I haven't had so much fun in ages,' he says.

But Miriam looks at him bewildered, feels the bloated, middle-aged body touch hers and is awakened into revulsion and shame. She finds herself shuddering. What a rotten way to behave. And to have continued while Peter's girlfriend was watching. But then, she reflects, it's so horribly out of character. Peter must have put something in my brandy. One of those date rape drugs. So it wasn't really me who did those revolting things. No, she decides. There is no part of me like that.

'Bronwyn,' she says blushing scarlet. 'What about Bronwyn?'

'Dear girl.' Peter climbs out of the bath and Miriam turns her face away so as not to see his ugly purpled genitals.

When they go downstairs, Bronwyn is in the kitchen, her eyes red in her pale, lined face. She brushes past Miriam, almost falling in her rush to leave.

Peter shrugs. 'She gets more impossible all the time. If I throw her out, she'll take me to the cleaners. It's a war of nerves. But I'll win, don't you worry.'

He is pouring Chablis when the doorbell rings. Miriam rushes to open it, her slightly soiled red skirt billowing around her. She buries her face in Derek's shoulder, kisses him again and again. Please ask if I'm alright, her caresses beg, but he shakes himself free. Her trembling lips, shivering body might as well be trampled undergrowth for all the notice he takes.

'We're in the kitchen,' she says dully, but Peter arrives to meet them, carrying a huge laden tray. Miriam cringes, takes a deep breath, and opens the sitting-room door. She fears that the signs of her recent lust will be visible everywhere, strings of vaginal juices suspended from the mantelpiece, from the edges of marble-topped tables; cushions, rugs, pictures in mad disarray.

To her surprise, all is as if they had never been in the room. Perhaps Bronwyn has cleaned it. That thought causes her to shudder again.

Prawns, smoked eel, ling, salads and cheeses are laid out on the table, but Miriam has no appetite. She takes a small portion of tomato, another of eel, moves the pieces around on her plate while Derek eats and drinks ravenously, then, with his mouth full, enquires about the origin of the colourful hearthrug.

'V'soske Joyce,' Peter says. 'The design's John Rocha. It was all provided by my interior designer. I gave her carte blanche. It seemed the easiest thing to do. I'm asking Miriam to take on one of my French houses. I think she'll be good at it, don't you?' Peter smiles across the low table at Miriam.

'France?' Derek says sharply. 'You're not going to run out on me, Miriam, are you? We have an agenda, you know.' Miriam sees the little tic working nervously in his cheek.

'It's a house in Pézenas,' Peter is saying. 'A bit of a wreck at the moment.'

'Oh really?' Derek pokes Miriam in the side, screws up his mouth in a moue of discontent. 'You're not going to Pézenas.'

Miriam says nothing. She looks down at the hearthrug, counts the concentric circles. When she looks up again, Derek is pulling a cigarette from a packet, lighting up. He lies back in his armchair, blowing smoke rings into the air. 'It's a load of cobblers,' he says. 'This romantic notion about finding yourself, paradise, happiness whatever, in France or wherever. If you haven't found it here, you're sure as hell not going to discover it there.' He raises a hand, slaps it down on the arm of his chair.

And then Peter and Derek are talking about fundraising, about sickness, about supporting bereft people. And Peter is offering a building on Arran Quay for a Sócúl drop-in centre. And Derek is smiling and he looks like a different person.

Miriam feels abandoned, raped and abandoned. Derek should be rushing to her aid. Instead, it is business as usual, as if nothing untoward has happened. Perhaps if she spoke up, she would be accused of imagining the whole thing. The only witness – Peter's girlfriend.

And suddenly she is being accused. 'Bloody Ireland,' Derek is saying. 'Rotten with carping. Bastard journalists, your stinking friend, Miriam. Just because we artists do something selfless, something pure; just when we put ourselves on the line. They want to say that we're idle and lazy, that we'll see the whole world going down the tubes and not raise a finger. And when we try to intervene, try to help, this is what we get. I'll shoot him. Wouldn't cost me a second thought. Just shoot him. Get the fucker off my back.'

Miriam looks at him and shakes her head. She doesn't understand what he is talking about. 'I don't speak to Paul Ryan,' she says. She would like to go home. She is not able for Derek today.

'I'll shoot him,' Derek mutters into his glass. And Peter seems to be nodding in sympathy, as if he regularly goes out and shoots people he doesn't like. Maybe he does, Miriam thinks. Finn seems to think it's possible, but then Finn would say that.

Derek refills his glass, stares out at the springtime garden. 'Carthage O'Shea,' he says abruptly. 'He's been kicked out of the hospital.'

Miriam feels her neck go tense. She has tried to explain to Derek that Carthage would prefer to be left alone. 'Please, Derek,' she says, 'he doesn't want to talk to us.' But Derek goes moody then, and refuses to speak to her.

Derek is putting out his cigarette, his hand shaking, and a gentle knocking is coming from somewhere. Miriam feels goose bumps rise on her arms. The door, she thinks; there's someone knocking at the door.

But Derek hears only the sound of his own voice. He is swiping the air. His hand brushes a glass from the table. 'Anywhere else, the untimely death of a cultured person would be a tragedy,' he snarls, 'but here in Ireland, it's worse. It's a catastrophe.'

Miriam kneels to pick up the fallen glass. She does not look at Derek; she imagines his tight breathing, the hand grasping his tortured forehead. She dabs the rug dry with her napkin – luckily it's white wine she thinks – and then the knocking comes once more, more intense now, and a pale face looks timidly into the room.

'I'm coming,' Peter says brusquely. 'Go out to the car. I'll be right there,' and the pale face disappears. 'Got to drive her to the doctor. Such a nuisance. You two don't have to rush away, do you? Make yourselves more coffee. Be my guests.' He crosses the room to shake Derek's hand, kisses Miriam on the forehead and is gone.

'I didn't make a great pitch,' Derek says. 'Not that you helped. I'm right off form. Bloody Carthage O'Shea.' He slumps back in his armchair and puts his feet on a glass-topped table. 'Odd wife; or is that the maid?'

'His girlfriend.' Miriam tries to focus on Derek. Her head feels confused; she finds it difficult to keep her eyes open. The brandy, she thinks, whatever Peter put in the brandy. 'What happened, Derek?' she says.

'What happened?' Derek stands up and begins to stride around the room kicking at pieces of furniture. 'What happened? You made us look like complete imbeciles.'

'I mean to Carthage?' she says.

Derek lights another cigarette and goes to stand by the mantelpiece. Miriam sees his manicured nails stuttering against the white marble. 'Yesterday morning. He was in the wheelchair and I was going to push him out onto the balcony for a fag. I don't know what set him off. It was awful. The staff nurse said you could hear him from the other end of the corridor. They thought he'd had a seizure.'

Miriam does not know what to say. She understands Derek's distress, how he needs to take his unhappiness out on someone else. She gets up and goes to look out of the tall window onto the irises, the fountain, and the statue of Cupid. As if Peter Brindley knew anything about love, she thinks bitterly.

'The fact is,' Derek is telling her, 'Carthage sees himself as a helpless victim of do-gooding fools like you and me. A lot was incoherent but the general message was that he'd specifically said he didn't want visitors, that it was his private suffering and he didn't see why I should be allowed to use his distress to make myself important.'

Miriam turns, stands now with her back to the window, her head bowed, her gaze falling on the shining parquet. Poor Carthage, she thinks. Being loved when you don't want that love is hard, very hard. She tries to smile at Derek.

'I talked to him out of the goodness of my heart,' he says. His voice quietens and he covers his face with shaking hands, 'The consultant came in on his rounds. Said Carthage would have to go. He'd been leading up to this for ages apparently. Smoking in the corridors, throwing his stuff around. The nurses are sick of him. The consultant says he'll be dead in a week.' Derek runs his fingers through thin black hair.

She is looking at the floor, then at the shiny toes of Derek's expensive black boots. And it becomes clear to Miriam that Sócúl does no one any good. Those who give and those who have charity thrust upon them become more wretched. Yvonne was right. Blaise Boothe was right. Even Paul Ryan is right. She should never have joined. Vanity, she thinks – that's what it was. *I was stupidly vain. I thought I could help change the world.* It's as if she had gone blind, and now the cataracts are removed.

'Come down to the kitchen.' She presses a palm to her forehead to try to ease the pain. 'I'll make us a cup of coffee.'

He stares at her as if surprised that she is still nearby, goes to follow her, and then stands a while to examine a Russian icon hanging above the hall table.

The percolator bubbles, Derek runs his fingers along hand-carved wooden fittings and Miriam wonders how she will tell him. Peter has given her a way out, but it is another sort of trap, though if Finn is with her, Finn and Jeremy, it will be alright.

'Finn?' she hears Derek say. 'How is he?'

'He's fine.' She stirs her coffee, forcing the words from her mouth. She tries not to see Finn sitting on the dark roadside, one arm around the redhead, the other holding a whiskey bottle to his lips. He had left a copybook on the kitchen table. In it Miriam had read neat, careful descriptions of ambushes, tortures, killings. She had thought at first that it was part of a novel.

Miriam looks into the dark coffee, stirs again. She stretches out her hands. All the hopeless elements in her life are expressed in their soft palms.

'Sparrow going splat,' Derek says. 'Maybe we could ask Peter here to rescue it? It'd be peanuts for him.'

Miriam does not look up. She does not wish Derek to see any expression of revulsion on her face. 'I can't ask him. He's giving us too much already.'

'Don't just think of yourself!' Derek says sharply. 'Sparrow's mine. How d'you imagine I feel now that it's gone?'

'I'm sorry, Derek. I didn't think.' She stands, leaving her half-finished coffee on the counter, walks into the hall, plucks her jacket and scarf from the closet.

'My new novel may just do the business,' Derek calls after her. 'I've dedicated it to you. And I got good news last night. Summer Twenty-Sixteen. I'm going to be in the festival. We should go out to celebrate.'

'Dedicated to me?' Miriam whispers softly to herself. 'Oh Derek, why are you so moody? And then lovely when it's too late?'

'Finn doing anything?' Derek has followed her to the hall, stands behind her carefully brushing, with Peter's clothes brush, the shoulders of his coat.

'He won't talk to the organisers.' Miriam buttons up her jacket, her eyes still downcast. 'He doesn't like the way Risteard O'Toole and Rosanne are getting all the limelight.' She looks at Derek, winds her scarf around her throat as she speaks. 'It's sweet of you to dedicate the book to me.' She kisses his cheek. 'Tell Philip I was asking for him.' She hesitates. 'Is he okay?'

'His appearance is extraordinarily improved. Pounds lighter, which is all to the good. Hadn't you ever noticed the flabby tumtum? Major turn-off, my dear. Which reminds me – our next amorous tryst? Thursday morning, we'll get our visits over early and then go back to my place. Philip has an appointment with the consultant.'

CHAPTER 16

A grey May morning in the school car park. Rosanne leaves her children to the classroom door, calls in to see the headmistress with whom she conducts a conversation in rapid idiomatic Irish, then returns to the car park to chat with other parents beside newly washed Mercedes, Volvos, SUVs.

Rosanne reflects on how satisfied she is with her children's Gaelscoil. In past generations it would have been a school for the poor or for the children of obsessed *gaeilgeoir* parents who refused to allow a word of English in their homes. Now it is the playground of openness, of the very best in Irish society. Many of the parents are artistic, gifted people, especially the mothers. Weavers, musicians, a cellist who gives recitals in the National Concert Hall, a number of excellent painters. The writers' group is made up of creative feminists who assert that there is a new world order in the making and that they will rule in this unfolding universe. They talk of women's sovereignty, of women's new contentment and lyricism.

The car park empties. Only Rosanne remains, sitting in her car writing careful notes in a small brown notebook. Nervously she looks at her watch, then closes the notebook, puts it into her briefcase, and gets out of the car. Her green tweed coat wrapped loosely around her, she walks backwards and forwards on the smooth tarmac. Until at last Finn Daly emerges from the school building, head bent, hands thrust into jacket pockets.

Rosanne's lips quiver. Her body grows warm, then cold, then warm again. 'Hello there,' she calls, trying to make her voice light.

He looks up, stares at her for a moment.

'I wondered … you're going away …, and I'd love us to have a chat. Maybe,' and then the words burst out in a rush. 'Would you come with me to visit the Devanneys?'

'What for? You brought me to visit them already. What's the point?' He stands beside her, his toe kicking at small stones on the tarmac. 'Anyway, I've to go to Cavan today. My aunt's expecting me.'

Rosanne opens the Volvo's passenger door. Finn gets in. They glide through the school gate; he does not look at her. 'I'll go to the Devanneys if you drive me to Cavan,' he says.

'You want me to drive you to Cavan?' Her warm thoughts cool.

'I have to be there before two,' Finn is saying, and she swallows and considers the situation. Rosanne is in a quandary. She has lent an electric heater to the Devanneys – a heater that belongs to her mother – and today she must get it back. It will be helpful to have another person to support her when she is insisting on its return.

'Your dad's feet get very cold,' her mother had complained on an unnaturally warm April day. Since then, small hints have prompted Rosanne to understand that the electric heater has become a solitary symbol of married happiness.

'Richard Cantillon,' she says as they wait for the lights to change at Portobello Bridge. 'I've been reading about him.'

'Wrote something on economics, didn't he?'

'Only the greatest eighteenth-century work on economic theory. Cromwell had confiscated his family's lands generations earlier. After that, the Cantillons decided that if they couldn't own land in Ireland, they'd make a damn good stab at owning and controlling most of the money in Europe.'

Rosanne feels Finn's glance and her skin tingles in response. She tells him about the millions Cantillon made, the houses he owned. 'Houses in seven European capitals. Imagine that!' She hears her voice running too quickly away from her, and she thinks: this must be love. I've never been like this with anyone else. Never. But her words are toppling into each other. A deep breath. Another deep breath.

Take it easy, she says to herself, her feet dancing on the pedals. Take it easy. Don't rush it. Between Harold's Cross and Clogher road, Mississippi schemes, stockmarket booms, South Sea bubbles rise and fall, until she gets to the place where she wants to be. 'Cantillon played the markets,' she finishes exultantly, 'but he knew when to sell his shares. The crash came, he called in his loans. Got revenge for past wrongs.'

Rosanne sits in the line of traffic, waiting for the lights to change. A wave of exhaustion flows down her neck, into her arms, her hands. 'Revenge,' she whispers, flexing her fingers, curling her toes, forcing movement back into her body. And she calls on the energy, and the energy flows back stronger and more vibrant. The small houses of Parnell Road slide away to her left, the canal on her right. She is describing the eighteenth-century smuggling trade in Kerry, the Molyneux manuscripts, the movements of peasants between Kerry and Spain. 'At the end of every summer,' she says, 'they came home with suntans.' And Finn is laughing a loud joyous laugh.

Rosanne laughs alongside him. 'A cosmopolitan society in Kerry,' she says. 'They spoke Latin and Spanish. The language they didn't need was English. I tell you, Finn, our history's been suppressed.' She stops at the traffic lights in Dolphin's Barn.

'I'll email lessons to you,' she says. 'I'll record them and send them to you. I'll teach you Irish.'

'Great,' he says. 'Okay.'

In a shifting fuzz of pleasure, Rosanne signals a left turn onto Crumlin Road. It is time to broach the subject of the heater. The memory of her mother's sharp, telephone voice prickles the back of her neck. She would rather shake it off, not weigh upon Finn's day.

'Now listen here,' Rosanne's mother had begun, without even saying hello. 'If that heater is not back with me by the weekend, there will be trouble. You have tried my patience too far. A very valuable article, that heater. Perhaps the likes of you and your husband cannot imagine what it is to be two old people on a small income. I won't be answerable if your dad gets a cold.'

Rosanne has priced the modern version in the local electrical superstore. She sees no reason to spend that sort of money; knows that if she does, her mother will not thank her.

'Derek,' she had said to his voicemail. 'You have to find me a solution. My parents are going crazy.' But Derek seldom returns Rosanne's calls.

Ever since that wretched Christmas party, Rosanne has noticed with sadness the falling away of Derek's friendship. Their monthly meetings have become an empty joke, for he is always busy. Perhaps it is Summer Twenty-Sixteen which has caused the estrangement. Rosanne is to be one of its stars, her poetry translated into thirty-five languages. She will spend July travelling through Vietnam, Cambodia and China speaking about her work, while William stays at home and looks after the children. A television documentary on her career is nearing completion. Her first play will tour Europe, the United States and the Far East.

Rosanne brings to the Devanney household friendly chat, occasional donations of used clothing, and generous advice on everything from cooking to contraception. She has asked several times for the return of her heater, but the Devanneys have pretended not to hear. Only once has she actually seen it. Gerry had been crouched over it, a blanket on his knees. That day Rosanne had enjoyed the warm feeling of her own generosity.

'Finn,' she says, 'I've a problem. I lent the Devanneys my mother's heater and she's driving me mad about it.'

Before she has even finished speaking, the spell is broken and Finn is telling her to let the Devanneys keep the bloody heater, that they are poor people.

'I can't,' she says. 'My mother wouldn't understand. It's the principle that's important. These people must learn to take responsibility for things they borrow. I wouldn't be showing them proper respect if I didn't insist. After all, I would insist with anyone else.'

Rosanne's one consolation in her weekly visits to the Devanneys has been her developing rapport with the local Daonnacht representatives. She sees one or more of these committed young men and women on nearly every visit, discusses with them the needs of the area, the work of instilling pride into the people, the necessity for moral compasses, and, if all else fails, the use of strictly controlled punishment to prevent actions that destabilise and debilitate the community. She has found herself becoming ever more convinced that Daonnacht is the political grouping of Ireland's future. A party that can help communities build up self-respect, which has the firmness of conviction to deal adequately with those who, through moral degeneracy, refuse the call.

Neither Rosanne nor the Daonnacht representatives with whom she has conferred support the violent excesses of the local disciplinary committee, whose secretary took a gun and blew away the kneecaps of the Devanney's eldest son. But the secretary has, in his turn, been punished for that excess. And Rosanne understands that, through such unfortunate experiences, Daonnacht has learnt a valuable lesson about the necessity for tighter controls on its personnel.

Mrs Devanney opens the door. A large woman with straggling grey-blonde hair. 'It's too good of you,' she mumbles unenthusiastically. 'Sure we don't deserve it at all.'

The kitchen-cum-living room is crowded: two social workers, who are saying their goodbyes, a priest, the three unmarried Devanney daughters and their babies, their wheelchair-bound brother. The large, pink-flowered sofa holds the girls and infants.

Rosanne stands at the edge of the sofa watching Mrs Devanney, who is leaning against the sink, arms folded, silent. Gerry is nowhere to be seen, but when Rosanne asks if her charge is still in bed, Mrs Devanney turns away without answering.

'You must be so happy about his eyes, Mrs Devanney – the way his eyesight's come back. You're a marvel, the way you look after him.' Rosanne whips enthusiasm into her voice. Each week she repeats the same phrases in one form or another.

During one of her sessions with the young man, as Rosanne declaimed her poetry into what she had previously experienced as a barren empty space, a searing pain in her head caused her to lose the thread of her poem, draw in her breath sharply. She had held her hand to her forehead and in that gesture somehow absorbed the knowledge that the tumour in Gerry's brain had stopped pressing on his optic nerve, that Gerry could see again and that his powers of thought had returned. At that very moment the young man had reached out to touch Rosanne's skirt, whispered some words.

Rosanne could scarcely breathe with excitement. At first she had wanted to call the whole family as witnesses, but then realised that this was her personal triumph, her own special magic. Tears dampened her eyes, and she had kissed Gerry on both cheeks. Her thanks rang out from that small, meanly furnished room, through aeons of time and space to her special mentors, the hag Garavogue of Sliabh na Caillí, Queen Medbh of Rathcruachan, Queen Áine of Cnoc Áine. 'The work has only begun,' she whispered to each of the ancient druidesses in turn. 'Together we will conquer the world.'

'You've been keeping up the eye exercises with Gerry I'm sure?' she says now in what she hopes is an encouraging tone. 'Every morning, every evening – just as the doctor ordered.'

Mrs Devanney does not reply. She searches for something in a drawer, her back to the room. The babies are as docile as ever. They sit sucking soothers, their big eyes staring.

Father Dessie stands up and rests a hand on Mrs Devanney's shoulder while she lays out the electricity bill for him to examine.

'I'm at my wits' end, Father.'

'Give me back my heater,' Rosanne mumbles. 'Then you won't spend so much.'

'The electricity's the worst of them. But it's all this too.' She shakes envelopes in the priest's face, 'The gas, the phone – we have to have it with our Gerry having to go to hospital at a moment's notice. And the grocery bills too. I'm goin' out of my mind. Gerry needs good food. To build him up like. And I have to send them few special little things to Johnny in Castlerea. It's all he lives for.'

'Well now,' the priest soothes, 'why do you think the good bishop sent me? Give me the electricity bill if that's the one that's worrying you most.'

Each time she visits, Rosanne wonders at the debasement of the Devanney family. The photos on the mantelpiece show well-dressed people living a life of social ease, but no one has ever responded to

Rosanne's questions about them. And now the only reality is aggravated burglary. Sending special little things into the prison? She's probably sending him drugs. Castlerea is full of them and they have to come from somewhere.

'My nerves is in rag order,' Mrs Devanney says to the kitchen in general, then pours the water from the kettle and starts to fill it again. 'They took Gerry back in yesterday. Poor lad was cryin'.' Mrs Devanney bangs down the kettle, plugs it in.

'And that heater you gave us.' Mrs Devanney turns and swipes the dirty tea-towel towards Rosanne. 'Eats money, the bloody thing. I nearly fell down in a weakness when I saw the bill. I had to hold on to the stairs to keep myself straight.'

'I'm terribly sorry, Mrs Devanney, but I really do want it back. It belongs to my mother. Maybe I could get you something more suitable.'

The kettle boils. Mrs Devanney spoons used teabags from the big teapot into the sink, adds some new ones, and pours in boiling water. One of the girls stands up, leaves her child propped on the sofa, and begins languorously to gather used mugs from windowsill, mantelpiece and floor. Rosanne can see cigarette butts floating in the dregs.

'Perhaps Finn and I could take the heater out to the car now, so that we won't forget it.'

Mrs Devanney sniffs. 'Lucky enough, my sister's done a swop. She's got a nice little gas heater that'll suit us, and she's taken ours.'

Rosanne presses her lips tightly together. She says nothing. Tea is poured into mugs and passed around the room. Chocolate biscuits are put on a plate. Father Dessie returns to the kitchen rubbing his hands.

'They're nice lads really,' he says. 'Stay of execution is what you might call it. Next month's the new deadline. And in the meantime we'll work out all the bills together. I'm not going to let anyone get on your back, Mrs Devanney. Sure I'd have to answer to the bishop if I did.'

'You're a good man, Father.'

'There's a small interim payment that I've promised for today. But don't worry,' he responds to Mrs Devanney's look of alarm. 'The three of us are going to take care of that.' He winks across the room at Rosanne. 'A fifty each will cover it.'

Rosanne chokes back her rage. She forces a smile, even a little laugh. She looks towards Finn. 'I'll see what I have in my bag,' she says firmly. 'And then we must go.'

They wave their goodbyes and walk to the car. Finn looks wistfully back at the front door. 'What a marvellous family,' he says slowly, as if he cannot quite believe what he has just witnessed. 'So interesting and complex. And mutually supportive. I admire them more than I can say. The mother astounds me.'

Rosanne does not reply. She moves around to the driver's side and gets in. For a moment she is tempted to drive off and leave Finn stranded.

'It just shows how blind our middle-class assumptions can be,' Finn says. 'You give someone a heater and think you're doing them a good turn. The more expensive the heater, the more you expect in gratitude, when really what you're doing is wrecking their economy. It took guts for her to point that out to you. The girls – so calm, did you notice? And the young man. He may be crippled but he's not going to let himself be patronised.' Finn laughs and punches the air.

Since Rosanne's first attempts at intercourse with Finn, she has taken steps to improve her performance. She has re-read the Kama Sutra and bought the works of the Marquis de Sade. She attends aerobics classes twice weekly.

De Sade has been a disappointment; Rosanne found herself wading through many tedious pages. The few passages of instruction had focused on anal intercourse as the very pinnacle of pleasure.

One night, Rosanne presented William with her bottom and a jar of Vaseline. In *Last Tango in Paris* they had used butter, but Vaseline seemed to Rosanne a more hygienic option. It had not worked. Her bottom had rejected William's determined thrusts. Rosanne had screamed aloud in pain. She had elbowed William hard in the gut as he ejaculated. The early hours were spent on the toilet, expelling air and yellow liquid with loud, machine-gun farts. Next day it was difficult for her to sit down.

The Kama Sutra is a gentler and more suitable text. Delicate scratching and biting replace the Marquis de Sade's violent whippings. Rosanne has become adept at the 'Yawning' and 'Rising' positions. 'Packed' and 'Lotus' were no trouble to her. Encouraged by these successes, she has embarked with William on the more challenging 'Splitting of a Bamboo' and 'Fixing of a Nail'. For, as Rosanne tells herself, with whom can she practise if not with her own husband?

CHAPTER 17

The Cavan countryside stretches across nondescript fields, low hills and polluted lakes. The unseasonal gloom of this May afternoon hangs over everything.

Finn stands in the long grass at the crossroads where Rosanne had dropped him. 'Phone me,' she had whispered as she touched his hand goodbye.

An ancient Toyota coughs to a stop beside him. His aunt keeps its bodywork polished and perfect. It had been her father's car, bought in 1990, the year of his death.

'I think the plugs need seeing to,' she shouts as he climbs in.

Finn's aunt claims to have been the beauty of the family, but in the few surviving photographs she looks little different from her dark-haired older sister, the two girls resisting the camera with nervous smiles. Finn has been unable to find a photograph of his own father among his grandfather's possessions, although there are several pictures of the younger brother, Larry. A lively, smiling young man.

They drive along a narrow road, slippery with wet cow-dung at each farmyard entrance. Bungalows are interspersed with shacks, mobile homes, decaying cottages. Summer is a rare visitor to this part of Ireland and the overcast day is turning once more to rain. Washing lines heavy with sodden clothing stand in desolate, unkempt yards, and on the muddied scar around recently finished bungalows. Unpainted walls merge with a sullen sky, scattered weeds dot the grey mud.

It is only beside the lake that prosperous houses with well-tended gardens appear. Vast timber decks, private moorings. Piers with sleek white boats project into the grey water. His aunt tells him that there is no view more beautiful when the sun shines. To Finn, however, this patchwork of villas seems more hideous than the squalid poverty.

'The pattern is spoiled right enough.' Finn's aunt contradicts herself with stabbing finger. 'A slut looking for a way to rise in the world. Where else would ambition lead but to the Dalys of Gurteen?'

On Finn's first visit, his aunt had sounded the car's horn to emphasise her words. 'It was then we should have told Daddy. He'd have put manners on Larry. Weeks roaming the countryside with that slut. Never went back to school. It wasn't that we were wealthy. Far from. But we had class. Daddy saw to that. We never let ourselves down.'

When they had reached the low white cottage, she pointed out the roof of a mock-Georgian villa, visible from the yard.

'I can't but think of Daddy's face if he'd seen it. It's the new vulgar class gets its way in this country.'

Aunt Eileen had shown him all the rooms of the family cottage, the big kitchen with dresser and long deal table, the small parlour where his grandfather's notebooks are kept. The children's bedrooms upstairs, their father's beside the kitchen. The large flower garden, embracing the cottage. Today, against the dank May air, it is a startling mass of colour and beauty.

'I'd never have let you in,' she tells Finn, 'but that you're the spit of him. I always went with older men. Then I came back to be with Daddy.'

'But I thought you didn't come back till after he died?' Finn is struggling to piece together the scattered elements of his grandfather's family.

'Bridie was eighteen when Daddy married Rita,' his aunt responds in her now familiar non-sequential manner. 'Before we knew it, she'd the whole place under her thumb. There were just the few times Daddy stood up to her; the few times he made her stop her nonsense. Sulking in the room. We'd be kneeling for the rosary, waiting for her to join in. She made a fool of him.'

Finn's aunt places her face in her hands and weeps noisily. Finn pats her warily on fleshy shoulders. He is afraid of making a wrong move.

On his first visit she made him a pot of tea, cooked a fry of sausages, black pudding and eggs before covering the deal table with a starched white cloth. Instead of sitting down immediately, Finn, mesmerised by the place, had strolled absently-mindedly into the parlour to check again the photographs of his father's family. When, after some minutes, he had wandered back into the kitchen, his dinner was already gone from the table.

'Is it a pig I brought into my father's house?' his aunt shouted. 'Without manners or grace?' She plucked Finn's letter from the dresser and started tearing it into shreds. 'I've no need of you here. I did very well before you showed up.'

Finn began to stutter apologies.

'There's the door!'

'But, Aunt Eileen, please, don't send me away now. Not when I've just found you. I beg you, please!' He knelt beside the straight chair on which she was seated.

The following week, sitting at the table, he had, in his nervousness, knocked a side plate to the floor. Quickly, he knelt to gather the pieces, then felt a sharp sting on the back of his head. Blows were raining down on him, on his hands as they tried to protect his head, on his back, on the backs of his legs. He crouched, dazed on the ground.

'I will not have plates broken in this house.' His aunt whipped and whipped again at the hands that were protecting his head. And just as suddenly the assault was over. Still crouched on the ground, he looked up at her from between his fingers. From where he knelt she seemed enormous, a giant Amazon who stood panting over him, her chest heaving.

'Kiss me,' his aunt said, leaning her mouth towards his.

He had risen unthinkingly to do so, placed his hands on her heavy shoulders, the situation so strange that this reflex seemed as natural as any.

'Now sit down and finish your dinner.'

He had drained his tea, then passed the cup to his aunt for a refill.

'After any chastisement,' she said, 'we always gave Daddy a kiss.'

Finn went back to the National Library to re-read old newspapers detailing his grandfather's campaigns. The National Archives held the police reports. As he sifted through these, the smell in his nostrils was of dust and decay – he saw himself as a detective in search of clues about a person whose life story Finn's own father had sought to destroy.

'We always served Daddy first. We ate after. Even on Christmas Day.' Aunt Eileen frowned. 'Until Rita came.' The familiar hard note came into her voice. 'Made fools of us girls, innocent poor creatures that we were. The one good thing she left us was the garden. Six months of the year I keep the altar in flowers from that little patch. It's a miracle. That's what Father O'Connor tells me. That's the trouble with today's youth.' She raised her voice. 'No discipline. I'll bet that father of yours never gave you a taste of the strap. He couldn't take it himself.'

'Aunt Eileen,' Finn began carefully, 'could I begin to look through Grandfather's notebooks today?'

'Yes, I suppose you might.' She looked at him, head on one side, squeezing her little clump of chins. 'You've been a good boy. One quick kiss and off you go.' And her mouth touched his.

The notebooks had been disappointing at first. Long lists of figures. Sometimes different purchases were mentioned by name, but generally the sums of money were not identified. Dates given occasionally. In the last notebook, the changeover from shillings and pence to decimal was marked by many crossings out.

'Daddy wrote down every penny. He hated waste.' His aunt came into the small parlour to stand behind him. 'It was *us* were blind. Never saw the signs.'

'The signs, Aunt Eileen?' Finn asked absent-mindedly.

'The signs. The signs,' she shouted. 'What are you going on about at all? If it wasn't for that bloody father of yours, she'd never have got past the door of the house. I can't stand a man who won't take a beating. If your father had stayed in the family, we'd have known what was right. We'd never have let Larry get away with it. He'd have been hauled back and beaten within an inch of his life. It's on our consciences, yes, but your father started the rot. Put those notebooks back. Now.'

Finn, startled, began to protest. 'But I've only just started, Aunt Eileen.'

Her face became livid with rage. She slapped the flat of her hand across his cheek.

'Have you never been taught to show respect?'

'Sorry,' Finn said.

It was all over as suddenly as it had begun.

'I'm off out to walk the fields,' she murmured, and was gone.

In the quiet of that afternoon. Finn was relieved and heartened to see words rather than figures. Written in a careful schoolboy's hand, it seemed the work of someone little more than a child. His grandfather wrote of the birds wintering on the lake, the text accompanied by crude, black and white sketches. A nature story began – *The blue curve of the sky fell before us*. It made Finn feel at one with his ancestor – carrying on and refining his tradition. Then came some diagrams of the sky at night. Finn pictured a young idealistic man, lying on his back in a meadow, gazing up at the starry blackness.

'You should have seen the cut of your father the day Daddy laid the gun across his bare arse.' His aunt, fresh from the meadows, giggled like a schoolgirl. 'He was never any good in the fields. The number of thrashings he had out there, rain streaming down on the pair of them as Daddy laid into him with whatever came to hand. I'm telling you, it taught us to be careful and quick when we were at outdoor work.'

CHAPTER 18

Finn stands outside his grandfather's cottage, staring at the slate roof, the white-washed walls. Two hooded crows, flying low, catch the edges of his vision. They have risen from the little copse beyond the haggard. He follows their flight path across the sloping meadows, the radiating lines of stone walls into the blue distance beyond.

'I don't want to leave you,' he tells the cottage and its fields. 'I don't want to go.'

Writers need stimulants. Finn knows this deep inside himself. Writers need stimulants – alcohol, drugs, sex – like a garden needs water. Miriam refuses to accept this elementary truth. Yet it was Miriam who had brought the redhead into their kitchen, held a cold facecloth to her eyes, fed her madness on sandwiches and hot coffee. When Finn entered the room that day, the redhead was sitting at the table sipping from her cup, while Miriam rinsed the facecloth in the sink. Finn had shuddered to see Jeremy's eyes, sparkling with excitement, dart from one to the other. He knew then that he would have to end it.

His aunt's large frame became a necessary refuge, his grandfather's notebooks a solace. In the cottage Finn was suspended in a childlike state, unable to do anything but submit. The alternative would be to leave and never return; to lose this vital contact with the past. And he had begun to find a secret pleasure in being beaten by a middle-aged woman.

'I take Daddy's gun some days and let off a few shots close to that monstrosity.' She gestured vaguely in the direction of the neo-Georgian guesthouse. 'We'll see how the fishermen like that. Magpies, I tell them. They're a terrible scourge around here.'

That day Finn opened another of his grandfather's notebooks. It was the first of the IRA period and he whooped with delight when he realised that he was on to the real thing. The oath was transcribed in full on the first page. On the second, a list of names with ticks beside them. Other pages listed police barracks, shops, private houses. These lists were sometimes accompanied by rough maps. Still other pages had further lists of names; some were circled, others marked with an asterisk. Finn ran his finger across the names as if his touch might reveal who these men had been: company commanders to be obeyed, or informers to be shot.

He rushed on to a second notebook, then a third: training instructions, advice on the handling of weapons, on encouraging the volunteers to practise, on the importance of familiarity with the feel of a gun. Here the writing had obviously been undertaken at speed, many sentences tailing off into nothingness. Finn imagined his grandfather sitting among rough, eager young men, chosen to command their own companies; perhaps by night, in a schoolroom, the windows blacked out with heavy sacking. A few lesser men would be left outside on guard. His grandfather's first hint of preferment. He would, years later, realise his ambition of marrying into land. Finn knew that he had been a fine catch. Married at fifty to a slip of a girl. A romantic hero.

That afternoon Finn hid one of the notebooks inside his jacket. He would bring it back on his next visit.

He sat at a desk in the National Library, assiduously copying. An injunction of Walter Benjamin sounded in his head: to know what has been written, we must transcribe the text and re-transcribe it. During the afternoon the redhead arrived and they walked into Trinity. He held her on his lap on the steps of the Pavilion, wanting her so much that he felt sick with it.

Finn felt a spasm of new fear when his aunt began once more to exult in his father's childhood humiliations.

'Standing there bog naked,' she said. 'It was a lesson for the rest of us, I can tell you. "How does that feel to you?" Daddy asked him. I can see it as if it was yesterday, though I was only about ten at the time. Funny the things you remember. "How does that feel?" Daddy asked again, giving him a good *sceilp* with the gun. He fell down on the floor, whinging and moaning, holding Daddy's ankles, slobbering big gobs of spit on Daddy's shoes. Daddy gave him a good kick in the face, then there was blood everywhere, and your father was sitting on the floor sobbing, with no shame. "You've killed me."

'"You can give up that yowling," Daddy said. "There's no one going to listen to you here." And he lashed at him with the gun. Your father was trying to get up. He was on his hands and knees, his body shaking and trembling, and he started to pray.

'"Our Father," he said, but Daddy shouted that it was blasphemy and slashed at him again.'

Finn listened with growing horror. 'What about your … mother, Aunt Eileen?' His voice sounded unnaturally high to his ears. He was stuttering with fear.

'I was too young. They told me that Daddy gave up the drink after her death, he was that upset. Couldn't bear to hear her name mentioned. The memory, you know. Thirty years his junior and as gentle and good a woman as ever lived. I always do the Easter duty for her. I've been inside the church more than out since I last saw you. And I was able to grace Our Lady's altar with the most beautiful display of tulips. All from my own little garden.' She looked misty-eyed at him. 'You know, I think I'm beginning to get fond of you.'

That week Finn was tempted to remove a second notebook. He had not yet returned the first. His aunt had gone out to the fields: there were fences to be repaired; the lambs had grown adventurous and were leading the flock astray. Eventually he decided against such a risk.

Later, as his aunt drove him to the bus, she mused aloud on the future of the farm. 'There's nothing in writing. The only one who could challenge me is Bridie, but she'll never come back now. You can't return here unless you've something to show for yourself.'

Finn pressed his aunt's hand but did not speak. He was afraid he might say the wrong thing.

At the crossroads that evening three other cars were awaiting the departure of the bus for Dublin. The unusual crowd, Finn surmised, must be because of the Easter holiday. His aunt drew up at some distance, then got out and walked across to chat to the drivers of the other cars. Finn was astonished at this show of friendliness.

'My nephew, Finn Daly, here to research his grandfather's life. He's going to write a great big book about him.' She looked proudly at Finn as he grimaced at the description. 'Modest as well. Doesn't like to hear his aunt bragging about him.'

Listening vaguely to the talk, Finn realised for the first time that his aunt was a woman of many parts. She seemed to be involved in a local home-visiting committee, was a member of the regional branch of the Irish Countrywomen's Association – not at all the lonely recluse he had imagined.

'I have to go away to France,' Finn told his aunt at the end of April. 'How will I finish the work?'

'Ah sure, who wants you?' She glanced sideways at him.

'I don't want to go,' Finn said, resenting her for not caring. 'Could I take some of the notebooks? I'll look after them. Send them back by registered post once I've transcribed the contents.'

'So you want to give my neighbours something to talk about?' Her voice rose sharply. 'Want to set their tongues wagging, do you? It takes the least little thing around here. They've nothing better to do.'

On that sun-filled April day, Finn transcribed with ferocious concentration, while his aunt tended her beloved flower garden. After a time his eyes began to sting with the effort and he wandered outside to stretch his cramped legs. The sun warmed his back with a delicious glow.

He had been copying a passage about the killing of an informer, an intimate of his grandfather, highly regarded until small clues had begun to make his comrades nervous. Finn's grandfather had been ordered to conduct the interrogation. *It was known that I would not flinch from my duty.*

The notebook analysed minutely the process of extracting a confession from a man already sentenced to death. The report was to be copied and circulated among different battalions and companies. Its purpose: a disincentive to betrayal.

Finn stood in the garden looking out on his grandfather's fiefdom. The trees had not yet come into full leaf, but the spring air was like perfume in his nostrils. He felt proud to be associated with a man who knew discipline and courage, who did not shrink from what had to be done.

His aunt looked up from a bed of tulips. 'I'm thinking of leaving you the farm. I'm off into Cavan next week to see the solicitor.' She rubbed clay-covered hands against her rough tweed skirt. 'Daddy wanted to bring us all together. He'd be always writing to your father, asking what his problem was, worrying at it, telling him to come back, that we could sort it out as a family. But your father would do nothing to help an old man die easy. We went on our knees. We begged him.'

Finn lies in the large double bed beside his aunt for the last time. He is thinking dreamily of his grandfather. His aunt sits naked beside him, thoughtfully sucking on a post-coital cigarette.

'I wonder did you count the notebooks?' she asks.

'Forty-three, I think.' Finn glances nervously at her.

'That's what I thought. I'd strap you for stealing, except that you're going away. You have to come back to your old auntie. She'll be waiting for you.'

'Of course I will. Just as soon as I can.' He sits up and kisses her large brown nipples.

In the study Finn opens a new notebook. He turns over pages, squints at the small, crabbed writing, then wanders back into the bedroom, where his aunt is nudging her slip down over voluminous knickers.

'From what I can make out,' he holds out the notebook to his aunt, 'it's your name, and Bridie's and a third name – Joan, is it? Repeated over and over with days and dates. Just those three names, they take up this whole notebook. Repeated daily, 1973 to 1978. Joan wasn't your mother's name, was it?'

His aunt flings the notebook on the bed and continues to dress. She fastens her skirt and fixes her face in front of the mirror before she strides past Finn into the kitchen.

The cloth on the table gleams whiter than ever. A large jug of splendid colourful flowers decorates its centre.

'Now I'm not depriving the church. I've just borrowed them for this day. I've promised Father O'Connor. I'll be straight down with them in the morning.'

'They're beautiful.'

'Every blossom from that garden is promised to Jesus and his Blessed Mother. So that while I work in that garden, I'm at prayer. It's as simple as that.'

Finn cuts through the tender, moist meat of a chop and chews carefully.

'Daddy had a special way of saying thank you,' she adds carelessly. 'Think of it. A long hard day at school, then the cold toil of the fields, weeding the cabbages, or picking stones from the clay. Homework finished, supper over, the rosary said, and we'd be called into the big bed. Daddy was just lovely then.' Finn's aunt sighs. 'I've often heard it said that men in those days could show no tenderness. Daddy wasn't like that.'

They sit in silence a little while, Finn chewing and cutting, buttering his bread, drinking his tea, careful not to interrupt the movement of his aunt's thoughts. She sits across the table, smoking another cigarette.

'Daddy was always fair. Never took one of us out of turn,' she says at last. 'Joan was the youngest.'

'You mean you've a younger sister?' Finn interjects despite himself.

His Aunt Eileen draws deeply on her cigarette.

'Daddy was wonderful, like no other person. There was nobody who could hold a candle to him.' She dabs at her eyes with a man's white handkerchief. 'Joan's in Dublin these thirty years and more.' She blows her nose and smiles at Finn. 'Aren't families the odd thing though? You coming home after all this time. It's going to be alright. It's all for you. Everything's for you.'

Finn travels back to Dublin. He carries forty-three notebooks in two Londis recyclable bags. He looks out of the bus window at the feast of dandelions in the low fields, the dark hedgerows speckled with white and pale pink hawthorn flowers. His aunt's garden in its luscious craziness is all wrong, he decides. Ireland was made for muted colours, grey walls. And through those muted colours, flashes of wild beauty like the yellow dandelions. Native flowers.

He closes his eyes, and in the inside of his head the bright vivid colours pulse and flash. It is his aunt's garden. The lure of it trying to take him back. And Joan, cast out into the multitude of Dublin city. He will have to start searching for her.

CHAPTER 19

The May school holiday is about to begin; the weather is warm and sunny with a little hint of a breeze. Miriam is standing in the schoolyard waiting for Jeremy. She is leaning against the wall, eyes closed, the predicaments of her life moving in and out of her head.

Jeremy's schoolyard is not always a welcoming place for Miriam. Sometimes she feels uneasy as she stands waiting for him. As if there is an invisible barrier between her and the other parents, as if Jeremy might be considered not the proper sort of child to be allowed to mix freely with the other children of his class. Then she shakes herself.

'I'll never understand why you didn't send him to St Mary's Primary,' Yvonne frequently says. 'It's an unpretentious sensible sort of school. And it's only down the road from you.'

Miriam buries her anxieties, and explains that she likes being part of an artistic and literary group of parents, who are also committed to the sorts of ideals that she and Finn consider important, such as women's issues, the Irish language.

As she stands in the warm sun, the dilemma of Sócúl assails Miriam. She should never have joined it. If she had not joined, she would not have become so close to Derek. That would have meant no sex, which would have been a very good thing. Because sex has destroyed their friendship.

The fundraising ball brought on the final disaster and Miriam winces as she thinks back to that night. Horse-drawn coaches, a fairytale evening in the great banqueting hall at Kilmainham. It should have been perfect. Armani models – twenty strange and beautiful men and women – wafted past the tables, close enough for Miriam to catch the scent of musk. She was sipping dessert wine, wearing a red Hervé Léger dress, given her by Peter Brindley.

When the parcel arrived, Miriam took the dress out of its wrappings and wondered should she return it instantly. But if she did that, she knew it would hurt Peter's feelings, and who could tell what the consequences would be?

She tried it on for Yvonne, and Yvonne shouted, 'Wow! I wonder would it look like that on me? Wear it for God's sake, flaunt it. You're fabulous-looking. Some prince will run off with you in that.'

Standing at the auction after the dinner, Miriam was aware of people's eyes on her, and for a while it was a glorious sensation. Then Peter Brindley stood beside her, and she felt ashamed, and wanted to go home. She knows now she should have followed that instinct. Instead, she had smiled at Peter, stroked his arm, and asked him to put money into Sparrow, because that was what Derek wanted.

Peter laughed raucously. 'No wonder it croaked if it's called Sparrow. That's a ridiculous name. You want me to bail him out so your poetry gets published? No problem.' Then he had kissed her on the cheek, and gone home, and Miriam felt as light as air, able to enjoy the rest of the evening without constraint. She had danced and chatted, sipped more wine, laughed her carefree laugh, almost unaware that Derek was watching her with bitter, jealous eyes.

Miriam presses a hand to her forehead in an attempt to shut out Derek's rage. She tries to fill her head with more important thoughts. Thoughts about people who are sick, people who need help. 'Bríd with your poor skinny bruised legs,' she whispers, 'I'll give you that red Hervé Léger dress. You'll like that. And I'll buy presents for your children. Some lovely clothes, so that you can all go out together and feel a million dollars.'

But Bríd, in her little house in Neilstown, is practically dead. She will never go out again. She will never wear Miriam's dress. Miriam shivers at the sound of Bríd's rattling cough, a crisp packet trapped in the school railings.

As Miriam stands in the schoolyard gusts of warm breeze touch her forehead, wisps of dark hair float across her face. The skirt of her dress, caught in a flurry, threatens to lift above her head, and she holds it down with two hands. The fundraising ball, she thinks, the ill-fated red dress.

Late that night she had gone looking for Derek. He was sitting alone in the courtyard, a glass of brandy and a cup of coffee on the small table in front of him. 'Derek, that was a fantastic success,' she said, kissing the top of his head. 'And I've more good news. Peter Brindley's agreed to put money into Sparrow. He says he'll work out a business plan with you next week.'

Miriam's hand was on Derek's shoulder. She was about to sit down beside him when his full coffee cup landed on the flagstones at her feet. She jumped back, startled. The cup broke and coffee splashed up, splattering her dress and legs.

'I'm not a whore like you,' Derek said, and left the shards of white china lying where they fell. Miriam dabbed at her bare legs with a tissue.

'That could have burnt me, Derek,' she said. 'Anyway, what do you mean? You don't believe in sexual fidelity.'

'You get wet for him, do you?' he asked in his coldest voice. 'Not the fucking frigid bitch I have to put up with. I'll kill him. I'll go out to his place and I'll kill him. Some dark night I'll go out there with a knife. I'll hang bits of his flesh from the bushes. I'll cut out his heart. I've been watching you, you two-faced bitch.' He raised his hand to strike her, but Blaise Boothe arrived just then and grabbed his arm.

'Give over, Derek,' he said.

Derek tried to hit Blaise, but fell, pulling the table with him, showering himself with brandy and bits of broken glass. 'You're fucking that bastard,' he screamed as he lay on the flagstones, 'to get your husband a free ride. Who d'you think you're fooling? He's a fucking pimp, that's what he is. Selling his wife so he doesn't have to pay his bills. The two of you were made for each other.'

Miriam grimaces. 'Horrible, horrible,' she whispers.

Carthage O'Shea is dead, after lying for five weeks on the hearthrug of his estranged wife's living room. Derek had kept vigil, read Dostoevsky's *Crime and Punishment* to the doomed man. Sócúl had attended the funeral in force. The members had wept to see skinny little boys in soccer gear forming a guard of honour.

And now Philip has died too – suddenly, unexpectedly. 'Poor Derek.' Miriam moves her lips soundlessly. 'First Carthage, and now Philip.' Since the fundraising ball, Derek has not spoken to her. And with the terrible blow of Philip's death, it is impossible to know if he will ever talk to her again. Maybe this part of my life is over for ever, she thinks. We'll live in France and these people, these friends, will come to seem like a dream, dreamt long ago.

'Mummy, Mummy, Mummy.' Jeremy rushes across the schoolyard. 'I want to go play with Robbie.' He pulls at Miriam's dress. 'Say yes, say yes.'

Miriam looks down at her son, his blond hair, beautiful grey eyes. Like Finn, she thinks. A Greek god. *'Conas atá tú*, darling?' she says. 'Let's speak a little Irish. You teach Mummy what you learned today.'

'I want to go play with Robbie.' Jeremy yanks the dress again.

'Please, Jeremy.' Miriam stands up straight. 'Mummy's *sciorta* is delicate. Don't pull it, pet.'

Jeremy drops his schoolbag on the ground, tugs the dress once more. 'Robbie's,' he says. His lower lip pushes out.

'Darling, you were there last week.'

Jeremy kicks the schoolbag, stares truculently at her.

'*Tá go maith*,' Miriam sighs; 'we'll find Robbie's mother.' She takes her son's hand, sets off across the car park.

Miriam put it to Yvonne – the dilemma between *doing good* and *being good* which Blaise had presented her with. 'According to Blaise, I've been destroying my own goodness by doing good,' Miriam explained. '*Being good* is where I should be putting my energies.'

'Sounds like rubbish to me,' Yvonne said.

'For me – when Blaise explained what it meant – the idea seemed a revelation. *Being good*, you see, is like the monastic ideal, where you try to perfect your inner self. For Blaise, that means perfecting the way he makes love to Wendy, the way he entertains his friends, the art works he buys to make their house beautiful. Whereas I, by *doing good*, join an unsavoury bunch of people whose actions, though perhaps for the best motives, have contributed to wrecking the world. Bernard Shaw and the Fabians, for instance, in quest of a more equal society, visited the Soviet Union in the nineteen-thirties and supported a Stalinist dictatorship.'

'Good job you've given it up so,' Yvonne said. 'If you'd listened to me, you wouldn't have got involved in the first place. I told you to get back to painting. You were good. And let's face it, poetry's never going to be a big seller. I know a woman who gets twelve thousand for a piece that she slaps together in a week, all tax free. It's the way to go.'

Miriam searches for Robbie's mother. Occasionally another parent greets her and she stops a moment to pick up a snatch of conversation. Then Jeremy drags her on.

'A sesame oil dressing. Of course I know Patrick uses it. And perhaps if Guilbaud's hadn't got so tacky.... But the way Cynthia ladled it on. Absolutely couldn't.'

'The baby's sweet. Rachel … episiotomy. Terribly painful. So we put our heads together. The answer's a condom filled with water, then frozen. Reaches all the parts…. So, so soothing.'

'Had to offload all the Mexican properties…. As much as we could do to hang on in Spain. George had too many business ideas in his head.'

Miriam does not contribute to these discussions. She stands and smiles a minute, then moves on, Jeremy's hand tugging at hers.

Between two parked cars a small trickle of liquid catches the corner of her eye: oozing across the tarmac, she thinks, like an amoeba on speed – an image for a new poem. She stores it away. Then she sees a man straightening up, fumbling with the zip of his trousers. She looks again, catches her breath. A man urinating in the school car park! Miriam suppresses the shout of condemnation which rises in her throat. It makes no sense, she thinks. Jeremy is clutching her hand, excitedly recounting the day's exploits, while a man exposes himself in front of them.

And there are Rosanne Roycroft's two daughters running through the car park towards this very spot. 'Quick, stop the girls,' Miriam tells Jeremy and opens her arms wide to shield them. But the girls evade her grasp, the oldest one catches Jeremy's hand as she passes, tousles his hair and swings him squealing into a twirl. Then they've escaped, and as Miriam turns to follow them, she hears their voices calling out joyfully, 'Gran, Grandpa. You're so lovely to come.'

'Look, Gran, I did a picture for you,' the youngest one is saying, and Miriam now sees that the man is Dr Roycroft, that his trousers are only partly zipped up, and that Mrs Roycroft is standing beside him. She is gazing down at a large sheet of paper that the little girl is holding out to her. The older child embraces her grandfather, presses her cheek against his.

'Oh, Grandpa, Grandpa, I've missed you,' she says. 'Was it a horrible drive up? I was afraid you wouldn't come … that Mummy'd find some reason.'

'Mummy says you're too old to drive, Grandpa,' the littler one is saying, and Miriam notes the damp patch on the front of the old man's trousers.

'Will you bring us to Kilkenny? Please, please.' The older child turns her pleading from the old man to the old woman. While she speaks the tips of her fingers explore the old woman's wrinkled face. 'Your cheeks are so soft,' she says.

And then Mrs Roycroft catches Miriam's eye. She smiles in recognition. Miriam is forced, against all her instincts, to smile back. She points exaggeratedly to her watch. 'I'm in a rush,' she calls, and walks rapidly away. There is something not quite right about Rosanne's children, she thinks. Their eyes are evasive. They do not respond when spoken to. Sometimes they have seemed to look *through* Miriam.

'*Dia dhuit*,' a child's voice says and Robbie is walking beside Miriam, smiling up at her. Jeremy reaches out, drags at his friend's school shirt. Miriam bends down to kiss Robbie's cheek.

'Let him go, Jeremy,' she says as Robbie's hand slips into hers. How did this gentle little boy come into being? she wonders. His mother is so different. Aggressive, leggy, good-looking, whereas Robbie is small for his age and not at all handsome. Robbie's mother is an extrovert, owns an art gallery, bought for her as a birthday present by her husband some years before. She has the reputation of having a knack with people. Her gallery sparkles with celebrities and society columnists.

'*Conas atá sibh?*' Miriam says to the women who are sitting together chatting on the grassy bank. '*Nach lá álainn é?*'

Robbie's mother turns lazily from the group, stands up and stretches.

'*Tá na laethanta saoire againn arís,*' she says at last, '*agus is mór an áthas atá orainn.*'

Miriam hesitates. She wishes now that she had not begun the conversation in Irish.

'I've been asking the girls what I should do,' Robbie's mother says. Her eyes focus for a moment on her son's hand holding Miriam's, then move to contemplate the wider world. 'I'm having my special *seomra* redecorated. A delicate pink for the walls, very light but true. And somehow it's thrown my walnut table off balance. Do come and advise me. I mean, you have a tiny bijou palace. You must have a solution for anything.'

'Not this afternoon, I'm afraid.' Miriam detaches her hand from Robbie's, leans a little away from him. 'I've to go to a funeral.' She is never sure whether Robbie's mother intends to be offensive, or whether it is just part of her famous direct style. As the boys wander off along the grassy verge to play, she tells the women about Philip's death, the planned cremation, and they shake their heads, little frowns creasing their foreheads. And then Miriam explains about Tina's vernissage this very same evening, how Tina had wanted to cancel the opening, and how her friends had dissuaded her.

As she speaks, Miriam is still asking herself why Dr Roycroft peed in the school car park? And his wife didn't even check that his zip was up. With grandparents like them, she thinks, maybe it's not surprising that Rosanne's children are so odd?

As Miriam ponders this question, Jeremy returns to tug at her arm, pulling her this way and that, so that she has no choice but to ask if he may spend the afternoon with his friend.

'Well….' There is a long hesitation in Robbie's mother's voice. 'The cremation? Is it … one of those people you look after?'

Miriam sighs. She does not feel like explaining that Philip is her friend, that there has been a battle for Philip's allegiance between Philip's family and Derek, or that Philip had chosen to re-enter the Catholic faith in the weeks before he died.

'I'm so glad that I attended your splendid fundraiser,' Robbie's mother says. 'I feel now that I'm playing my part, in my own little way. But what I don't understand is why people are still dying? I absolutely know I read somewhere that the whole scare is over. People are getting well again.'

'Just one of those wretched things that we can't understand.' Miriam holds out her hands helplessly. 'Only a week ago he seemed perfectly healthy....'

'I could never be as brave as you, darling. I couldn't touch those people, I know I couldn't. I'm a coward really, but the food was absolutely delicious. I was relieved. My husband.... You know what men are. It was such a trouble dragging him out. And then he enjoyed himself no end. Now, children,' Robbie's mother claps her hands vigorously, 'into the car. Come along.'

Miriam walks to the almost new Audi which Peter has insisted she borrow – 'A friend went bankrupt,' he said, 'and you've got to have reliable wheels. We're not in the Stone Age.'

Miriam still feels soiled and embarrassed when she drives the car, though Yvonne laughed at her for being so conventional.

'There's got to be some payback,' she said.

As Miriam moves away, Robbie's mother turns again to her friends. She shrugs elegant shoulders. 'Isn't it a relief they're off to France!'

CHAPTER 20

As she drives home, Miriam blames herself for having snubbed the Roycroft grandparents. I completely overreacted, she tells herself. It's horrible to have to be suspicious of everyone.

She parks the Audi in the street outside the house. And there is Finn, waving to her from the open front door, and she cannot help but catch her breath when she sees his smile.

'Jeremy's gone to play with Robbie.' She smiles back at him. And then he grabs her hands and waltzes her into the house.

'We can tell him to fuck off,' he whispers. 'We can tell him to fuck right off.' And he embraces her, kisses her, and she does not understand what is happening.

'The book,' he exults. 'The book. They're making a film of the book! Blaise Boothe, you know the film-maker, skinny ugly little guy?'

'Finn, he's a friend of mine. I thought you hated him.'

'There'll be megabucks.' Finn flings his hands up in the air; his palms open as if he is flinging bundles of money up to the ceiling. He strides up and down the room. 'You don't know the relief. Bloody Pézenas. I'd have gone out of my mind.'

Miriam stands, trying to rethink everything, while Finn talks about having a meeting that very evening with Blaise Boothe and an American producer at Tina Foley's opening.

'I'll be signing a contract,' he almost screams, reaching to embrace her once more.

Miriam can feel his erection through her dress. She pulls away. It would be terrible if he decided he had to have sex now. That would cloud everything. If only she could clear her head, decide what to say. It's extraordinary if it's true, she thinks. But if it isn't true? What if it's just another of Finn's fantasies?

'Peter paid your fine,' she says. 'It was a sort of condition, wasn't it, that we'd go to France? Didn't we agree that it would be good for you to get out of Ireland?'

'Not to fucking Pézenas. We don't need Peter any more. We'll never need fucking Peter again. Or fucking Aosdána. Hallelujah!'

Script, film. The words keep jumbling in Miriam's head while she mechanically strips off her summer dress. If Finn goes off with Blaise Boothe, she thinks, what guarantee is there that he will ever be paid? Because Blaise has money problems. That is what he told Miriam. And if they don't go to France, what will she say to Jeremy? She has promised him a swimming pool, orangina, ice-cream.

She searches the wardrobe for her blouse. And there is Finn behind her, his hands caressing the cheeks of her bottom.

'Please, Finn.' Miriam zips up her skirt, pulls on her blouse, buttons it.

'Not to have to be dependent on that rich bastard's charity,' he exults, embracing her again. 'To be able to ditch his fucking memoir; his boring fucking memoir! Just one little moment, my love.' He is opening the zip of her skirt, pulling down her knickers. 'Just one little moment.'

Twenty minutes later Miriam slides into the driving seat. Her breath is coming in gasps. She bites her lip. He has crushed the cream silk blouse. Deodorant, she thinks – I'll give myself a blast of perfume when I get there. She should have taken a shower, but there was no time.

Outside the crematorium people stand in the sun – Tina, Wendy, Rosanne, Blaise Boothe and several young men whom Miriam does not recognise. William is away at a conference in Sweden. 'The Advanced Study Collegium,' Rosanne explained carelessly to Miriam. 'Where all the great world intellects gather.'

What if we don't go to France? Miriam thinks. Her eyes skate across Rosanne's strong features. After the cremation she will explain to her what happened in the school car park. But maybe Rosanne will be unkind to Dr Roycroft if Miriam tells her. No, she decides. I'll tell William when he gets back. Her fraught eyes move to Blaise, who is standing quietly among the young men, head bowed. I'll ask Blaise straight out, she decides. At least then I'll know if it's true. A Daonnacht representative is standing a little behind Blaise. Miriam recognises the distinctive armband. And another young man behind him again, also wearing the armband.

As Miriam looks around the little group of mourners standing in front of the crematorium, she feels there is something amiss, an unnatural stillness in the air. People stare at the ground and scuff the dusty gravel with the toes of their shoes. She touches Derek's arm. He recoils from her as if stung.

'Philip's gone,' Wendy murmurs from behind her.

'Yes,' Miriam answers sadly.

'His body's been stolen.' Blaise's ponytail sways in the early summer breeze and Miriam's mouth opens in shock.

'Catholic parents are loathsome immoral creatures.' Blaise's voice is high and light. His ponytail swings from side to side, his pimples shine in the sun. 'They spirited him away in the small hours. And now his poor corpse putrifies in a Catholic Church somewhere … Donegal, Kerry, Monaghan, who can tell where to find him?'

Derek is kicking at the ground. His Louboutin shoes are covered in grey dust. 'We can't just leave it at that,' he says, and Miriam's heart breaks for him. 'How will we find him?' he growls. 'What if his family have told the priests to keep it quiet? A conspiracy. No information.' In his anxiety Derek dribbles spittle down his chin.

'I know one priest,' Miriam says. 'He's a friend of my mother's. I'm sure he'd help us.' She looks around at her fellow mourners. 'Sorry, I…. I left my mobile at home.'

Rosanne plucks a phone from her pocket. Hands it to Miriam. She dials, all eyes on her.

'No reply,' Miriam says dejectedly. She listens sadly to the small trickle of conversation as the mourners drift away.

'Priests are cunts,' Tina growls.

Miriam tries the phone again. 'Sorry', she says. 'Still no answer.'

The Daonnacht representatives walk quietly behind them. One comes forward and touches Derek's shoulder. 'The funeral's tomorrow morning in Inchicore,' he says. 'We've located the body.'

CHAPTER 21

Tina sits in the back seat of Inchicore parish church, swallowing Nurofen and bottled water. Last night's opening revisits her in vivid splendid flashes. A packed room. Even Wendy had been unable to stay away. Tina had heard her voice, glanced in that direction, then turned aside.

Blaise Boothe introduced, with a sly wink, the Fitzpatrick sisters. 'Loaded,' he whispered, 'Mater Private – Caroline's a skin specialist, Serena fixes hearts.' They bought six paintings. Nine other canvases had sold.

For Tina the best part of the evening was spent down in the men's toilets, snorting coke and drinking champagne with Finn Daly and Blaise.

'*The strong should take what they want.*' She spread her legs. Her urine flowed down onto white tiles. '*My works are a summary of destructions.*' Tina held the champagne glass aloft like a consecrated chalice. 'For this is my blood,' she called out, 'which will be offered up for all of you.' She lowered the glass, peered into the effervescent liquid, its tiny necklace of bubbles on top, and the champagne seemed to be of the most exquisite beauty, each of its infinitesimal spheres separate from the next, tiny perfect entities of carbon dioxide in solution.

She touched a finger to a line of cocaine. 'My body,' she said, snuffling up the particles of white dust. 'My body.'

Then there was commotion in the midst of revelation – Miriam in the toilets, Miriam speaking earnestly with Finn, Finn's voice raised. Tina held two dusty fingers reverently to Miriam's nostrils, but Miriam squirmed away with a cry of revulsion.

'It's wet down there' – Tina had found herself speaking from a trance. 'I pissed all over it.' A sense of ecstasy pervaded her entire being. She felt her urine to be the waters of baptism. 'Come to me and I will feed you the bread of life.' She held out her hands, white dust clinging to her fingertips.

Tina closes her eyes. Blaise – a night of crazy, drugged sex. Blaise Boothe. A tingling sensation of pleasure courses through her body. A certain way he had of touching her breasts. The quick slide of fingers, the soft tongue, her nipples still quiver as Mass begins.

Tina presses fingertips to her breasts to ease the memory of shuddering pleasure, opens her eyes slowly. There is sunlight on the bench in front of her. Other light falls haphazardly across the congregation. And now Tina becomes aware of the bright air held in the shaft of sunlight closest to her, the air populated by a million tiny particles. Photons without mass. Minuscule ships floating on a sea of light.

A gust of breeze from an opened door and a wave of particles swirls away from her. The particles are lightships sailing across an ocean, which is almost always invisible to Tina, but today she has been given sunlight, she has been invited into a new dimension.

Her moment of pleasure cannot last. A delicate body moves into the seat in front – elegant black suit, wide black hat.

Tina lowers her gaze. She does not wish to encounter Miriam this morning. The human body settles, and Tina gradually raises her eyes to a new raft of bright particles. Light waves, light particles, she thinks. How can light be wave and particle all at once? And she thinks of the millions of dimensions outside in the world just beyond her eye. Bewildering new dimensions where, if Tina's senses were not sequestered and limited, she would be able to peel the skin from her eyes, and step outside herself into the beautiful crazy worlds around her.

And now the lush harmonies of Ravel's *Daphnis and Chloë* drown the words of the Mass. People stand up and look around for the source of the music, and Tina's particles are driven this way and that, then forced upwards to the nave's high ceiling. The music softens to a whisper and the congregation can hear Derek sobbing from all corners of the church.

'For Philip.' His choked voice at last enunciates the words. His hands shake as he holds out several crumpled pages in front of the microphone.

'For Philip, whose dark moment has arrived….' At first the words pour out in a flood, then trail off into blurred grunts and half-sentences.

Derek wipes his eyes with the back of his hand. The priest approaches, touches Derek's arm. Tina holds her breath.

'Resist him, Derek,' she whispers, and, as she watches, Derek pushes away the priest, turns back to the microphone. His head bows. A heavy groan reverberates around the church.

'He has stepped into the black boat on the shadowed river.' He is weeping again and the microphone shrieks as his mouth comes too close. He takes a step back, rubs his forehead and stares into the body of the church. Tina, standing in the centre aisle, can see the priest talking with a group of men to the side of the altar. The priest is shaking his head, his hands spread wide in a gesture, which could be sympathy for Derek's plight, or even a counsel of restraint, for the men do not move.

Tina holds her breath, watching, waiting for Derek to continue. But Derek is looking around, searching for someone or something in his audience.

'Go on, Derek,' she whispers silently. 'Speak or they'll take you down.'

Someone whistles, others clap, but Derek's head continues to jerk this way and that. Finally it becomes still. He stares at his notes, searches for something in his jacket pocket.

'The black boat rides low in the water … dark water,' he says softly. 'Philip….' His voice descends into an incomprehensible murmur; he stretches out his hands to the churchgoers, stands silent, then stares once more at his notes. 'His coin of passage cold in already coldening hands.' The pages drop to the tiles.

CHAPTER 22

A June morning in Brittas Bay. Long miles of shadowed beach light up, then sink into shadow once more. Among the pale dunes, soft sanded ridges sprout wiry grass. The sky plays out the great cosmic struggles between good and evil, light and dark. Gulls, oystercatchers, sandpipers shriek and glide over sand and water.

Rosanne flashes her Loyalty Card at the car park entrance, glares into the camera. She parks the Volvo, takes the beach paraphernalia from the boot and mechanically distributes it between herself and her two daughters. Laden down with cool bags, flasks, windbreaks, towels, buckets, spades, the three trudge through scrub-grass to the dunes.

In a hollow, Rosanne spreads her beach mat on raked and cleaned sand, then removes her clothes and lies goose-pimpled and sun-lotioned on the leeside of her windbreak. She pays a yearly contribution so that the gated enclosure will remain clean and safe. No parties, no dogs, no stereo systems. Beach security services break up teenage gatherings. Prosecutions follow. Recalcitrant young thugs are sent to inland prisons.

Gusts of bracing June wind whirl around her. The windbreak billows under the wind's force, the canvas sheeting collapses. She stands to right it and is whipped by grains of sand caught in the gust. A violent blustering and there is sand in her eyes, her mouth. She bows her head and sinks back, defeated.

Finn Daly had disappeared as Rosanne knew he would. She mourned the loss of him for two long weeks. Then a phone call from Berlin revealed that he was stranded there without funds. Some confusion with his bank. Rosanne had dropped everything, flown to offer him the use of her credit card.

'You've got some nerve,' her mother said when Rosanne told her that the children would be coming to stay.

'Please, Mother. You know William's in Argentina and their minder's gone for the summer. If you won't keep them, I'll have to send them to Kilkenny.'

'I've warned you,' her mother answered. 'You know what age that child is – almost eleven years old. I'll not have them in this house till Maeve has her Communion made.'

So the children had gone to William's parents in Bennettsbridge.

'Gran brought us to a play, Mum,' Maeve announced as soon as they had driven out of her grandparents' imposing gateway.

'It wasn't like a play,' Deirdre said. 'There was just this man in a shiny tracksuit sitting on a stool. And it was only a room. Not like a theatre.'

'What did you expect? It was down the country, stupid.'

'Don't speak to your sister like that,' Rosanne said automatically. Her thoughts were on Finn, his strong shoulders, T-shirt revealing golden-haired bare arms, the cleft in his chin. She wanted to stop the car and weep.

'Hmm. Anyway this fellow in the tracksuit told us about a dwarf that got his legs shot off.'

Rosanne remembers how she and Finn had strolled around the Reichstag, peered into Hitler's bunker, examined the remains of SS headquarters. And afterwards? Afterwards, nothing. Nothing.

'It was Daonnacht that did it. And Gran says they hold huge meetings to get people under their spell. And they have this salute that everyone has to do. It's like brainwashing.'

'Daonnacht did what?'

'Shot the dwarf's legs off. Then the guy told us that he had stolen cars, about fifty of them, and took them up on a bridge and burned them all in a big bonfire, that you could see the flames for thousands of miles. And

Daonnacht wanted to shoot his legs off too but he stayed at home that day. So they gave him an appointment. Like with the doctor.'

'Daonnacht doesn't do that sort of thing, Maeve,' Rosanne exclaimed. 'Maybe by mistake once or twice. But the people who did it were punished. They shot them in the knees. It wasn't nearly so serious.'

By the Reichstag, at the end of the third day, Rosanne had sat at the fountain and sobbed great gulping sobs. She knew then that there was no choice but to return home.

'Afterwards,' Deirdre explained, 'I started to cry because Maeve wanted to give me an appointment. But Gran said it was no joking matter, that Daonnacht's an evil organisation.'

'They pretend they don't shoot people,' Maeve interrupted, 'but they're lying. Gran says everyone's innocent until they're proved guilty. And destroying people's bodies is wrong for any reason. They want people to be afraid. That's why I shouldn't joke about giving Deirdre an appointment. Gran asked me how I'd feel if Deirdre couldn't walk any more. She showed us a thing in the newspaper about a girl having her two arms broken with a stick because she didn't do what they told her. We'll all have to shut up or have our legs shot off. Do you think that's true, Mum?'

'Of course it's not true, Maeve. Gran gets a bee in her bonnet – that's the way old people are. And I must say the play sounds entirely unsuitable. I'll have to find out who wrote it. People can't be allowed to go around spreading lies like that.'

Ridiculous old people, Rosanne thinks as she grits chattering teeth and dips her reluctant body into a cold choppy sea. Did the old bitch write the play herself? she wonders. Bad enough to have demented parents-in-law; she had known from the start that William's parents would be difficult – she had expected it. But both sets of parents crazy, that was beyond everything. She tries not to look at the heavy cloud bank moving in from the horizon, sets out on a rapid crawl, then turns on her back, and suddenly relishes the intense cold against her head. Her own parents, her insane ghastly parents. Turns once more, strikes out for the deep, while the girls make castles with the wet, cold sand. Her mother's lumpy form in flower-patterned dress, her pale cold eyes staring at Rosanne through the dark unhappy water, standing hands on hips with a little bubble of white saliva on her lower lip, calling out the rosary from the kitchen while her children kneel and respond.

'Possessed by the devil,' Rosanne's mother would utter solemnly, which meant that another family member was being dropped from the list of prayers. First it had been an uncle who had somehow become involved with a dissolute woman. There had been others – divorcees, blasphemers, political deviants. Each in their turn suffered excommunication from the night-time liturgy.

As the family came of age, Rosanne's younger sister had been tracked (as a favour to her mother) by a distant relative, and discovered living with her boyfriend in a London squat. The frenzy of her sister's consignment to hell had shocked Rosanne. Even as she continued to keep her mother up to date on which of her brothers and sisters were failing to attend Sunday Mass, Rosanne had felt the first twinges of religious doubt creep into her own soul. She turns for the shore once more. She has swum out farther than she had intended, and must battle against a receding tide. Head down, she forces herself onwards. Stroke after stroke, a quick breath, then head down once more, until she sees the stick insects that are her children. They are running now in the sand, chasing each other with long strings of seaweed.

'Stop it, Maeve,' she shouts as she runs up the beach. Then without waiting to see if Maeve is obeying her, she crouches in the dunes, dragging off her wet bathing togs. Her blouse and jeans stick to her body, to her damp shivering skin.

The sky darkens to deep purple, the wind drops. Rain begins in a thin stream, then grows thicker and heavier until it is pouring in a drenching surge. As Rosanne gathers beach equipment, the two children are racing away from her, along the wet sand to the protective outer fence. They intertwine their fingers in sections of latticed wire, shake it as best they can and scream joyfully at the billion droplets they have made.

Their journey home is never pleasant – continuous backseat skirmishes of pinching and teasing while Rosanne threatens general retribution. She would hate to be seen as that type of mother who reaches into the back of the car and strikes her children in an abandonment of rage. I'll show them the new cottage, she decides; that'll distract them. We'll light a fire, and I'll try to cheer up. It isn't far.

On a blue-skied afternoon in May, Rosanne and William had completed the purchase.

'I can hardly believe it,' William told the solicitor. 'Five acres of unspoilt land and a perfectly restored cottage. The price is so small, I'm almost embarrassed, but then I remind myself that it's for a good cause. I've always wanted to give the children space to run wild, to let them be free. A space apart. A space for happiness.'

William and Rosanne have been down twice since they bought the cottage. They have employed a local handyman to put in new locks and build a fence.

Rosanne switches on her indicator and turns left towards the mountains. The girls cheer, but a sharp word from their mother sends them back to their books. She wonders is she pinning too many hopes on this forlorn cottage and its boggy site?

At Glenealy the road begins to climb. Rosanne negotiates the bends, peers through a film of water at the brambles on every side, the dejected low-slung cottages. There is the ghostly image of a car in front of her, at a standstill on the shoulder of a corkscrew bend. She slams on the brakes, sounds her horn, dimly makes out a rain-soaked figure in the roadway waving its arms.

'Take the number, Maeve. Write it down,' she shouts as they pass. 'That car's breaking the law.'

'Mummy,' she hears Maeve cry. 'There's someone on the road. You nearly hit him.'

Rosanne slows to a halt. 'What are you saying, Maeve? The man's a fool to be standing there. I couldn't see him.'

A red petrol can clangs against the body of her car. A drenched face looks in. Rosanne presses the accelerator and the car leaps forward.

'He said your name, Mummy,' Maeve shrieks and her mother again brings the car to a halt.

The two girls are kneeling up now, escaped from their seatbelts. Wide-eyed, trembling with excitement, they stare out to where a rain-soaked man is picking himself up from the roadway.

'I think you're very mean to that poor man.' Maeve points an accusing finger at her mother. 'He's all covered in dirt and wet. And it's your fault.'

'Rosanne.'

She turns slowly. Paul Ryan, journalist, with sodden hair and matted beard, stares in at her.

'I've run out of petrol.' Ryan stands in the roadway pleading with Rosanne through a crack of open window.

'You can sit in here beside me.' Maeve tries to open the back door. Her mother presses the central locking switch.

'For heaven's sake, Maeve, he'll destroy the upholstery.'

'We're sorry you fell,' Maeve says. 'Mummy made a mistake. She didn't mean to drive away.'

Rosanne fumes as she drives into Rathdrum with Ryan's petrol can in the boot. Paul Ryan is a nobody. He had once been important, had talked the grand rhetoric of knowledge, ideas, technology – all freely circulated across borders. Then he'd resigned in a pique when a protégé of his was refused entry to Ireland. An unknown philosopher deported, and Ryan had made that senseless gesture.

At the petrol station, a thin teenage boy responds to the sound of her horn. She notices Maeve's window wide open, her bare arm held out to the rain. 'What are you doing, you bad child? Close the window immediately.'

'The money,' Maeve explains, drawing in her hand as her mother presses the window control. 'I opened my window and he gave it to me.'

Her mother snatches a wet banknote from her daughter's hand while the boy screws tight the cap of Paul Ryan's petrol can. Rosanne takes another twenty from her purse. 'Here,' she says. 'You'll find the car stopped on the first bend towards Rathnew. You can tell the owner I'll be reporting him to the police.'

The road from Rathdrum to Laragh follows the course of the Avonmore river, but Rosanne and her children never see the swirling dark water. Dense belts of conifers on both sides of the road hide all topographical features. Rosanne cautiously negotiates each bend. She thinks about Paul Ryan. It had been a stupid mistake all those months before to invite him into their home. She'd had a vague idea of giving him a hand back up. A ridiculous idea.

William had served *coq au vin*. Afterwards, Rosanne had sung for the company, and William had played Irish airs on the violin. She had chatted with Tadhg Ó Cuinn on the living room sofa, and watched Ryan carefully. When she judged the moment right, she shooed Tadhg away and patted the cushion beside her.

'Come and talk to me, Paul. Let's discuss the poetic impulse.'

He sat down beside her. 'Francis Stuart,' he said. 'Mediocre writer, unrepentant fascist, anti-semite. Why did Aosdána make him a *Saoi*?'

Rosanne focused her attention on the Basil Blackshaw painting across the room. 'I was very young then,' she said. 'I'd only just become a member. I hardly knew what was happening.'

'Everything about Stuart was bad,' Ryan said. 'Yet the Irish President awarded him a collar of gold. Stuart bitterly opposed Jewish children being allowed into Ireland in the thirties; went to Germany to work for the Nazis in 1940. Putting it simply, he chose evil over good at a crucial point in world history. And, knowing all this, the members of Aosdána made him a *Saoi*. I'm trying to understand why.'

'I had nothing to do with it, Paul. Honestly.'

He sat back, gnawing his thumbnail, and Rosanne wondered how to get the conversation restarted on a less difficult plane.

'*There are storms that are promised that never come,*' he said eventually.

'I couldn't agree with you there,' Rosanne answered. 'We were given ample warning of the storms. I mean, didn't Morgan Kelly spell it out over and over? Every chance he got – I'd say he began back in 2007 … just after we bought our house actually – he warned us that the economy was on a disaster course.'

'It's a poem by Dermot Healy.'

Rosanne poured more wine. She was not interested in Healy's writings.

Ryan seemed to be quoting the full poem, and she briefly wondered had he taken some strange drug.

> *'And some not promised*
> *That do:*
>
> *They come out of the blue*
> *Out of the blue*
>
> *Because they are true,*
> *Because they are true:*
>
> *Oh they are true to their word*
> *The storms not promised*
>
> *And they wreck you,*
> *They wreck you,*
>
> *They do.'*

As Ryan spoke, Rosanne reflected on how to present her poetry through him to a mass audience. She might ask him to adapt the piece from her Japanese residency.

'The editor's wife,' he said then; 'we had this big bust up. Something I wrote. Something I wouldn't write. So she hates my guts. Anyway, I swim. Every day if I can. I'm not a great swimmer, but I love the feel of the sea. We were in Courtown one of those bracing days last week. I decided to get in. There I am splashing around – it's choppy, a bit of a swell. Claire and the boys have gone shopping. They all think I'm mad to be swimming at this time of the year. There's a woman standing on the beach. I don't take any notice. And then I do. And I feel like she's staring at me. There's a cold sensation around my heart. It drags me down. Suddenly I'm drowning.'

He put a hand on his chest and Rosanne noticed the stumped fingers, nails bitten to the quick. She had refilled their glasses, reached for a raspberry tartlet, popped it into her mouth.

'Luckily it's more panic than anything else. I'm not out of my depth, so I stand up, feel a bit of a fool, get out of the water. The woman's walking away. But when I look at her again, I think it's the editor's wife. And when I try to run after her, it's like a concrete block on my heart. I can't go on.

I'm clutching my chest, thinking this is it. It's a heart attack. Imagining myself dead on a winter beach in wet boxers. Thirty seconds later the pain and the woman are gone.'

'Have you tried these, Paul?' Rosanne nibbled another tartlet. 'They're awfully good.' Her fingers stroked the sleeve of his jacket.

'I look after the Devanneys, you see.' She had felt, probably because she was already a little drunk, that Ryan's confession merited one of her own. 'The Devanneys,' she said again. 'I use magical rites to help them because there's nothing else that can get through to them. Prison and babies. That's all they know. Sickness, prison and babies.'

Ryan sighed, blew his nose in a yellowing, tattered handkerchief. 'I should go for a check-up,' he said. 'Heart beating too fast. Fibrillation or something.'

'I read my poems for Gerry Devanney, my irredeemable savage. To open him up to experience. The way you'd clear someone's sinuses. New sensations. I want to do good, you see. I want to use my talent in every positive way I can. I need to go beyond – to where the poetic incantation has a material effect.'

She felt at that moment – though this was again probably the fault of the wine – that Ryan was looking at her with something approaching admiration.

'I may yet cure his disease. I am the one who sees. I, the druid, the *file*, can call Wind, Earth, Water, Fire to do my will. Every day new powers pulse through me. Already they have moved the tumour from Gerry Devanney's brain. The magic rites are powerful enough to give him back his sight. I go into the room with him, try out new poems in Irish, because the language matters.... I work out the rhythms. The family think I'm praying and I don't disillusion them. It's the incantation that transforms.'

She had heard Ryan mutter something about having to get home, but when he'd tried to stand up, she had dragged him down by the back of his jacket. 'I hate that family. They're a poison in society. The power of the creative spirit – I always felt inside me that I had it. I go home with a photo of him, concoct little potions, enact the magic rites of the *fili*.'

Paul Ryan had refused more wine, covered his glass with his hand.

'The tumour has moved,' Rosanne exulted. 'Gerry can see again.

Shadows so far, but it's improving, and he's beginning to talk sense. And Paul, I'm grateful to Gerry Devanney for teaching me something about myself. Because he's shown me that I can do this transforming thing. I can use the ancient powers of the druids. I am their present-day incarnation. It's an enormous responsibility, Paul, and I have to carry it.' She had started to cry, overcome by the wine and the weight of her inheritance. When she recovered herself, she was alone on the sofa. Paul Ryan had gone.

At Cullentragh the road becomes little more than a narrow track. Sublime, Rosanne thinks, as the mist thickens, but even though she loves this swirling mist, feels it like a protective cloak around her, there is something in the damp air that makes her hesitate. And at Knockrath junction she stops a moment, almost turns for Laragh and home. Then she takes a deep breath, switches on her fog lights, hugs the edge of the boreen, and urges the car forward.

CHAPTER 23

'Are you sure we're going the right way, Mummy? I think we're lost.' Maeve's voice grates on Rosanne's strained nerves. She presses her lips tightly together, stares into the mist. Pools of water at the road's edge glimmer in the light of her fog lamps. The road surface disappears into a filmy ether.

'I don't like it. I want to go home. It's scary and I can't see anything.' Deirdre starts to cry.

'Don't be such a baby,' Maeve tells her sister. 'We'll throw you out and leave you here if you're not quiet. And then the wolves'll get you.'

'There are no wolves in Ireland. Deirdre, honestly, how could you believe such nonsense?' Deirdre's muffled whimpers echo in her mother's ears.

They have reached a summit, for the grey space beyond the headlights becomes a void. It is hard not to feel nervous, although Rosanne knows that they must soon be descending into Glenmalure. She tries to remember how it had been when she and William had first followed this route in their quest for a holiday home. She remembers little about it, apart from their exclamations at the beauty of the valley. Surely it couldn't be more than a mile or two?

In Rosanne's garden Wendy accepted the weeding trowel, which Rosanne thrust at her, then knelt to begin the careful removal of dandelions and scutch grass from the base of the musk mallows. 'I'm helping Derek with Sócúl,' she said. 'And I'm trying to write a piece on gay love.' She took a pale violet petal in her hand. 'I was outside Derek's toilet,' she said. 'The door slightly open, two men kissing just inside.'

Rosanne lifted her head from the sweet-peas, stared at Wendy. She had not wanted to be dragged from the delicacy of the flower garden into a world of carnal appetites.

'One had his trousers around his knees, and he was sliding his foreskin backwards and forwards.'

Rosanne there and then decided to make it clear that some things are unacceptable. 'Wendy, I don't want to be told about the revolting events that I imagine go on hourly in Derek's house,' she said. 'He's coked up to his eyeballs these days. You should keep away from him.'

Wendy looked at her in surprise. 'I thought it was beautiful,' she said. 'But I can't write the article that way. I've got to make it sexless and sentimental.' She bent once more over the flowerbed, clearing each separate dandelion root.

'Homosexual love is a wild other world,' she said. 'You're not going to have babies, so sex is free. That's the choice you make, and it's an exultant sort of choice. No snags, so long as you avoid disease. Sex and commitment don't have to hang together. You can fuck just for the joy in the other's body.'

'Enough,' Rosanne hissed, and at last Wendy looked up, gesturing with muddy hands.

'Sorry,' she said, 'it's just that when I'm gardening, I find it easier to think these things through.'

Rosanne descends the mountainside, stares into the gloom, follows carefully the pools on either side of the boreen. In the back of the car Maeve is reciting for her sister the story of Little Red Riding Hood.

'Nice soft skin, dearest. Grrrh. Let me have a feel of it, dearest. Grrrh. Wooooh.'

Rosanne sees in her rear-view mirror Deirdre squealing as Maeve's fingers pinch her neck.

'Stop that immediately, Maeve! Leave your sister alone.'

The car lurches and Rosanne thinks: this is how mothers hurtle to their doom.

'I'm telling the story and you're spoiling it, Mummy. The granny can't see very well. That's why she has to touch Little Red Riding Hood – so she'll know if it's her.'

'Stop it now!' her mother shouts. 'My goodness, when I get the car off this damned road, you are going to learn a very serious lesson.'

Wendy had been kneeling, bending over the herb bed. She straightened, raised her arms, swung them up above her head. 'Ooh,' she said, 'that's better. What moves in the garden of delight?' She gestured across the road to the leafy park.

Rosanne turned from the poppies where some as yet unidentified canker was causing the buds to fall before they opened. 'What do you mean, Wendy? It's a park where children play. I don't understand what you're insinuating.'

'And it's a place where gays go cruising.' She sat back on her heels and reflected for a moment. 'It's that wild gay world. Imagine it, Rosanne. Someone in there is taking down his pants.' Wendy turned to look at the rose of Sharon, which was being crowded by new bamboo shoots. '*I am the rose of Sharon,*' she said, '*and the lily of the valleys. I sat down under his shadow with great delight, and his fruit was sweet to my taste.*'

'If you continue this sort of loose chatter,' Rosanne hissed into the back of Wendy's head, 'you can get out of here.' But Wendy took no notice.

'A bit early in the day for sex in a public space though,' she said, looking at her watch. 'Probably just a chat. Gay men are great about sex. Nothing's off limits. They'll talk about queens, sucking off; they'll grade penises. Lesbians seem so joyless by comparison.'

Rosanne had taken a deep breath to regain control. 'Rust on the Souvenir du Dr Jamain,' she said, holding an orange-patched rose leaf up to the sun. 'We've still got some of that seaweed solution, haven't we? You can spray it on tomorrow.' She had looked Wendy full in the face. 'And this topic of conversation is over.'

Wendy had smiled as she loosened the soil between the dill and the *Rosa rugosa*. 'I love the garden,' she said. 'It's the place where I've always been happiest.'

The road levels out and Rosanne is able to discern the grey mass of the old barracks across the Avonbeg river. Drumgoff barracks. Part of a chain of fortifications through the Wicklow mountains, built in the opening moments of the nineteenth century to protect the British from the avenging Irish – Glencree, Laragh, Glenmalure, Aughavannagh. Massive, remote, all of them abandoned within thirty years of being built. Glencree used by the new Irish State as a reformatory, housed 300 delinquent boys. Drumgoff was taken over by miners.

Rosanne grits her teeth. Her own lunatic father still talks with pride about rescuing delinquent children in a post-colonial world. That great purifying reformist energy, the Catholic Church, called on to spearhead the movement. Religious orders who plucked children from stricken lives, who offered them a new way forward.

'If there were excesses,' he shouts, 'it was a few bad apples. You can't use them to tarnish the whole barrel.'

She thinks with a little shiver of the fields around Glencree – those rectangular patches of green, which stretch from the old reformatory into the valley. Vivid fertile fields against the carpets of grey-brown bog which drift to the mountaintops on either side. Green rectangles created by the bare hands of children.

The barracks disappears – a new sweep of mist across the road and everything is hidden. Rosanne peers from the car, her foot on the brake, her eyes screwed up in an effort to make out the tilt of the road. And now her father's gaunt face stares into the car, and the grey air moves new shadows through the mist.

'Go away.' Rosanne whispers. 'Can't you see I'm trying to drive.' But the face comes closer, long yellowing teeth, thin grey lips. She bangs her hand down on the steering-wheel in frustration.

'The Church,' he is telling her, his skinny finger hovering outside the windscreen, 'never reckoned on that possibility. Children so mired in corruption that nothing could save them. So far gone in fetid knowledge that they could drag whomever down into the devil's pit. Satan's spawn, Rosanne. Worse than rabid dogs.'

Rosanne opens her mouth to answer, but her father waves his hand in a gesture of dismissal.

'The young men sent to bring these monsters into God's house,' he is shouting now, as if she had interrupted him, as if he must urgently contradict her. 'Those young men could have had no knowledge of what they were facing. Innocent young fellows, recruited from the countryside, enlisted to serve God as holy Brothers, in the flower of their youth. They thought they were dealing with children. Seed that had fallen on thorny soil, children who, with good example and correction, would return to the ways of God.'

Rosanne stares through the mist at the looming shadow of her father.

'How could the Brothers have triumphed against such concerted evil? Even with special training, how could they have triumphed? The creatures who were sent to the reformatories weren't natural. They weren't children; they were young devils. Soiled in vile practices from an early age, well trained in the devil's art of prostitution, they knew all the tricks, how to insinuate themselves into the Brothers' affections, how to pick out the weakest of them, how to flaunt their bodies, torture those pure young men until they gave in to the sins of the flesh. No wonder the Brothers tried to whip it out of them. And even that wasn't sufficient. Evil reached out from Satan's flock, held the community in its grasp.'

Rosanne signals a right turn. She shakes her head and her father's image fades. Through a thinning veil of mist, she begins to make out the few bungalows that line the road. Maeve's voice digs deeper and deeper. It is little more than a whisper. The tiny miaows that escape from Deirdre cause beads of sweat to appear on Rosanne's forehead. She clutches the steering wheel. 'Stop it,' she moans. 'Stop it.'

'She was a clever old granny.' Maeve is barely audible. 'Like Granny Flynn. She didn't let the wolf gobble her up. She smashed him on the head with a frying pan, then pushed him into the wardrobe and locked the door.'

Rosanne feels her breath coming in little gasps. 'I can't bear this,' she whispers to herself. 'I can't survive this. She's doing it deliberately. She knows I'm at her mercy. Torturing me. She's got to be made to obey me.'

'Daddy rushes in. He's on the other side of the bed, so he can't see Little Deirdre Riding Hood. He thinks Granny Flynn's the wolf, and that she's gobbled up Little Deedee Riding Hood. So he gets his big hatchet and chops off Granny Flynn's head. And blood spurts out all over the bed.'

'Jesus Christ!' Rosanne screams over Deirdre's wails. 'I am going to go mad.' Her eyes search for a place to stop. Not near a house. It has to be in open country.

Wendy held up a small yellowing leaf for Rosanne's appraisal. 'I was reading a thing about the historical context,' she said. 'At the turn of the twentieth century men like Casement, Wilde and Eulenburg were extraordinarily charismatic figures. Loved and fêted by heterosexuals – women and men – at all the best parties. And everyone knew they were gay, accepted it, no problem. But as soon as they were outed, they became untouchables, despised by everyone who had adored them. That's the problem with gay love: there's too few boundaries. It frightens people when it gets visible. Ouch.' She held up a finger. 'A nettle got me. Even though heteros do more weird sexual things to each other than gays do.' She had sucked the finger reflectively. 'I'd look for a dock leaf but I don't really think they work,' she said. 'Yet heteros are a byword for normality.'

Wendy had carefully clipped at stray shoots of lilac, which were forcing themselves through the lavender. 'I want Blaise to get a place in the country,' she said. 'He's promised he'll think about it when we get back from Australia. We're going to renew our marriage vows.' She held up another leaf, this time browned and atrophied. 'These days all sex is legal, but gays are leaping back into the closet.'

'Put away that leaf, Wendy,' Rosanne said; 'it's withered, that's all. What do you mean, closet? Gays have never been more free. Not since ancient Greece.'

'They've dragged themselves back into domesticity. That's the closet. They want to be married, have babies, for God's sake! Appear normal, like heteros do. Pledge devotion to one partner – it's weird! The great thing about being gay used to be that you weren't domestic.'

'Daddy chops and chops, searching inside the wolf for Little Red Riding Hood until Granny Flynn is chopped to bits. Like steaks. Daddy's so busy chopping, he doesn't notice the real wolf. It sneaks out of the wardrobe and gobbles up Little Deirdre Riding Hood.' Maeve's voice trails off as she notices that the car is slowing down. Deirdre's hiccupping sobs continue.

'Good story, wasn't it, Mummy?' Maeve offers conversationally. 'Have we got there? Why are we stopping? And Mummy, you're wrong; there are wolves in Ireland. They're in the zoo. And I bet some of them escaped. I know they'd come here if they did.' She turns to poke her sister. 'So they'll get you, so they will, crybaby. There! There!' Then she points excitedly out of the car window. 'I see one, I see one. Oh, there's lots. Oh! Oh!'

Wendy stood up and rubbed earth-stained hands against her skirt. 'I have to go,' she said, 'to feed my puppy.' She waved at Rosanne's elder daughter, who was balancing on the stone balustrade beside the front steps. 'I'm off to Australia for three weeks,' she said. 'Would you like to look after my puppy while I'm gone?'

Maeve jumped from the balustrade and ran to Wendy. 'Of course we would,' she said. 'Can I come to see it today?' She held Wendy's bicycle. 'You could give me a back carrier. I'll wear my helmet, Mummy.'

'Go back to your room, Maeve.' Rosanne glared at Wendy. 'We will *not* be looking after any puppy.'

'If it's okay with you, Rosanne, I'll bring Maeve to see it?' Wendy said.

'Get back to your room, Maeve,' Rosanne snapped. 'And please don't interfere, Wendy. You women who have no children can be incredibly irresponsible. You said you were in a hurry to leave. Go, will you. Get on your bike and go.'

Rosanne makes to pull the Volvo on to the verge, but she is moving too fast. The car staggers a little; a noise of crunching comes from underneath. One front wheel sinks and the car tilts forward.

'Oh, my God, you little bitch! See what you've done.'

'I didn't do it, Mummy. You weren't looking where you were going. And you said a bad word.' Maeve begins to snivel.

Deirdre's sobs grow louder. Rosanne attempts to start the car. There's a grinding noise, but the wheels do not catch. She tries once more, then opens the door and gets out.

'Come out here.' Rosanne stands in the road, white-faced, pointing in at Maeve with a stick picked up from the ditch.

'I don't want to. I'm sorry, Mummy. I didn't mean to.' Maeve starts to struggle as her mother drags her from the car. 'No, Mummy, no! I'll tell Daddy on you. You're not allowed. Stop it, Mummy! Stop!'

'There's nobody to hear your whinging.' Rosanne pulls Maeve's knickers to her ankles and hits the first blow. 'Wait till I tell your father that you dared to invite a strange man into our car. He could have killed us all or done worse.'

'You knew him,' Maeve sobs. 'You knew him, you did. He said your name.'

'Your father will say I was right.' She strikes downwards again. Maeve shrieks. She struggles to free herself from her mother's grasp, but Rosanne is too strong for her.

In the car Deirdre, face pressed against the back of the seat, holds the palms of her hands against her ears to keep out the sound.

Rosanne stands on her lawn in the fading light. She hears rustlings from the bushes in the park across the road, feels her flesh crawl with the certainty that in that quiet space nocturnal activity has already begun.

Vile and depraved, they lurk in the bushes. Foul images crowd her mind. Dirty and smelly, urine and faeces everywhere, waiting for their moment. The boy at the railings turns, holds out an erect penis. They converge on him. One kisses him on the mouth, a second licks his testicles, a third his penis. A fourth kneels in the grass and licks his anus. And these beasts want to marry. They need to marry, need to father children in order to hide from the world of decency their loathsome degeneracy.

Hateful, hateful.' Rosanne shudders as she beats her daughter. Women are not like that. Lesbians are not like that. Rosanne will get up a petition. Have the park patrolled at night.

The stick works hard at its task of retribution. Red marks appear on Maeve's skin, her screams rise in the saturated air. A trickle of blood runs down one leg. The stick hits the child again, breaks, and she slips from

Rosanne's grasp into the ditch. Rosanne stands in the roadway, staring in confusion at the short portion of stick which remains in her hand. It is a thin, stringy, miserable thing, strips of pale bark peeling away from it. She cannot identify what sort of tree it comes from.

Maeve is lying in the wet grass without her knickers. There is blood on her bottom, and thick red weals.

'I'm sorry,' Rosanne whispers. 'I didn't think the stick would be that vicious,' and Maeve's sobs mutate into thin bleats.

But now there is a sound of someone approaching along the road, and Rosanne feels panic rise in her chest.

'Get up, for God's sake,' she whispers. 'There's someone coming. You don't want to make a fool of us.' She pulls Maeve to her feet and shakes her, tries to pull her knickers up over her shoes, but they catch and tear. 'For God's sake, Maeve, can't you help me here?'

A woman can be seen now, running towards them through the mist. 'We heard screams.' She is panting from the effort. 'Are you hurt?'

Rosanne steps in front of Maeve to block the woman's view. 'Thank you … we're perfectly all right. My daughter took a little turn and got upset. We had a mishap with the car. I wonder would there be anyone who could help us get out of the ditch.'

The woman does not answer. She seems to be mesmerised by the sight of Maeve crawling through the wet grass to the car, her knickers dragging from one ankle.

'She's fine,' Rosanne says. 'It's the car I'm worried about.'

'I could phone for someone.' The woman does not take her eyes off the child, who is now climbing painfully into the car, pulling the door shut behind her.

'Thanks, thanks,' Rosanne says distractedly. 'Could you phone the AA? I don't know if my mobile will have coverage.'

'Aren't you the people who bought the Whelan's place at Ballinafunshoge?' the woman asks.

'Yes…. It…. We have.' Rosanne hesitates. 'I'll just try my phone.'

'I know the house well,' the woman says. 'My brother, Martin, did your fences.'

CHAPTER 24

The bus, the confusion, the hot shimmering July air. Tina drags her worn blue suitcase on its wretched little wheels through the town of Pézenas. The streets pass in a blur. *Molière* – she sees the name in huge lettering on a wall. She is far too hot to care what plays he wrote, or if he was born in these over-manicured streets. The tourist office. She holds the little map in a shaking hand. Chemin de St Siméon, her finger stabs the spot, and she struggles on.

A kilometre out of the town, along the Route de Roujon, the handle of Tina's case begins to tear the skin of her palm. Her arm trembles, sweat drips from her eyebrows. In a sort of trance, it seems to her that the road dancing ahead of her, hot leafy vines on either side, is the road home: the Sligo road her feet had tramped so often that it came to seem like her own body. Bramble hedges, fresh damp air, sunshine after rain. The darts of sun, warm and mellow as they lit the puddles, the drops of water glinting on leaves. And if she was out early enough, the cobwebs would be still intact, mistily enveloping the hawthorn. The First Sea Road – as a child, she had believed that it was the first road ever in the world.

She stands now and raises a hand to wipe sweat from her forehead. Her back is wet with it, her tee-shirt soaked through. Flies circle around her head. She is too tired to brush them away. A car approaches and she puts out a hand in an attempt to stop it, but the driver refuses to understand her desperation, and the car passes by.

She staggers on, sweat in her eyes, pulling the little suitcase, lost in the hallucination that she is walking past her own home, the neo-Edwardian villa that her parents bankrupted themselves to build. Tina stands with her head down, revolted by their enthusiasm, ashamed of the ugly house on its bare single-acre site.

She had made them send her to boarding school. In her dormitory bed, during those first few weeks, she clenched her teeth. Separation, she discovered, was painful. Her mother's fat cheeks and bright lipstick became beautiful to her, her father's stiff remote form attained some magical power to make her sad. And, as she told herself often, these were the people she most despised in the world. That was something she could not bear; she must harden herself, fight her own weakness. She had decided then to become another person.

The spray from Atlantic waves does not rise to bathe Tina's cheeks. There is no relief from the blanket of heat that presses on her head. Then, when she is almost ready to sink down in the roadway and die, someone is talking to her, helping her as she stumbles, giving her water to drink, wiping her chin.

'Thank you,' she whispers, and she climbs into a car, hands over the slip of paper she has kept clutched in her hand, feels the cool pleasure of air-conditioning.

They are speaking French, a middle-aged man and woman, and Tina cannot understand a single word. The woman is fat and blonde and Tina's mother wobbles once more unbidden into her sights. She had come to visit the school every week. Tina could not shake her off. On sports day, there had been a new ugly hairdo, a new appalling dress.

'This is nice, pet,' her mother murmured over Tina's belongings. 'It's very plain, though. Very sparse. And when I think of the lovely home you left…. Do you know I've a little piece of pink satin that I could work up into a frill for around your bed. Make it a bit special.' And then Tina was outside the dormitory, locking the door carefully, walking away. That year she had won the hundred metres.

Tina opens her eyes to see an entrance, huge pillared gates. Miriam standing in a paint-splattered shirt peering into the car, answering the French couple with stumbling broken words. And then Tina is out, dragging her suitcase through the garden where a little boy glowers from a distance, his blond hair bleached by the sun. Thin brown body, bare toes scuffing the gravelled path.

'She's dirty, Mummy.'

'Poor Tina,' Miriam tells him. 'She was lost for three whole days.'

Tina looks down at her bitten legs. 'I thought you weren't going to let me in,' she says.

'A misunderstanding,' Miriam explains quickly. 'For a second I didn't recognise you. Come and sit in the pergola. It's lovely and cool.'

'Your voicemail,' Tina says. 'I thought I was going mad. You never answered. I had to phone Blaise Boothe to get your address.'

Miriam's eyes flicker. 'It's my French mobile,' she says, and takes off her painting shirt, revealing string top, shorts and long brown legs. 'It's unreliable. I don't always pick up the messages.'

Tina kicks off her sandals, lies back on the cushions, holds out a shaking hand for a glass of wine. Miriam pours and Tina drinks, feeling the cold sting of it in her throat. And now she's able to look around, take in the gardens, the *terrasse*, the small child scraping the dusty earth nearby.

'It's big,' she says and holds out her glass again. She looks beyond the garden to the vineyards, and for a little while Miriam's words sting her cheeks. Then there is no sound, only the mouth moving in lisps and starts. It is a curiously pleasant sensation.

'There's a party nearly every night,' Miriam is saying. Tina holds out her glass for another refill, and allows herself to listen. 'I used to bring Jeremy, but he gets so tired. That's why Peter suggested an *au pair*. Tonight she'll take him down to her place.'

'Mummy, I want ice-cream.' Jeremy is standing now, and, as Tina watches, he flings a handful of pebbles towards her. They strike the tiles and ricochet against the walls of the pergola.

'Darling,' Miriam says, and Tina is aware that her voice has an anxious quality, 'we'll have ice-cream later. I told them to bring some for you when they're delivering the party.'

'He misses Finn,' she says then to Tina. 'Finn hasn't got here yet. I don't suppose you've met him?' And Tina sees her eyes cloud over, her mouth contract.

'Party?' she says, ignoring the question. 'What party?'

'The one I was telling you about. Peter planned it, but then he called yesterday and said I'd have to go it alone. Some business crisis. They're going to set up tables at the edge of the vineyard.'

'I want ice-cream now.' Jeremy flings another handful of pebbles.

'We don't have any ice-cream, lovie.'

Jeremy sits back down in the grey earth. He hunches over, holds his knees tight against his chest.

'You see,' Miriam tells Tina, 'it's such a long way to town. I tried driving Peter's car, but going on the wrong side and with such narrow roads, I was a nervous wreck. Anyway, Pézenas gives me a creepy feeling. The last time I was there an old woman was on a street corner, begging. And the moment after I gave her something, the police arrived. People told me that the *gendarmes* can arrest you just for giving someone a few euro. And maybe she was there to trap people like me who don't know the law. After that, I didn't really feel like going into town any more, so now I stay here and paint. They deliver the shopping or, if I need something urgently, the *au pair* gets it for me.'

'I'm here for a while.' Tina watches for Miriam's reaction.

'Mummy….'

'Go and find Nicole, darling,' Miriam says. 'Mummy has to talk to Tina. And wash your hands. They're a sight.'

'I need a rest,' Tina says. 'I'm worn out.' She looks around the patio. Jeremy has not moved. His nails scrabble the earth.

'Blaise Boothe is gone, Tina,' Miriam says. 'He came looking for Finn. I didn't want to let him in, but he's employing Finn so I had to.'

'So?' Tina closes her eyes.

'He's not to be trusted. I found that out back in Dublin. He's got wads of money and he thinks he can buy anyone. I hadn't realised … till he told me how much he'd paid Finn.' Miriam shrugs, a thin cream strap slips from one bronzed shoulder.

Tina's eyes open a fraction. Enough to register the droop of Miriam's body, the quick recovery, the way she picks up an olive in delicate fingers, nibbles at its shiny green surface.

'These are the local ones. They're called *lucques*.' She spits the stone into her hand. 'I love having olive trees near the house.'

Tina gazes at the distant hills. Christ, she thinks, Blaise Boothe.

❦

'I'm crazy for you,' Blaise Boothe told Tina on one of those long June evenings. They stood for a while on the edge of the Grand Canal, looking into its still, black water. Then it was time to return to the Landrover where Boothe laid out the coke in careful lines on the dashboard.

'I'm crazy for you,' he said again and rubbed his thin pimpled face against her hair.

Later they lurched from club to club, ending in a Docklands penthouse. 'Give up the flat,' Blaise kept up the whisper as they fucked. 'To help me out. I'll find you another. You can trust me.'

Tina snuffled up another dusting of coke. She allowed Boothe's chin to rub her thighs, his shoulder to rest in the crook of her arm.

'See you in Pézenas,' Boothe said, kissing her goodbye. 'I've stuff to sort out with Finn Daly. We're bringing a film crew – the Irish *outre-mer*. We'll film you in the sun. Your paintings as backdrop. Then let's us two go down to Barcelona.' His tongue penetrated deep into her mouth and withdrew. 'I want the flat, Tina. I have to sell. Please.'

Tina, refreshed from her bath, blocks out those repellent memories, sprays herself with Miriam's perfume. Miriam offers her a choice of dresses, but the zips will not close, the waists will not button.

'I'm getting fat,' Tina says, kneading the lump of flesh at her midriff between forefinger and thumb.

'It's just that I've lost weight,' Miriam says. 'Being in a new country. There's a different diet here. Anyway, I've just the thing for you.' A silk kimono is unearthed from a drawer, still carefully wrapped in protective cloth.

'How lovely you look,' Miriam says as Tina tries it on. 'Peter brought it back from his last business trip to Tokyo. He says it's an antique – he wants to hang it somewhere – but I think it's better to wear it, don't you?'

To Tina's surprise, the mirror reflects a figure she hardly recognises, a regal magnificent creature. She turns this way and that. 'It's amazing,' she says. 'It might have been made for me.'

Her make-up complete, Tina goes out to stand in the garden's fading

light, watches the *au pair* lead the protesting child to a small car. She sees
Miriam's party arrive in an articulated trailer. Uniformed men unload the
flowers, the toilets, the dance floor, the garden lights, the folded linen
napkins. Salads are ranged on trestle tables. A barbecue, sizzling steaks
and fish. A string quartet. Champagne piled on the earth, amid rough-cut
slabs of ice.

Soon shadowy guests begin to fill the garden spaces, clinking glasses,
nibbling food, chatting lightly. The string quartet plays Mozart.

'I want to sing,' Tina says. Over the ethereal sounds of the quartet, she
sings of a doomed child's bonny cheeks, a mother's impotent love. Her
voice, husky from twenty years of cigarettes, produces a sound that startles
the throng of guests. The song finishes. The partygoers remain silent for a
moment, then 'Encore,' they shout and the violins fade away.

'*Speak low, speak low, the banshee is crying.*' Her voice fills the garden;
the string quartet is silent. '*What shadow flits dark'ning the face of the water?
Oh list' to the echo, she's dead, she's dead. Gone, gone is the wraith of the
Geraldine's daughter.*' And again her audience calls for more.

As blue dawn lightens the vineyards, Tina sits at the swimming-pool,
her legs dangling into dark water. The water laps against her knees, soaking
the bottom of the kimono. Kimono, she thinks, I love you. You're mine;
I'll run away with you.

'Sebastian asked me if we're gay.' Miriam is coming towards her a little
unsteadily, carrying glasses and a brandy bottle. She sits at the water's
edge, her toes rippling the dark surface. 'He doesn't understand how Finn
can leave me here all alone.'

Tina sips the brandy that Miriam offers her. 'I was seduced by a
housewife once,' she says. 'She came to my first exhibition, bought
a painting, invited me to lunch. A Rathgar housewife with impeccable
children. I think she was on the school board. Tulips in her front garden,
springtime.' Her fingers come to rest on the warm skin of Miriam's leg.

'One day her husband was there. I was sitting on the counter, watching
her as she moved around the kitchen, her hair tied up in a loose roll, little
wisps of it escaping down her neck. A white T-shirt over jeans. I couldn't
bear the helpless way she looked at him, the idea of them sharing a bed.
Talking about me, I suppose – the things we did.'

Tina touches Miriam's cheek with the tip of a finger, her other hand rises to a warm breast, her mouth opens in a kiss. Tongues touch and Miriam is clinging to Tina, the Baccarat glass slipping from her hand, floating a moment, then disappearing under the rippled water's surface, her strength draining away down her legs, into the dark pool.

CHAPTER 25

At first it is just a small child sitting in a supermarket trolley. It could be anywhere, and Finn has been turning over the problems of slavery in his mind. Slavery – endemic, so far as he can tell, in all societies throughout history. He is lying on a beach; lying in the hot sun on burning sand, trying to see this world through a slave's eyes.

The child in the supermarket trolley is somewhere in the distance. And Finn is crossing an immense car park, which stretches to a railway line. A vast open space, almost empty of cars. There are white markings on the tarmac. He is carrying two bulging shopping bags. And he sits up with a jerk and he's back on the beach, blinking his eyes, trying to think about slavery in Ireland, the way it thrived right up to the twelfth century. Saints came out of it – Patrick, Brigit, Ciarán – so why don't the Irish want to accept its existence? Criminals, debtors, prisoners of war were taken as slaves. During war the men were killed. Women and cattle were the real booty. They needed women slaves – for all the menial work, and for sex. Cúchulainn, when he should have been defending Ulster, was off screwing Fedelm's slave woman. And if they wanted to make a statement about power or if it was a bad harvest and they couldn't feed the slaves, they massacred them. For public pleasure. Dionysian rampages. Just like in the castle of Rechnitz. Except in Rechnitz it was because the war had ended and the Nazis wanted to murder all the Jews they possibly could, before escaping over the border to Switzerland. Party time.

The car park reappears through the mangled limbs of slaves. There in front of him is the shopping trolley with the child in it. And the car park clears of blood. And he doesn't think to ask himself what the child is doing in an empty car park under a hot sun. It seems so far away and Finn's shopping bags get heavier and heavier, he has to rest.

A young man is clutching the side of the trolley. Finn stares. He cannot understand how he did not notice him before. Something exhausted in his face: thin, shiny with sweat. Finn realises with a start that the man is unable to walk, that his legs in stained jeans are emaciated, that he is clutching the trolley because otherwise he would fall down, and that the child has blond curls. There appears to be a plank laid between two blocks on which the man can sit, and in fact the man is sitting on this plank in the middle of an empty car park. And Finn is standing beside the trolley, looking at the young man and trying not to look at him, trying not to look at his legs, and the young man is trying to stand and is dragging himself up on the side of the shopping trolley and he is smiling and saying something. And then the young man is vomiting a great splash of red mucus on to the ground, leaning over and vomiting again, and the child is looking at him with love and terror in his face.

Finn's eyes open, his body recoils from the hard stone with a jerk. He is lying on a beach, and he cannot remember why he is here. The dream flashes vividly in front of him, but he cannot tell what the truth is. 'Slavery,' he says and he is sitting surrounded by its works.

Arrived in Pézenas, Finn walks through the town as Tina had, weeks earlier, trudges along the Route de Roujon, head bowed, the hot sun beating on his head. He goes too far, stops a cyclist to ask for help, then retraces his steps, finds the small turn he should have taken, and at last he is standing at the pillared gate, speaking into the intercom.

The gate opens. Miriam stands in the driveway.

'You've got thin,' he says, but what he sees is her skin, her glorious beauty. He's pressing her to him, and she is in his arms; her body is melting into his, and he lifts her from the ground into his embrace. He tries to hold her tight. 'How's Jeremy?' he asks. 'I had such fearful dreams on the train.'

'We've been waiting so long for you,' she says. 'Nicole – she's the *au pair* – brought Jeremy to her place. You can collect him tomorrow.' Her voice has a dreamy quality, and Finn stares into her eyes. She's been hypnotised, he thinks. And then her arms encircle his neck and that glorious body is part of his once more.

'Oh, love, love,' he whispers, pressing his face to her warm hair, kissing her cheeks, her eyes, her forehead. His hands on her slender back. But she is stiffening, pulling away from him. And standing there inside the huge gate, she is shaking her head.

Her face is sad and she turns, walks slowly through the pale oak front door into a high entrance hall, and from there into a sitting-room. He tries to take her in his arms again. 'I'm here to love you,' he says. 'I'm here to be your slave.'

It is as if she does not hear him. She walks through glass-panelled doors into the garden, and Finn can see Peter Brindley's red, fat body stretched on a sun-lounger. He shudders and backs away.

Finn goes upstairs, prowls through the bedrooms, searching them for signs of Jeremy, of Miriam. He finds the little boy's bedroom, turns up the air-conditioning, lies on Jeremy's bed.

Through the open window he hears the sound of voices. He hears Miriam say the word 'Byron'. He flinches and curls himself up in the bed, his hands over his ears.

'Byron,' she says the word again, and no matter what he does, he cannot prevent her voice penetrating his brain. She seems to caress Brindley with the word. And Brindley is wooing her with idiot talk – about lost Mediterranean islands, hidden grottoes, beaches of pale sand, yachts as big as liners, cabins walled with pale sycamore, blue marbled bathrooms.

Finn sleeps, and later, when he opens his eyes, the room is very dark. He lies still for several minutes, trying to remember where he is, then gets off the bed, stumbles over building blocks, makes his way out onto the landing, letting the door bang behind him.

For a moment he is lost, and then Miriam is beckoning him from a lighted room. 'I heard the door bang,' she says. 'I didn't want to wake you.' She is standing in front of him in bare feet.

'I've got to find Jeremy.' Finn is still disoriented from sleep. A sense of desperation overwhelms him. 'You should never have sent him away.' He stumbles against a cupboard, and hits it with his fist. 'Where is he?'

'I'm sorry, Finn.' She is rummaging through the wardrobe, holds two pairs of shoes out to the light. 'Peter's yacht wouldn't be suitable. And Jeremy likes Nicole. I couldn't think what else to do.'

'Miriam,' Finn whispers, holding his hands out to his wife, 'why have you deserted me?'

'It was you that deserted me,' she says and he knows for certain that a dark rift has come between them. 'I couldn't get you on your phone, and you never answered my emails. I didn't know if you....'

Finn presses his head between his hands. It was the redhead, he wants to say. I had to work the thing out. I had to bring it to an end. He sits on the bed, watches her push the thin straps of her beach dress from her shoulders, sees it slither down her body to lie in a small pile around her ankles.

'Peter's stopped your money, Finn. You weren't helping him with his work.' She is standing in front of him in bra and panties, then these too are removed, and Miriam is naked, walking away from the little heap of clothes to look at herself in the mirror. She twists around to examine her thigh, and he sees a purplish stain on the bronzed skin. 'Anyway,' she says, 'he probably thought you didn't need it.'

'What happened?'

'It's almost gone. It's fine.'

'Did that bastard hurt you?'

'Of course he didn't,' she says quickly. 'It was just a stupid thing I did. A few weeks ago some Roms were camping in the field down the road. I didn't know they were there.... I was out for a walk.'

'You should have turned back,' he says.

'I did, but as I was walking away – I didn't want to run – there was this terrible noise of shouting and screaming. I looked back, and I saw the *gendarmes*, people being punched and battered. Children. A woman with a little baby.... It was awful.'

'Keep away from that sort of thing.' He is frightened by what he has heard. 'You can't help.'

She shrugs. 'That's what I found out.' She touches the purple-tinged skin with the tips of her fingers. 'And by the way, Peter showed me the interview you gave *The Irish Times*.'

'I was drunk.' He lies down on the bed, stares at the painted window, dark sky, shadowy leaves. 'Some fellow phoned me.'

'You were boasting that you'd been given a hundred thousand as an advance for your new novel.'

He turns over, presses his face into the pillow. He has a sensation of nausea. She looks down at him, touches his back, and he turns to her, takes her hands in his.

'If you have some of that money left,' she says, 'I'll go home with you.' There is a softening in her eyes, and her voice takes a hopeful bound. 'If we had enough to live on for a few months….'

But he shakes his head and she pulls her hands away.

'You spent it all by yourself? You left me and Jeremy alone and spent all that money?' She raises her head, pushes her hair out of her eyes. 'I have to shower.'

Peter's scarlet face; white, too even teeth; pale eyes; insinuating, bullying smile. The whole ghastly picture forces itself into Finn's head.

'Peter's planning to get involved in the festival.' Miriam's hand is pushing open the bathroom door. 'In Summer Twenty-Sixteen. As a backer. He told me today. So it's probably just as well you don't want to be part of it, because he doesn't feel very happy about you at the moment.' She turns to him, and her delicate navel, the mole on her thigh, the dark pubic hair, seem to him indefinably poignant.

'Peter says the only way forward is to monetise Irish culture. We've got the best assets – poets, writers, artists. He wants to sell the Irish mind, the same way you'd sell Irish crystal.'

He presses his face again into the pillow, pulls its edges up over his ears. 'Slavery,' he says. 'Slavery.'

She closes the bathroom door and Finn hears the key turn in the lock. How many kicks would it take to break it down? he wonders. But he does not move. He lies on the white linen sheet, listening to the sound of the shower, the water caressing her beautiful pliant face, her perfect body.

'She understands nothing,' he whispers. 'She is the splinter of ice lodged in my heart.' And he thinks how strange it is that a lousy writer like Graham Greene could have found that perfect phrase.

CHAPTER 26

In Pézenas, time passes slowly for Finn. He sunbathes, plays in the pool with Jeremy and drinks Peter Brindley's wine. In the mornings, while the *au pair* takes Jeremy to the beach, he listens to Rosanne's podcasts, follows the written texts with his finger, tries to pronounce the words *as gaeilge*, and then gives up, cursing his own stupidity. Every day is the same and the tedium weighs on him.

But now at last Rosanne has arrived. Finn is reading aloud from her latest book, and she is lying in the sun-lounger listening to his confused rhythms, his laboured, stuttering pronunciation. You would label him a weak pupil if he was at school, she thinks; he understands none of it. But that does not matter. He can mispronounce every word, the mistakes cause no dent in her happiness. She smiles at his awkwardness, his pleasure in reading her words. Little by little she explains a phrase here, an idiom there, until the poetry comes alive to him, and he reads it again and again.

An image of Rosanne's younger self floats on the pool's surface in a haze of sultry heat. The manuscript room of the National Library. She had toiled in that room for long months, day after day. The analogues of the *Immran Brain* lay on her desk, the uncompleted thesis. The light fading on Kildare Street. Friday, and she wanted to go home, but the thought gave her no pleasure. A week without achievement, a week of blankness. And she hated the *Immran Brain* with a deep, stomach-churning hatred.

Among the piles delivered to her desk was a thick manuscript of some unknown Gaelic poet. She cursed, because this would be just another wasted moment. The mere act of ascertaining that it was not what she needed enraged her. She grasped the unasked-for pages, squeezed them between her hands, wanting to tear them into shreds. Then she quickly flattened them out again on her desk. Don't be so childish, she warned herself, then sat, hands on the desk, looking at nothing. After several minutes she looked down at her hands, found herself inexplicably drawn to the words that peered through her outspread fingers.

As she read, a veil of incomprehension lifted, and she became aware of a voice echoing in her mind, her heart, that came to sound like her own voice. She was reading the most extraordinary poetry. She was reading *her own words.*

A catalogue number? Rosanne had asked herself. But she could find none. The pages had been tucked in, lost among the analogues. In that instant Rosanne knew that these jumbled, handwritten pages belonged to her. They were her path to salvation. She must stop toiling at her thesis, and start to write poetry.

Late that evening she left the library with a sparkling feeling of optimism. As she descended the stairs, she felt herself give way to a giggle of delight. In the Beinecke Library at Yale University the manuscript folders would have been weighed on issue and again on their return. The National Library had no such procedure, so Rosanne could fit the manuscript snugly under her sweater, and hold it in place with the waistband of her skirt. The perfect work will be one that is constituted only of quotations. Walter Benjamin's enigma was at last comprehensible to her.

I have fallen in love for the first time in my life, she told herself as she stood completely still outside the little Huguenot graveyard on Merrion Row to listen to the beating of her heart. I have fallen in love, she told the thrum of passing cars and buses. I have fallen in love with a voice. I have discovered it is my own.

'Rosanne.'

She lifts her head from the sun-lounger, looks dazedly up at Finn. Then down at the patches of bright sunburn on her stomach and legs.

'What's the point?' Finn says. He is standing above her, the book held in his hand. 'I'm reading the poems to you and you fall asleep. What use is that? How can I know if I'm pronouncing the words right?'

'You must have lulled me.' She smiles at him. 'Maybe your pronunciation was perfect, and I was hypnotised. Though I wasn't really asleep. I could hear the words as you read them, and they seemed to me more rich and beautiful than I ever realised.'

'Lunchtime,' he says and he smiles too. Then stands and flexes a naked body so bronzed and beautiful that she has to restrain herself from dragging him down on the tiles beside the swimming pool, drowning him with lust. He offers her his hand, pulls her to her feet. 'Come on,' he says. 'We'll have ours before the kids get back.'

She walks beside him to the kitchen, watches in a dream as he sautés courgettes, peppers and onions, notes the way the muscles in his back flex as he bends over the cooker, the curve of his elbow, the thrust of his strong chin. He is all mine, she thinks. For this short time he is all mine.

Rosanne and her two children have been in Pézenas a week. She had not been able to resist. Finn in Pézenas, Finn and Jeremy together. When he called her, she had to come. Impossible to do otherwise.

He takes *saucisson* from the fridge, slices and fries it. She stands behind him, lets her fingers brush his bare shoulder. 'When I give readings,' she says, 'I feel that I'm carrying on a sacred tradition. That my words are the words of others who have spoken through the centuries. That, somehow, I have caught their traces on the air, absorbed them into my own body, then written them.'

'Risteard O'Toole is shit compared to you,' Finn says. 'Grab the two frying pans. I'll carry the tray.'

Rosanne had taken the children to Galway on the day after the Glenmalure débâcle. Maeve's wounds had to heal, before William, or anyone else, could see them. Never lose your temper. Never punish in anger. She had looked again at the weals, at the purple bruising and found it hard to believe that she, a mature adult, could have been the perpetrator. Although Rosanne is aware that a chasm often exists between people's beliefs and their behaviour, she had always previously imagined that this chasm existed for others, not for herself. When people come to write her biography, she fears, that is the secret flaw to be discovered.

In Galway, Rosanne did what was needed to efface the memory of her demented outburst. Two turns on the giant wheel in the fairground, rides on the bumper cars and a chocolate bar. They played crazy golf together, raced across Silverstrand beach and leapt into the sea, laughing and shouting. She bought them pizzas on Middle Street and giant banana splits.

It is so easy, she thought, as they queued for ice-cream cones on the promenade, to make them love you again, to make them forget the bad things as if they had never been.

'I love this world,' she says as Finn distributes the food. 'Should we keep something for the *au pair?*'

'She'll eat with the kids. She likes fish fingers too.'

Rosanne bows her head and chews. She will not say that she would prefer Maeve and Deirdre to eat proper food. She will not break the spell.

In the misery of Glenmalure on that foggy day in June, Rosanne felt shame. Deep shame. She held her head in her hands. 'The woman's only a local,' she told herself. 'It really doesn't matter.' She contacted the AA on her mobile, and tried to keep her voice light, as she sat in the tilting car, unpacking the large picnic box. Then the sound of an approaching engine.

'Well, they *have* come quickly.' She felt cheered by the unexpected efficiency. 'Isn't that great, children? It's the AA and they're going to pull us out of this ditch.'

A car parked in front of them. Not the familiar bright yellow tow-truck, but a dingy blue wreck. Paul Ryan, dirty and dishevelled, stared in at them once more.

'You all right?'

It could hardly have been worse.

'Go away, Paul,' Rosanne said. 'We don't need anything. The AA are coming. What gave you the right to follow us?'

'You okay?' Paul Ryan reached into the car, touched Maeve's tear-stained face. She cowered back from him. 'I live here,' he said. 'My wife … heard there'd been an accident.'

CHAPTER 27

William Roycroft stands in the arrivals hall beside his airport trolley, and holds out his arms in the time-honoured way. He is perplexed to see the little family group remain motionless. He thinks once more of the final lecture in his Yale series: 'Reinventing Ireland's Avant-Garde'. The lectures spanned the period from the ninth century up to the present – Eriugena, Swift, Berkeley, Wilde, Beckett. William, in his *coup de grâce*, succeeded in cutting through twelve hundred years of Irish thought to reconcile the scandalous neo-Platonism of Eriugena with the cultural fragmentation detected in the doppelganger tactics of Banville and his nom de plume, Benjamin Black. He received a standing ovation from his audience.

The applause fades, William pushes the trolley towards his wife and daughters. He kisses Rosanne, looks into her shadowed eyes, her pinched reddened cheeks, then bends to the girls.

'No, William, no.' He hears the tremble in his wife's voice, sees her mouth contort in an involuntary spasm. 'Don't touch them. I'm afraid we have two very bad children.'

He looks at the sad, down-turned mouths of his children, the red eyes. 'Oh dear me,' he says. 'What's been going on?'

Ten minutes pass in a blur of suitcases and driving, and searching for parking places, then in an air-conditioned café-bar overlooking the marina at Palavas, William waits for his wife to direct him where to sit. She sits beside him, the children opposite. He has not slept for two days and there is a headache nagging at the back of his eyes.

Revisionism? He sips at a large, steaming cup of café crème. He has been pondering the question over the past several weeks. A revisionist? Yes, he had been a revisionist back in student days. The girls sit beside each other. His eyes move from one bowed head to the other. They are silently dipping teaspoons in cups of hot chocolate, trailing patterns of brown milky liquid across the table. He hopes Rosanne will not notice.

Revisionist – that cynical thing that saw cause and effect in the narrowest of contexts, which saw self-interest as the motive for all historical action. But I've changed, he tells himself, stirring sugar into his own steaming coffee. I've come to imagine something more. He reaches across the table, wipes with his napkin the brown trails of liquid his daughters have made. Nationalism is where I've arrived by a long and tortuous path. Twenty-Sixteen, the history of our nation. Nationalism explained as an act of magic – the sympathetic alchemy that makes a nation, even for post-modernists. We can see magic as a game. Play that game.

And now he sees that Rosanne is surreptitiously slipping headache pills into her mouth. She's been drinking, he realises. It does not bode well.

Twenty-Sixteen the History. It has been handed to William as he knew it would be, and a sensation of quiet satisfaction calms the throbbing ache behind his eyes so that he can scarcely feel it. His appraisal of the 1916 Rising will work itself into today's Ireland. First he will look back to 1798. He will show that Wolfe Tone's republicanism set the agenda. I'm taking it away from the French model, he decides, and smiles a half-smile. For William, Tone's republicanism is firmly grounded in the American Revolution, in freedom, not equality.

In another world, his wife is buttering a croissant with hard strokes. A dab of apricot jam, a swift bite. And she's telling him a story about an afternoon on a beach, swimming, lying in the sun, building sandcastles, playing ball games. A perfectly good afternoon, as far as William can understand. Except that she is spitting the words, and there are little flecks of croissant on her lips, some flecks too on her chin.

The children are sitting in front of him, perfectly healthy, if a little sad, and William remains caught in the slipstream of his intellectual life. She'll tell me some silly story of pinching and teasing, he thinks. She does get all in a fuss about nothing. Jetlag, he thinks then, and his mind contemplates the American roots. That's the way it has to go. American roots as backdrop, Daonnacht as the logical continuation of Wolfe Tone's vision. It has been portrayed by its denigrators as populist and reactionary. But in reality it's a rational organisation, the synthesis of all that is great in nationalist ideology. Daonnacht, he believes, moves us beyond flawed reactive movements like Sinn Féin, which nevertheless have had their place in attempting to safeguard the honour of the Republic.

William reaches carefully around the table. His fingers touch Maeve's knee. He winks at her, and feels her two hands clutch his.

'Marseillan Plâges,' Rosanne is saying. 'A gorgeous little restaurant. They could choose anything they liked. Milkshakes, huge ice-creams for dessert. We gave them everything, a wonderful, wonderful day.'

'Yes, love,' he says. Yes, he thinks, that's how I'll play it. Our struggle has always been the same struggle. Against that irrational hatred, that system of apartheid that was this whole island. He wishes he had a page beside him to record his thoughts. He wonders could he take out his notebook but, glancing again at Rosanne, decides against. He will have to remember. Apartheid, he tells himself – a key word – because after 1921 apartheid retreated northwards. Northern Ireland became its bastion. There, to be a nationalist was to be treated like an animal. Strange, he reflects, that after two sleepless days his brain cannot stop. Ruling elites, he thinks, all over the world, ruling elites stood idly by. The IRA campaign was a crude, confused struggle. The ideals were honourable, but the means were often sordid, sectarian, murderous, just as the blacks in South Africa struggling against white supremacy tried to defend the use of *the necklace*. Yes, the IRA made serious errors. It became crazed and out of control, but its intentions, its intentions….

Rosanne is beginning to sob aloud. What can be wrong with her? he asks himself. Premenstrual tension? William removes his hand from his older daughter's grasp. He is certain that this historical moment is the golden opportunity for the philosophical historian to unite the country behind Daonnacht's mission. We must give the people a focus, he tells himself, a real focus, and to that end we have to learn to be comfortable with stretching facts. Our modern media create blurry shadows on the wall, and the philosopher has to be prepared to manipulate these shadows in the service of a greater truth. Daonnacht's truth.

'How can I tell you when I know you'll blame me?'

These words come at him out of nowhere. He feels his head tottering, his ideas crashing against a brick wall. What is she talking about? His glance takes in a run of fluid from one of her nostrils. He looks away, down into his cup, into the melted grains of sugar. He would like to order another coffee – hot, bitter, strong – so that the brick wall can melt, the first blows can strike. The first blows struck courageously in 1916. Then came 1921 and a treaty which deformed us, which spilt our blood over and over again. Freedom fighters. Republicans. Regrettable things happened.

'Have you a tissue?' he hears Rosanne saying. 'I don't think you're listening.'

'Darling, of course I'm listening.' He hands her his chocolate-stained napkin, looks on anxiously as the skin around her nostrils reddens with the angry scrubbing. Another sip of coffee, another bite of jammed croissant. Why will she not just come out with it? he wonders.

The highways and byways – he thinks with a sense of loss for those marginal spaces. Those spaces for free thought. Because now he must cloak the strong Republican heartbeat. The people still scarred by memories of inept and pointless violence cannot yet appreciate Daonnacht's great ideals, its passionate wish for the regeneration of the Irish race, so that Daonnacht must work in other ways to entice the Irish public into its orbit. In a time of economic distress, people strike out in terror against the outsider. They are told that immigrants bring disease, crime, prostitution, disorder. They fear the stranger in all his aspects. We must work with these fears, develop them for the good of the nation. A demon must be created to focus the energies of the population. The rule of war, he thinks. The great rallies. A doubting individual submits himself to the kinetic energy of the crowd, emerges fortified, no longer doubting. The wisdom of crowds.

'Stand up, Maeve,' Rosanne says. The words bounce off the edges of William's head. He glances at his daughter. She is sitting perfectly still, no bad behaviour, no pinching.

'Stand up.' This time Rosanne's voice seems to be cracking, and the child hurriedly stands. 'Turn around and lift up your dress,' she is saying, and William is shuddering. He sees Maeve shake her head, back away from her mother, a thin, freckled child with mousey hair. William sees that her face is white under the freckles, her hands joined as if in prayer. And there at the corner of his eye is Rosanne's frantic mouth, globules of milky spit appearing on her lips.

And now she is shaking her head. 'No,' she says, 'No. I'm going insane. I'm sorry, William. I'm sorry. Let the dress down, Maeve. Just don't look at me.'

'Rosanne, what have you done?' William says softly. 'We're on holidays; we're supposed to be enjoying ourselves.' He strokes her hand in an attempt to calm her.

'Deirdre.' He hears Rosanne's voice crack again, and he sees that his younger daughter is crying silently. 'It's been going through my head all night.' Her voice is running fast, out of control again, and William clutches her hands to try to restrain her. 'We're sitting there in the restaurant having a lovely evening, and the girls disappear with Jeremy. Of course I thought they'd be back in a minute, but they weren't. We're looking everywhere, calling frantically. Then they appear around a corner in one of those bloody bicycle carriage things. Maeve was driving, and when I put out my hands to try to stop her, she just kept going. She tried to drive over me.'

She frees one hand and rubs her forehead with the same napkin. A brown stain appears on her skin. The white globules on her lips are jumping again. And there is a fluid squelching inside William's head. Spontaneous baptisms in bog pools, the idea somehow floats in cranial juices. A golden age – eighteenth-century Connemara. Bodhrán sessions in mossy woods, dances on great turf ditches. If we got back to that innocence, all the tawdry words of today would be as nothing. But it is not to be, and William looks sadly at his wife.

'When I was lying in the roadway, the children laughed. They humiliated me in front of Finn. In front of everyone.'

William's fingers tip his daughter's knee again. But he feels Rosanne's eyes strafe him, and quickly withdraws.

'When everyone had gone to bed,' her voice continues dully, 'I took her into the vineyard and beat her. But Finn heard her screaming. He told me that his aunt had beaten him and that it had weakened him. It had no benefits, he said.'

Rosanne's face lies against the crumb-covered tabletop. Her red fleshy shoulders heave. 'We were having a lovely time,' she whispers. 'Everything was going so well, and then she ruined it.'

Their daughter turns away. Her gaze goes out to the blue horizon, to a scudding yacht on the wide sea, its white sail.

CHAPTER 28

Summer holidays are over. After sweating and burning on the beaches of the Costa del Sol, the Algarve, Sicily, Majorca, Crete, the exhausted populations straggle home to a welcoming Irish September. 'Indian summer,' they all say. And they decide not to put away their shorts, tiny tops and holiday dresses. They eat ice-cream cones, stroll on Irish beaches, swim in the sea.

During that September, on a balmy evening, Tina Foley stands in the kitchen of her new apartment, cooking badami roghan josh. She has been reading about the Higgs boson, and the idea that one of those bosons, one of those tiniest of particles, could of itself, without having any weight at all, give mass to others. It seems to her an intensely beautiful idea.

She glances out at early evening sun-dapples on wide footpaths and turning leaves, then drops cloves, peppercorns, cardamom seeds into the oiled pan, watches them swell and pop. Bosons, fermions – with these minuscule particles Enrico Fermi helped create the atomic bomb, saw it dropped on Nagasaki and was satisfied that it had worked well. She stirs in pieces of lamb. Wendy is coming to dinner this evening. The estrangement is over. It will be Tina and Wendy's first meal together in months. Tina sings softly to herself. She has missed Wendy more than she cares to admit.

There are spices to be roasted. Tina takes out a heavy, iron frying pan. Fermi got out of Italy in 1938, after he had won the Nobel prize for Physics. Carrying the mass of his fermions. Weighed down by the past. Why did he take the fermions for himself, when bosons are free and weightless? The frying pan, sitting over a high flame, black and solid. Packed with fermions, she supposes. So where are the bosons? Flitting all around her? Splitting the atom? She imagines the bosons exploding, speeding to destroy. Then throws two teaspoons of cumin, another of cardamom into the hot pan, swirls the grains so that they roast, but do not burn, lifts the pan off quickly. Greedily sucks in the smell. Roghan josh is Wendy's favourite food.

At first, Tina had not recognised Wendy. She had been sitting in Davy Byrnes on Duke Street, three brandies already down the hatch, and a warm sense of well-being percolating in her stomach. Something made her look again at the stained jacket, the blotched and scrawny neck, the mousey, listlessly straggling hair.

'For heaven's sake,' Tina said, 'how are you?'

'A bit tired.' Wendy smiled wanly. 'Listen, maybe we could meet? I can't talk here.'

The next day in Bewley's, Tina arrived early and managed to park herself in a roomy alcove, soft, plush, deep red. She ordered coffee, and waited. Wendy appeared just as she was deciding to give up.

'Sorry. I had a bad night.' Wendy slumped into the cushioned seat.

Tina noted the white face, dark shadows under eyes, a purple mark high on one cheek. Jesus, she's sick, she thought. Cancer – it couldn't be cancer?

'What'll I order?'

'I'll have tea. Nothing to eat, thanks.'

Tina glanced at Wendy, then looked away. It was too wretched. Her gaze settled on the Harry Clarke windows, the stained-glass fantasy of birds and pedestals and winding garlands. The pot of tea arrived and she was still looking at the windows. She was beginning to wish she hadn't come.

Wendy was brushing her hair and squinting into a compact mirror. 'I look terrible,' she said.

Tina watched as Wendy poured in milk, stirred, added sugar, stirred again. Eventually sipped at the tea.

'I've got horrible morning sickness.' She pushed the cup away. Her eyes were damp. 'Except it goes on all day with me.'

'You're not pregnant?' With the shock, Tina's voice came out high and shrieky. She cleared her throat. 'You're not pregnant?' she said more softly.

'He's trying to make me get rid of the baby.'

Foetus, foetus, foetus. A couple of cells. Baby – let's not use that emotive language. Tina shuddered to herself and repressed the words.

'He tried to persuade me last night. That's how I got this.' Wendy pointed to the purple mark on her cheek and opened the compact once more, dabbing at her tears. 'I'm sorry I'm behaving like a fool. And that's not all.' She snapped the compact shut, pulled up one sleeve of her jacket, revealing livid pinch marks. 'He's very upset.'

'Oh my God. Who *is* he?'

Wendy reached over to touch her hand. 'When I came back from Australia, he'd sold the house. He was supposed to follow me … to renew our marriage vows. I was a fool, Tina, to believe him. I never thought I'd be that stupid. But now that it's clear, I can admit you were right. Blaise is a bastard; he always was a bastard.'

Tina found her mouth opening and shutting. For a while no sound emerged. 'Blaise?' she eventually squeaked. 'You can't be serious?'

'And the book I was writing about drug addiction and collapsed populations in the inner city. Remember he said he'd help me. He didn't have time in the States, so in the end we decided we'd do the work this autumn. But before Blaise sold the house, he got builders in. They threw out all my recordings, all my notes.'

'Jesus.'

'And then I thought if I had his baby, I'd at least have got something out of the marriage.'

Fresh okra from Mary Street Asia Market. Tina slits them open lengthways, then deftly, with finger and thumb, presses into each narrow opening the delicately flavoured stuffing. She repeats the action over and over, until her largest frying pan is filled with the tiny objects, lying in a single layer, slits upwards so that aromas of coriander, fennel, mango rise to Tina's nostrils.

Hiroshima and Nagasaki. The names circulate as aromas in Tina's head. The cities chosen because they were clean. A couple of firebombs on Nagasaki, but by and large untouched till Fat Man smashed it. They needed pristine sites so they could see the bombs' full effects. Fermi, in some desert place, working obsessively. Fat Man, how did they choose the name? she wonders, and sets the mixing bowl on the countertop. Dough for the naan bread is next. Milk, sugar and yeast. She stirs them together. Secondary neutrons, chain reactions, and then Fat Man gets so fat that he bursts. Fermi dropping paper shreds on the ground to show the yield. She stirs the mixture a little more, then leaves it to stand, returns to her frying pan. The doorbell shrills and she lifts the pan off the heat, runs to the window. Down below she recognises the scarlet-coated figure of her mother.

Wendy scrabbled in her bag and pulled out a crumpled magazine. 'I think I might have an incompetent cervix.' She leafed through pages.

'*Woman's Way?*' Tina exclaimed. 'What's wrong with you?'

'Stole it from the hairdressers.' Wendy pushed the magazine across the table. Tina looked in horror at the pattern for a baby's cardigan.

'I've got to get my act together,' Wendy said. 'Say goodbye to drugs and booze. Otherwise it's miscarriage, stillbirth, mental retardation, physical defects – the works!'

'What's happened to your forehead?' Tina asked. 'You never used to have lines like that.'

'Old age, stress … who knows? There's another problem. Over thirty-five. It's a minefield. That's why I've taken up knitting.'

Tina had added so much sugar to her coffee, it was undrinkable. She hadn't done that in years.

Then Wendy told her about the psychotherapist. 'I had to talk to someone,' she said.

Tina grimaced, but said nothing. There was nothing to be said. 'Better the devil you know,' Wendy said apologetically.

The doorbell rings yet again.

'Shut up,' Tina mumbles. The yeast has frothed the milk up nicely. The dough is ready to be made. To calm herself, she takes a can of beer from the fridge. She flicks the remote control and the television's comforting blast helps drown out the bell's shrill sound. She strides around the living room, willing her mother to go away. Tina's new flat, with its real fireplace, its compact cosy kitchen and its small but decent bedroom, is on the second floor of a Victorian terrace. Big windows, bright and airy – what more could a woman ask for?

The deeds of the flat are with Tina's solicitor. She could not have imagined a more satisfying conclusion. The perfect use of tactics. She glances at the television. Images of burnt-out buildings around the Robert Emmet bridge – Halal butchers, a Moroccan restaurant, an Indian takeaway. *The cause of the fire is unknown.* Tina stretches and yawns. A few beers, the tantalising exotic smells of India, Wendy will be a push-over. Chop out the cancer, Tina will say. It's the sort that doesn't return, and we'll all be as we once were.

'Love me?' Blaise will ask, when next he visits for their Wednesday rendezvous.

Tina will yield as always to the fingers stroking her T-shirt, will look at him through a haze of smoke. Wild, wild for her body, Blaise will tell her. And she will laugh again at the idea.

Tina's mother sits into the tall armchair – Tina's favourite. 'I was ringing for ages, pet. Did you not hear the bell?'

'I was cooking.'

'That kind neighbour of yours, so good of her to let me in. I haven't met such lovely manners since your Daddy died.' Mrs Foley's hands shake. Her lipstick makes a wide gash in her face.

'Lay off,' Tina says.

'You mustn't speak badly about your father. It was difficult for him moving to Dublin. He wasn't a young man. But shutting me up in that house in Mount Merrion, that was a crime. Only five minutes from the hotel. And there I'd be all alone. Cleaning and scrubbing for him, ironing his shirts.'

'More fool you.' Tina looks at her watch. 'How did you find me, for

God's sake?'

'It's just that I wanted to talk to you, love. Father McCarthy came in to me this morning.'

'I'm not listening.' Tina turns away. 'Don't, I warn you.'

'When I think of the contributions. "Fifty for this, Mrs Foley, one hundred for that. I don't know what we'd do without you, Mrs Foley." He kept telling me I'd leadership qualities, invited me to join the widows' group, said I'd help the others, get them out of themselves.'

Tina goes into the kitchen and measures out the flour, baking powder, yoghurt and salt. She adds them to the bowl of frothed milk, stirs the mixture. She has forgotten the egg, breaks it in on top and begins to bash the thick mixture with her fists. Her mother's face has got horribly thin. Tina tries to smash out that face, that shaking voice, as she punches the dough.

'They're not my class of people.' The wheedling tones will not stop. 'And when I think of the sort of people your Daddy and I used to mix with. Pet, do you think I could have a drink? Just one, love, then I swear I'll go. Cross my heart.'

Tina comes to the door of the kitchen, hands covered in floury dough, watches her mother's trembling fingers trace a cross on her breast. 'You've got to get out of here,' she says.

'Three shabby old women. It looks bad for a young thing like me to be seen in that sort of company. I should never have gone out with them. And Father McCarthy had the cheek to say I was drunk.'

'Jesus, Mummy, this is ludicrous. I told you I've a friend coming.' She grabs her mother's arm, trails floury fingermarks down the sleeve of the red coat, pulls her from the chair.

'I don't know where I got you from at all. A most unnatural child.' Her mother clutches the door handle. 'That friend of yours. What's her name? The tall skinny one?'

'I don't know.' Tina pushes her mother out into the stairway.

'She followed me into the toilet. I had to do a wee and she was there right behind me. Started dragging at my arm the way you are now. That's what reminded me.'

'For Christ's sake, Mother, shut up!' Tina opens the front door, forces her mother into the street.

'It was she told me how to find you. And I may have raised my voice but who wouldn't? Rita, Lizzie and Brenda. They're the three I was with. They didn't know what was up, with the management and all coming into the toilets. And nor did I. Very small toilets, love. There were a lot of people in there. I mean, when you're having a night out. We had no choice but to leave the restaurant. That'll tell you. And not even our main course served. Wendy, that's the name. Wendy. Drugs, I thought. Of course I didn't give her a cent. I was careful, pet. And you should be too. I don't like you to have nasty friends. I worry, you know.'

'Goodbye,' Tina says.

'Goodnight, goodnight,' her mother mutters as she totters along the street in her stilettos, lacquered hair rising in little clumps in the evening breeze. 'Goodnight, Christina.'

'Goodbye, Mother,' Tina calls aloud to the dwindling figure. 'You've got thin, Mummy,' she says silently to herself.

Tina had met her father by chance a few nights before the car crash that killed him. He'd been his usual nervy self. Standing outside Hartigan's, smoking restlessly, a dark-haired woman with him. He did not seem pleased to meet his daughter, and when Tina enquired after her mother, he had drawn a finger across his throat.

'Not a word between us in three months. I forgot her birthday.' He hustled the woman away, one hand on her shoulder, the other waving Tina goodbye.

'Call in and see your mother,' he came back along the pavement to mutter in Tina's ear. 'She's a bit lonely. Can't get used to city life.'

He had died only two years ago. Pissed at the time. On the road back to the old home in Sligo, apparently. Nobody knew why. And alone. Tina had caught a glimpse of the dark-haired woman at the funeral. Her mother, huge in those days, had wept in the front bench of the church. Tina had wept too.

Tina rolls the dough in oil, covers the bowl with clingfilm, then returns to her vegetable pilau. She heats oil, sizzles the cumin seeds, adds potato, carrots, green beans, stirs and sautés. Those two old people, she thinks, alone in a foreign city. Before they moved to Dublin, they had been excited, like children fantasising about a dream holiday. Tina adds the drained rice, turmeric, ground cumin, coriander, cayenne.

'It's the chance your father always deserved,' her mother had exulted to Tina's voicemail. 'I told him it would come. Quality like his will always be recognised in the long run.'

Three years later her father was dead. Tina stirs in chopped green chilli, grated ginger, mashed garlic, adds water, stirs again and waits for the mixture to boil.

CHAPTER 29

September comes to an end and storms roll across Ireland from the south-west. They beat the coast with such ferocity that people are carried away by rogue waves. The beaches become designated danger zones, the government sends army units to patrol the foreshore, and warn people to keep away.

During this tumultuous autumn, when the worst of the storms have abated, Finn, Miriam and Jeremy Daly return to Ireland. Each night after their return, they dream of bougainvillea, sun-soaked land and iridescent seas. Each morning they awaken to smells of damp, mould on the bathroom wall, a leak in a pipe, blocked drains. Downstairs the kitchen paint is peeling, the sash window swells and will not open. The furniture is laden with piles of papers and books, the floor covered in broken toys. There's a thin layer of dust on the shelves.

They try to find work. Miriam calls The Female State repeatedly. The phone rings and rings, but no one answers. She walks to the offices in Drury Street. The windows have been boarded up. Now she searches the newspapers for jobs, reads ads in shop windows. Finn sends articles to literary journals and newspapers, but most of his energy is spent writing the final draft of his new book.

Jeremy goes back to school.

On a sunless October morning Finn walks home through Donnybrook with Jeremy on his shoulders. They look into shop windows, discuss the fixtures posted outside the rugby ground, and Finn glances at the contents of the bin in the petrol station, in case a newspaper might have been dumped there.

The front door is ajar. Finn ducks so that Jeremy will not bang his head. He has lost his key. He does not want to tell Miriam, so he has left the door on the latch. In the sitting-room, he bends his knees, leans forward and catapults the child head first onto the couch. 'Keep your coat on, Jeremy.' He presses the television's remote control. 'I'm not lighting the fire.' He collects the post from the hall floor and goes upstairs.

In the bedroom he watches Miriam's eyelids flicker. He knows that she is trying to wake up, trying to escape from a nightmare that has plagued her since their return, a nightmare where Jeremy is lost and will never be found.

'Jeremy's downstairs,' he says. 'He's watching television.'

Immediately Miriam is awake. She sits up in a fright and the duvet falls away, slithers onto the floor. Shivering, she reaches out to it, and lies down again, huddled in the bed. She covers her face with her hands.

'Why isn't he in school? You didn't forget his lunch, did you?'

He tries to keep his temper. 'The school's shut,' he says. 'Did they not tell you yesterday when you were collecting him? Alright, Jeremy,' he goes to the door and calls downstairs, 'you can change the channel.'

He drops Jeremy's schoolbag and an assortment of letters on to the bed. 'That fucking school,' he says. 'Supposed to be non-denominational and it's packed with fucking Catholics. They'd a notice on the door today that Catechism classes are starting up.'

'I thought we'd agreed to limit TV?' He's been so hyperactive since we got back. His teacher hasn't been mean to him again, has she?'

'There wasn't any school,' he says through his teeth.

'But why?'

'Teachers' in-training.' He begins to rip open envelopes.

'Everyone seems to have changed since we came back.' Miriam's voice comes to him plaintively from under the covers. 'They used to be so friendly, so good-natured. I could talk to everyone.'

Finn grunts.

'It's something to do with speaking Irish.' She pushes away the duvet. 'Finn, I hate Irish. Before we went away, Robbie's mother was practically my best friend, and now she's just horrible. I was sure she'd want to exhibit my paintings, but when I asked her yesterday, first of all she pretended she didn't hear me, then she splurted this big stream of Irish, and I had to run after her across the playground to ask her what she meant.'

Finn looks at the envelopes. There are too many bills. Nothing at all to pay them with. 'So?' he says. 'What did she mean?'

'She meant no. And then I asked her could Robbie come to play with Jeremy. I mean they were inseparable last year, and she did another big stream of Irish. That meant no too.'

'That bitch was never your friend.' Finn rapidly scans a typed page. 'Invitation from the Roycrofts. For December. What's wrong with these people?' He throws it on the bed.

'They're all taking Irish lessons,' Miriam says. 'And Rosanne's got them into magical rites and transcendental knowledge. That's what Wendy told me. Imagining themselves as reincarnations of Yeats, Raftery and O'Carolan.'

'Jesus!' He glances at her, tears open another envelope.

'Derek won't speak to me, Finn. He still blames me because I went away.'

He puts a hand to his head. These people are rubbish, he thinks. Miriam gets sucked in every time.

'Oh yes.' She glances at him. 'I'll be out from midday.'

'For Christ's sake.' Finn brings his fist down on the dressing-table, scattering Miriam's face creams. 'It's not my day.'

'Finn, I thought he'd be at school.' She sits erect in the bed, stares at him. 'I can't cancel it. It's a new gallery on the Quays. And I can't bring Jeremy.'

Finn picks a large brown envelope from the floor, holds it up to the light, opens it slowly. 'Jesus, my articles on Europe's shift towards ultranationalism – *The Irish Times* has rejected them: "Would not appeal to our readership." I wrote them because of that bloody Roma incident you had to put up with.' He looks at the letter again, feels the paper with his finger, as if that might reveal something to him. 'Last year they kept begging me to write,' he growls. 'What's wrong with them?'

'You've written a disgusting book that no one will ever publish, let alone read.' Miriam does not look at him as she speaks. 'That's what's wrong, Finn: you don't think things through.'

He watches as she gets out of the bed and picks up the cosmetics, replacing them between the patches of dust on the dressing-table. 'Please don't knock over my stuff,' she says.

'Look at my fucking letters. You've scattered them all over the floor.' He picks out another envelope. 'This one's for you,' he says. 'Peter Brindley.'

She doesn't want to take it. He can see that. He holds it out to her. She climbs back into the bed. 'Take it,' he says and drops it on the duvet in front of her. 'It was my fault too. I should never have had anything to do with him. Toilet paper magnate. Jesus!'

'He's diversified,' Miriam says. 'He's into renewable energy, and baby wear.' The letter is in her hands. She is holding it, opening it, reading it, and as Finn watches, tears begin to roll down her cheeks. 'He says I damaged his car.' She turns her face away from Finn. 'And remember I told you that Tina took a kimono thing. He wants money for that too.'

'Christ!' Finn picks the piece of paper from the bed. 'Forget this drivel, Miriam. He's just trying to get his own back.'

'You ruined it on me,' Miriam says. 'You wrecked it.' She is lying on her side, facing away from him, her voice choked.

'No, Miriam, no.' Finn sits on the bed and strokes his wife's hair. 'I rescued you. You didn't want to screw that fat fuck. You know you didn't. Remember, you wanted to come home with me.'

'I couldn't come home with you. You'd squandered all the money.'

'It wasn't a good life, Miriam.' He is holding her in his arms, kissing her hair, the back of her neck, her shoulders. 'It was disgusting.'

'I wore lovely dresses,' she murmurs. 'Chloé, Alice by Temperley, Just Cavalli, Balenciaga, Versace.' He hears her say the words like a litany of saints. 'He knew the names of all the fishes in the sea, the birds in the air. He took me to Cairo and Istanbul; he danced beautifully. I'd have lived in a palace.'

'You had to come back to me, Miriam. To rescue me. From Rosanne. She'd her clutches right in. Jesus. And then fucking William arrives. You had to come home.'

He is leaning over her, kissing her forehead, little tiny butterfly kisses; he is stroking her back.

'Peter was jealous,' she whispers now. 'He pinched me when I talked to other men. Once he dug his nail into my back, and I wanted you to come and rescue me.'

Finn is caressing her bottom and her thighs, he is kissing her eyes, pressing her back in the bed. And at last they are touching each other, loving each other, and Finn is kissing her breasts, and she is pressing herself into his body.

'Thank goodness Jeremy didn't hear us,' Miriam whispers when it is over. She raises herself in the bed, looks at her watch. 'Oh God, I'll be late for the gallery! Finn, could you hand me a mirror?' And Finn knows that the spell is broken.

'My face is a show,' she is saying now. 'I'll never be able…. Fetch me a basin of cold water and a flannel, please.'

He bangs the red plastic basin down on the bedside locker. Water slops over the edge.

'Careful.' She lays the flannel across her eyes. 'I'll need a towel. There's one on the floor near the wardrobe.'

Finn finds a towel under a pile of clothes, and as he straightens he watches her take a deep breath, prepare herself for the next onslaught. 'About your manuscript, Finn.' She is lying back on the pillow again, the cold wet facecloth covering her eyes. He can see little rivulets of water trickling down the sides of her face to dampen the pillow.

'You have this beautiful story,' she is saying. 'Your grandfather, the simple life he lived, the fields, the natural world, his perceptions about Ireland, about the future. And suddenly you make the whole thing repulsive. My stomach turned. It's as if you don't understand that some things are totally wrong.'

'That's the whole point. You caught it in one. There is nothing wrong. It's all part of a continuum. A beautiful honourable continuum.'

'Having sex with little children is beautiful? You don't mean that. I know you don't. Otherwise, you'd be advocating the foulest crime. Which would be all wrong, completely against the spirit of all that is good.' Miriam takes the flannel from her eyes, checks her appearance in the mirror, dips the flannel in water and again replaces it over her eyes.

'Recalcitrant fact against the bourgeois lie. It's like….' He is searching for an analogy. 'It's like a transgression. Transgressing all the taboos. Without blame, without judgement, without irony. Just recording the facts with complete acceptance.'

'For God's sake, Finn. It's not going to be acceptable to anyone. Remember I was telling you about William's father – the one who's dead. Well, when he peed in the school car park, I thought he was a weirdo, but now I know it was only a kidney infection. We're over-sensitised these days. So, please, you could easily rewrite those sections. Because if you leave it in, it makes all the rest repulsive. He's looking at the sky, he's describing the new moon, and you're thinking: he's going inside to feel his children's bottoms, put his fingers up their ... no, it's too horrible. I can't. Bring my make-up case over. The little one on the floor beside your foot.'

He throws the make-up case on the bed. 'I met Paul Ryan in town yesterday.' He can see that the name makes her nervous – she's fiddling with the catch of the make-up case; her fingers are reaching up to touch her hair. 'I asked him to do a background piece – Cavan roots, that sort of stuff.'

She is looking into the mirror, applying cream to the skin around her eyes. 'Please don't give anyone the manuscript till we've sorted this out. Please, Finn?' Now she is fumbling with the lid of the cream, twisting a lock of hair between her fingers. And he is trying to explain that Paul Ryan is okay; he's an independent voice. It's too small a country. Too many cultural vampires; you need an independent voice.

But she won't listen. Everyone hates Ryan, she insists. Rosanne has warned her friends to keep away from him, and she's trying an exorcism by rubbing potions into his effigy.

'Rosanne makes us sick, so why would we care what she thinks?'

'It's her children I can't bear. Jeremy's got so difficult, and I think it's because those girls are in school with him every day. Maybe we should move schools, Finn.'

'For Christ's sake, they're just ordinary children, Miriam. It's Rosanne who's the imbecile.'

'We might get exorcised too.'

'Who'd take any notice of such cretins?' Finn kicks at the base of the bed. 'I discovered a few things about Ryan over the summer. He's out of their league. That's why they hate him. He was one of the brains behind the Festival de Beauté in Avignon back in 2000. He did stuff with the Eileen Gray house in Roquebrune Cap Martin.'

'None of that matters. I want us to keep away from him.'

'But, Miriam, he's been all over the Middle East, Africa, film festivals in Burkina Faso. He's talented like none of them are. And now he's got the sack, so he's going freelance.'

She's sitting up in bed staring at him. 'Sacked from his job?' she says. 'Are you sure?' And then almost silently and in awe: 'That was part of Rosanne's plan.'

CHAPTER 30

The typescript has been submitted, but there has been no response. It is already November, and Finn's barrage of follow-up letters remains unanswered. He discovers that his publisher is somewhere in Turkey climbing a mountain, that the typescript has gone missing, and he stands transfixed a moment in his cold, unfriendly bedroom, then goes out and drinks himself into a stupor.

He scrapes around to find work. A few hours are offered teaching English in a language school. He hates the grind of it. Miriam will not speak to him. She will not even look at him. Instead, she embraces Jeremy with exaggerated demonstrations of motherly love, and communicates to him the messages she wishes Finn to understand. Jeremy participates uncertainly in this charade, watches nervously as his mother packs her suitcase and places it threateningly close to the front door.

After another wild weekend of alcohol and sex, Finn's chest is heaving, his feet are as heavy as lead. A message on his phone tells him that he has to collect Jeremy from school, but the tram terminus is miles from where he had found himself a doorway to sleep in, and his body is collapsing. He is running and running, and he wants it to be a nightmare. He wants desperately to wake up, and discover that he is not dashing across roads, racing into traffic, listening to the squeals of brakes, the angry shouts, the honking horns.

In the real world he finally reaches the station, but his lungs are refusing to suck in air and he hunches over, pressing his two hands to his chest. He grasps the tram doors just before they close, hauls himself on, lurches across the carriage, falls on his knees, drags himself up, stumbles to a seat. He sits there gasping, staring down at his muddy shoes, filthy jeans. Then he stretches his legs to the seat opposite. 'Where is it from?' he whispers to his shoes. 'Where did the mud come from?'

He tries to think about where he has been, but thinking makes the pain more intense. It's a cramp, he tells himself, and he rubs his hand against his chest to ease it.

Thankfully the tram is moving. He presses his two hands against his heart, and the pain recedes. It is probably not a heart attack, but there is a jagged red cut on the back of one hand. He had been climbing through barbed wire. The phone in his pocket vibrates against his leg.

'Finn? William here. Good to get your message. Great to have you in Dublin again.'

Finn closes his eyes; the pain is still gripping his chest. He forces himself to breathe slowly as William talks.

'Phone powered off all weekend. Only just got your message. Maeve and I … we took a holiday together. Her eleventh birthday … that sort of thing. She's been a bit run down. My Dad's death … one thing and another.'

The pain in Finn's chest settles to a dull ache, the smell from his clothes rises to his nostrils, a dirty musky smell. He asks himself if he has been sleeping rough for days.

'One of those madcap things.' William's voice comes through the thick fog that has submerged Finn's brain. A darting pain between his eyes. He moans, presses a hand to his forehead, shakes his head as if that might help to clarify something.

How long has he been gone? Finn wonders. Can he remember taking a tram or a bus out to that wasteland? And all the time William's voice droning on.

'Maeve and I went west. Not a cloud in the sky, the sun as soft on your back as a lamb's fleece. Lough Corrib at its most placid. Inchagoill. Then Cleggan, Inishbofin.'

'Jesus,' Finn says. He puts the phone in his lap. The buzz of William's voice continues from far away as he tries again to understand what has happened to him. He must have been drinking. Drinking to oblivion. And then there was a woman: fair-haired, young. A shadowy image in the throbbing ache that goes deep into his brain. He sniffs at his blackened fingers, trying to identify her, trying to place her in his mind.

'Harmony, spiritual quest, magic.' Little snippets of phrases jump from the phone to hit Finn's forehead. 'Resurrecting a golden age. Eighteenth-century Connemara.' And then he picks up the phone again and William's voice flows around his earlobe. 'I've talked to you about that idea before, Finn. But this time it really happened. We became part of that paradise of the poor.'

Finn sees the young woman now. There is a whiskey bottle in his hand and they are walking up a lane. He trips and falls into the brambles and the whiskey bottle breaks and he holds up the jagged glass and roars at her. And she starts to run away. He wants to tell William that Miriam has cut him out of the family, that she will not talk to him until he changes the typescript. That whoever may judge Finn must accept that whatever catastrophe may befall him will be all Miriam's fault.

'Irish revolutionaries through the centuries.' The words pour into the side of his head. A bag laden with shopping knocks against his shoes. He moves his feet off the seat, watches a middle-aged woman wipe dried mud from it.

Finn and the young woman had walked for miles. They had found an off-licence. Finn had sent her in, but they had refused to serve her. So he had taken off his filthy coat and strode in. 'No problem,' he said when he returned with the whiskey bottle.

'For Christ's sake, William,' he growls.

'It was expensive, Finn. And we only had spaces for twenty people. Stayed in Delphi Lodge. Walked the Famine Road, knocked at the door of the big house. And we weren't turned away.'

With the young woman, Finn had been looking for the lead mines. But by that time he was too drunk. And the girl was from somewhere else. She didn't know anything.

Dundrum. An inrush of passengers. Finn hunches his shoulders against the preening women, the *Petit Bateau* and *Château de Sable* brats. These are the greedy, he thinks. These are the bitches who suck the state dry, these are the parasites who don't pay taxes. He wants to spit at the designer coats. Instead, he hunches over again and closes his eyes.

'I've been landed with Twenty-Sixteen the History. Could need a bit of help there because America's been calling. Harvard want me to teach for a term. A hundred thousand – you can't turn your back on it with the way things are.'

'Jesus,' Finn grunts. He remembers now that she had stood in front of him, and they had wandered off somehow to a dirty little bed-sit out in the suburbs. Finn rocks forward in the seat, examines the rough herringbone under the dirt of his coat. 'It's not my coat,' he mutters. 'It's someone else's coat.' He's running his hands along the dirty torn jeans, looking at them, wondering who owns them.

A child pushes at Finn's leg, sits on the floor of the tram, pulls Finn's shoelace, and talks gibberish to himself.

'Jeremy,' Finn mumbles. 'Jeremy.' The phone slips from his hand, falls. The child picks it up, holds it to his ear. The purr of William's voice continues.

'Give me the phone,' Finn says.

'No.' The child presses buttons, cuts off William.

Finn is suddenly wide awake. 'For Christ's sake,' he says. The little boy clutches the phone, twists and wriggles to get away. Finn holds on to his sleeve.

'I've to collect Jeremy,' he says. 'I need the phone.'

'Mummy!' the child screams. The passengers look down in disapproval, but no one arrives to claim the child.

'Mummy!' the child screams again.

'I have to collect Jeremy,' Finn says. He squeezes the child's wrist and snatches the phone from him. The child's mouth opens in a howl of rage and pain.

Finn peers out of the tram window into suburban gardens. He is lost. The terraced houses beside the track look alien to him. He doesn't recognise the grassy spaces and narrow lanes.

'Where are we?' he asks, panic rising in his chest. Jeremy must be collected.

The man beside Finn stares at him. 'It's written up there,' he says, pointing at the overhead screen. 'Can you read?'

Take it easy, Finn tells himself, pressing his hand to a pounding heart. His head burns but the world seems to be coming into focus at last. The phone vibrates once more in his palm.

'Sorry,' William says, 'had to put on the potatoes.'

Jeremy, blond hair, skinny legs, he sometimes looks as if he suffers. That look sets Finn into a blazing fury. Bloody Miriam, he thinks, using the child as her weapon. Bloody kid stealing my phone. The child's angry, frightened face comes into focus again, and Finn shakes his head to dislodge the image.

'Rosanne's hoping you'll do a bit of research for her. A family history. Some poor deranged woman thinks that Rosanne has stolen her personality. It's a theme, she thought, that you could use for your fiction.'

He'll send the school a message, telling them he'll be late. Where do I get off this bloody tram? They won't let Jeremy out by himself in the street. They'll hold him a few minutes till I arrive.

'Rosanne doesn't want to call the police. That would be too cruel when this person lives in a world of fantasy. Rosanne wants to find out a bit of background, what her connections are. Detective work. Think you'd be on for that, so she can discover how best to intervene? I felt you might have time. My work too you see.'

'I've got to get off,' Finn says. 'I've to collect Jeremy.'

'Between the two of us, say … three mornings a week for the next couple of months. Mine is more … long-term.'

The tram is slowing. Finn stands, forces his way towards the door. The child reappears in front of him like a judgement, this time in the arms of its blonde mother. He sees the fingers of nearby passengers pointing at him.

'Ahem,' William says. Finn is pressing at the button, but the door will not open. 'Rosanne's proposing you for Aosdána at the next meeting.'

Finn presses the button again. Other people are standing behind him. The doors are stuck.

'And Finn, we want you and Miriam to come for dinner.' In Finn's exhausted brain the thought comes into focus: Miriam will forgive me. She'll start talking to me again. I'll change the book, and I'll take work from William. She'll stay with me.

'Just the four of us,' William is saying. 'Such a shame the French holiday had to be cut short. Just as everything had got back on an even keel. We'll take stock, firm up the work arrangements, put our heads together for Miriam. A bit of lateral thinking…. What about Friday?'

Finn presses the button again. Now the door opens and he stumbles out onto the platform. There he stands quite still, his arms limp, and looks behind him into the crowded carriage.

CHAPTER 31

Miriam and Finn sit at William and Rosanne's table. Miriam eats dutifully, but somehow she is too tired to attempt conversation.

'Don't show me the new book if you're not ready,' Rosanne is saying to Finn, 'but I am looking forward to it. I'll just put everything else to one side.' She pours Finn a glass of Mas Julien 2002. 'I picked this up in Rathmines. They told me it grows north-east of Pézenas. Did you try it at all while you were there?'

'For Christ's sake,' Finn growls, then turns back to contemplating his cutlery.

At least some things have improved, Miriam thinks. Finn has agreed to remove the repulsive sections of his book. Her suitcase has been unpacked. She and Jeremy will be able to stay. It is a sensation of enormous relief. Finn has been in a black mood ever since, but for Miriam this is a small price to pay.

'I think it's important to serve red wine with fish,' William says. 'I've only started to do it recently, but I find it very rewarding.'

'For me the potatoes were the real triumph,' Rosanne says. 'William adapted the recipe from a sort of tart that an old peasant woman made for us. The recipe isn't recorded anywhere. William's searched for it all over the internet. Not a trace. Luckily he'd watched her until he worked out the method. Remember when we went off for those few days before poor Daddy Roycroft died. Well, we found this amazing old farmhouse near Mont Ségur. A film crew were staying in the converted stables, doing a remake of *Moby-Dick*. The girls were fascinated. We all were, especially when we discovered that the ugly misshapen little fellow in the corner was Captain Ahab, and the beautiful tall one with the ponytail was only a cameraman.

'I hear Peter Brindley's gone belly up,' William says, and Miriam glances at him in surprise. She looks down again at the muted glow of the table's surface, squeezes a lock of hair between two fingers. Her other hand describes a circle on the table, then touches the delicate cutlery laid across her plate.

'I could never get used to his body,' she told Yvonne. 'And he was old. When you've once had Finn, that's impossible. And he was cranky. He was so used to having everything his own way; he'd get into a mood if the tiniest thing went against him.'

'But isn't that exactly what Finn's like – always in a rage about something? And look at him now? I mean the two of you are skint, and what's he doing about it?' Yvonne was kneeling down painting the skirting-board of the sitting-room. Now she sat back on her heels and looked up at Miriam. 'If he was my husband, I'd dump him.'

'That's not fair. Finn tried to teach in a language school, but the director was horrible. Then I got a couple of mornings doing receptionist in the dentist. The trouble is Jeremy. I can't do a full day. Now Finn's looking for something else. And, Yvonne, I'll never leave him no matter how difficult he is. He's part of me and that's that.'

She did not tell Yvonne about Finn's book. About the passages so abhorrent to her that she had obliged him to remove them. She did not tell Yvonne that she had refused to speak to Finn for a full three weeks.

Yvonne returned to her work and Miriam spoke to her black curls and her narrow curved back. 'I suppose I forget to take account of how incredibly jealous men are,' she said. 'Because Finn isn't jealous at all. At the harbour in Barcelona I was chatting with some young men, and Peter kicked me in the ankle and then walked away. He didn't come back all night.'

'If you couldn't stand his body, it's for the best. So what about the paintings you brought back?' Yvonne reached for the masking tape, stuck a length of it to the floor. 'They might bring in something.'

'It's hopeless. The galleries say they'll get back to me but they never do.'

'I was thinking about that *being good* and *doing good* thing that you were going on about.' Yvonne expertly painted a length of skirting, laid the paintbrush on the lid of the paint tin, while she stuck down another length of masking tape. 'We were staying in a B&B in Sligo, and the woman who's running it turns out to be an American with an Irish great-grandfather, one of these frontiersmen who set off across Wyoming and Montana. She showed us some incredible photos. Anyway, the woman and her husband had bought this ruin in Sligo, done all the restoration themselves. Grew all their own vegetables – the food was fabulous.'

'And you thought that was what I meant by *doing good*?' Miriam asked tiredly. She wished then that she had never mentioned such things to Yvonne.

'No, no, no. That was *being good*, because afterwards she talked about her mother, and that's what struck me – the difference between them. Early each morning her mother would wash the clothes and bake the bread, then she left the house to do what she saw as her real work – fighting for the rights of native Americans, prisoners, blacks. She was *doing good*. The daughter described her mother as an egotist. Working for the underdog gave her a sense of power, an ability to control the destiny of others. But she wasn't *being good* because by doing this work for the wretched of the earth, she neglected her real responsibility – herself, her own children.'

Yvonne sat back on her heels once more. 'I'm moving to Sligo,' she said, 'selling the house.'

'But why?' Miriam asked. Please don't leave me, she wanted to say.

'I've been offered a job with Daonnacht. And I've found a school for the kids. Dublin's a dangerous city these days; actually the whole country's gone to the dogs. And Sligo's home. We Irish need a short sharp shock, and I'm joining Daonnacht because they've promised to give us just that. They're going to rouse us from our defeatist whinging and revive our sense of national pride. People who can pull it all together are useful to them, and I've always been good at organisation. Not that I'll neglect the kids, of course.' And she had laughed.

'There's a whole world of corruption in an Irishman who can afford to own a French château,' Rosanne says. 'I'll find a gallery for you.'

That careless phrase causes Miriam to sit up straight. 'A gallery?'

'And I'm proposing Finn for Aosdána next week,' Rosanne continues. 'There won't be a problem.'

William talks about finding a publisher for Miriam's poems. 'It's a shame the way you've been let down,' he is saying. 'I've contacts in Dark Island.'

Miriam takes a deep breath. 'Thanks,' she says and sits digesting this extraordinary news, while Rosanne attempts to rouse a dormant Finn, who is slouched over the table, sunk in gloomy introspection.

'Alethea Gyles,' Rosanne is saying. 'Wilde suggested she call herself Althea Le Gys. He said her rustic surname made him shudder. Then when she visited him in Paris, he confessed himself surprised to find her quite clean and charmingly dressed. His words. I can only imagine he was being ironic. After all, Yeats said her Waterford family was so haughty that the neighbours dubbed them the royal family.' She pours herself another glass of dessert wine.

'Talking of royal families,' she says. 'Derek's taken up with Risteard O'Toole. They're collaborating with Damien Hirst on a series of vignettes. *Tree frogs and Reparation.* Really, it is funny. Because I told Derek six months ago that we would drag him into Summer Twenty-Sixteen by hook or by crook. He didn't believe me then. He's taken to aping the great Risteard – brocade waistcoat, rose in the lapel, down-turned mouth.'

When Miriam hears Derek's name, she shifts in her seat, tries not to feel the cold fingers that take a new grip on her heart. Derek has responded to none of her messages. He has frozen her out of his life.

'It does show us what an immature society we still are,' Rosanne continues. 'A row in a Catholic Church and suddenly Derek's picture is splashed in the newspapers and he's interviewed on all the chat shows. Not that he doesn't deserve it. I actually love this for Derek. At the moment he desperately needs adulation. It makes him feel whole again. The attention fills the void left by Philip's death.'

'If you're talking about Alethea Gyles,' Finn says abruptly to Rosanne, 'tell us about her for Christ's sake. Don't leave it hanging in mid-air. She's some sort of nutcase who hung around Yeats, isn't she? But what's interesting about her beyond that?'

'Well, as you know, it's the spiritualist element that fascinates me. All her life she was on a mystic quest, though she never formally joined the Golden Dawn. She designed the cover for *The Secret Rose*. Her sensibility was directed towards abstract images of love and penury. A creature of infinite unreason, according to Yeats, so she must have been seriously mad!'

At least things don't seem terrible any more, Miriam reflects as she looks around the table. When Derek hears that a gallery wants to show her work, and a publisher is interested in her poems, he'll get over his rage; of course he will. Finn will have Aosdána, and a part to play in William's research. We'll be able to pay the mortgage. And maybe the paintings will sell. Even though Finn still hates what she does. 'What's the point?' he says. 'Painting a photograph, why do you bother?'

'I use the photograph as an *aide-mémoire*,' she tells him.

The others are laughing together at the thought of Alethea Gyles falling from the arms of a drunken pornographer into the clutches of Annie Horniman. They laugh at Aleister Crowley, another lover of Gyles, who believed Yeats' poetry vastly inferior to his own, of Yeats' black envious rage on reading Crowley's verses. They laugh even more when Rosanne describes the mad woman who believes that she is the author of Rosanne's poems. The woman who stands each day in the park across the road staring at the upper windows of the Roycroft home.

'She's got some connection with UCD, so I asked them to check her out. They tell me she's insane, beyond help. They shut their office doors when they see her coming. And even then she doesn't get the message. Apparently it's only a matter of time before she's locked up.'

None of them hears the soft swoosh of a letter landing on the hall floor. It is half past nine in the evening, way past the time of postal delivery. The kitchen door opens and a small figure sends the letter flying towards them. 'It's the post,' Deirdre announces. 'It's come late.'

'Say goodnight to Finn and Miriam,' Rosanne commands. 'And then it's bedtime. You can tell your sister to come down for a minute.'

Deirdre looks warily at her parents' friends. 'Maeve's asleep,' she says. 'She told me she's worn out.'

Miriam looks at the child. You sly creature, she thinks.

'Alethea Gyles couldn't get her poems published,' Rosanne remarks as she looks at the envelope. 'Wrong street number,' she notes. 'Did one of the neighbours drop it in? First of all, Gyles refused to correct the proofs.' She tears open the letter. 'And then she wouldn't remove some ridiculous dedication to Oscar Wilde. He was dead by then. I know you won't fall into that trap, Miriam.'

Rosanne frowns at the handwritten sheets in front of her, turns the pages to look for a signature. 'I'd better get my glasses,' she says. 'They're in the bedroom.'

'Leave it, love,' William suggests. 'It can hardly be anything important. Probably that ridiculous woman.'

'I just want to see who it's from,' Rosanne calls from the stairs.

William puts on his glasses, stares at the signature. 'Paul Ryan,' he says wonderingly. 'Why is he writing to Rosanne?'

'He's lost his job,' Miriam says.

'Oh dear me,' William says, as Rosanne returns to the room. 'The writing is difficult to read … even with glasses.' He looks over the top of his spectacles at Rosanne. 'I'm sorry, love, but it appears Faber has commissioned Paul Ryan to write a book of critical essays on Irish writers. He wants to include you. You'll have to think very hard about that.' He turns over the page. 'Lord,' William murmurs. 'Lord!'

As Miriam watches, Rosanne gets up from the table again, stands with her hand covering her mouth, her forehead tight with anxiety, looking at her husband. 'There's something wrong.' Her eyes seem to implore him. 'Tell me what's wrong?'

'Summer Twenty-Sixteen,' William says heavily. 'If we're to believe this letter, Ryan has just been appointed its director. They're announcing it next week.'

Rosanne snatches the pages from his hand, stares intently at the cramped writing.

A few minutes later Miriam and Finn are walking down Ranelagh Road. 'That felt as if we were being thrown out,' Miriam says. 'Like stray dogs that you dump in a river.'

Finn raises his face to the dark sky. It seems that his mood has lifted. 'Ryan in charge. Wow!' he says. 'That's thrown the cat among the pigeons. Wow! Maybe there is a God after all.'

'We're back a whole month, and the Roycrofts don't even phone us.

Then they're suddenly all over us. And now they've thrown us out. What does it all mean?'

'Ryan's the most important man in Dublin,' Finn says. 'And that lot are imbeciles. I've told you over and over. This beats everything. Maybe I'll take part in the festival after all. I'll send Ryan the manuscript tomorrow.'

'You've got to show me it before you send it.' Miriam stares at him across a glistening pool of rain-water at the kerbside. She clenches her fists, holds them out to their reflection in shimmering water. 'You've got to show the new version to me.'

'Read it tonight,' he says, 'if you're so hung up.'

In her perfect kitchen Rosanne presses her hand to the Aga's hot ring. 'Aaaah,' she screams, lifts her hand, stares at the broken red flesh.

'But you're still participating in the literary festival, love. If you put your hand under the cold tap, that always helps. Your readings are the centrepiece.' William moves nervously behind her, attempts to touch her shoulder, holds out the anti-burn cream. 'Even if Ryan is the director, he hasn't tried to interfere with that.'

'You and your stupid self-confidence!' Rosanne shrieks as water pours over the red stinging mess of her palm. 'You said you had the festival under control.' She sits again at the kitchen table among the wreckage of the meal, rubbing silvadene cream into her burnt flesh. Her body trembles. William's hands move towards her with hesitant gestures.

'Of course I'm participating,' she says at last. 'I'm too important for him to get rid of me just like that. But look who he's invited on to my panel.' She shoves the letter under William's nose. 'He's rooted out the two people who have given me hostile reviews.'

'But the three other panellists are your allies,' William pleads. 'It's just a bit of theatre.'

'What about that mad bitch? Is that fun? She's on the panel too. I can't believe that Ryan's done this to me. I'll have to get a private detective. Finn would never be up to it.' Rosanne drags the letter from her husband. From her mouth comes a bleak howl.

'You can't put a madwoman on a public discussion panel,' William insists as he tries to reassure his wife. 'You'll see, love: Ryan will have to drop her.'

Rosanne begins circling the kitchen again. 'It's memory,' she says as she paces. 'How you construct memory – that's crucial. I have to focus on that. What actually happens doesn't matter. What happens is trivial. It's how things are remembered. We're on the cusp, William.' She turns to her husband with a wild look in her eyes. 'And I will not be dragged down.' She opens her fists, stares again at the burn, holds her hands up in a gesture of supplication, then makes a frenzied dash to the study. William, hovering in her wake, sees Rosanne unlock the drawer where the deeds of the house and their wills are guarded. She plucks out a naked doll, tears off its head and legs.

'The gloves are off, Paul Ryan,' she sobs.

William gathers up the little sticklike portions of doll, moves close to his wife, and strokes her back with a pudgy hand. 'It's alright, darling,' he says. 'I'll put it all back together again.'

CHAPTER 32

Miriam shivers. The theatre's heating has not been adequate for a cold December evening. She climbs the stairs to the bar. And there is Derek standing, drink in hand, staring through the oval window to the street below. She moves towards him, touches his shoulder. He spins around, but when he recognises her, he takes a step back. He does not smile.

'I came out early.' Miriam's cheeks go red, but she keeps talking. 'My feet were freezing.'

He drains his glass of scotch and turns away from her to replace it on the counter. He stands with his back to her. She touches his sleeve. He shrugs off her hand, removes a fleck from where her fingers had lain for a second on the fabric.

'Don't you want to find out,' he flicks a beer mat away across the counter, 'whether I too have a place in the sun?'

Miriam winds strands of her hair around a finger. 'I know you're taking part in the festival,' she says. 'Well done.'

He turns and walks past her to the stairs. 'You have heard that Blaise Boothe is gunning for Finn?' he says over his shoulder.

'No,' Miriam says and she follows him down the stairs.

'My dear, you are so out of the loop. You will have to teach Finn the rules, since he does not appear to be bright enough to learn them himself. The curse of genius, I suppose.'

'Could we be friends again, Derek?' Miriam asks. The world is falling in around me, she wants to say. Please come back to me.

Derek looks contemptuously at her and Miriam cringes. He pauses at the foot of the stairs, looking to the auditorium where the doors have just opened and people are emerging, at first in ones and twos, then in a concentrated mass.

'Blaise paid him an advance for the script,' Derek says as the audience streams around them.

Miriam leans close to try to catch his words. 'And…?'

'And no script! But since I'm feeling generous tonight, perhaps I'll allow bygones to be bygones. Finn's new book? He can start afresh. I will give it a plug, but only on the strict understanding that I get nothing in return.'

All the time he is speaking, he is looking beyond her into the crowd, probably checking, she thinks, which important person he will abandon her for. And she doesn't understand at all what he has said.

Without warning, Derek embraces Miriam, whispers in her ear. 'Hold me,' he pleads. 'Hide me.' And Miriam lovingly enfolds him. Her lips kiss his neck, his hair, his ear, her cheek presses his, and she wishes deep inside her that she might return to that past friendship with him. There was a time before sex, before horrible jealousies intervened, when it was a perfect friendship.

He shuffles to one side. She follows, her arms close around him, and sees Wendy walk past in a pale green skirt. And Miriam understands the reasons for Derek's embrace. Averting his eyes, Derek pushes Miriam away, walks out of the theatre.

Miriam rushes after him. 'Rosanne was supposed to propose Finn for Aosdána.' She catches at Derek's jacket as he stands under the theatre canopy, trying to open his umbrella. 'But she didn't turn up at the meeting. Since Paul Ryan became head of the festival, she doesn't answer her phone. We need a little help, you see, just to tide us over. It's the mortgage. We're six months behind….' The words shoot out into cold wet air. They hang there a moment, then fall exhausted to the pavement.

'My dear, I am not a charity. It is ghastly that a tiny bit of success comes one's way and suddenly one has hangers-on.'

'I'm not a hanger-on, Derek,' she says. 'Wendy thinks you might still have some of that money we raised? The Sócúl money.'

Derek bangs the umbrella against the edge of the footpath, trying to activate the opening mechanism. 'If you're threatening me, don't bother. Try to remember that if I ever fell, so would you. Though I would never have believed that even you would stoop so low as to blackmail your discarded lover.' Tiny droplets from his mouth sprinkle Miriam's face. 'Remember last year? How we were caught *in flagrante* in a little child's bedroom?'

'I'm not trying to blackmail you, Derek,' Miriam says. She puts a hand to her mouth, shivers at the cold aggression in his voice.

'Such a short time and all is changed. Derek Garvin, once a failed publisher, now a superstar. There is a special providence in the fall of a Sparrow!' Derek's hands tremble as he stands under the theatre canopy trying to open his umbrella. And Miriam sees the little tic working in his cheek, the drop of moisture at the end of his nose. Despite everything, his fame, the money he's earning, he's worried, she thinks. He's afraid. She puts a hand to her neck, touches its thin contours, and feels her throat contracting. 'What's wrong, Derek?' she asks.

'They're blaming immigrants for spreading it.' Derek bangs the tip of his umbrella on the ground, hammering words into the concrete, either to bury them there or to lay them out for all to view. 'Every globule of immigrant spit is being analysed. Though you and I know, of course, that the bloody Irish are able to spread the plague without any outside help. Jenny O'Shea … that wretched creature.' A laugh that sounds like a scream. 'You recall my infatuation with her husband, the wondrous Carthage? The woman's got whatever he had. She's going to die.'

Miriam's chest tightens. 'I had a horrible thought,' she says before she can stop herself. 'That it's our fault. We made Jenny take Carthage back when he was dying. Sometimes I get nightmares. He was living in her sitting-room. And what about their children? What will happen to them?' She steps back to avoid being hit as Derek waves his still unopened umbrella.

'Bought it this morning. How does the damn thing work?' He presses angrily at the umbrella's stem and it unfurls. He holds it high above his head and walks away into the night.

Miriam looks down at her leaking Prada slip-ons against the dark footpath. She walks slowly back upstairs to the theatre bar, feeling the cold against her feet. A headache is forming behind her eyes, a gnawing pain in her stomach. She stands alone at the top of the stairs, watching the theatre audience mingle. William Roycroft is there with Finn, and she moves like an automaton in their direction.

'Deep entryist,' William is saying as she approaches. 'I believe they're called sleepers. Ryan resigned from the European Commission so that he could hover in a third-rate newspaper till he saw his chance. Nothing to do with defending a principle. Because, you know, he couldn't be better qualified for the job. That's the appalling vista. He's managed festivals all over Europe. Kolbe Ryan. An alter ego, apparently, which he adopts for his theatrical work. And we didn't put two and two.... Very successful. Avignon, Berlin. A multi-linguist. Campaign of vilification. Standard practice I know, but when one is the butt.... Rosanne has written to the publisher, asking that no chapter about her writing be included in Ryan's book. I have legal advice on this. It is that serious, Finn. So I've decided not to go away this year. Harvard's put off till next year. No work for you till then, I'm afraid.'

As Miriam approaches, William, with outstretched hand, is beckoning a third person into the conversation. It is Mrs Roycroft. Miriam quickly turns away. And at that very moment someone grips her elbow, pulling her backwards, and she finds herself sitting down hard on a leather sofa, Tina and Wendy on either side of her.

'I've a bit of a cramp,' Wendy is saying, 'so we thought this would be a good place to sit. And then we saw you....'

'Hello,' Miriam says. Her voice sounds unsteady and frightened. She rubs her hands to stop them from shaking.

Wendy is massaging her pale green skirt with the flat of her hand, and Tina is reaching out to touch Miriam's cheek. She cringes away so that her head butts lightly against Wendy's.

'Sorry', she says. 'We're a bit squashed,' and she tries to stand. But Tina is holding the back of her dress.

'Wendy,' Miriam says, 'I loved that card you sent me from Australia.' But as she speaks, she sees Wendy's shoulders droop, her face cloud over.

'Are you okay?' she says then, and Tina drawls out an explanation for Wendy's unhappiness. Then leans over and licks Miriam's nose.

'Stop,' Miriam whispers. She pats her nose and cheek dry with a tissue, turns to Wendy to say that she is sorry. But Tina's fingers are on her knee.

'Have you heard the sensational news?' Tina is saying while Miriam pushes away her fingers, presses her knees tightly together.

'Ryan. Paul Ryan heading Summer Twenty-Sixteen. The Minister picked

Ryan because he knew that'd give us a kick in the balls. Wanted to piss off all the artists.'

Miriam can do nothing but concentrate on pushing away Tina's fingers. She tries to hold her dress close to her skin. 'I heard he got the job because his wife is the Minister's first cousin,' she says.

'They're putting zillions into it,' Tina says. 'All set for next June. Apparently he's sifting through everything – little known and unknown, even unpublished. Works to be translated into every possible language. Inviting an open submission for artwork. Got some guy from Turin curating, whom no one here has ever heard of. The shows will go everywhere, along with the artists. It's the relaunching of Ireland Inc. We'll make zillions.'

'Ryan's name is big in Europe.' Wendy's voice seems to come from a faraway space. 'I think that's why he got it.'

Again Miriam pushes Tina's hand away, and this time she manages to pull the back of her dress from Tina's grasp and stands abruptly to avoid further caresses. William's mother is standing in front of her. The meeting is inescapable.

'Oh, Mrs Roycroft,' Miriam says. 'Finn and I were sorry to hear that Dr Roycroft had passed away.'

As Mrs Roycroft murmurs a reply, Tina's fingers make a new foray, this time on the delicate skin at the back of Miriam's knee. Miriam steps to one side. 'Did you enjoy the play?' she says in order to say something. 'I wonder would that have been a good way to live? Travellers seem to have such romantic lives.'

'They're tinkers, Miriam.' Tina's voice comes mockingly from behind her. 'It's *The Tinker's Wedding*. That's what Synge tells us. They're drunkards and thieves, live in filth and ignorance, and dump shit around themselves for the rest of us to pick up. Tinkers call that their culture.'

Miriam blushes at Tina's ugly words. She cannot understand how she could have let herself be seduced. How could she have? That first time she had been drunk. It had not been entirely her fault. But afterwards she had been too weak to say no, to explain to Tina that, for her, sex with another woman was a revolting idea, a cosmic aberration. And the awful thing about it was that each time, once the sex got going and she had blanked out the fact that this was Tina, she had actually enjoyed it. But Jeremy had come into their room. He had stared at them together in the big bed. He had wanted to know why Tina would kiss Miriam full on the lips.

Miriam thinks of the mistakes of last summer as Mrs Roycroft leans to one side, and responds to Tina. Words like tolerance and common humanity, Nazi Germany and fascist Italy, pass in and out of Miriam's consciousness. *Being good.* Perfecting the way that you make love. When she thinks of the idea now, it seems revolting to her. She looks at Finn, slouched over the bar, and a little shiver of misery runs across her shoulders. She fears that he has not taken the evil out of his typescript.

When she had looked at it that night, pages were missing, sections crossed out. But for all Miriam knows, Finn may have pasted back all that he had excised. And now he has sent it to Paul Ryan.

'Picturesque versions,' Mrs Roycroft is saying, 'Synge with the Travellers. Stereotypes. Maybe their culture is far more complex and interesting than Synge allows.'

'Traveller filth and indigence is complex and interesting?' Tina snarls, and Miriam flinches. Tina is furious. She is taking her fury out on Mrs Roycroft because she imagines that Miriam feels some affection for her. 'Our iconic painters and playwrights who've tried to make Travellers a little more attractive, noble even, are concealing some higher truth. Is that what you're saying?' Tina is almost spitting in her rage. She's getting fat, Miriam thinks, watching the bulging cheeks, the wet mouth uttering sharp angry words.

Miriam looks at the cheap brooch on Mrs Roycroft's sagging jersey dress, at Tina's too black hair, the pouches under her eyes, at Wendy's hand rhythmically massaging her cramped stomach. She would like to slip away but she is hemmed in, trapped. If only Yvonne were still around, she thinks; at least then I'd have one true friend. But Yvonne has moved to Sligo and is too busy organising her new home and the local Daonnacht network to talk over the phone about Miriam's difficulties.

'Storytelling, music-making,' Mrs Roycroft is saying, 'expertise in herbal medicines and healing – that's all been removed from the record, and we're left with the crude folk images of a Jack Yeats painting or a Synge play. We impound their horses, and now with all the new legal restrictions, we're making it practically impossible for them to travel. Their last remaining freedom is being taken from them. I believe they're challenging that ruling in the Supreme Court, though I can see how hopeless it is.'

'You want to sit back and let them rot?' Tina asks.

'I'm writing an article on that theme, Mrs Roycroft,' Wendy says. And Miriam notes the mottled skin, the dank greasy hair. Poor Wendy, she thinks. She was always so beautiful. And now she's separated and she looks wretched.

'The moral choices we make when we intervene in people's lives,' Wendy is saying. She is pushing a strand of limp mousey hair behind one ear and Miriam sees that the skin of her neck is scaly and unwashed.

'On the one hand, we're told that Travellers are destroying themselves, that they're heavily alcoholic and opposed to education. That they wreck the new pre-schools built for their children. On the other hand, there's this quest for freedom. I'm afraid my newspaper isn't very keen on that side of the argument.'

'For Christ's sake, they're pathological, dysfunctional,' Tina says. 'If we had any sense, we'd give them hard labour, and take their children into care.' She stands up, looks impatiently over Mrs Roycroft's shoulder, and at last a little space opens up, so that Miriam can slide to the outside of the group.

'You're talking sentimental garbage,' Tina says to Mrs Roycroft. And now she is nudging Wendy, pointing to where Risteard O'Toole is making his entrance, arm in arm with the play's director. 'Europe's going down the tubes, and all you can do is bleat on about tinkers. That scum are giving Europe's governments all the reasons in the world to clamp down. They're handing them the moral high ground on a plate. So try not to be so stupid.' She pushes her way through the crowded bar.

Miriam looks back at Mrs Roycroft's shapeless drooping figure. The old woman is raising a hand to her eyes, taking off her glasses, rubbing the lenses with the sleeve of her dress. Her wrinkled cheeks are pink.

There is a desolate empty space around Miriam's heart, and for a moment Mrs Roycroft's pain seems to echo inside that space. A sudden urge to take the old woman's hand in hers, stroke with her fingers the furrowed cheeks, as she had seen Rosanne's children do in the school car park.

Miriam resists this urge. I'm pathetic, she thinks. Always looking for somewhere to rest my head, imagining that others can make things alright for me, when I'm the only one who can help myself. She turns and walks towards the stairs.

2016

CHAPTER 33

Another hurricane batters Ireland with the arrival of the New Year. Through the course of a day and night, rivers across the country burst their banks, power lines collapse. There follows a week of havoc. Boats move along unlit submerged streets, carrying those who wish to collect belongings from their drowned houses. Looting is widespread and homeowners struggle to defend their property.

Small battalions of volunteers travel to the riverside inland towns worst affected by the flooding, paddle canoes and rowing boats up and down the streets, call with loudspeakers to trapped residents. Those who, despite the order to evacuate, have returned in their homes to protect them, attack the volunteers. Rival gangs stage battles in waterlogged villages. In the aftermath of skirmishes, corpses are carried by the currents through suburban streets; blood stains the brown water.

During the following weeks newspaper articles and television programmes analyse this unprecedented outbreak of violence. The government reveals plans to introduce a new identity card system, each card with a tagging device embedded. Honest citizens, the government insists, will not object that we monitor their activities. They will be grateful for the protection we offer.

The clean-up begins. Inhabitants emerge from damp, candle-lit shelters into the dark, cold air. Electricity is restored. Cafés, cinemas, bars reopen and life continues much as before.

Café en Seine on Dawson Street has cleared the sandbags from its doors and late in January Tina sits at an outdoor table hunched against seeping cold. She draws in deep lungfuls of smoke, watches the women passing along the street – tall and straight, with long slim legs. They are too young, too thin, too good-looking. Tina sips coffee, stubs out her cigarette, lights another. The waistband of her skirt cuts into her stomach. She opens the button, releases trapped skin and fat. Her hair is cut jagged and short. A new dye has caused tufts of hair to fall out.

Particles invade Tina's life. By day she walks the streets, or sits slumped in Grogan's or Kehoe's. She thinks incessantly about tritium, plutonium, uranium, wrestles with neutrons and creates virtual explosions. Little Boy. They called it Little Boy and smashed Hiroshima. A hundred and sixty thousand dead. *A little boy with his toys destroys.* The words are trapped in her mind.

She had come to the door of Wendy's psychotherapist, talked about her father's death, stammered and fell over words. It was ridiculous because, even as she remembered, she knew that she didn't give a toss. Tears had come into her eyes.

Rain starts. Tina lights another cigarette. Kyoto, she thinks. City of culture. No air raids, no atomic bombs, no divine disintegration. 'We honour culture,' the Americans said, and preserved Kyoto intact. An immaculate suede coat is approaching from Nassau Street.

'Hello there, aren't you freezing?' Wendy's elder sister, Gillian, stands in front of her. 'Do let's go inside.'

'So sorry I'm late.' Gillian divests herself of coat and St Laurent scarf. 'The traffic was woeful, and I can't leave the Merc on the street. Mummy and I were just saying that people don't know the difference between right and wrong any more. I mean whatever faults the Church may have had in the past, it did spell out wrongdoing in large letters. Waiter,' she calls out, 'I'll have a camomile. You'll have something, Tina?'

'A brandy.'

'Are you well, Tina? I like that blue. For us forty-somethings it's a good choice. Not too harsh. I always tell my girl in BTs....'

'Thirty-seven.'

'Beg pardon?'

'I'm thirty-seven.'

The camomile and brandy arrive. Wendy's sister drops an artificial sweetener into her cup.

'Arthur's dreadfully strict. Up on that weighing scales once a week. He says he won't have me turning into a lump of lard. And so many women our age do, don't they?'

Tina sees the significant look, but she is in another space, thinking about Gillian's body breaking into all its constituent particles. Then it would be beautiful, she acknowledges. Unconsciously she takes out a cigarette, lights it.

But Gillian's unbroken face is staring at her. 'It's illegal,' she's whispering.

Tina shrugs. 'No one cares any more.' She takes two deep drags, stubs it out, looks at the satisfied, toned face, carefully highlighted hair. She tastes the brandy and grimaces.

Gillian clears her throat. 'I have to admit that we were flabbergasted when Wendy told us.'

Inside the disused church Tina had swallowed two lysergide pills, lain on a mattress facing the wall. Soft music came from speakers high in the walls. She was thinking about uranium – heavy, dense, radioactive. Wondered what it would feel like if a uranium atom lay in her hand. Ninety-two protons and ninety-two electrons. Fissile, she had moved the word around in her head. Isotopes.

But then the music became drumbeats, sounds of people crying and moaning. And Tina herself was part of the sobbing. Protons and electrons, each a single sob, together a vast tumult. And the music got louder, wilder – babies crying, people screaming in pain. And Tina was screaming, and the isotopes were screaming too. Flashes of flame on her skin, her clothes burning. A tiny, tiny Tina whose feet didn't reach the floor, an infant in a Sligo kitchen.

The flames turned orange, and Little Boy was exploding in the air over Hiroshima, the shock wave smashing buildings into tiny fragments. And she was fighting her way through the flames. The skin on her legs had turned orange. And she was becoming a burning orange carrot with green shoots instead of hair. Screaming and screaming, and then her voice had grown thick, choked with snot and thick black soil. Soil in her mouth and she was gagging, suffocating, and the psychotherapist had set her shaking frame on all fours. He pressed her stomach muscles with his open hand.

'Vomit it out.' He held a metal bowl before her face, and she had retched till her stomach ached. In the bowl, floating in her clotted orange vomit was a little black metal numeral – the number three.

'Daddy,' she called out with a despairing howl, 'Help me.'

'Are you sure you're all right?' Gillian shades her eyes against the light. 'Can I say this to you very confidentially, Tina? Drugs. We feel that Wendy may have a problem. Have you noticed her eyes? Separated from her husband and pregnant all in the same moment. She says it's his baby, but then why would they separate? We've searched for Blaise, of course. Hopeless trying to find someone who doesn't want to be found. Part of the fault is ours, we admit that. Should have intervened immediately…. Because we did sense there was a problem. Just couldn't cope. My two teenagers in different Christmas plays and me busy, busy. Have to be constantly on the ball. It does take its toll.'

'Why don't you talk to Wendy?' Tina feels for her cigarette packet, pushes it to the bottom of her bag. Tritium, she thinks. That beautiful little atom with mad energy. Could she put her hand into the air and, without thinking, without trying, hold tritium in her palm?

'But that's just it.' Wendy's sister leans forward, her voice shaking with anxiety. 'Every one of us has tried. I've known Wendy longer than you have, and I can tell you she could have had anyone. At the time, none of us thought Blaise was right for our sister. But of course she never listened to us. And to give Blaise his due, he has made good. He's worth real money, Tina.'

'I'll have another brandy.' Tina's fingers touch a drop of water on the table. Surface tension, she thinks. The hydrogen atoms running away from mother oxygen. A whole play of love and revulsion. Tritium must be in there somewhere.

'We've been phoning her constantly.'

Out of the corner of her eye Tina notices the face fragmenting, the careful make-up disintegrating to show the raw angry molecules underneath.

'Are you listening to me, Tina?' The molecules pulse. 'Astonished to see that the house is gone. She's moved to some grotty flat, but we haven't been able to find her there either. Arthur's in touch with a colleague in London.

I do hope you will forgive me calling a spade a spade. Wendy will be well looked after. A rehabilitation programme – detox. Arthur checked that.'

'I'll have another brandy,' Tina says again. Tritium. Lights in watches, rifle sights, nuclear weapons. Tritium vital in all of them. She thinks of the rifle sights, lines up Gillian in front of her, pulls the trigger, and the disconnected face collapses into black night. The coincidence of molecules disintegrates.

'All Wendy has ever wanted is to cause embarrassment and pain to us, her own family. I mean, how do you think we feel? Our sister, who is almost forty.' The face is completely fragmented. When Tina squints, lipstick reforms for a second, then falls apart.

'Thirty-six.'

'Almost forty,' Gillian stabs her empty cup with her spoon, 'and probably a drug addict, decides to leave her husband, and have a child. It could be anyone's! It'll most likely be an idiot, and then she'll be begging us to help her out. But how? Every one of us is a busy professional person. If she'd been a proper wife, looked after her husband … a successful man like Blaise has needs, Tina. Wendy just goes her own way. She's never understood team play. Never.'

'She's in hospital.' Tina tastes the brandy. It's good, she thinks. 'For observation.' She tastes it again, then looks at Gillian's disintegrated face and body. If Tina holds her eyes almost shut, she can see a new form begin to emerge from those blundering particles.

'Why on earth are you squinting at me like that? I really don't understand.' Gillian takes out her mobile phone. She sits wide-eyed, presses the phone to her ear and waits.

'Goodbye, Gillian,' Tina murmurs. As she stands and fastens her skirt she wonders about the new form Gillian's body will take. She puts on her raincoat and stands for a moment in the doorway of Café en Seine. Tritium and uranium particles fly to and fro. Penetrate our bodies, invade our cells, conquer them, set them to self-destruct. After that annihilation, cockroaches will be all that remain.

She walks up Dawson Street and along Stephen's Green imagining Kafka's cockroach. What had weighed on Gregor Samsa's mind was how he would keep his job.

CHAPTER 34

The foyer of the Shelbourne Hotel – brocade wallpaper, gilt sofas, plumped up cushions. Tina hesitates at the door of the Horseshoe Bar. 'Christina, pet.'

She turns sharply, and there is her mother tottering towards her, high heels, jagged red mouth.

'Christina, you didn't see me. I was sitting there in the lounge. I look up, you know how hard it is to catch the eye of these Shelbourne waitresses, especially since your poor Daddy passed on.' Tina's mother sighs and clutches her daughter's arm. 'And there you were in the doorway. Come and have afternoon tea with your Mum.'

Tina flinches. 'Actually I was looking for you,' she says. 'Just don't touch me.'

'I'm off the drink,' her mother says, fluttering after her daughter. 'It's been two whole months. And Father McCarthy let me back into the widows' club. They've all been very kind, very forgiving.'

Tina glances at her mother's face. The cheeks no longer seem so gaunt and starved. 'You're looking better,' she reluctantly volunteers. 'Not so thin.'

'I've a lovely comfy corner. We can see everyone. Sit in here beside me now, pet.' Tina's mother pats the sofa beside her. 'Lean over near me and I'll tell you a secret.' She looks furtively around the lounge. 'I'm seeing a shrink,' she whispers. 'Father McCarthy put me on to him. He's called Hermann and he's a dote.'

'How can you afford a shrink? I thought you'd no money.'

'That's another thing Father McCarthy did for me. We had a long chat, and I told him everything. A sort of confession, really, though it was in his sitting-room. He gave me absolution at the end. So it turns out that he knows Mr Whirdy well. They're in that religious thing. What do you call it? Corpus Christi, is it?'

'Opus Dei?'

'The very thing. Just one phone call and Mr Whirdy called me in the next week. It seemed I had misjudged him, poor man. He's been sick. That's why I had difficulty getting to talk to him. And he says there's nothing to worry about. It's natural he says that my capital should go down in the short term. Deplete he calls it. But it's a ten-year investment and the last five are always the best. After five years the money starts pumping back in. Nothing to do with the economy. It's the way it's all arranged. And I'm only in my second year. He was a gentleman, I will say that. And you see, pet, giving up the drink pays for the shrink. And all I do is go there and talk about anything I like. It might be the weather or the widows' club, or that father of yours, though I do like to keep it light. Once I start crying, the make-up goes to hell. And I want Hermann to see me at my best. Because you know he's very fond of me. He says he got a sense of *déjà vu* when I first came in the door, as if he'd met me in another life.'

'Jesus Christ, you'd fall for anything.'

'And do you know what else he told me? He thinks I'm bursting with life, so I have to live up to it, don't I? Hermann says most of his other patients are dead inside, but I'm so lively, I make him feel lively too. European gentlemen never mind an age-gap. And I was told only yesterday I don't look a day over fifty. What do you think of that?'

'You're sixty-two, Mother, and you look every second of it! That's what I think.'

'You're very harsh, pet. Don't make me cry now. Fifty-five is the very most I'll stand for.'

Stupid old cow, Tina thinks, kicking the leg of the table.

'Careful,' her mother says, 'you'll spill the milk. Have one of these little sandwiches. They're gorgeous. Or do you prefer the scones? I've had a few good chats with Hermann about you. We share our worries, he and I. He's separated. A very difficult situation. He told me that he and I were lucky to find each other. And do you know what else he said? That I have *gestalt*. He's German, so it could have been that I am *gestalt*, that sounds more like it, doesn't it? I thought it was a very sweet compliment.'

'You don't have a clue what he meant,' Tina exclaims, racking her brains for the meaning of *gestalt*. Something to do with an undivided perception, she thinks, something which can't be expressed in terms of its parts. She shakes her head. Her mother is for Tina the ultimate non-perception. No logic, no rational thought. A formless amoeba, squelching its way through the world.

'I think Dad abused me,' she hisses, wondering now if there is any point. Her voice is shaking. She puts a hand to trembling lips. Particles, molecules, they are too good for her mother, she realises now. Strange how a monster like Wendy's sister could at least have the saving possibility of disintegration.

'What's that, pet?'

But Tina is staring across the room. She notes the beautifully cut suit shimmering with droplets of rain, the cane he holds in his right hand.

'I want to order those nice éclairs,' her mother is saying, 'but that wretched girl, every time I think I've caught her eye, she just flits away. Could you try, there's a dear?'

Tina looks at the ground, shakes her head in an attempt to steady her racing brain, and at that moment Derek's elegant fingers brush her shoulder. She flinches at the touch.

'Honoured to meet you.' Derek kisses the air somewhere near Mrs Foley's hand, gestures extravagantly across the room to where a group of people are divesting themselves of raincoats and scarves. 'I've interviews back-to-back over the next two hours. *New York Times*, *London Review of Books*, and our very own *Irish Times*. They're livid that I've taken a few minutes off to come and greet old friends. They can wait on me. It's my privilege now.'

He leans forward and enunciates his every word in Mrs Foley's direction. 'My first excursion into opera. An elegy for Philip. In memory of that glorious day when we fought the forces of reaction and we won. A return to the pagan truths. *The Gayboy of the Western World*. The bitter-sweet comedy of our relationship. An outright attack on the pinched philosophies of political correctness, victim culture and intellectualism. Thus the finished product will be ribald, absurd, impossible, commonsensical and, in a bewilderingly varied number of ways, dead right.'

'That sounds lovely,' Mrs Foley says.

He smiles at her. 'Aha, you see I have learnt quite a lot, dear Mrs Foley. In the American, and now in the Irish, market, the more absurd the claims, the greater one's credibility. Massage the media. Milk the media. I tell you, I adore the whole business. The only cloud on my horizon – that loathsome director of Summer Twenty-Sixteen. Having to deal with Paul Ryan makes me shudder.'

Tina looks at the carpet. Paul Ryan isn't the problem, she thinks. It's me. It's my imbecile mother.

And then a minuscule Blaise Boothe flutters out of nowhere and squats on Tina's shoulder. 'Come back to me,' he whispers. 'If you want your work to dazzle the world, come back to me.'

'If Ryan were to be removed from the celestial orb,' Derek is blithely saying, 'my cup would veritably overflow. Should I take out a contract? Blow him away?' He stands up, kisses his fingers towards Tina's mother.

'Did I tell you, Tina, that Philip left me the most extraordinary collection of paintings? Had them stored in a warehouse for years. You'll be astonished, I promise.'

'That's a charming young man.' Mrs Foley's eyes follow Derek. She raises her hand in a farewell wave. A waitress approaches and takes an order for éclairs and more tea.

'No, he isn't.' There is a pain between Tina's shoulders. She tries to ease it by moving the muscles of her back up and down. 'I think Dad abused me,' she says, though she feels now that a vital momentum has been lost.

'Your father was a law unto himself, pet. And I was very young at the time. I've often felt that I'd have done a better job with you if I'd been that bit more mature.'

'You were twenty-four for Christ's sake! If you'd been seventeen I might have some sympathy.' Tina stares wildly at her mother. 'So tell me about it. Go on.'

'About what, pet?'

'How did the bastard abuse me?' She wants to bang her mother's head against the brocaded wall.

'Your Daddy did nothing, pet. That was the whole problem. It was as if the two of us didn't exist. Running around on his hotel business. How

I endured it I'll never know. You can sin by omission just as much as by commission – that's what Father McCarthy says.' Tina's mother reaches for an éclair, but Tina's hand clamps down on the outstretched fingers. The white-haired couple at the next table glance sideways in frigid disapproval.

'Oh dear, pet, you've hurt my fingers.' Her mother rubs at her knuckles. 'I've a touch of arthritis there.'

'He raped me when I was three,' Tina whispers into her mother's ear.

'Well, pet, I don't like to contradict, but if memory serves me…. Your father took leave of absence when you were very young. Never even came back for Christmas. One of those African places. Me stuck in the house in Sligo, and the neighbours, God damn them: "Where's your husband, Mrs Foley? He's been away a long time, Mrs Foley." I thought he was gone for good. Two years go by and he waltzes back without so much as a why or a wherefore. Your brother arrived nine months later to the day.' Tina's mother sighs and pours them both another cup of tea.

'For Christ's sake.' Tina lies back in the armchair. The pain in her back shoots downwards. She gasps and her eyes close to a crack. Her mother's body sways.

'In those days, pet, you never saw them with their clothes off till it was too late.'

'Don't talk rubbish, mother.' Tina tries to sit up straight, shrugs her aching shoulders. 'Everyone was having sex in the seventies.' The pain retreats into a dull ache, and through half-closed eyes she sees that in her mother's warm crotch something is hatching. Tiny blue-black beetles are crawling outward through the material of the flowered skirt. Raising minuscule heads. Disappearing and reappearing among the roses.

'Well, pet, I may have had sex, but I didn't take my clothes off before I tied the knot. And nor did your father. We were very refined like that.'

As Tina watches, the material of her mother's skirt evaporates, leaving knickers, suspender belt, pasty stringy legs in full view. Beetles swarm through the knickers, cluster on the suspender belt's clips, ooze down the wrinkled legs, form blue-black lumps under thin stockings.

'Your father used to have red hair,' her mother seems to be saying. 'That was a long time back; I hardly remember. I screamed the first time I saw it. I think that hurt your father, but I couldn't help myself. He was very orange down there.'

'Did it look like a carrot?' Tina finds herself panting as she attempts to concentrate enough to put the question. 'I've a fixation about carrots, and it's driving me insane.' She cannot take her eyes from the mass of blue-black beetles pulsing from her mother's knickers.

'Well, pet, I always felt it was more like a nasty little red worm. It used to give me the creeps. And all that orangey hair. Like one of those tropical plants, the fly-eating ones. I used to keep my eyes shut tight.'

Beetles slither down her mother's bony shins, pour over her ankles, and disappear into the space between shoe and foot.

Squelching, Tina thinks, turning into blue-black mush in my mother's shoes. 'A little red worm?' she says. 'That doesn't fit. It won't do.' She feels her breath coming in short gasps. The beetles are attempting to climb from her mother's shoes, damaged, squashed. But still their scrabbling feet try to gain new footholds.

'Your father was fixated on the carrots too, lovie. The pair of you are very alike that way. He came back from foreign parts with some sort of crazy theory that carrots were a complete food, that you didn't need to eat another thing, and he used you for his guinea pig. Now he lasted only a month at it because you were turning orange yourself, as well as screaming the place down. Every time I'd have you in the shop and you'd see a carrot, you'd go mental. These little éclairs, pet. They're gorgeous.' Tina's mother pops a second éclair into her mouth. 'Disappear in a second though. Will I call the girl to get another one for you? Hermann thinks I'm too thin, God bless him. So I've got good reason to put on a bit of flesh.'

Tina opens her eyes wide, the beetles fade and disappear. The flowers of her mother's skirt come slowly back into view. 'What are you talking about?' The plump complacent room reappears as a cage around her, the walls beat against her distraught nerves. She looks despairingly at her mother, drags her fingers through her cropped hair.

Mrs Foley dabs her mouth with a napkin. 'I think you should get your hair done, pet. It's very bitty. And it needs some colour. The dyes you get in the supermarket always let you down in the end.'

Before the final therapy session Tina had taken two more lysergide tablets. The heavy breathing had begun, the sound system delivering as always the loud weeping of millions in pain. Tina was one of many, all lying on mattresses, some already screaming, others unnaturally still. And she started to cry in the familiar desolate way, as though no explanation could ever come, as if her whole body had evaporated into its constituent elements, only her voice retaining strength. Then everything turned orange and she became once more a burning carrot, licked and scorched by orange flames. Sickening explosions – tritium and uranium bombarded her liquified breasts. Her carrot throat filled up with earth and cockroaches. She was choking, dying. And in her death she lay still, stretched out on the mattress, her arms crossed on her breast, the black metal numeral on her forehead.

'Let thy will be done.' The murmur seemed to come from inside her own soul. Those words had brought her back to life.

The psychotherapist had shaken his head. 'No, no, no,' he said. 'You have been abused.' He patted her knee. 'The clues we've picked up: your father, a carrot, the number three, those Catholic incantations you keep calling out. The great ordeal of those abused, is that not only do they suffer the abuse, they grow to accept it, even to believe that it is necessary to their well-being. You must struggle through this nightmare.'

Tina grasps her mother's wrist. The skin is hard and wasted. Amoeba, she thinks, out of the water too long; scrunched into a wrinkled mess. 'I want to know everything,' she says. 'If you don't answer me properly, I'm going to twist your wrist like this.'

'Aahh, pet, please,' her mother yelps. 'You wouldn't hurt me, would you?'

CHAPTER 35

On a bleak February day the doorbell rings, and rings again. Miriam descends the stairs of her Donnybrook home. She examines her face in the hall mirror, puts a fingertip to her eyelashes to remove a tiny excess of mascara, smiles at her reflection in the mirror. Beautiful, she tells herself, beautiful. Tonight when she dines in New York, people will stare at her, appreciate her, envy her. The cases are packed, a little one for Jeremy – they will collect him from school on the way to the airport – a large one for herself. They will live in a hotel for the first few weeks, while the Manhattan apartment is being done up.

Miriam quickly checks the belt of the tight-waisted Armani suit, opens the front door, raises her mouth for Peter's kiss. There is nobody there. She steps out onto the rain-soaked path, walks the few paces to the gate. Nobody. No steel-grey Porsche, only the rain blowing against her in fine droplets. She puts a hand up to protect her hair, then retreats up the path to the house, but a gust of wind slams the front door.

'Hello.' Wendy's head appears from the window of a small yellow Fiat. 'I was ringing the bell like crazy.'

Miriam hardly hears her and continues to push at the front door.

'Get into the car,' Wendy shouts, and Miriam, after several moments' hesitation runs towards her, ducks into the back seat on top of a mess of sweaty sports clothes, water bottles, apple butts. She pushes them aside, tries to find a clean place to sit.

'Don't worry about anything back there,' Wendy says. 'It's only my ante-natal stuff.'

Miriam stifles an anxious wail. 'What am I going to do? The key's inside.'

'Listen, I have to tell you something,' Wendy says, and as Miriam looks at her watch and imagines having to break down the front door, the news slowly penetrates her that Jenny O'Shea is dead, and that her three little children will be taken into care. 'The relations won't look after them,' Wendy is saying. 'They're not able.'

Miriam's hand goes up to her mouth; a deep plaintive sound emerges from her throat. 'I'm so sorry, Wendy. I … I won't be able to go to the funeral. I'm going away with Jeremy. Finn and I…. It's a trial separation.' She hears herself say these words, and a sensation of bitter desperate regret – about Jenny O'Shea's death, about her own collapsing marriage – threatens to overpower her.

'As a separated person,' Wendy's hand caresses her stomach as if consoling the unborn baby. 'I can tell you separation's not much fun. Where will you go?'

'Friends in the country. I don't want Finn to know where. He'll only try to find me.' And in her regret and desperation she is, without intending to, telling Wendy about the book. 'It's a hymn to child abuse,' she says. 'And Finn thinks it's going to change Ireland, change the world. I think he's gone insane.' She shakes herself, glances at her watch. Peter will be here any second, and this is not the way that she wants him to find her.

'Listen, Wendy,' she says. 'If you've your phone, we could call a locksmith. You must know someone who could help?' And then Wendy points to the sitting-room window.

'Is that window a tiny bit open? Or am I imagining it?'

'Oh Jesus, God,' Miriam whispers. 'Why did this have to happen today? 'It's been stuck for ages,' she says and gets out of the car with Wendy's tracksuit top over her shoulders, a pair of nylon shorts covering her hair. The pouring rain beats at her as she struggles with the window, all the time praying to a God, in whom she at least half-believes, that Peter Brindley will not drive down the road at this moment.

Wendy arrives to stand beside Miriam. She holds out an umbrella. 'Found it in the boot,' she says, but Miriam is already soaked.

'Finn's supposed to be getting treatment, Wendy.' She desperately tugs and pushes at the sash window, drips of water trickling down her neck. 'Arrested on the Luas for hitting a child. He left Jeremy stranded at school and hit someone else's child. Imagine that – a three-year-old child. And he never even told me. The mother called … it was awful.'

'Finn went on the Luas?' The umbrella slips from Wendy's fingers, a spoke catches in Miriam's hair, knocks the protective nylon shorts from her head. Miriam wants to shout out: this is my moment, my moment of escape. You made me slam my door, Wendy, and now my hair's destroyed and Peter will arrive before I can sort myself out. Instead, she picks up the shorts, replaces them on her wet hair, drags at the sash with all her strength, and this time she feels it move a little.

'He went on the tram?' Wendy is asking again. She has not picked up the umbrella, and is standing with rain pouring down on her, staring at Miriam. 'He's one of our main signatories. If he used the Luas, our protest would make no sense at all. We have to stand together – if we don't….'

'Wendy, please pick up the umbrella. You'll catch a chill.' The rain penetrates Miriam's suit; her shoulders are cold and wet. The sash moves a little more, and she tugs harder. 'I know the Luas should never have been privatised, and I know that the Loyalty Card system isn't fair. Of course it's not fair that they won't allow some people take the trams, but I'm talking about the collapse of lives. Finn's and mine and Jeremy's. Our human lives. The protest is a different thing. It's ideological, theoretical. This is real. And listen, go back to the car. You're getting drenched.'

'Ideology's important.' Wendy stands in the rain, seemingly unconscious of the fact that the water has made dark stains on her clothes. Her wet sweatshirt clings to her pregnant stomach. 'If we use the trams, we stand by while other people are publicly humiliated. In a system of apartheid, it becomes easy to assume that the weaker group deserves to be degraded.'

'I can't change it, Miriam,' Finn told her. 'I've tried, but I can't. I'd be betraying the dead, betraying children who lived a rough, hard life. The work had to be done or they wouldn't eat. Their father had to be rigorous, demanding. And in the evenings after dinner, after the rosary, he'd call them into his bed. Their night clothes laid out. They'd have all the warmth and tenderness that he couldn't afford to show during the day. Can't you see that, Miriam?'

'The rosary?' she had said. 'You can't be serious, Finn? Surely that shows you how depraved the whole thing was.'

The window sash creaks and shudders; it moves again. The space is big enough, Miriam estimates. She looks around for something to keep the sash up.

'I'll hold it,' Wendy says.

Miriam looks doubtfully at Wendy's bulging abdomen. 'No. We'll put a stick in it. You've got to be careful with the baby.' She breaks a branch from their only tree. 'I'll take off my skirt,' she says. 'It's too tight.'

She crouches down to slide off her skirt, then glances rapidly around. No one. She pulls off her jacket and blouse. She does not notice that in a house across the road curtains are being drawn back. A man's face presses against the glass.

For Miriam's neighbour Geoff, this is a moment of unexpected pleasure. He turns once more to the screen of his computer. He checks his facebook, looks at the Daily What, then tweets to the world his pleasure in the contours of Miriam's rain-drenched figure. *La Bohème* comes to him as if in a dream. Mimi, shivering in the cold dawn, hides from Rodolfo. The music resonates through his heavy frame. He sits back on the edge of his bed, sets up the video camera, hums Rodolfo's anguished aria. I'll post it on my site, he thinks, and films Miriam's anxious glance towards his window as she slides her skirt down over wet thighs. Moments pass in slow motion. He focuses in on the clinging slip, the slim legs. Singing Mimi's sad renunciation of her lover, Geoff pulls down Calvin Klein boxer shorts, strokes a hand along the length of his penis, turns the video camera to contemplate his erection. Miriam stands forlorn in a creamy satin slip. She crouches below at the open sash.

'Act Four.' Geoff checks his updates, Miriam forces her way through the small gap. He rubs the palm of one hand quickly back and forth across the glans. Mumford he whispers and the lyrics float to him through heavy bedroom air. Mimi is dying. She has come back to be with Rodolfo at the end. '*I will hold on hope,*' he sings, '*I won't let you choke on the noose around your neck.*' Miriam's body disappears. A piece of cream material tears and remains caught on the window-frame. Geoff watches the pregnant woman carefully peel it off. '*Now let me at the truth,*' he sings, '*which will refresh my broken mind,*' while across the road a tailored suit flaps in the rain on iron railings. He repositions the camera, holds the measuring jug ready, his eyes turn dreamily upwards.

'*Sono andati,*' he sings. '*Fingevo di dormire.*' In a little while he will note on a chart, which he keeps in the bedroom cupboard, the amount of semen produced today. He places modest bets with himself. On a winning day he cooks a special dinner for himself and his mother.

CHAPTER 36

Her eyes and mouth made up again, Miriam stands in a Stella McCartney trouser suit, then sits, then stands once more. The rain stops and a shaft of sunlight reaches in through the window to touch her cheek and forehead. She stares blindly through it, waiting for a man who will not arrive.

At that same moment Finn is peering into a Dalkey bay-window, a house perched over the sea, with a long winding driveway, set among immaculate lawns, daffodils and crocuses. Its name is Paradise.

'Aunt Joan,' Finn calls, tapping on the window pane. 'I'm Tom's son. Your brother's son.'

A thin blonde woman, engaged it seems in a game of Patience, looks up. Finn sees her turn and rush from the room. He walks on flag-stoned paths to the back of the house, surprised that his aunt looks so young. By his calculations she should be fifty, grey-haired and heavy, like Aunt Eileen.

Finn stands now at a kitchen window, looking in at ancient terracotta tiles, copper saucepans hanging, immaculate dark slate surfaces, oval pine table.

Miriam phones Peter's mobile, his home, then his office. Peter's secretary comes on the line. 'Mr Brindley has just left for the Cayman Islands.

He asked me to convey his apologies. There's a courier on his way with something for you.'

Miriam waits, rocking herself on her brightly coloured settee.

The first blow stuns Finn, and he falls, face downward into a flowerbed. He is pressing his hands into the earth to try to raise himself when another blow thrusts him forward and his face grinds against the wall of the house. The cartilage in his nose cracks, blood pours from his nostrils and he slides back to the ground. He screams once. Short and sharp, then a kick to the head silences him.

Miriam signs the receipt the courier holds out for her. In the sitting-room she opens the letter. At first everything is a blur. Then words begin to come into focus. *Double-dealing, betrayal, shame.*

'Oh, God,' she moans. She has struggled through three months of grovelling apologies, careful flattery, a hand resting casually on Peter's arm, his knee, while she listens with rapt attention to his every word.

You were seen. Don't try to deny it. Kissing and fondling. Stringing me along while you and your despicable husband laugh behind my back.

Could Finn have told him? Miriam asks herself. Would Finn have done that for spite? There had been a night, maybe two weeks before: Peter was away and she had gone to Grogan's, and stood irresolute in the doorway. And there was Finn. He had held her hands in his, and then his warm lips kissed her mouth, her neck, his hands caressed her hair. Against all her resolutions, she had found herself kissing him back, welcoming the little drips from his glass that spilt onto her coat.

The account is closed, the letter finishes.

Oh God, please, she says to herself. Surely Finn wouldn't have done that to her. She had been careful not to let him know she was leaving him, so there could have been no reason. What a fool she has been, she thinks now. A grinding noise from outside, and Miriam runs to the front door, opens it. On the roadway her Audi is being lifted onto a truck.

'He says you're his Auntie Joan, Mother. And we only did what you told us to. Good job the garage door's strong. Now let's get it straight. This poor deluded fellow was knocking at our drawing-room window. He was calling your name.'

'I was in fear of my life, darlings. And, boys, do not interrogate me in my own home. Daddy's being paged. He'll know what to do. Justin, Oliver, listen to what I say. Do *not* open that door.'

'Doesn't sound like the usual suburban killer,' Justin grins, 'though perhaps those are the bits they keep out of the news, how the killer knocked gently on the back window, calling, "Auntie Joan, Auntie Joan, I'm your long-lost nephew" before committing murder most foul.'

'Ruined our school uniforms, Mother. That'll cost you.' Oliver examines his blood-stained trousers, and smiles. 'Though he did deserve a beating. It's like the story of the wolf and the seven little kids. Pass me another slice of quiche, Justin, and I'll take some tea.' He tilts his large frame to hold out the cup for a refill. 'Remember when the wolf pretended to be the kids' mother? "Open the door, dear children," Oliver adopts a high feminine voice, "for I am your mother and I have brought something home for each of you." And when they let him in, he gobbled them up.' He makes a sudden lunge across the table.

His mother delicately slaps at his hands. 'Careful, Oliver, careful – you'll spill your tea.'

Miriam strides around the room, fists clenched, forcing herself to contemplate the worst possible outcome. She phones the school. 'Jeremy's to go to after-school,' she says. 'Yes, I know I said I'd be collecting him early, but I've had a change of plan. Problems with the car. Sorry.'

Next she calls Wendy. 'Wendy, I wanted to tell you: I've decided to give

Finn another chance. After talking to you, I realised it wouldn't be fair.
And I know I didn't make it clear, but it was last October Finn had the
row on the Luas. Way before they put in the Loyalty Card system. And I
will be able to go to Jenny O'Shea's funeral. I'll definitely be there. And
… about Finn's new book, it's alright. He's explained it to me now, and
it's … it's a metaphor. It's just that I misunderstood.'

Rosanne Roycroft's voice has a strained quality to it as she answers
the phone. 'No, Miriam, I'm finished with all that. You'll have to find
someone else to bring you to the funeral.'

Rosanne holds the phone to her mouth and sighs. Her distress has grown
in recent weeks. She can find no consolation in the world of literature,
although poetry in the Irish language is now more fashionable than she
could ever have imagined. As recently as the previous October her existence
had been a smooth unruffled sheet. Summer Twenty-Sixteen. Rosanne and
William together. William with History, Rosanne with the Arts. And what
if Rosanne were named *Saoi* – the youngest *Saoi* in Aosdána's history? She
had giggled to herself at the thought, and the world seemed a supremely
satisfying place. A mere four months later, everything has been turned on
its head. Rosanne is struggling to stay alive.

She has done almost everything right. She has written a tender, poignant
account of her own childhood, which has touched people in ways she
could scarcely have imagined. Excerpts have appeared in international
newspapers, and the response has continued to be extraordinary. Radio
talk-shows, a television interview. Strangers had stopped her in the street
to congratulate her. Her publisher has decided on an immediate large
reprint.

The maquette of Paul Ryan has been made whole again. William had
reconstructed it while the girls were out at a Hallowe'en party. 'There,
love. There,' he had soothed as head and arms and legs were repositioned,
glued, covered with *papier-mâché*. 'I don't think the girls will notice too
much wrong with that.'

Each morning Rosanne takes the reconstituted maquette from its
drawer and sticks large pins into it, intones three short incantations, then

immerses the doll in ice cubes and water. She has visited Rathcruachan, entrance to the spirit world, place of Medbh's palace, made her way past grazing cattle to lie full-length on the high grassy mound, whispering imprecations to the warrior queen. She has crouched on Sliabh na Caillí, prayed to the goddess Garavogue as the rays of the equinox sun reached in to touch her body, and light up the ancient carvings. On the summit of Cnoc Áine she called out to Áine, queen of druidesses. She has summoned the *glám dichenn* curse and borrowed the *fe fiada*, the magic mantle of invisibility, for the time that she may need it.

'Summer Twenty-Sixteen,' Rosanne whispers as she touches the warm phone to her mouth. 'I will survive it. You want to meet for coffee?' she says now. 'You're going to give me Finn's typescript? Well that's marvellous. I can't wait.'

Miriam makes the phone call to Derek.

'What are you crying for?' Derek asks irritably, and with her fists Miriam rubs her eyes, smears the last of her make-up across her cheeks.

'Wendy just told me about Jenny O'Shea,' she says. 'I should have done something. I should have understood how sick she was. I know you told me, but I just let it all slip past. And now she's dead and I'll never be able to make it up to her.' There is silence at the other end of the phone. 'And her poor children,' Miriam whispers. 'How awful it all is.'

'I'm busy,' Derek says.

'Can I see you, Derek? I'm sorry Jeremy bit you.'

'I had to have an anti-tetanus. You never know with children these days. Worse than dogs. Thursday at ten in the Italian Quarter? You can buy me coffee.'

Justin looks up from his crossword. 'My theory's quite different.' He tosses fair hair from his eyes. 'I think Mummy's natural child has come back to find her. The adoption agency told him not to frighten her, so he called her Auntie and got beaten to a pulp for his pains. That'll teach him to try and take our Mummy away.'

'Darling,' Joan Meehan answers her husband's call. 'We've had an incident. Now I don't want you to worry. I'm fine. The boys dealt with it. Their Irish grinds were cancelled, so they were already on their way when I phoned. Apparently he climbed over the wall…. Of course the boys are taking their Irish classes seriously, darling. They understand how important it is, they really do. The teacher had to go to a meeting, that's all. The problem is, the man we've locked in the garage keeps shouting out that he's my nephew…. We can't call the police…. I don't want the boys' names to be mixed up in anything nasty…. Now don't interrupt, darling, please. I've never seen him before. You have to come home straight away. Tell them it's an emergency…. No, darling, no. It's worse than that. Please come now.'

CHAPTER 37

G rey Atlantic sea, scuffling uncertain wind. March tides have flung an oily mess of flotsam on flat bright sand. Broken bottles, car parts, disintegrating shards of metal and plastic in indiscriminate union with black and deep green seaweeds.

The neo-Georgian villas of Glasoileán look worn, in need of paint. Garages are stacked with turf, upstairs windows shuttered as if families have moved to the ground floor in an effort to keep warm. Weeds grow in the sheltered roof valleys of faux-thatch cottages. A lone swimmer is labouring against the receding tide. Gulls rise and scream above the water.

Paul Ryan emerges from the sea, his hair flattened to his head, his beard dripping, body reddened from the cold. He picks his way through the debris, stands shivering for a moment, staring out towards the islands. Then he rubs his chest and arms with an old green towel. He slaps his legs to restore the circulation, pulls on shorts, tee-shirt and runners. Behind the line of sea-borne rubbish he begins his shambling run up the track to the road.

Past a sprawling ranch – peeling Doric columns hold up its front porch. Steel bars protect latticed windows. The garden enclosed by wooden fencing has grown wild. Some crossbars have come adrift and hang crookedly, others have been stolen for firewood. The Connemara ponies, bred for French dinner tables, are held captive by barbed wire stretched between the uprights. Occasionally some escape, to run wild on the hills.

Ridged and pockmarked mountains rise behind Glasoileán, heavy greens and browns colour Benchoona and Garraun, a sudden rainbow rises erect from Benchoona's peak, the silvery marks of streams slip down through the ridges to russet bogland. Paul Ryan jogs in a slow shuffle through the derelict holiday village, built by a local business magnate who wanted to give something back to his community.

'Greatman's Bay – *Cuan an Fhir Mhóir*' is emblazoned in red neon on the enormous leisure centre. The lights no longer work. The 'B' has slipped down the façade and hangs crookedly a few feet from the ground. Roofed over like an aircraft hangar, the disused building fronts a fairground – a crazy golf course, a hall of video installations and gaming machines. In a field, where donkeys now graze, the ice-cream booths, the waltzers, the bumper cars, the paraphernalia of summertime had appeared for a few brief, frenzied seasons, then disappeared forever. The beach bars and restaurants are boarded up. The Grianán, the Pink Lobster, the Moule Marinière, the Café del Sol.

Ryan slows to a walk, then sits on a rotting bench and looks over bogland, mountain and sea.

Ryan's children have told him that this is their worst holiday ever. 'This place is rubbish, Dad,' they say. 'What did you do here when you were a kid? You must have been bored out of your mind.' They sulked when they were forbidden to explore the derelict holiday village. They complained that the sea was icy when they dipped their toes in the water. Now they are playing soccer on the springy grass above the beach while their father swims and jogs. Claire, their mother, has walked to Letterfrack to visit a friend – an opera singer down on her luck. Given the choice of which parent they should accompany, the children reluctantly chose their father.

As Paul Ryan sits, he is aware of the sharp light, the potholed road, the bog stretching across the hillside, the warning sign nailed to a post, bleached by wind and weather. He feels the veins in his forehead pulsing, and tilts back his head in an attempt to ease the rush of blood.

The Ryan family have been staying in rooms above a pub in the village of Tully for the past week. These are the same rooms where Ryan passed childhood holidays. In the field beside the primary school he played football with the local children, while his father satisfied his passion for scuba diving from the farthest reaches of Carrickduff.

Each day Ryan goes trawling for information. He calls to decaying houses at Glasoileán, stands awkwardly on doorsteps, making conversation. He brings his children to visit Renvyle House, and while they play their own version of croquet on the lawn, he swims in the freezing outdoor pool.

They sit in the hotel bar and Ryan jots notes on a page as he chats to the barman. He calls to houses in the villages, asking about family names, old books. For his children, it all seems random.

'Dad's no fun any more,' they tell their mother. 'He doesn't sing for us like he used to.'

Some families invite Paul Ryan to look in their attics. He climbs up ladders and emerges with folders and photographs. The Tullycross library preoccupies him for a while. On the afternoon of that investigation he visits the parish priest. Claire drives the children through the rain to Clifden, where they find a little more to amuse themselves.

'We'll buy board games,' she says.

They return to the cramped bedrooms over the pub and bicker cheerfully during a lengthy game of Monopoly.

Ryan visits the graveyard at Tullycross, where the dead gaze down the steep grassy slopes towards the sea. He walks carefully between headstones, noting names and dates.

Rain moves in from the ocean as Ryan sits on a decaying bench gathering his strength. Drizzle envelops the fields around him, and eats away at the rusting structures of the dead village. Gusts of wind blow needle spikes of thin rain into his face. Seagulls keen and glide overhead. He jogs back to his children and, as he runs, the rain fades and he sees, as he did when a child, the rainbow through a spiral of mist.

It is low tide on an afternoon when the wind has dropped and the air is motionless. A cloud-bank darkens ominously over the horizon. Sea birds swoop and dive and cry. Paul Ryan walks the beach with his children trailing behind him, collecting shells, skimming pebbles across the grey surface of a suddenly still sea.

They are walking towards the island which the nun had described to Ryan, towards those gulls' nests with their bluish-green and grey eggs, those pathetic skimpy, makeshift nests that in her madness she wishes to restructure. It is a matter of real pain to her that the gulls seem incapable of building more resilient nurseries. The nun has told him that at low tide a narrow ridge of sand joins the island to the beach. Once the sea turns, the waves roll in, and in a shorter time than one can easily imagine, the causeway is again covered by water.

The tide is far out. He calls to the boys to hurry. He will bring them to search for nests on the small island without trees, low, as he appraises it across the causeway, with a gradual rise towards the humps of the dunes where tough beach grasses grow.

But even as they cross the precarious ridge of soft sucking sand, the sky darkens to a deep purple, and it seems that a million gulls rise and shriek, a silver-grey chaos over the island, rising and falling in a demented fury, with the roar of beating wings.

'We'll have to go back,' Ryan tells his children as huge drops of rain fall, and gulls and terns descend on them in furious, elegant curves. 'I didn't realise it was so wild here.'

Bewildered by the cacophony, by the swoops and jabs of the gulls, the little family rushes back across the causeway under drenching rain. Lightning flashes in the dark sky, and the gulls rise in new swarms, opening their beaks wide. The gulls' shrieks pursue them back along the beach, where the rain blots away the turfy hillsides, the mountains, the neo-Georgian mansions. Even the rocky outcrop fades to a shadow.

'Here.' Ryan raises his drenched head and points to the dim outline of a house above the beach.

He carries Ben, the youngest child. Jumps a jagged piece of wire, feels his chest overwhelmed by the effort to expel air. The others follow him up a thin path through the rocks, stumbling, falling and half-crying as rain and wind batter them. Another flash of lightning and they see the house clearly before it vanishes again. An explosion of thunder and they cover their heads with their hands.

Rain is dribbling from Ryan's mouth. 'Knock at the door,' he says, trying to prevent his fear becoming visible to his children. A veil of water moves across his face.

They stand dripping in the dark sitting-room of the house. There is no fire and the floor is bare grey concrete. Ryan holds a hand pressed against his chest, trying to slow his heartbeat. Matthew asks for a towel, for the loan of a bag in which to place his shells. The woman, who has reluctantly opened her door to them, picks a blanket covered in dog hairs from a couch whose seams have split and from which the stuffing oozes. She offers it to the child. The dog, an ancient collie, snuffles blindly around their feet, licking at the water that drips from their anoraks.

Ryan shivers in great spasms. His wheezing chest forces air out of his lungs, and sucks it in again. His children sit on the decrepit couch, their shells laid out in front of them on a small greasy table. They make occasional alterations to the patterns, talk in low voices about shapes and sizes.

To distract himself from his body's suffering, Ryan stands up, counts to ten for each inward and outward breath, stares at the photographs on the wall above the mantelpiece. They tell of a dark and poky huckster's shop where a previous generation sold everything from shoelaces to creamed rice. The shopkeeper's three children, two boys and a girl, stare from their picture frames into the sitting-room as if it were alien to them. Some of the photographs depict horse races on the beach, others a crab-catching competition between two families. One presents the primary school choir as if it were in the middle of a song, their mouths open for all eternity. The girl's achievements are gloried in. Her school prizes, her Confirmation ceremony, her graduation from university.

Her brothers had not continued at school, the woman tells Ryan. They had been in a rush to get away. She points to a photo sent by one brother from the United States – a thickset, red-faced young man with a blonde woman. *Fiancés*, he had written on the back of the photo. But the relationship had not lasted and his sister has not heard from him in many years.

The storm abates. They emerge from the house into a dripping world where a glimpse of sun has created new mist spirals and rainbows. The woman closes the heavy door behind them, shuts the bolts with grinding noises, creaks and clicks. Ryan makes his way to the car. The children run ahead, their shells stuffed into anorak pockets.

Later, back in the bedroom above the pub, he lies exhausted on the bed.

'It was brilliant,' Matthew tells their mother. 'All the birds flew up like a new sky. And a white shower of feathers came down on us, soft feathers like snow. Then the storm came, so we never found their nests. Dad says we can go back tomorrow if it's fine.'

'We had to scarper because of the thunder and lightning,' Ryan says ruefully. 'You didn't get caught in it, did you?'

'Myra gave me a lift back.' Claire looks into his grey, drawn face. 'With the country in the state it's in,' she gestures towards the window, to the dark air beyond, 'what's the point in having a festival of culture?'

'It's a local collapse. When the holiday park failed, everyone who'd invested from around here collapsed too. They took huge risks because they thought it was a sure thing. A group from Clifden are putting on an event for the festival, recounting the Glasoileán story in some novel way. We're supplying a fleet of buses.'

'Returning to a childhood holiday destination … it wasn't even a good memory for you. So coming back doesn't make sense.' Claire sighs, touches her husband's dark, dishevelled hair. 'This area is derelict. In Letterfrack they've to boil the drinking water. The primary school's been closed since Christmas.'

'A mad nun from Lettergesh claims that Rosanne Roycroft is a fraud. That's the real reason we're here.' Ryan lies on his side looking into his wife's eyes. 'The nun's an authority on the *Immran Brain,* so I tried to put her on Rosanne's panel.'

'And?'

'Rosanne went crazy. Would you blame her? The nun's a crank. And there are always cranks out to get famous people. My enquiries had to seem casual. I didn't want to go trawling around by myself in a place where they watch your every move.' He pats her hand. 'Thanks for giving me cover.'

'And you never bothered to tell me.' She looks away from him resentfully.

'Don't be like that. I couldn't, not till now. Not till I was sure I'd drawn a blank.' He ruffles her hair, gives it a sudden pull.

'Ouch.' She puts her hands to her head. 'Stop that.'

He holds two fingers pressed together up to the light. 'Look, it's a grey hair.'

She makes a grab at his fingers and he releases the long silvery hair which glides slowly to the tattered carpet, becomes invisible as it merges with a worn flower pattern. Claire gets off the bed, goes to the mirror to stare at herself. 'You're sure the nun's got it wrong?'

'Who knows? The woman existed alright – all the details as the nun described: Mary Heanue, born in 1868 at Derryinver. Prodigiously intelligent, educated apparently by one of the Anglo-Irish families from

Renvyle, until something went wrong and she was dumped back home. All that I was able to verify. What I haven't been able to find is any hint of the poems. The nun says that thirty-five years ago she found Heanue's manuscripts in the National Library, stuffed into a folder with the analogues of the *Immran Brain*. No separate catalogue number. At the time she was still a student, didn't realise that she should have told someone. So she just put them back where she'd found them. She discovered afterwards that herself and Heanue are from neighbouring townlands.'

'It sounds like a fairy story,' Claire says, lying down beside him again, touching her hands to his face, which is slowly regaining its colour. 'You're still pale,' she says. 'You'll have to take better care of yourself.'

'In 1985 the nun was sent off on the missions. She went to Sumatra and didn't come back till last year. A recurring tropical fever, so they retired her out of it. By that stage she'd read Rosanne's poetry, realised there was something fishy and decided to investigate. When she went to look for the manuscripts, they'd disappeared from the *Immran Brain* folder. No catalogue number. The National Library threw up their hands when she enquired.'

'Does it matter who the author is? The Heanue person is dead. She won't care.'

'Both Rosanne and the nun think it matters a lot. They've been hounding me for months. Rosanne's pretty hard-edged, and it always struck me as slightly incongruous that her poetry does the mystical yearning thing.'

'It's worked for her, hasn't it?' His wife laughs.

'Where would you search for clues about a missing poet? The nun's back in Dublin looking for allusions in unpublished PhD theses. And I'm here searching for needles in a haystack, when all the time I know that there's a ninety-five percent chance that the whole concoction exists only in her addled head.'

'It reminds me of that Friel play *Dancing at Lughnasa*,' Claire says. 'Do nuns and priests go mad more easily than the rest of us?'

CHAPTER 38

Derek had asserted in the pages of *The New York Review of Books*: *The fluent voice and brilliant metaphor light into the mind like night flares.* And for those who read *The Irish Times*, Rosanne had written: *A keeper of the artistic estate, a custodian of grief and wonders. Finn Daly's prose reads more and more like absolute music, and once the long second sentence rolls in, with its description of the strange tones of the titular soil, you are sunk, seduced even by sound alone.*

The guests at the book launch applaud when Finn and Miriam pose beside tall piles of *The Titular Soil*. Press photographers snap and snap again. A television camera follows the couple, and records detailed close-ups. It moves to capture the reactions of the audience, rests a minute on Wendy nervously cradling a tiny beautiful baby boy in her arms, creamy skin, blue eyes, a thatch of dark hair. Wendy's eyes flicking from the child's face to the crowd around her.

'Your Daddy's here somewhere,' she whispers.

The camera lights on Tina, resurrected, statuesque. Smooth cheeks, henna-red hair. Abandoned by her psychotherapist, her childhood traumas reduced to the banal, Tina has dieted, gone to aerobic classes, botoxed her face back to beauty. She stands staring defiantly at an uncomprehending world.

Now the camera floats towards Derek and his bevy of beautiful young men. It comes to rest on Derek, as he declares his allegiance to the new nationalism. '*O assembly of foolish mortals,*' Derek intones. '*Came there not unto you apostles from Daonnacht, setting forth signs, and warning of the Day of Judgment fast approaching? Did you hide from truth in the darkness of mean streets? Did you creep through the forests?*

'*"We were blinded by the life of this world," you will say when you are brought to trial, "we were deceived." So, against yourselves, you will bear witness that you rejected Daonnacht.*' He beats time with his forearm, and his voice rises to a crescendo. '*Remember all ye that Daonnacht speaks of lilting Gaelic melodies, of comely maidens. Learn our language fast* mo cháirde*, or be for ever* damanta.*'

Blaise Boothe lurks out of sight of television cameras, estranged wife and gurgling baby. Hidden among the travel literature he thinks only of erotic destinations. He raises a gloved index-finger above the bookshelf. Tina recognises the signal for their tryst. The previous week she had filmed his hairy body, then follicle by follicle demonstrated the hair-removal process. Until Blaise was smooth and pink all over … and irresistible.

From Landscape to Depilation. This will be the title of Tina's exhibition in The Douglas Hyde, its centrepiece a waxing parlour. She steps confidently to the travel section. Blaise removes one sleek leather glove and, hidden by glossy pages, rubs the back of a smooth pink hand against Tina's navel.

'If you marry me,' he promises, 'I'll buy us a villa in Thailand, and stay hairless for ever.'

Rosanne is late for the book launch. She and William had sat for hours, it seems, waiting in the foyer of the Taoiseach's office.

'I'm not getting involved,' the Taoiseach said when he arrived. 'Sort it out between yourselves, but don't drag me into it. Summer Twenty-Sixteen is supposed to be good news. Ireland as cultural dynamo … that sort of thing. We're marketing the Irish mind, not nasty squabbles. I've enough headaches as it is. Somebody's exaggerating the infection stats and it's causing mayhem. Our reputation is being destroyed again … the festival has to go well. And I'm trusting Paul Ryan to make sure it does.'

'But that's just it, Taoiseach,' Rosanne said. 'Paul Ryan's going to accuse your government of fomenting hatred, of aiding and abetting the racist attacks. All over the world everybody will hear what Ryan has to say.'

The Taoiseach picked up the phone. 'Get me the Minister for Culture,' he said. 'I want a transcript of Ryan's speech.'

'But don't you know he'll ad lib? He's unreliable. He'll just throw away the text.' Rosanne tried to emphasise her point, but the Taoiseach was already shaking her hand. 'I'm going home for my tea,' he said. 'Mary's expecting me.'

He's a weak and pathetic fool, terrified to rock boats, Rosanne tells herself as she runs along Stephen's Green. He won't face facts. She reaches St Anne's Church, slows to catch her breath. William has been left far behind. The sky threatens rain, and the gloom of evening is settling on the street. Rosanne glances at her watch, then walks rapidly on.

Outside the bookshop an old nun stands waiting on an uneven pavement, sheltered by the half-light of cloud and darkening sky. Paul Ryan emerges from the shadows to stand beside her. 'Just a minute, Rosanne,' he says.

'No,' Rosanne moans, forcing herself erect. 'I can't stand it. I'm going to Finn's book launch. I've to meet my mother-in-law. Leave me alone.' She stands facing her adversaries, looks wretchedly from one to the other. The muscles of her jaw constrict and, as she stares at them, a sense of the hopelessness of everything threatens to crush her.

'Sister,' Ryan nods in the direction of the nun, 'wants to explain.'

'To destroy my life,' Rosanne stands looking down at grey stains of chewing-gum on a grey path. 'My life destroyed ... just as I approach my zenith. You despise poetry, Paul. You know you do. You think it's just another obfuscation created by the elite to help them stay on top. So why should you care about my methods? My life ... one long struggle. Dragging myself into knowledge against the terrible weight of the world around me. Parents so mean-minded and fearful that if they saw any sign of independent thought, they squeezed and squeezed until it was dead. A school whose fundamental aim was to enforce cretinous conformity.'

'Did we not all go to that same school,' the nun asks, 'along the eternal lanes and footpaths of youth? Into those same classrooms, taught by the dreary hopelessness of middle-age? But then at what moment of all our moments is life not utterly, utterly changed, until the final most momentous change of all?'

'What are you saying, you old fool? Are you trying to tell me I had the same chance as anyone else?' Rosanne takes a step forward on the grey footpath, presses her face close to the nun's. 'Well, I did not.'

The nun backs against a glass shop-front. 'At first I thought Mary Heanue a wraith of my imagination,' she says. 'The poems come down from God, like a sudden revelation. But when I went west, I found her name, and heard the sound of bare feet running on floorboards, and a girl laughing.'

'How can a woman manage to be intelligent in this world?' Rosanne's hands are held out, in a gesture of entreaty, to Paul Ryan, to the fading light. 'My mother-in-law? She's supposed to be here. You encouraged her in this stupid festival stuff, so she over-reached herself. And now she's hobbling around on a crutch and I've got to bring her to the station.'

'Yesterday had been sombre and wet.' The nun, in sign language, makes rapid movements with her fingers. 'But afterwards the spray came up and the evening was naked light and tawny shadows, the scrub grass dripping with jewels and a boat with a maroon sail out on the bay.'

Rosanne's fingers bunch on the sleeve of Ryan's jacket. 'Women, like this fool here,' she glances resentfully at the nun, 'ignore logic and rational thought because they can't do them.'

'In the darkening sea,' the nun's voice runs on, 'that seems to arch its back like a beast as the night fast advances from the fogged horizon. The feel of dampened ash….'

'Why don't you shut up?' Rosanne's stare shifts from the nun's face to the refractive shop fronts across the street, to Ryan's badly cut jacket, to his bearded face.

'A child stands over the rain barrel to wash midnight-black hair. Her mother has one hand cupped under the heavy fall of hair, the other pours a dense silvery sluice of water from a chipped enamel jug.'

'Sister, please,' Paul Ryan says. 'Say what you've come to say and I'll take you home.'

The nun looks down into the space between kerb and road where sweet papers, squashed plastic bottles and cigarette butts coexist in the dark mud. 'This morning the sky was misted white all over with a flat pale-gold disc of sun. The air was still and I recognised at last what God wishes that I should do.'

Rosanne raises her shoulder-bag, presses it to her cheek. 'I'm trying to explain, Paul, if only you'd listen. A nineteenth-century west of Ireland woman was better educated than I was. Try to imagine what that felt like.

All those years she lay in hiding. Waiting, yearning for me to liberate her.'
She pauses for breath, drags a hand through thin orange hair. 'And at last
we found each other. The Androgynes, Paul. I had searched the world.'

'El Greco's Toledo,' the nun says. 'The celebration of landscape, a calvary
of soft hills and jagged grey stone.'

'For heaven's sake, Sister,' Paul Ryan interrupts. 'If you won't tell her, I
will.' He looks at his scuffed black shoes, then at a thin old lady emerging
slowly, painfully from the bookshop. 'It's Mrs Roycroft,' he says.

Mrs Roycroft looks up with a start. 'Ah, Paul. Rosanne. Dropped my
keys. They seem to have melted into the path.'

The nun silently plucks the keys from the kerb, places them in Mrs
Roycroft's hand, stands watching the little group – Rosanne placing
herself directly in front of her mother-in-law.

'The book launch, mother?' she asks sternly. 'I'll just drop in to say
hello, then I'll bring you to the train.'

'Isn't William here?' Mrs Roycroft says.

'Gone home to give the girls their dinner,' Rosanne replies.

'I've found a film crew,' Mrs Roycroft tells Paul Ryan. 'They'll be there
every day during the restoration.'

Paul Ryan scratches his head. 'We've a project manager concentrating
on transport. We're scheduling mini-buses to transport people to the
different shows. They'll do a circuit, drop people off, pick them up.'

'Anyone I know is boycotting the festival,' Rosanne says. 'If you go
ahead, Mother, you'll make a complete fool of yourself.'

'An exhibition by Pierre Hugyhe inspired me,' Mrs Roycroft tells the nun.
'Are you familiar with his films? He influenced our ideas about combining
opera and film with the building of homes. The sense of celebration
involved.' Mrs Roycroft steadies herself on her crutch. 'It's an amazing
outcome, Rosanne, lots of volunteers working patiently together to restore
abandoned buildings. I want people to appreciate the possibilities lying all
around them, so boycotting the festival wouldn't make sense.'

'For heaven's sake, Mother.' Rosanne's voice echoes more loudly than
she had anticipated. She pushes at the nun who has come too close. 'And
really, Sister, I do wish you'd go away.'

'Let us forgive each other for all that we are not.' The nun reaches forward and touches Rosanne's cheek. 'What more could be expected in this vale of torment and tears? I give you the poetry. It is yours.'

'I've always been fascinated by set-building and opera,' Mrs Roycroft says while Rosanne stares at the nun.

'Is that what you've been trying to say all this time?' Rosanne grips the nun's shoulders, looks into red-rimmed eyes. 'You've put me through torture and now…?'

'Lack of evidence,' Paul Ryan says shortly. He disengages the nun from Rosanne's grasp, links her arm with his. 'Nothing to give flesh to the claims. She had to tell you in her own way.'

'You let that mad old woman wreck my life,' Rosanne calls after Ryan, 'and you're supposed to have principles.'

'We'd no evidence,' he calls as he turns towards the corner of Nassau Street. 'No evidence until now.'

CHAPTER 39

In the hours before dawn, Miriam and Rosanne drive south from the city. Kilmacanogue, Roundwood, Annamoe, Laragh. And still they continue, travelling on roads that Miriam has never driven before. She loses all sense of where she is, except that the car is in low gears, climbing a mountain, negotiating difficult bends and curves, then descending through more acute turns, more frightening blackness. 'I should be in bed,' she mutters, but Rosanne does not answer.

Three o'clock in the morning. Miriam cannot explain it to herself. Today will be the day of the grand opening ceremony of Summer Twenty-Sixteen. She grasps the steering wheel, indicates left and right as she is directed. And the little hired car does its bit in the dense black air.

They stop at last. Miriam turns off the engine, flexes and unflexes her hands, opens the car door. Cool damp early-morning air envelops her. 'Should I turn the headlights back on?' she asks. 'I can't see a thing.'

'No,' Rosanne hisses through the blackness that surrounds the car.

Miriam shudders at the touch of cold wet plants against her ankles and arms and, moving slowly, feels her way towards a rough dry stone wall. 'Ouch.' She recoils as a nettle stings her ankle. She can barely make out Rosanne's large form ahead of her. She bends down in the darkness to rub her leg.

'Welcome to my nightmare,' Rosanne says. She shines a torch around the interior of the cottage. 'I haven't had a day's luck since we bought this bloody place.' She pulls on heavy overalls and a pair of black wellington boots, encases her orange hair in a woollen hat. 'Do you want overalls?' she says. 'You can wear William's.'

Miriam shakes her head. 'Why would I need overalls?'

'No reason,' Rosanne says. 'I like them. Come on, we'd better get going. Take a pair of boots from the pile.'

A pair of boots in her hand, Miriam steps outside the front door of the cottage, and looks towards the hired car's dark curves. She would like to get back into its warmth, turn on the radio. Instead, she pulls on the boots, places her Prada slip-ons on a windowsill. Black bog stretches all around. 'Rosanne,' she says as they walk towards the fence. 'I thought you said we were collecting something. You never told me we were going to need wellingtons. I haven't even brought a jacket. Maybe I should go back for the overalls?'

'No time now,' Rosanne says. She is holding up barbed wire with gloved hands, sliding between the strands. 'Sorry for rushing you.' Her torch shines on the wire. 'You can get through here.' She holds the barbed wire in place. 'Hurry up, Miriam. Hunker down; it's easy. Did I tell you that Granny Roycroft's gone off her rocker?'

She is talking and talking and Miriam is crouching down in her thin T-shirt, trying to avoid the spikes of barbed wire.

'Georgian house,' Rosanne is saying.

'My T-shirt – is it catching?' Miriam asks, and then she hears the material tear.

'The land's rolling fields,' Rosanne says. 'Not like this muck.'

'Ouch.' Miriam puts her two hands to her head and disentangles strands of hair from the wire. She straightens up slowly. 'I'm not very good at cross-country.' She puts a foot forward into wet bog, gestures ahead of her at the clumps of sedge, cotton grass and heather stretching up the dark hillside. I'm pregnant, she wants to say. But she does not say it, because the pregnancy is still a warm happy secret between herself and Finn. A new miraculous life.

'Here, put on my sweater.' Rosanne opens the overalls, pulls the red sweater over her head, hands it to Miriam. 'That'll keep some of the wind off you. William used to have a little punt when he was a kid – explored for miles up and down the river Nore. The small canals that go off into the hinterland. A whole navigation system to individual farms. William mapped it when he was twelve. *The Waterways from Bennettsbridge to Kilkenny*, he called it. And now she's sold the place…. No, don't go that way, Miriam. Bogholes. You won't see them in the half-light. Follow me and you'll be fine. We'll be on more solid ground when we get to the edge of the pine wood.'

Miriam's eyes search for a firm surface to walk on. As she picks her way in Rosanne's wake, a dreadful image of Finn's face rises from the pools of dark water. His nose is bloodied and broken, his eyes bloodshot, his beauty destroyed. He turns his face away from Miriam in revulsion, and she sees that the back of his head has been shaved. There are ugly purple stitch marks in his mottled white scalp. 'I'm sorry, Finn,' she whispers. 'I never believed Peter would do such a cruel thing.'

Finn's head becomes ether, his naked body remains glistening in the bog pool, cuts and angry bruises all over it. It's like the Crucifixion, she thinks and looks away quickly.

On Miriam's left a line of heavy black conifers glowers at her under a sombre sky. She stumbles in the squelching undergrowth, puts out a hand to save herself, and finds herself kneeling in the dark turfy pool. Finn's body dissolves.

'You're alright; it's only a bit of water.' Rosanne takes a used tissue from her pocket and wipes the knees of Miriam's trousers, smearing the watery mud. 'I know you saw the marks on Maeve's legs,' she says, and Miriam looks at her in bewilderment. She tries to stand up, trips again and falls forward more heavily than before.

'For heaven's sake, Miriam, concentrate, can't you? We haven't got all day. Maeve had weals on her legs. I might as well be straight about it, because I know you saw them.' She drags Miriam to her feet.

The sleeves of the sweater that Rosanne has lent Miriam are sodden. Her saturated trousers cling to her thighs. She looks down at wet, scraped hands. Her head feels fuzzy and uncertain.

'If kids are mollycoddled all the time,' Rosanne's voice snaps and snaps again, 'how will they ever learn to cope with the vicious side of human nature? How will they survive in the real world? Maeve hurt me and I hurt her back. It's as simple as that. I showed her there are consequences. We've this ridiculous pretence that a caring family provides the child with soft cushioned space. In reality of course, it doesn't. And it shouldn't. Do you understand that, Miriam?'

And suddenly Miriam does understand. Yes, she thinks, I was guilty there too. She had seen the thin legs in the bathing suit, the way the child had tried to hide the purple marks. But Rosanne's daughter seemed furtive and strange, and Miriam had hated the way Jeremy nuzzled up to her. If I had spoken out, she tells herself now, Rosanne would have become my enemy.

'This stupid festival,' Rosanne says.

Oh dear, Miriam thinks, why won't she stop? Please let her stop.

'I am taking part. I've told them. I'm not going to be intimidated, just because my mother-in-law is a fool. She calls it an opera. Apparently she wrote the score and libretto when she was an intern in Ballinasloe hospital.'

Miriam wipes her slimy hands in the coarse grass. 'If we're going to the opening,' she says, 'I don't know what we're both doing out here. We're going to be in a terrible state. Why can't I go back? Wait for you at the cottage?'

'When you asked me to take the perversions out of Finn's book,' Miriam shudders as she hears Rosanne's teeth scrape together. 'When you asked me to subtly rewrite whole chapters, so that no one could guess I'd ever touched it, did I say no? Did I say it's too hard? Did I say it's going to wreck my fingernails? And today I'm asking for a small commitment from you. And just because the ground's boggy, don't think you can say no.'

'I was only trying to explain that I'm not used to boggy countryside.'

'Muckraking,' Rosanne shouts, 'could destroy Finn. For heaven's sake, Miriam, if his book is to be the symbol of Ireland for the twenty-first century, it's got to be irreproachable.'

Miriam says nothing, picks her way cautiously. Slowly they skirt the edge of the forest, the debris of tree-felling littering their way. What is happening to me? Miriam asks herself. She had sat in the car – hired on Rosanne's instructions – waited at the triangle in Ranelagh. Waited and waited. Then Rosanne had slid into the back seat. 'We've to collect something,' she said.

'Nice to have company.' Rosanne is speaking more quietly now. She squeezes Miriam's hand. 'Mother Roycroft sold her house and land. She bought up a street in Kilkenny city. Big substantial houses, all derelict. With yards and stables, she told me, so the Travellers would have somewhere to keep their caravans and horses. And now she's got a whole bunch of asylum-seekers down in Kilkenny restoring the houses. They were supposed to be back in their home countries six weeks ago, and she persuaded some fool in the Department of Justice to offer a stay of execution. And now they've got work permits and visas and can't be budged. All Kilkenny's in an uproar, but does she care? I heard her maundering on, but I'd no notion she planned to do something for real.'

Miriam struggles through the debris of the forest. Rosanne seems to move effortlessly ahead of her. Forests in Miriam's mind, even if dark and intimidating, should have smooth paths between tall trees. But here the ground has been churned by monstrous machines. Branches and wads of black plastic are scattered on devastated earth. The ground is cut into deep water-logged trenches. There are no paths, and there never were.

'Okay, here's the house.' Rosanne is a little way ahead, her arm outstretched, and Miriam stands still at the edge of the pine trees, breathing heavily. She looks down the rough hillside in grey early morning air.

'How's that for taste?' Rosanne exclaims. 'And they have *him* running a culture festival.'

It is bright enough now for Miriam to see the low pitch of the tiled roof, the ill-proportioned dormer windows. She hears again Paul Ryan's words as if from another era. He was talking with admiration of the contradiction between the filth and confusion of an artist's studio and the beauty of the work that emerges from it. And as Miriam stands shivering in green wellingtons on a Wicklow mountainside, her gaze fixed on the laden clothesline, a vision of the young Ryan comes back to her. In a lecture theatre chatting with the students, his head thrown back in a laugh. The curve of his open mouth, his white teeth. But that was before everything. A different world from the tracksuits, socks, underpants that billow and subside in the brisk wind's ebb and flow.

'Blacks and Romanians,' Rosanne is saying, and Miriam's attention switches tiredly back to her, 'never miss a trick when it comes to getting something for nothing – staying in Bennettsbridge as Granny Roycroft's guests while the bloody restoration work goes on. She set the whole thing in train last November without telling any of us. Sold William's birthright. She's moving next month to some tiny house in Kilkenny city. Come on,' Rosanne slips through the garden fence, pulls Miriam after her, then checks her watch. 'We'd better get in and out fast.'

Finn had woken up in hospital. He could remember nothing of what had happened. All he knew was that when he opened his eyes, a kindly man, who asked to be addressed as Uncle Thomas, was looking down at him. Miriam stood on the other side of the bed, weeping.

Uncle Thomas, Miriam explained through her tears, was a neurologist, who had watched over Finn while he was x-rayed and stitched. 'They found you unconscious in their garden, Finn. At first they thought you were dead.' And she had gone into a paroxysm of distress.

When Finn's wounds had healed, and he no longer looked – in his newfound cousins' words – like the Elephant Man, Aunt Joan had welcomed him with Miriam into her home. They seemed a warm gentle family, and Miriam had felt a sudden ray of hope. For herself and for Finn; for their future together. Aunt Joan and Uncle Thomas are so generous, she had thought, and her face had crimsoned with shame, because she believed that the assault on Finn had been her fault, and that Peter Brindley had organised it.

That same night Miriam and Finn had created their new being. So far he or she is little more than the size of Miriam's thumb, but with such promise, such luminous promise for the future.

'I'm not going in there, Rosanne,' Miriam says. 'I'm not breaking into Paul Ryan's house.'

'We need that early draft,' Rosanne says. 'His study's right there.' She points to a curtained window narrower than the others. With a growing sense of horror, Miriam realises what she is required to do.

Bicycles lean against the side wall of the house. A stack of flowerpots, an upturned tricycle, a pile of sand to the side of the path, all these things, innocuous and banal, warn her not to trespass any further.

'I don't want it.' She struggles to detach Rosanne's hand from her arm. 'Let me go, will you?' she says. 'I'm not even sure that Paul Ryan has Finn's manuscript. Why would he keep it here? Why not in his office in town.'

'Do you think we haven't looked?' Rosanne's grip gets tighter. 'For Christ's sake, Miriam,' she hisses, 'think of the great tradition of guerrilla warriors, those who have had to achieve by stealth what was theirs by right. The manuscript is yours. It's not his. If it's here, you have to get it back.' Keeping a vice-like grip on Miriam's elbow, she steers her to the front door, takes a key from under the mat, opens the door silently. Before Miriam knows what has happened, they are standing inside, and Rosanne is holding a finger to her lips.

'Find that script,' she whispers and pulls off her wellingtons, carries them between finger and thumb, tiptoeing in her stocking feet down the narrow corridor to the kitchen. The door shuts softly behind her.

Miriam stands trembling in the dark hallway. In contrast to where she is now, her whole life seems to have been childlike and innocent. She can identify which room is Ryan's study, but she is paralysed. The manuscript is mine, Miriam tells herself, takes a deep breath and inches forward. Her cheek brushes something and she almost cries out. But it is only an anorak, hanging with many others on coat-hooks nailed to the wall.

'I can't do it,' she whispers. 'I just can't.' If she were a braver sort of person, she might creep upstairs, try to find Ryan's bedroom, and warn him about Rosanne. Her eyes begin to adjust to the interior darkness. Now she can make out the line of boots at the front door and a sweeping brush against the wall. There are shoes stacked higgledy-piggledy on a shelf above the boots. A toy robot on the floor beside them, a football still muddy from its last game.

Beside her stands a little telephone table. She could phone the emergency number and then creep back out through the front door. She would tell them that she has broken into Paul Ryan's house under duress. 'I can't do that,' she whispers. Very quietly she moves towards the front door. When I get outside, she decides, I'll call the police on my mobile, and then I'll run to the neighbours.

Her hand is rising to the door knob when she realises that a dim light is shining from the other end of the hallway. And there is Rosanne standing at the open kitchen door beckoning her.

'You didn't even look for it?' Rosanne pulls Miriam into the kitchen, closes the door behind them. Miriam sees Rosanne lift a large saucepan onto the solid-fuel kitchen range. She watches stupefied as Rosanne begins to stir its contents. And now Rosanne is uttering words and phrases, chanting an incantation.

Miriam stands numbly as Rosanne stirs. And then she is, without wishing to, moving towards the cooker, staring into the saucepan, mesmerised by the hot swirling liquid.

'Stir it.' Rosanne thrusts the ladle into Miriam's hand, then disappears through the kitchen door. It looks like oil, Miriam thinks, like boiling oil, and she peers at its bubbling surface. Minutes later Rosanne is back in the kitchen, placing a sheaf of handwritten sheets of paper on the table. She takes the ladle from Miriam's hand.

It does not seem real to Miriam that she can be standing in a small, dishevelled kitchen, a kitchen with empty bottles on the draining board, jars of sauces and mustards on shelves, plates and cups stacked on a homemade dresser.

Rosanne takes the little maquette of Paul Ryan from her pocket and tosses it into the saucepan. She finds a plastic bag in the cupboard under the sink, stuffs the sheaf of papers into it. Miriam looks on helplessly. It's a nightmare, she thinks. I'll wake up soon.

'We're off,' Rosanne whispers, pulls Miriam quickly out through the back door, shutting it behind them. She takes off her gloves, folds them in her pocket, jogs down the back garden carrying the plastic bag, and slips through strands of wire out onto the bog. Miriam is still standing at the back door. It is only now as she feels a blast of wind on her face that her senses begin to awaken. Instinctively she runs to catch Rosanne, then stops beside the laden clothesline, touches her fingers to a small blue pyjama jacket. It is almost dry. She looks nervously back at the house, its speckled pebbledash, its broken gutter hanging low over the kitchen window. Her head is in a fog of confusion and her body is shaking with huge shudders.

The dawn is almost up and everything is pale and lit by an invisible sun. Miriam tries to find firm places to put her feet, but every tuft of grass sinks under her weight; the bedraggled heather tries to snare her boots and trip her.

'The only weak link now,' Rosanne looks down at her, 'is the aunt in Cavan.'

Miriam struggles to catch up, but the land seems wetter than before. With every step she takes, her boots drag. Her legs are tired, her head is blurred. She tries to say that Finn's aunt has died, but Rosanne is staring down at her, like an enormous predatory creature. Miriam feels all her energy drain away. Her voice comes out weak and exhausted. 'Aunt Eileen left Finn her cottage. He wants us to go and live there.'

She looks up to the line of trees. There is a mist rising with the sun. She can see it swirl towards the tops of the cotton grasses. We'll get lost, she thinks, and we'll die of exposure.

Rosanne is suddenly back at her side. With careful, quick steps, she leads her onwards. When Rosanne walks on the bog, it is as if she is on solid ground. 'What happened?' Rosanne asks. Her arms reach out to grasp Miriam's shoulders.

Miriam recoils but cannot escape the grasping hands. 'She died,' she says quickly and Rosanne shakes her hard.

'How did she die?'

'She kept everything in lemonade bottles. She thought she was having a drink of lemonade and it turned out to be sheep dip. Leave me alone, Rosanne. Stop shaking me.'

But Rosanne presses hard fingers into Miriam's skin. 'Why didn't you tell me?' she is shouting. 'You fool.'

Miriam twists away from Rosanne's grasp, struggles up through the sedge towards the line of trees, her feet heavier in her boots with every step. 'It's not my fault that Finn wants to live in Cavan,' she gasps. She can feel Rosanne's step behind her. She is frightened, but the fear cannot make her move faster. She stumbles in a clump of heather, falls into soggy moss.

I'll have a miscarriage, she thinks; I'll have a miscarriage, and our new vows will come to nothing. She is prostrate on the ground, her stomach and chest soaked in turfy water. Her trousers have torn all down one leg. Blood oozes from a long scrape on her knee. She looks up helplessly into Rosanne's laughing face.

'Don't you see?' Rosanne exclaims. Her face is livid, the freckles lost in the reddened flesh. She bends down and caresses Miriam's arms. 'I've done it in the end of all. I am the *file*, the minister of truth. I can call on the elements, Fire, Wind, Earth, Water, to destroy the refractory ones. I do it for you and Finn, Miriam. Everything I do is for you and Finn.'

CHAPTER 40

'Ladybird, ladybird, fly away home.' Miriam taps her foot on the polished floor of the State Apartments. Vast spaces, frescoes, flags, a TV crew with lithe black-clad men and women. Dublin Castle echoes with voices. 'Your house is on….' She stops abruptly. 'Please, Finn, I'm feeling so strange.' Her hand reaches out to touch her husband's cheek. 'That horrible nursery rhyme, it's driving me mad….'

From the painted ceiling a bearded figure stares down at Miriam, demanding her as a sacrificial offering. A fire is fed among rough stone columns. Hard flesh tones, heroic postures. She tears her gaze away from the painted ceiling's mythic scene to the splendours of the room itself and even here she cannot be at ease. The deep blue walls, the gold pillars set up a staccato rhythm denouncing her.

'How did you scrape your hands?' Finn asks.

'Thorns.' She sits on them so that he will not ask her again. 'You're fine,' he says then. 'It's probably your hormones. Calm down.' He pats her knee. 'Where the fuck is Ryan?' He looks around the great room. 'Why isn't he here?'

Miriam shudders. During the struggle back across the boggy hillside to Rosanne's cottage, she had found herself looking over her shoulder, dreading that flames from the Ryan bungalow would stain the heavens. But all was calm, quiet. And even as they drove away on their homeward journey, the house looked like any other ugly bungalow in the unflattering early light of a grey June day. Perhaps her imagination had run away with her. The worst that could happen would be that the saucepan would boil dry. It might give Ryan a fright, but nothing more.

'Drop me at the Festival office,' Rosanne had said. 'I've to pick up invitations.'

Her mind blank, Miriam could not even say goodbye. Caught in rush-hour traffic, she had driven slowly towards the city. She had pulled out a single page from the plastic bag that Rosanne had placed on the passenger seat and there in front of her was Finn's crabbed handwriting. It had taken her a minute to absorb it. Had Rosanne done this for Miriam and for Finn? Had she risked herself to retrieve the manuscript? 'Thank you,' Miriam whispered into the traffic that blocked her way.

She had thought about her exhibition: *Roll-call of the Dead*. Photography, paint, mixed media – each piece named after the people dead from disease, the wretched ones whom Sócúl had tried to help.

'Haunting,' Derek had said. 'Powerful.' Miriam knew then that her transgressions had been forgiven. Derek would once again be her true friend. As she drove towards Dublin, that thought alone thawed her frozen heart.

Mrs Roycroft stands in her Kilkenny kitchen preparing supper. She washes lettuce and tomatoes, peels a hard-boiled egg, butters slices of brown bread, looks out on the storm which is pounding her herb garden. She will be sad to leave all this behind. Rosemary, thyme, dill, parsley, mint, lemon balm – growing wild now. The dill and mint and purple flowered chives have colonised large areas where more delicate herbs once flourished. A rambling rose grows against the far courtyard wall. As Mrs Roycroft watches, the rain strips red petals, lashes them to the ground. She switches on the television, sits and eats her evening meal, watches the opening moments of Summer Twenty-Sixteen. The cameras survey the great crowds, the magnificent State Apartments of Dublin Castle.

'For Jesus' sake, what are we waiting for?' Tina says. She is sitting beside Blaise Boothe in the middle of the great room. His pink hand rests on her knee. Thin hairless fingers slide up her leg, linger under her skirt. 'No babies,' she tells him. 'Babies disgust me.'

She holds out her left hand, waves her fingers so that the diamond of her engagement ring glitters in the light.

Derek turns from the row in front. '*Sodomacht*, darling,' he says. 'Perhaps Paul Ryan has left his speech at home? Perhaps he has run away to a better life?'

'Why does Miriam always get the cream?' Tina grumbles. 'Look at her preening herself up there. As for that imbecile husband of hers…. You're not to give him any more work, Blaise.'

'After tonight,' Derek says, 'I hardly think that Finn will need Blaise or anyone else for that matter. He is set on a course for certain sanctification. Just six short months ago … whoever would have thought it?'

Wendy is sitting beside William. She is holding a notebook, ready to record the evening's events.

In an antechamber to the Apollo Room, the Taoiseach glances at his watch, turns to his advisors. The Minister for Culture speaks to the linen-suited woman by his side.

'We'll have to get started,' the Taoiseach says. 'I don't want to be here all night. Mary's come down with the flu, and I promised I wouldn't be late.'

'Paul Ryan hasn't arrived yet, Taoiseach.' The Minister for Culture shakes his head. 'Can we begin without him? My people have been trying his mobile. They can't get anything.'

The storm's fury increases. Mrs Roycroft listens to the wind in the chimney, the rain from the south-west. She shudders when a sudden blast slaps the branches of her alder against a window frame, makes a note to herself that she must have it cut back or it might crack the panes.

The Kilkenny houses are ready. New roofs, new windows, new floors, new kitchens. Everything is pristine. Thirty-five men and twenty women – Travellers, Eastern Europeans, Africans – have been working on the opera for the past six weeks. Singers, dancers, actors, film crew are in Kilkenny for their final rehearsal. Next week the ceremony for handing over the keys to Traveller families will take place. The film crew is French, the director

Brazilian. The wide mix of nationalities will, Mrs Roycroft hopes, bring international media coverage and ultimately protect the project.

The film crew, which arrived to record the derelict Kilkenny street, the restoration project, the opera rehearsals, the finished houses, is continuing to film the city. Now it concentrates on the racist slogans painted on walls and hoardings throughout Kilkenny; the posters that depict Mrs Roycroft as a witch, an aged crone, a madwoman; the huge mound of pig slurry which lies in front of the restored houses. The film crew invites the Concerned Parents to give their views on Mrs Roycroft's project, and explain why they are organising a protest march through the city. They interview the local Daonnacht activists who patrol the area. These serious young people explain that they have no prejudice against Travellers being well housed. They joke that they would be grateful if a philanthropist would offer them houses half as good. They are there, they explain, to help keep order should a problem arise. Mrs Roycroft believes that members of the Garda Reserve are among them.

'There's a call in.' The Minister for Culture – tall, red-faced, a former hurling star – stares at his linen-suited assistant. 'Some local guard realised what was what ten minutes ago. They say he's dead. A fire at his home. They found all the family dead.'

'Jesus.' The Taoiseach turns away from his advisors. 'He couldn't be a target, could he? This is supposed to be the feel-good factor. Jesus,' he says again. 'Supposed to take our minds off…. You know as well as I do, Jim. We're not going to last this one out. Another bunch of shops torched last night. People dragged from their beds.'

Mrs Roycroft pours a second cup of tea. She thinks about her son, her grandchildren, the passing on of value systems, the cultivation of intelligence. Does rational thought give insight into the human condition? she wonders. Does it help to make one more just? More fair? More honourable?

'I am prepared.' Rosanne takes the Taoiseach's arm and quietly offers herself as spokeswoman. 'I will speak on Paul Ryan's behalf. Afterwards, Taoiseach, you will give Finn Daly his award.'

'But … with this disaster…?' the Minister for Culture stammers. 'Can you cope? Without alluding of course…. No tragedies…. We can't assume it's true.'

'I can cope,' Rosanne declares. 'Be assured.'

Mrs Roycroft clears the table. She watches rain flowing down the kitchen window. There is a crash in the courtyard. A slate must be down, she thinks. Her eyes flick back to the television. And now she sees the rain-drenched grounds of Dublin Castle, the entrance gates, Dame Street. They're filling in time. Mrs Roycroft looks at her watch. There must be some delay. The voiceover laments the weather. The open air party, the fireworks will have to be deferred. Passersby, noticing the cameras, quicken their pace, shield themselves from view with lowered umbrellas.

'Festival?' One woman, careless of being seen, turns at last in response to the reporter's query. 'What do I care about a bloody festival?' She waves her hands at the scurrying furtive throngs. 'Look at them. Look at them,' she shrieks. 'They're everywhere. Polluting our water, giving us disease. Vermin, that's what they are. They've got to be got rid of. Stamp them out! That's what I say. And then we'll have reason for a festival.'

The radiant blue of the State Apartments fill the screen. Cameras focus on Rosanne Roycroft slowly moving towards the podium.

'What's happened?' Mrs Roycroft asks her television set. 'What's gone wrong?'

Summer Twenty-Sixteen, Rosanne's voice exults. *Ireland in this young century proclaims her culture throughout the world.*

'Jesus,' Finn says. 'Miriam, what's happened to Ryan?'

Miriam shrinks back into her seat. 'I don't know,' she says. 'I don't know.' She stares at Rosanne's ecstatic face and tries to push the dread away from her. Rosanne isn't that sort of person, she repeats to herself. But I went there. I was with her in Paul Ryan's house. I burnt Finn's manuscript in our fireplace this afternoon. Terrifying uncertainties crowd upon Miriam. She finds herself weeping into her cupped hands.

Rosanne gazes out at Mrs Roycroft from the screen. Her words are confident, vigorous. They strike a note of defiance, of triumph over adversity.

For twenty years I defended Irish culture by standing watch against Catholic authoritarianism.

Mrs Roycroft stares into the television, trying to decipher Rosanne's face, trying to understand the words that her daughter-in-law is uttering with such force.

After the shipwreck of the Irish priesthood, we had years of relative peace, years of repose, years of quiet gain. But then a day arrived when greed became our new god.

Derek whistles a low incredulous whistle. '*Quel horreur*,' he says. 'I'll have to climb back into her lap. Become her Pangúr Bán. Rub my fur against her chin. Ugh.' He shudders.

'I'll tongue her orange bush,' Tina says. 'I've always wanted to screw an orange bush. Or will I rape her digitally? What d'you think, Blaise? Which finger will I use?' She holds out a hand, opens her fingers wide. He leans over, sucks in the long red nail of her index finger, through thin colourless lips. He holds the finger in his mouth, and Tina gives a little moan of pleasure. 'But who'll hold her down?' she whispers. 'Who'll spread her legs for me?'

'The very idea of penetrating that *tor oráiste*,' Derek whispers, 'makes me feel nauseous.'

'Once in a toilet I touched her cunt,' Tina says. 'She was wearing a g-string, and all the fluffy bits stuck out around the edges.'

Wendy stands up from her place in the audience. William's extended hand tries to pull her back. Her face is white as she shakes herself free.

'She's gone very plain,' Tina says as Wendy twists away from William, and strides towards the exit.

'For Christ's sake stop crying,' Finn says to Miriam. 'It'll look ridiculous. When I stand up on that podium, I'm going to shout out that you're pregnant. I'm going to tell the world that I'm celebrating love, integrity, equals standing together. Isn't that what this bloody festival is supposed to be about? You're nearly three months gone, Miriam. That's what I'm going to say. I'm not keeping it secret any longer.'

'No, Finn, no,' Miriam pleads. 'It's not the right time. I'm feeling so awful, you see.' She presses her face against his chest. 'It's only ten weeks. Please, Finn.'

Pausing between sips of tea, Mrs Roycroft is spellbound by the power of her daughter-in-law's delivery.

There is only one force of history that can break the reign of materialism and greed, and that is the force of culture. We, the poets and singers, the film-makers and musicians, the novelists and playwrights have not brought about the present disaster. But we shall selflessly fight to rescue our unhappy country, to bring about our vision of the good. The difficulty of the task is no excuse for avoiding it. And we shall not avoid it.

A knock at the door. 'Come in,' Mrs Roycroft calls. No one enters, and she goes to investigate. The hall is empty. 'Who's there?' She stands waiting.

Our influence is considerable and we shall use it confidently in culture's cause....

'Daonnacht,' Mrs Roycroft says. 'She's talking about Daonnacht.' She closes the kitchen door once more, sits at the table and stirs her cold tea. 'I am Cassandra.' She speaks aloud to the empty kitchen. 'I call out in warning to people who cannot hear me.'

Some have questioned the global appeal of culture but we – we the intelligentsia – should never be surprised by the power of our ideals.

Mrs Roycroft reflects silently, and sees herself, a dead old woman half-sitting by her own front door, blood oozing from a wound in her neck.

We do not accept the persistence of ignorance because we do not accept slavery. Some have unwisely chosen to test our resolve, but they have found it firm.

And now Mrs Roycroft sees that a man is standing beside her.

'The Travellers whom you wish to house,' he tells her, 'will never be allowed to take up residence. There will be riots outside your opera on its opening night. People will die, and it will be your fault.'

Is it her son, William, who is looking down at her, an expression of sorrow on his face?

'The spirit of the age,' he says, 'is too strong for any individual to fight against it. And Daonnacht is the spirit of this age. The rule of war prevails, and I have created demons to focus the energies of the people. So that good can ultimately triumph, and Ireland can once more become a proud strong nation. I have done this in the clear knowledge that history will not judge me harshly. I will not build gas ovens.'

We will rise from the fionn uisce *as the phoenix rises from its all-consuming fire. We are a victorious army bringing Irish culture to the ends of the earth.*

Finn's arm encircles Miriam's shoulders. 'Sssh,' he's saying and he finds a tissue in his pocket and starts dabbing at her eyes.

'I'll have to go to the Ladies to do my face,' she whispers, and Finn strokes her knee again. She does not move. She cannot move. And as the events of the early morning flow inexorably through her mind, she remembers that Rosanne had worn gloves. Miriam's fingerprints will be the only ones they might find. In the kitchen, all over the telephone in the hall, and when Miriam came out of the bungalow she had touched a pyjama jacket that swung from the clothesline. The washing was almost dry. She had wanted to take it in, leave it piled on the kitchen table.

We honour those who have suffered fire for culture's sake. Those flames are called clear water, and that pure water washes our hands clean.

Mrs Roycroft stands rigidly still. She must, she tells herself, silence these gathering voices, this nightmare of the future. Tired out, she turns from the television and wanders out towards the rain-filled air.

'Struggle on tomorrow,' she murmurs. 'Tomorrow.'